To Sar

Stay HOT!

HOT PURSUIT

A *HOSTILE OPERATIONS TEAM* Novel

Lynn Raye Harris

LYNN RAYE HARRIS

Copyright ©2013 by Lynn Raye Harris
Cover Design Copyright © 2013 Croco Designs
Interior Design by JT Formatting

www.**lynnrayeharris**.com

Printed in the United States of America

First Edition: July 2013
Library of Congress Cataloging-in-Publication Data

Harris, Lynn Raye
    Hot Pursuit / Lynn Raye Harris. – 1st ed

    ISBN-13: 978-0-9894512-1-5

    1. Hot Pursuit—Fiction. 2. Fiction—Romance
    Fiction—Contemporary Romance

DEDICATION

*For my handsome military husband, who always
believed in this story..*

PROLOGUE

Two months ago...

SOMETHING WAS WRONG.

It wasn't anything obvious, but Captain Matthew Girard felt it in his gut nonetheless. It was an itching sensation across his skin, a buzzing in his belly. Perhaps it was simply the weight of this mission pressing down on him. Though the Hostile Operations Team always performed critical missions, this one was even more so. Failure was not an option.

Beside him, Kevin MacDonald lay in the sand, his camouflage-clad form as still as marble until the moment he turned his head and caught Matt's eye.

Kev's hand moved. Doesn't feel right, he signaled.

No, Matt signaled back. Count on Kev to pick up on it too. They'd been on a shitload of ops together. Matt knew that if his second-in-command was picking up on this weird vibe, it wasn't just him. Yet the mission was too important to scrub without more than just a gut feeling to go on.

"It's awful quiet in that compound." Jim Matuzaki's voice came through the earpiece a few moments later.

"Yeah," Matt answered into the mic attached to his helmet. Almost as if the tangos inside knew that a HOT squad was coming and had abandoned the compound.

The stone structure thirty meters away rose two stories high and lacked windows. The roof was flat to enable gunmen to look out on the surrounding territory and defend the building.

But there were no gunmen. Not tonight.

In the surveillance photos, the gunmen were so plentiful they'd stood out against the pale roof like a porcupine's quills. And now...

Nothing.

Though it was quiet here, gunfire exploded in the distance at regular intervals. A pitched battle between a pocket of enemy forces and a Ranger battalion raged a few miles away. HOT's mission was quieter, but no less deadly.

They were here for Jassar ibn-Rashad, heir to Freedom Force leader Al Ahmad. But this mission was different. Usually, they killed the target. Tonight, they were extracting him. The rumored new Freedom Force mastermind was wanted higher up in the chain, and Matt didn't question orders from the Pentagon. They wanted him, they were getting him.

Matt and his team had planned the mission to kidnap ibn-Rashad for weeks. Down to the last damn detail. And then they'd gotten word just a few days ago that ibn-Rashad was moving to this location.

The intel was good. Damn good. And their contact had been reliable on more than one occasion.

But this time?

The bad feeling in Matt's gut was getting stronger by the second. He'd thought the kid seemed more nervous than usual the last time he'd gone to meet with him. The kid had always been nervous, but he'd seemed to trust Matt's word. And Matt had trusted him as much as he was able. Trust, but verify.

Which the CIA had done. All the chatter indicated that ibn-Rashad had moved to this location. Nothing indicated that the Freedom Force had any idea they were being targeted. And in spite of the niggling feeling he'd had about the whole thing, Matt had chosen to press forward with the op.

Just then, a light flashed up on the roof and blinked out again. Male voices carried in the night, followed by a bark of laughter.

"Two men," Marco San Ramos said over the headset. "Smoking."

Marco and Jim were closer and had a better view through the glasses.

"Richie?" Jim's voice came through the headset again, calling Matt by his team name.

He knew what the other man was asking. What they were all waiting for. In another location close by, Billy Blake, Jack Hunter, Chase Daniels, and Ryan Gordon also waited for the signal to go or to retreat. The timeline was tight, and if they didn't go in now, they'd have to scrub the mission. They had precisely twenty minutes to infiltrate the compound, kill the tangos, and extract ibn-Rashad.

If they were going in.

"Mission is a go." Matt made the split-second decision in spite of the acid roiling in his belly. What if they didn't get a second chance at this? Lives hung in the balance with ibn-Rashad remaining free. This mission had always been risky, but what did they ever do that wasn't?

Failing was simply not a part of his genetic makeup. Maybe he got it from the old man—that combination of stubbornness, meanness, and sheer cockiness that wouldn't let him back down unless there was no other option. He wasn't stupid, but he wasn't a quitter either. And people's lives hung in the balance.

People he could save. He'd made a promise, long ago, and he'd kept it. He was still keeping it.

"Repeat," Matt said, his jaw tight, "mission is a go."

"Copy," Jim replied. The rest of the men chimed in. Seconds later, two cracks rang in the night. And then Billy's voice came over the headset. "Targets on roof neutralized."

Matt let out a breath he hadn't realized he'd been holding. Jack "Hawk" Hunter could always be counted on to make the difficult shots. The dude was probably the best sharpshooter Matt had ever seen. Thank God.

Everything went like clockwork from that point on. They converged on the compound from their separate locations. Kev set a charge on the door and then it exploded inward. Billy tossed a flash-bang into the opening. It went off with a loud crack, the light flaring for a split second as bright as a nuclear flash. Whoever was in that room would be temporarily blind and disoriented after that baby went off.

The team rushed through the door, going right and left in succession, guns drawn, as pandemonium reigned inside. HOT worked like a well-oiled machine. Each man knew instinctively where to shoot, could have done so blindfolded.

Within seconds, the terrorists lay dead and the scent of spent gunpowder hung heavy in the air, along with the odors of smoke and stale sweat.

Sweat also trickled down the inside of Matt's assault suit. He didn't have time to be uncomfortable. Instead, he and Kev raced up the steps along with Marco and Jim, searching for ibn-Rashad, while the other guys secured the perimeter.

A methodical sweep of the rooms proved futile.

"He's not here," Marco spat. "There's no one else."

"Goddamn." The skin-crawling sensation Matt had had from the beginning of this op was now a full-blown assault on his senses. Kev looked at him, his face bleak behind the greasepaint, his eyes saying everything Matt was thinking.

Jassar ibn-Rashad was supposed to be here. He'd been reported here as of this afternoon, in fact. There was a price on the man's head and no reason to move from this location... unless he'd been tipped off they were coming.

Sonofabitch. Matt suddenly felt like he was standing in a lightning storm, holding a steel rod in the air. He wasn't necessarily going to be struck down, but the possibility was damn good.

"Do another sweep for intel. West side. Three minutes, and we're out," Matt ordered.

"Copy," Marco said. He and Jim headed for the west side of the house while Matt and Kev split up to cover the rooms at the east end. Matt swept into each room, weapon drawn, helmet light blazing. There was nothing. No papers, no computers, no media of any kind. Nothing they could use to determine what ibn-Rashad was planning next.

He hit the hall again and met up with Kev, who shook his head.

Jim and Marco arrived next, empty-handed. The four of them pounded down the stairs. Another quick sweep of the rooms on the ground floor, and they were back into the night with the rest of the team, running for the extraction point five miles away.

They hadn't gone a mile when bullets blasted into the air beside them. A hot, stinging sensation bloomed in Matt's side. He kept running anyway. Until they crested the dune they'd been traveling up and came face-to-face with a series of rocket-propelled grenade launchers pointed right at them.

ONE

"MM-MM, LOOK AT THAT GIRARD BOY, all grown up and better looking than a man ought to be," said one of the ladies under the row of hairdryers.

Evie Baker's heart did a somersault. *Matt Girard. Dear God.* "Careful," Stella Dupre yelped as warm water sprayed against the side of the sink and hit her in the face.

"Sorry." Evie shifted the hose.

She was a chef, not a shampoo girl, but she didn't suppose that distinction mattered anymore since the bank now owned her restaurant. Shampoo girl in her mama's beauty salon was just about the only job she could get at the moment, in spite of the resumes she'd blasted to every culinary school contact she could think of. The economy was bad and no one was hiring—and she didn't have the luxury of waiting for something else to come along.

She didn't think her skills would rust anytime soon, but it hurt not to be cooking right now. She should be

1

playing with recipes, tweaking the flavors, and experimenting with new combinations. Instead, she was rinsing hair for a host of Stella Dupres—and doing it badly, apparently.

Mama glanced over at her, frowning even as the snip-snip of scissors continued unabated. The ladies in the salon swung to look out the picture window as Matt strode along, and the chatter ratcheted up a notch. The odor of perming solution and floral shampoo surrounded Evie like a wet blanket, squeezing her lungs. Her breath stuttered in her chest.

Matt Girard. She hadn't seen him in ten years. Not since that night when he'd taken her virginity and broken her heart all at once. She'd known he was back in town—hell, the whole town had talked of nothing else since his arrival yesterday. She'd even known this moment was inevitable, except that she'd been doing her best to avoid all the places he might be for as long as possible.

They'd had an easy relationship, once. The kind where he could tug her ponytail, drop a frog in her shirt, or tease her endlessly about her buckteeth—which, thank God, she no longer had. But that had been when they were kids. Then she'd gotten breasts and started blushing whenever he looked her way, and things had changed. Or at least they had for her.

Matt, however, had been determined not to see her as anything other than little Evie Baker, the tomboy he used to play with when her mama went out to Reynier's Retreat every week to fix his sick mother's hair. He'd apparently persisted in that belief until the night she'd asked him, after a single shot of whiskey to give her courage, to be her first.

2

She'd had so many stupid dreams, and he'd crushed them all. But not before he gave her what she'd asked him for.

"Heard he got shot out there in Iraq," Mrs. Martin said as Evie's mama rolled a lock of gray hair around a fat pink curler.

"Yes indeed, got a Purple Heart," Mama said. "The senator was right proud, according to Lucy Greene."

"That's not what I heard!" Joely Hinch crowed. "Miss Mildred told me he's being kicked out of the Army because he didn't obey orders."

"Fiddlesticks," Mrs. Martin said. "That boy bleeds red, white, and blue. Same as his daddy and every last Girard that ever was born up in that big house."

Joely crossed her arms, looking slightly irritated to be contradicted. "You just wait and see," she said smugly.

"Shush up, y'all," Mama said. "I think he's coming in."

Evie's heart sank to her toes. She wasn't ready for this. Not on top of everything else. She was feeling so bruised and battered after her failure with the restaurant. She did not need Matt Girard swaggering back into her life and making her feel all the chaotic emotions she'd once felt for him.

She finished Stella's shampoo and wrapped her hair in a towel. "I'm not tipping you, Evangeline." Stella sniffed. "You have to be more careful than that."

"I know. And I don't blame you at all." Except, of course, she desperately needed every penny she could get if she hoped to escape this town again. It wasn't that Rochambeau was bad—it's that it was bad for *her*. Always had been.

Here, she always felt like the awkward kid who lived in a tiny cottage with her mama and wore secondhand clothes because that's all they could afford. Didn't matter that the clothes were no longer secondhand, or that she wasn't a kid anymore. Or that she didn't care if the girls who lived in the nice big houses with the manicured lawns didn't like her; she still felt like that girl who wanted so desperately to fit in.

And the biggest part of fitting in had, at one time, relied on the man striding toward her mama's salon like he didn't have a care in the world. Evie's heart did a somersault as he reached the door.

Magazines snapped open in a flurry as the ladies tried to appear casually disinterested in the six-foot-two hunk of muscle about to open the glass door. More than one pair of eyes peeked over the tops of glossy pages as he stepped up to the sidewalk from the street.

No way in hell was she sticking around for this. It wouldn't take these ladies more than a few moments to remember the scandalous rumors about her and Matt, and she didn't want to be here when they did.

"If you'll excuse me, I have to get some things out of the back." Without waiting for a reply, she strode toward the stockroom. Rachel Mayhew, Mama's regular shampoo girl, looked up and smiled as she passed. Rachel was only twenty, so she probably didn't know about Evie's disastrous night with Matt. Or maybe she did, considering the way this town talked.

What should have been Evie's own private shame had all too quickly become common knowledge back then. Part of that was her own fault, and part was Matt's—but she still wasn't sticking around to endure the sidelong glances and whispered conversations.

Life had beaten her up enough recently and she wasn't in the mood to feel like a wounded teenager today.

A month ago, she'd said goodbye to her dream. It still hurt. Her lovely little bistro in Florida was now in the bank's hands, and all because she'd trusted a man. Or mostly because she'd trusted a man.

Her restaurant, Evangeline's, hadn't exactly been doing a booming business, but things had been getting better and growth had been steady. It had, for a time, flourished under David's management, which was how she'd grown to trust his insistence that he knew what he was doing and that she should spend her time perfecting her recipes instead of worrying over the mundane details.

David was cocky, charming, and utterly confident. She'd found that intriguing. One thing had led to another, and they'd ended up sharing a bed from time to time. She'd liked David, thought they were on the same page. He was an accountant who loved to cook, who knew a lot about social media and advertising, and who increased her profits by a few simple—or so he'd said—marketing tricks.

All of it lies. He'd increased her profits, yes. But then he'd robbed her blind. She'd seen the books on a regular basis and never known anything was out of whack. He hadn't meant her to know, of course, but it still bugged her that she hadn't seen through David's schemes.

No, she'd been so thrilled with the way things were going that she'd spent more time doing what she really loved—cooking and creating recipes for the Cajun fusion dishes she'd become known for in their community. A mistake that she still kicked herself over, even though

David had covered his tracks too well for her to see anything amiss.

She'd trusted him. But how had she not known he was bad news? How had she let herself be fooled by a handsome face and charming manners?

She'd learned in the aftermath of the destruction he'd wrought that the authorities thought he had ties to organized crime. He'd been skimming money, along with other more nefarious schemes such as money laundering and extortion. She hated to think about it. Evangeline's had been everything she'd ever wanted when she'd broken out of her hometown and gone to cooking school a few years ago.

But here she was again, back in Rochambeau and washing hair in her mama's salon, just like when she'd been in high school. *Loser.* All she wanted was to get out again at the first opportunity. Before that loser feeling wrapped around her throat and squeezed the rest of her dreams away.

Matt reached for the door, and Evie darted behind the stockroom curtain. Her heart slammed against her ribs as the tinkling bell announced his arrival. She turned to lean against the doorjamb and pushed the rose-print polyester aside with one finger. She was being silly. He wasn't here because of her. He was here because his sister had sent him on some errand or other for her wedding.

Hell, he probably wouldn't even blink twice if he ran smack into her.

Evie frowned. Her eyes slid down his body and back up again. He was still something to look at. Something easy on the eyes and hard on the senses.

He'd changed in ten years, but some things were still

the same. That cocky swagger as he'd approached the shop. He'd always walked like his daddy owned all the oil in the Gulf of Mexico. Which he damn near did. The Girards had been Rochambeau's wealthiest family for as long as anyone could remember.

Matt's dark hair was cut very short, and his shoulders were much broader than when he'd been seventeen. The fabric of his white cotton T-shirt stretched across a wide chest packed with muscle. His bare forearms made her throat go dry.

Something quivered deep inside her, the way it always had from the moment she'd become aware of Matt as more than a boy she played with. Something hot and dark and secret. Evie squashed the feeling ruthlessly.

He pushed a hand through his hair, every muscle of his torso seeming to bunch and flex with the movement. She would have sworn she heard a collective sigh from the ladies in the salon. Rachel absently ran water in her sink, cleaning out the soap bubbles from the last shampoo. When she got too close to the edge, the water sprayed up into her face.

Evie would have laughed if she too weren't caught up in Matt's every move. She'd adored him ten years ago and worshipped him until the night she'd given him her virginity.

What a mistake that had been. Not because the sex had been awful. No, it'd been pretty exciting, all things considered. It was what had happened afterward that ruined it for her. The shift in their relationship hadn't been what she'd expected. And then he'd been such an ass about it.

"Afternoon, ladies." Matt tipped his head to them.

"Afternoon," they murmured in unison, voices sugary and lilting, eyes assessing and cataloging him.

"Miz Breaux." He took her mother's hand and kissed it like a courtier.

"Oh, shoot." She smacked him playfully on the shoulder. "What do you want? Don't you know this is a beauty parlor? Sid's Barber Shop is on Main Street."

"Well, ma'am." He grinned that devil-may-care grin Evie remembered so well. "I figured Old Sid can't see so well anymore and I'm still fond of my ears. I'd much rather have a lady's touch, if you know what I mean."

"Oh my." Mama giggled. *Giggled.*

Evie rolled her eyes. No wonder she couldn't pick a decent man. She came by the defect genetically. Mama had been divorced three times. She'd gone back to using her maiden name after the second one in order to avoid confusion. Evie had her daddy's last name, her sixteen-year-old sister had a different name, and Mama had yet another one.

"You don't even look like you need a haircut," Mama was saying.

He scrubbed a hand over the nape of his neck. "My sister thinks I do. And it's her wedding."

Mama giggled again. What was it about that man that turned even the smartest woman into an airhead? "Well, we can't let Christina be disappointed then, can we? But you'll have to wait until I finish with Mrs. Martin."

Mama gestured toward the pink vinyl seats in the front of the shop, and Matt gave her the famous Girard smile that used to melt the female hearts of Rochambeau High School. Evie felt a little hitch in her own heart, in spite of herself.

Why did he still have to be so damn good-looking? Was it too much to ask for him to be balding or growing a potbelly? Apparently so. Mother Nature was cruel.

"Sure thing, Miz Breaux."

Before he'd taken three steps toward the waiting area, Mama said, "You remember my daughter, Evangeline, don't you? She was a year behind you in school. Y'all used to play when I'd come out to do your mama's hair every week."

Evie's heart crashed into her ribs. The ladies in the shop grew quiet while they waited for his answer. She knew what they were thinking. What they were waiting for. Why should it bother her what they thought? What any of them thought?

It had been ten years ago, and it didn't matter any-more. She was grown up. Matt was grown up. Who cared?

Except that's not how Rochambeau worked, and she knew it. It might have been ten years, but he'd humiliated her. He'd broken her heart and tossed her to the wolves when she wasn't prepared to deal with the consequences of her actions. Not that anyone knew for sure what had happened, but rumors were usually enough in Rocham-beau.

"Yes, ma'am, I sure do. How is she?" He didn't sound in the least bit remorseful. But why would he? He'd departed for college a week later, and she'd been the one left behind to pick up the pieces.

"Evie's great," Mama announced. "Been living in Florida, but she's home now. Maybe you can talk to her while you wait. Y'all can catch up."

Evie's stomach plummeted to her toes. Oh no. No, no, *no*. What if she went into the bathroom and refused to come out? Or just quietly slipped out the back door and disappeared for a couple of hours? It was time for her lunch break, and—

Coward. Evie stiffened her spine. She wasn't running away. If it wasn't now, it'd be some other time. She couldn't avoid him forever. And far better to get this over with in public, while she could maintain her dignity and show the good people of Rochambeau there was nothing left to talk about.

"That'd be great," he said in an *aw shucks* way she didn't buy for a second. He might talk smooth and act all friendly and *gee-whiz ma'am*, but she knew better. God, did she know better.

He was nothing more than a self-centered, arrogant jerk with a giant sense of entitlement and no mercy for those he considered beneath him. A little corner of her heart still hurt like it had been yesterday, but she ruthlessly stomped on the feeling until it stopped.

"Good," her mother said as if it were the best idea in the world, her gaze sweeping the shop. "She was here just a minute ago. Evie? Evie?"

"She went in the back," Stella offered with what Evie was convinced was a hint of glee. Bitch.

Right. There was nothing Evie could do except face this particular blast from the past. Because there was no way on earth she'd ever let Matt Girard humiliate her again. She'd learned the hard way, but at least she'd learned.

"I'm right here, Mama," she said, whipping off her smock and pushing back the curtain.

TWO

MATT STILL DIDN'T KNOW WHAT he was doing at the Cut 'N Curl, but the second Evie Baker walked out of the stockroom, he felt as if someone had dropped a truckload of cement on his head. He hadn't seen her in ten years, not since the night he'd taken her virginity in the back of his daddy's Cadillac.

He'd never forgotten that night, never forgotten what a dickhead he'd been. He didn't expect she had either, which is why he wasn't surprised that she was currently glaring daggers at him.

Little Evie Baker. Not so little anymore.

He remembered the first time he'd ever seen her, when he'd been seven and his mama had first gotten sick. Norma Breaux always brought Evie with her when she came out to Reynier's Retreat. He hadn't known any of the kids in town because he'd been in private school then, but when Evie didn't scream after he dropped a worm on her, he knew he'd found someone fun to play with. His sister always screamed and hated even a speck of dirt to land on her pretty clothes, but Evie had been as good as any boy when it came to getting dirty.

Matt's temples throbbed. He'd never wanted to hurt her, God knew, but he'd been in a bad place back then. No, he'd been an arrogant, entitled prick. He knew he shouldn't have touched her when she'd asked, but he'd done it anyway.

By that point, he'd been trying for years to ignore the way she'd changed—one day she started wearing dresses and blushing whenever he looked at her; the next she had breasts and curves and he had no clue what to say to her anymore. But then she was there, standing before him with her eyes flashing and her cheeks flushed, and she'd just been so damn pretty, and so damn exciting, that he'd taken her hand, led her out to his daddy's car, and drove them away from the party they'd been at.

He'd felt guilty every moment since, but it was simply another thing to add to the heap of guilt inside his soul. Later, when he'd gotten his head on a bit straighter, he'd thought about calling her to apologize, but too much time had passed. By then he'd figured it was better to let it stay in the past.

A mistake, he thought now. This woman was not happy to see him. There was no pushing aside old mistakes, no going back to a simpler time when they'd gone fishing for crawdads together or sat in a tall tree and watched the gators glide through the bayou.

This Evie Baker was not in a forgiving mood, and he didn't blame her at all.

Still, a very male part of him couldn't help but appreciate her on another level. The level that had gotten him in trouble in the first place.

Evie had been a lovely teenager, but she'd blossomed

into an even lovelier woman. And he shouldn't do a damn thing about it, no matter how much he might want to. If he'd met her in a bar, he'd do everything he could to get her to go home with him.

But she was not a woman in a bar, and he owed her more than that. Matt focused on her pissed-off posture and flashing eyes.

"Evie." She stopped in front of him, arms crossed.

Jesus. She was all curves and sleek skin in a pair of cut-off jean shorts and a body-hugging pink tank top. Her legs were still long, still built to hug a man's waist.

Shit. He didn't need to be thinking that way.

And yet, no matter how hard he tried, he couldn't help it. It was the first thought that sprang to his head when his gaze glided over those legs. He'd kick himself for it later. Right now, he had a bigger problem: keeping his body from responding the way it wanted to at the memory of the last time he'd seen her.

She'd been naked, her lush form arrayed before him, her skin hot, silky, and damp with sweat. She'd been so damn sweet, so innocent. And it'd been a long time since he'd had any sweetness in his life.

"Hi, Matt."

"You're looking all grown up." He could have bit his tongue off when her eyes narrowed.

"It's what happens in ten years." Hostility swirled around her like a tornado.

He stretched his arm along the back of the chair beside him with a casualness he didn't feel. *New tactic.* "So how have you been?"

"Great. You?"

She was smiling now, but he wasn't fooled. Violet

eyes looked back at him with a mixture of embarrassment and fury. He'd done that. He'd put that look on her face, and it bothered him more than he could say.

God, he had a lot to answer for.

"Great," he said, parroting her like an idiot. "Why don't you have a seat?"

She shook her long black ponytail. He remembered wrapping his fists in that hair and tugging when they'd been children. And then he remembered wrapping his hands in her hair for a completely different reason.

"Thanks, but I can't stay. It was nice to see you."

"Wait a minute," he said as she moved away. She stopped and half-turned toward him. He glanced at the ladies watching them. They were just out of earshot, but he leaned forward and pitched his voice lower anyway. "What's your hurry? We've hardly said two words to each other."

He knew the reason, but he didn't want her to go. Not yet. There was something about having her near, something that sparked inside him and made him feel somewhat human again. He didn't know why, and he didn't know if it would last.

But he liked it. For the first time in months, he felt as if he could breathe again. As if he'd come home for real instead of simply going through the motions.

She sighed and turned to face him completely. He got the distinct impression she was calling up some sort of internal armor system in order to deal with him. Definitely not what he was used to in a woman—but then nothing about his relationship with Evie had ever been normal.

Usually, with other women, he was the one with the internal armor. He was the one who pulled away, because he had nothing to offer beyond a few stolen nights before he was back out on a mission.

But dealing with Evie felt completely different.

Her chin thrust out, her eyes flashing cold fire. "It's not personal. I'm just busy. And there's really nothing to say, is there?"

Matt stood. Hesitated when she seemed to shrink away from him. His height and size could be intimidating, he knew, but he hadn't expected that reaction from her of all people. As if she were afraid of him. She'd never been afraid of him, even when he'd jumped out from behind a tree and screamed bloody murder. She'd shrieked, of course—and then she'd socked him.

But this, here and now… it loosened any remaining restraints on his tongue.

"I'm sorry." He hadn't known quite what he would say if he ever saw her again, but that was certainly the least of what he owed her.

"For what?" The question surprised him, though perhaps it shouldn't. Evie Baker never had liked to show any weakness. She glanced over her shoulder to see if anyone was listening, lowered her voice another notch. "I came on to you, remember?"

At least she didn't pretend not to know what he was talking about. He admired that. And he also admired the way she always tried to take responsibility, even when it wasn't her fault. It was frustrating as hell, but so was Evie. She'd never backed down from a challenge in all the time he'd known her.

Still, she wasn't the one at fault here. He was. "Yeah, but you probably didn't expect me to brag about it."

Anger slid through him. He'd been such an arrogant

young fuck back then. Stupid. She'd given him her innocence, and he'd trampled it in the dirt like it was his due. He still had no idea what he'd been thinking when it was over and he'd swaggered back to the party.

He was leaving in a week, going off to West Point, and he remembered being so ready to escape. Ready to get the hell out of his father's house and be his own man. He'd been drunk, stupid, and filled with a rage at the world that he couldn't explain.

Evie shrugged. "What guy wouldn't have told his buddies, especially at that age? It was a long time ago."

He stepped closer, lowered his voice as Rachel Mayhew turned off the taps to her latest shampoo customer and cocked an ear in their direction.

"Maybe so, but I shouldn't have done it. We were friends and then—"

Her gaze snapped to his. "Were we? Were we ever?"

He felt her words like a barb to his heart. He deserved them. "I thought so. But I fucked up. I'm sorry."

He didn't bother to tell her he'd been falling-down drunk when he'd spilled the details of their evening to his friends. It wasn't an excuse.

She drew in what he assumed was a calming breath. And then she lifted those lashes and speared him with her pretty eyes again. "You did fuck up. Bad. But nobody gave you a hard time about it. They reserved that for me."

Shame rolled over him. "I know the guys made your life hell after I left."

"Not just the guys. Oh, they thought I was an easy mark, that's certain. But the girls weren't particularly nice either. Well, some of them. It hurt. A lot."

Before he could even begin to answer, to find the

right thing to say, she seemed to shake her head as if clearing away the fog of pain and anger. "Ancient history though. Over and done and not your problem." She glanced down at her bare wrist. "Oh, hey, look, it's time to get going. As much as this little reunion has buoyed my spirits, I gotta run."

"Evie—"

The door chimed then and a petite blond woman barreled inside, stopping Evie in her tracks and cutting off any further apologies Matt tried to make.

He recognized her cousin right away, but Julie Breaux didn't even spare him a glance.

"Hey, Evie, can you see if there's room to fit me in? I want to get my highlights done before the party tonight."

"Sure, let me check the schedule." Evie turned away and the woman started to follow, then came up short as if she'd just realized he was there.

If looks could freeze a guy in his tracks, he'd be stuck here into the next millennium. Julie arched an eyebrow, coolly assessing him.

"Heard you got a whole battalion captured out there in Iraq."

Jesus. There was nothing this town didn't blow out of proportion. Though what he usually did for the military was top secret, the Department of Defense propaganda machine had to work overtime once the Freedom Force took to the airwaves with news of their captives. By the time the DoD was done, Matt and his team looked like average G.I. Joes on a rescue mission rather than part of an elite counter-terrorism unit.

Which was precisely as it should be. There was no compromising the identity of HOT. Ever.

"Nope, it was just a platoon," Matt replied with a sarcasm he didn't feel. Jim Matuzaki and Marco San Ramos weren't ever coming home again because of him. Because he hadn't listened to his gut that night.

Not a day went by when he didn't think about them. Two guys he'd shared dusty foxholes and claustrophobic caves with, who'd watched his back more than once. He'd failed them by not scrubbing that mission. He'd wanted to get Jassar ibn-Rashad and save lives, but he'd lost two instead.

Ibn-Rashad was still out there. Still planning to kill.

And Matt might not ever get a chance to do a damn thing about it. His future with HOT was shaky at best after the failure of the last op. His team had been inactive for weeks while other HOT teams came and went. They'd had to sit and watch others go into the field, knowing they'd failed at their task, knowing others were in danger because of them.

Soon, he'd find out his fate. Next week, when he left Rochambeau, he had to attend a hearing on what had gone wrong out there in the desert. He would take responsibility for what had happened to his team, and he might never go on another operation again. His days in HOT very well could be over.

The place where he'd been shot still throbbed. The bullet—a long, ugly mother called a 7.62x39—had pierced the skin, but it had lost momentum going through his assault suit and gotten stuck without passing into his body. He'd been lucky that day, even if he hadn't deserved it. And luckier still when another HOT squad infiltrated the camp and rescued his team before the rest of them could be killed.

Standing here now, in a beauty salon in Rochambeau, was surreal at best. That sense of unreality he'd been living with for the last couple of months grew stronger. What the hell was he going to do if he got assigned to a desk for the rest of his career? It would, in effect, be a demotion, even if they never stripped him of rank.

And it would mean the end of everything that made any sense to him.

"So how's Christina doing?" Julie asked. "I haven't seen her in a couple of weeks now."

"Fine. Nervous, maybe, but fine."

"That's good. She's nice, your sister." *Unlike you* remained unspoken.

"She is indeed."

Julie's gaze dropped over him then. "So you gonna be at the lake tonight?" she asked, switching gears on him so fast he had to shake off a sense of whiplash.

He looked at Evie, didn't miss the look of disbelief that crossed her face as she glanced up from the appointment book. Her cousin had just performed a one-eighty turn at ninety miles an hour, going from hostile to flirtatious in a heartbeat.

"Probably not."

Julie stuck out her lower lip. "Too bad."

Definitely a sexual vibe there. He tried to imagine it. Couldn't. But he could imagine it with Evie. It'd been far too long since he'd had a woman, and though Evie was the wrong woman for a variety of reasons, he couldn't help but think about it.

"Great news, Jules," Evie said. "Mama can fit you in in about an hour."

"Sounds good," Julie said as she went and leaned on

the counter beside Evie.

"Will you be there tonight?" Matt asked Evie as she penciled her cousin's name in the appointment book. He didn't know why he was asking, since he had to attend a formal dinner for Christina and her fiancé tonight. But he wanted to know.

She looked up, her gaze locking with his, and he felt the jolt inside, right at gut level.

"No."

Julie pinched her arm. "Yes, you will. I promised everyone I'd bring you. You've been in town for almost a month and you keep promising to go. It's been so long, and everyone misses you."

Evie looked skeptical and Matt felt a throb of irritation at her cousin. "I really don't think—" Evie began.

"Aw, Evie, come on. It's just one night. Don't be so stuck up."

"We'll talk about it later." Evie was clearly not happy with the idea. She put the pencil down and grabbed Julie's arm. "Let's go get some lunch. Give your sister my congratulations, in case I don't see her before Saturday," she said to Matt.

The two of them headed for the back of the shop, disappearing behind the same flowered curtain she'd emerged from earlier. Matt turned and sank down on the pink vinyl seat again, feeling oddly numb and out of place.

He was home in a pink nightmare of a salon, Evie hated him, and Jim and Marco were dead. The contrast was so stark, so gut-wrenching. Half the time he just wanted to shout at everyone that they had no idea what kind of things happened out there in the world and how dare they go on as if everything was normal, but the rational part of him knew they wouldn't understand. Not only that, but they'd also think he was crazy.

He thought of Evie's dark hair and flashing eyes. For a few minutes, she'd made him feel grounded. Real. Now he felt the way he had for the past two months: as if he were walking around with his guts on the outside.

"You ready, sugar?" Norma Breaux said then, whipping Matt from his dark thoughts. She shook out a hot-pink plastic smock and wrapped it around his neck as he sat down in her chair.

He was ready for anything these days.

And none of it good.

French Quarter, New Orleans

The files were gone. The computer. Everything. He'd been careless. David West melded into the shadows of the building, peering into the dark alley. Rivera's grunts had been in his room. He couldn't go back, nor could he verify what he knew to be true. But he didn't need to. He'd seen them, seen Brianna Sweeney leaving with her two thugs in tow.

Once, he'd been one of them, doing as he was told, moving into an area and enforcing Ryan Rivera's will. He'd been the bean counter, much higher on the brain meter than any of those three, but he knew them intimately. Had worked with them countless times.

Most recently with Brianna in Florida at a place called Evangeline's. He thought he'd evaded the organization this time, but sonofabitch if he hadn't quite done it after all.

He'd wanted out, but apparently once Rivera had a hold of you, you never got out.

Cold sweat dripped down his spine. He'd blown it. He should have moved on by now, but he'd holed up here for the past two weeks instead, indulging in the decadence and sin the Quarter had to offer. He'd gotten cocky, and he'd gotten stupid. He'd been so sure he'd covered his tracks. He was going by a new name, and he always paid in cash.

He'd left Florida five months ago, moving around constantly until he'd landed here. He'd been *safe*, goddamn it! Certain he'd pulled it off. How had they found him?

He shook his head. It still swam from one too many absinthe drips. He pressed a hand to the damp brick to steady himself and swallowed down a flood of acid in his throat. The sounds of revelry and jazz wafted down the alley from Bourbon Street. The air was hot and sweet, saturated with humidity, liquor, and the smells of spicy food.

David sucked in a sharp breath against the bile rising in his throat. Brianna had his files now, the bitch. Panic flooded him. Briefly, he wondered if she would negotiate. If she would consider a cut of the money he'd taken to give them back again.

He put his forehead against the brick and breathed deep. Fuck no, she wouldn't negotiate. He knew that. He'd tried once before when he'd sensed she was as sick of working for Rivera as he was.

But Brianna was tough, and she wasn't caving. And now he was out here with his dick swinging in the wind. He had no guarantees without those files. The money wouldn't do him a damn bit of good if he was dead.

It had taken years to build the dossier. It was his protection, his assurance that Rivera wouldn't send anyone to kill him. So long as he had the files, he was safe. Or so he'd told himself—except that he hadn't quite believed it enough to live out in the open under his own name.

He should have set up an online backup, but he'd been too worried it would somehow fall into the wrong hands. He didn't want evidence of Rivera's crimes—and his by extension—sitting on a server somewhere just waiting for the Feds to find it.

It was different if he traded it for immunity, but to have the Feds get all the info without him having it as a bargaining chip?

Not happening.

Goddamn it!

Right now, he almost wished he'd taken the chance. If he *had* parked those files somewhere online, he wouldn't be standing here and cursing himself six ways to Sunday. He'd only be a simple download away from replacing the evidence, but instead the files were gone and he was as vulnerable as a virgin in a whorehouse.

He should have moved to a new location by now. That was the second dumbass thing he'd done. He'd stayed here when he should have gone south and kept going until he nearly fell off the tip of South America. He was tired of doing Rivera's dirty work, tired of being the brains behind the financials and getting nothing in return.

23

Hell, Rivera hadn't even recognized how valuable an asset he could be.

But David had gotten the last laugh when he'd skimmed a cool ten million for himself out of the Florida operations. He wasn't greedy—Rivera was worth far more—but he wanted his due.

Yeah, he'd run Evie's business into the ground in the process. Maybe he shouldn't have done it. Her paltry earnings were only a drop in the bucket of his ten mil—but it had gotten him what he wanted faster than if he'd waited another few months to skim the money out of Rivera's operations. Simply put, he'd had no choice if he wanted his freedom. And he wanted that far more than he'd wanted anything else.

David shook his head again. It wasn't too late for him yet. Rivera probably thought he had him between a rock and a hard place. But Rivera didn't know a damn thing about him if he believed that.

There were other kinds of backups. Other ways to hide information. David just had to go and sweet-talk Evie one more time. A much more difficult task this time around, not only because she was pissed at him but also because Brianna Sweeney was on his ass.

But desperation had a way of making a man do whatever it took. He *would* get those files back again.

And then he would disappear for good.

THREE

EVIE FROWNED AT HERSELF IN the mirror as she turned this way and that.

"You look gorgeous, Evie. Now let's get moving."

Evie turned to her cousin with a sigh. "It's a lovely dress, but I'm not quite sure it's appropriate for an evening at the lake."

What she really wanted was to pull on her faded jeans and a T-shirt, but Julie wouldn't hear of it.

As expected, Julie scoffed. "Please. We'll be at the pavilion—and the other girls will be dressed up too, you'll see."

Julie smoothed a hand over the denim mini she wore. She'd paired it with a silk tank and a pair of pink platforms, and she looked gorgeous. Julie was petite and cute, whereas Evie was tall and not so cute.

Evie tugged at the hem of the dress. It was a pale pink color with wide straps and a skirt that was a hair too tight. And short. The three-inch heels Julie had talked her into wearing didn't help either. "It's a bit short, don't you think?"

Julie shook her auburn ringlets. "No. It looks amazing on you! That dress has never looked as good on me. Blush is *so* not my color."

Evie sighed and gathered the tiny purse Julie had insisted she carry. "This really isn't me, Jules. I'm a chef. I work in hot kitchens all day and I wear comfortable clothes."

"You aren't a chef right now," Julie pointed out. "Think of it like you're on vacation. Everybody gets dressed up on vacation, right?"

"Yes, but I don't feel like I'm on vacation."

Julie huffed. "Is this about Matt Girard and what happened back in high school?"

Evie felt a tiny pinch in her chest. "Of course not."

Julie looked militant. "Good. Because that was high school, Evie, and we aren't there anymore. No one gives a good goddamn that you slept with Matt our junior year or that he bragged about it. Half those girls would have dropped their panties in a New York second if they'd thought he'd give them a lay. Still would."

Evie's skin was hot and she wasn't quite sure why. Because Julie was right, and she really didn't give a shit what people thought about her these days—her reaction in the salon notwithstanding. She wasn't sixteen anymore, and she couldn't be hurt by whispers and rumors.

No, her issues with this town were the same issues she'd always had—the ones where she felt like there was a box she was supposed to stay in and she just didn't want to. Aside from that, her only problem today had been coming face-to-face with the boy she used to love and remembering the way he used to make her feel.

"Fine, I'll wear it. Let's go."

"Excellent," Julie replied. "Besides, you look hot—and you want to impress Matt, don't you?"

Evie's stomach bottomed out. "Why would I want to do that?" She waved a hand. "He's old news. Besides, he's not coming, remember?"

Julie laughed, her dark eyes sparkling. "Right. Didn't you see the way he was looking at you today? He'll be there."

"He wasn't looking at me *any* way. We were just talking."

Julie shook her head. "Girl, I think the heat in those kitchens has gone to your head. Matt Girard is just about the hottest thing on two legs, and he was definitely looking at you with interest. He wants in your panties again, trust me." Julie grinned. "And if you're smart, you'll let him."

Evie felt as if her cheeks were six shades of fuchsia. The last time she'd let a man in her panties, she'd lost her damn restaurant. And though the thought of Matt there made her body tingle in ways it hadn't in a very long time, there was no way she was going to repeat the mistakes of her past. They might not be teenagers, and she might not give a damn what anyone said these days since she was no longer vulnerable, but sleeping with Matt was just a bad idea all around.

Her feelings for Matt had always been a giant tangle, like a ball of Christmas lights buried in the garage all year, and she really didn't want to start sorting them out again.

"He won't be there, Jules. Mark my words."

Julie sighed. "Fine. But he will be in town for a few days, so do yourself a favor and don't push him away when he comes around. You definitely need to get laid."

Evie shook her head. "Maybe so, but he's the wrong

man to do it."

Julie snorted. "Well, I can promise you one thing. If he looks at me that way, I'm not saying no."

"Go for it," Evie said, though a little twinge of jealousy speared into her at the thought.

"There's always Jimmy Thibodeaux, if you insist on saying no to Matt. He's been asking after you since he got back."

Evie frowned. Jimmy had been one of the worst back in high school after Matt had left. Always calling her Easy Evie and grabbing her ass. She'd hated him then. She didn't much care for the idea of him now since she'd heard he hadn't changed much. Thankfully, he'd been away in Montana on a hunting trip for most of the month and she hadn't yet had the dubious pleasure of running into him again.

"I'll pass."

Julie shrugged. "Probably best. Jimmy's not been quite right in the head lately. He pulled a knife on Ginny Temple a couple of months ago."

Evie's heart somersaulted. "What do you mean?"

"She said something about his hunting dog crapping on her lawn and Jimmy waved that knife around like he was some kind of avenger. But nothing came of it."

Evie shook her head. Damn crazy Cajun redneck. She hadn't missed that about Rochambeau at all. "And you were seriously suggesting I should sleep with him?"

Julie's mouth turned down. "Of course not! I was kidding. Geez, you've lost your sense of humor lately."

"It hasn't been a good few months, Jules."

"Which is why I said you should get laid. Take your mind right off it. But no Matt and definitely no Jimmy."

28

She patted Evie's arm. "We'll find someone."

"I'd rather we didn't."

Julie grinned. "We'll see. Now let's stop talking about it and get going."

Evie's little sister looked up from her position in front of the television as they walked through the living room. Evie's heart twisted at the look on the girl's face. Evie had been home a month now, and Sarah was still sullen and withdrawn.

Not that she could blame the kid. There was ten years difference in their ages, and Evie hadn't exactly been around for the past few years. No, she'd been off doing her own thing and calling home on occasion rather than making an effort to be a part of her little sister's life. She hadn't thought of it much at the time, but being home and seeing the effects—well, it made her feel rotten every time she saw that wary look on Sarah's face.

"Where are y'all going looking like that?" Sarah was curious, but her tone said she couldn't care less.

"It's a party." Julie put her hands on her hips. "For adults."

Sarah snorted. "Yeah, I figured that."

"I don't have to go," Evie said, though Julie made a noise when she did. "Is there something you want to do tonight? We could go for pizza, or maybe a movie?"

Sarah turned back to the TV and pressed the channel button. "I ate pizza for lunch. And there's nothing at that lame theater I want to see."

Evie sighed. "Mama's at the Moose Lodge for the evening. Are you sure you don't want me to stay?"

Sarah's eyes flashed. "I know where Mama is. She's been going to bingo every week for the past four years.

Not that *you* would know that."

Julie bristled. "You need to lighten up, little girl. Your sister's had a bad time of it and she could use your support."

Sarah shot to her feet. "Yeah, well why do I have to be nice to her when she's never thought twice about me and Mama? Went off to that fancy cooking school and forgot all about us. Now she's back and thinks we're supposed to care? Like hell." Sarah tossed the remote onto the couch and stalked toward her bedroom.

Julie's dozen or so bracelets clinked as she popped her hands on her hips again and stared after Sarah. "That little brat. You want me to go get her and make her apologize?"

Evie shook her head, even as she swallowed the lump in her throat. "No, forget it. She didn't get mad overnight, and she won't get un-mad that way either."

"Your mama's been too indulgent with her. She would've paddled your behind for acting that way, no matter how old you were."

"Mama's busy, Jules. And I doubt Sarah acts that way toward her. Me, on the other hand..." She sighed. "Maybe if I *had* been here, she wouldn't be so hostile. I can't really blame her for not trusting me."

Julie snorted. "Don't kid yourself, girlfriend. She's a teenager. Brattiness is practically a requirement." Julie tossed her hair over her shoulder and peered up at Evie. "C'mon, you ready to go get laid? That'll certainly help your mood, I promise."

Evie laughed, though inside she still stung from Sarah's rejection. But there wasn't much she could do about it. Even if she stayed here, she'd get nowhere with the kid. Sarah would hide in her room until Mama came home later. "God no. But I'll go out to the lake with you and have a beer or two. Then I'm coming home. *Alone*."

Julie rolled her eyes. "Your loss. Especially when Matt Girard shows up."

"He's not coming, Julie."

"Bet he does. And when I win, you have to cook your famous gumbo for me."

Evie rolled her eyes. "He won't."

Julie looked smug. "We'll see..."

Rochambeau Lake had a split personality. One side— the side with picnic tables, charcoal grills, and a big pavilion—was clear and calm. But the farther you went across the lake, moss-draped cypress trees crowded together like shadowy sentinels and the lake became a bayou. Gators swam deep in the cypress, down the long winding fingers of murky water that branched and stretched for miles throughout the parish. Snakes coiled in the trees overhanging the water, sometimes dropping in on unsuspecting anglers.

Evie couldn't see the people splashing in the dark, but she heard them laughing. Crazy to go swimming in the middle of the night, even if it was hot. A flash of murky water and the black S-curve silhouette of a snake flowing toward her were the most vivid memories of her last foray into the bayou.

Evie shuddered. She wasn't getting into—or onto—the bayou ever again. She'd never been particularly squeamish, but that afternoon when the snake had fallen out of the tree and into the little canoe—which she and Julie then proceeded to overturn in their panic—had seared itself into her memory.

Just then, Jimmy Thibodeaux reappeared with a beer and a wine cooler, and Evie gritted her teeth. So much for avoiding Jimmy. He'd made a beeline for her the minute they arrived and he hadn't let her out of his sight in the fifteen minutes since. He'd been nothing but polite, however, so she couldn't exactly get away from him without being rude.

And she wasn't prepared to be rude just yet. She kept thinking of him pulling a knife on Ginny Temple, but she didn't think he was crazy enough to do something like that here with so many people around. The other guys would tackle him if he tried it.

Evie craned her neck, looking for Julie, but her cousin had slipped into Steve LaValle's arms and didn't look as if she was slipping out again anytime soon. She didn't think Julie had meant to leave her with Jimmy, but that didn't change the current situation.

"I know you said beer, but I thought you might like this better." Jimmy handed her a wine cooler and sat down on the bench beside her. "I know how you ladies like foo-foo drinks."

Evie's jaw felt like it might crack. "Thanks." She scooted down the bench as much as possible. The crowd closed to hide Julie and Steve from her view.

Damn it.

She turned and tried to smile politely at Jimmy. He

wasn't bad-looking, with his dark hair and dark eyes, but she'd never liked him. He was loud, brazen, and a bit too macho. Always had been. If she had to hear another story about him bagging a gator—or a moose in Montana— she'd probably scream.

"So," Jimmy said, his hand skimming across her bare knee and up her thigh. "You back in town for good?"

Evie pushed his hand away and kept smiling. There wasn't an ounce of friendliness in it, but she knew Jimmy was too dumb to see it. No, he leered and groped like they were back in high school and she was still Easy Evie. More than anything, it made her mad. Livid.

"Nope," she replied through clenched teeth. "I'll be leaving again soon."

She didn't know that for sure, but it was definitely the plan. The sooner, the better. She felt a pang of guilt when she pictured Sarah's sullen face, but that was life. *Her life* dictated that she had to get out of Rochambeau or go crazy.

"That's a shame. Maybe we could get together before you go." He leaned in a little more, his fingers skimming the side of her breast.

Evie shot to her feet, and Jimmy barely managed to catch himself before he fell into her vacant seat. "No, thanks." She said it politely when what she really wanted to do was sock him. "I'm not ready to start a relationship."

"Who said anything about a relationship?" Jimmy blinked up at her, clueless as usual. But there was something in those eyes, something cold and mean. It made her shiver. "You got time for sex, ain't you?"

Warning bells rang in her head as she faced him down. Her smile could have cut glass. Maybe she should

33

have socked him anyway. "Oh darn, I took a vow of celibacy two days ago. Look, there's my cousin."

She spun on her high heels, thankful she didn't trip and make a mockery of her grand exit, and walked away without waiting for an answer. She didn't turn around to look at Jimmy, but she could feel his eyes on her as she stepped into the pavilion. She'd pissed him off, that was for sure.

Evie breathed a sigh of relief as she skirted the make-shift dance floor where couples gyrated to the music someone played using an iPod and two great big speakers. She didn't think Jimmy would pull anything, but she liked having a crowd around her just in case.

She searched for Julie, finally spotting her again. Julie leaned back against Steve, her head on his shoulder, her lips tilted up to accept a lingering kiss.

By the looks of it, Julie wasn't going to be willing to leave just yet. Julie had probably had sex with Steve a thousand times, but they still had to go through this ritual-courting thing first. They got together, broke up, then made up a few days later with wild monkey sex. This looked like a monkey-sex night, but there was a protocol to follow. Why they couldn't just admit they were hot for each other and go for it, Evie would never understand.

Evie set the wine cooler she'd nearly forgotten she was still holding on top of a table as she skirted the crowd. She'd go hang out in Julie and Steve's corner until they were ready to leave. If she were lucky, it'd be a matter of minutes before they couldn't keep their hands off each other and wanted to go back to Steve's place. Before they did, she'd get Julie's keys and drive herself home.

"I think you lost your drink."

Evie knew that voice. It slid over her like hot silk and she spun to find Matt Girard standing behind her, holding the bottle she'd just ditched. Why did her heart skip the second he showed up? And why did he have to look so *delicious*?

"I didn't lose it."

He stood there in faded jeans and a dark T-shirt that molded to his hard pecs and biceps. But it wasn't his clothing that got her attention so much as his eyes. There was something in them, something she didn't remember seeing when he'd been seventeen. He'd been part of this crowd long ago, much more than she had, but he no longer looked like he belonged—in spite of the longing looks some of the women were casting in his direction.

His gaze dropped over her before rising again, slowly, and her body reacted as if he'd brushed his fingers over her. There was something hot, sharp, and thrilling in that gaze—and she was way more susceptible to it than she wanted to be.

Once, she would have given anything for him to look at her like that. Now, she wasn't certain she'd survive the experience.

"Great dress." His voice was silky.

Evie swallowed. She was tingling, and that wasn't a good thing. The last time she'd tingled over this man, it had not turned out so well. "Thanks. I think."

He grinned. "It's definitely a compliment."

Evie crossed her arms and tried to look cool. "Thought you weren't coming tonight."

"Now what made you think a thing like that?"

Her blood slogged like molasses in her veins. "I believe you said 'probably not' in response to Julie's query."

His teeth flashed. "Yeah, but that's before I knew you'd be here."

"What do you want, Matt?" Her heart thrummed like she was sixteen again.

His gaze dropped once more. "Maybe I'd like to see what's under that dress." His voice sounded low and sexy. It pooled in her belly and sent hot waves of need spiraling outward.

"Forget it," she said with a conviction she didn't quite feel. "As I recall, the last time didn't turn out so well for me."

"I know, and I'm sorry."

"You said that earlier."

"I did."

She tossed her hair over her shoulder. "So why'd you come then? I heard you the first time."

He sighed. "Evie. Jesus." He raked a hand through his hair, and her blood hummed at the ripple and flex of muscle. "I just got back from the desert. Life out there is… unpredictable. It makes a man think. And I've decided that I don't like feeling like a shithead for something that happened ten years ago. I want to clear the slate."

Evie let out a breath. She'd been so hurt; then she'd been angry. But it was a long time ago and she couldn't hold a grudge forever. Even now, she recognized that most of her feelings about the incident were still tied up with having her love so cruelly flung back in her face. The other stuff, while definitely unpleasant at the time, hardly mattered anymore.

"We were kids, Matt."

"I hurt you."

She didn't flinch from his gaze. "You did. But I'm not sixteen anymore. And like I said today, it was my fault too. I asked you to do it. And I told a couple of my friends about it, so it wasn't just you telling the boys." She shrugged with a lightness she didn't quite feel. "What happened was probably inevitable. The guys thought I was easy. The girls who were jealous said I was a slut. They made my senior year difficult in some ways. But what hurt the most was never hearing from you again."

There, she'd said it. She'd told him what really hurt, and she'd given him a window into her feelings back then. He'd have to be an idiot not to know, but it was always possible he hadn't.

"I should have called you."

The music changed, the beat slowing. Evie took a step backward instinctively, but Matt caught her hand and held it tight. She tugged once, then stopped. They faced each other across a few feet of space. Around them, couples began to slide together, fitting into each other.

Evie's pulse beat harder. Her skin sizzled where they touched, his big hand engulfing hers, his palm calloused in a way that shocked her. He was a Girard—rich, entitled— and he had a workman's hands.

"One dance."

Her insides melted a little more. "I'm not sure it's a good idea."

But what she really wanted to do was say yes.

His eyes were bright. "Why not? We're adults now, Evie. No one's getting hurt here."

He said it like it was so easy, but was it really? Wasn't she still vulnerable on some level? She was down on her luck right now, feeling like a loser, and here he was, the same gorgeous, cocky, beautiful creature he'd always been.

Except, no, he was more than that, wasn't he? There was something behind his smile now. Something dark and sad. Pain flared in his gray eyes and then was gone so quickly she wondered if she'd imagined it.

It shocked her. She suddenly wanted to know what had happened to him. She'd heard about him being held captive by terrorists. How could he not be affected by something like that? Of all the things she'd expected Matt Girard to do with his life, putting himself into danger had not even occurred to her. He had everything. Why would he want to risk his life that way?

She remembered when his mother had died. He'd been twelve. Mama had taken her to the wake out at Reynier's Retreat. There were so many people crowding the beautiful rooms of the mansion. The house was heavy with sadness and thick with grief, and it had scared her. She'd escaped to run down the wide lawn. She'd known where to find Matt. He'd been curled inside the hollow of a tree they'd found a few years before.

He'd been dressed in a black suit, his dark hair slicked back carefully, his gray eyes wide and wounded as he looked up at her. Her heart had lifted into her throat then. She'd only been eleven, but she'd felt something in that moment that rocked her world—and would continue to rock her world until she was sixteen and shattered by his casual cruelty.

But not that day. That day, she'd slid into the hollow and sat down beside him. When she'd put her arms around him, he'd turned his face into the crook of her neck and wept.

Evie sucked in a breath. How could she walk away from him now, knowing there was something behind those eyes? He was hurting again, and she didn't know why.

"One dance, Evangeline," he said softly when she hesitated. "Make a soldier's night. I just got back from the desert a few days ago. I'd like to dance with a pretty woman and forget about that hellhole for a while."

Evie swallowed. "That's not fair."

He grinned. "Because you can't say no now?"

She nodded.

"Good for me then."

"Just one dance and we go our separate ways, got it?" Because she didn't want to feel this tangle of emotions again. This tiny blossoming in her heart that said she was going to be in so much trouble if she didn't shut it down quickly.

"If that's what you want." His voice was rough.

He took her other hand then, ran his palms up her arms to her shoulders. Little sparks of sensation swirled in her belly, lighting her up like the Fourth of July. He pulled her into his arms right there on the edge of the dance floor.

Evie braced her hands against his chest, pressed back when he tried to bring her closer. It was already overwhelming to be so close to him. To feel his heat and hardness next to her body.

To feel everything she'd once wanted so much.

"I don't bite," he murmured. "Unless you want me to."

"Hardly." But heat flowed through her at the thought. Evie closed her eyes. This was insane. Why had she agreed? It was like she'd stepped back in time and gotten caught in all her girlish dreams.

She was in Matt Girard's arms, dancing with him in public. Poor Evie Baker and the rich senator's son. The boy most likely to succeed and the girl who would never amount to anything. What a pair.

She should have refused, no matter how much she ached for him. No matter how much history flowed between them.

But he'd trotted out that returning soldier line and she'd caved like a fallen soufflé.

She should walk away right now, but she couldn't seem to make herself do so. Instead, she tried to keep distance between them, stood stiffly in his embrace with her hands on his shoulders until he grasped her arms and twined them around his neck. "At least look like you're having fun."

"What if I'm not?"

He laughed. "Pretend."

They swayed to the music without talking. His body was so hard, like he'd been carved from marble. He was lean and lethal, a finely honed military machine. From the hard contours of his shoulders to the flat planes of his abdomen, there wasn't an ounce of softness anywhere on him.

His hands were in the small of her back, caressing her as they moved. She became acutely aware of her breasts pressing against his chest. When she tilted her head back to look up at him, his eyes were intense. She turned away even as a thrill shot through her.

"I've missed you, Evie. I didn't realize how much until I saw you today."

"Don't lie."

"I'm not lying."

A bead of sweat trickled between her breasts and her skin grew hot. She'd forgotten how steamy Louisiana nights could be. Why did these morons still party at the lake? They weren't teenagers anymore, and they had houses.

"We haven't spoken in ten years. I hardly think you missed me that much."

Matt's hands slid across her back, leaving a trail of flame in their wake. "I said I didn't realize it until today. That's the truth. You were always honest with me, Evie. I liked that. Needed it."

Evie snorted, more to cover the riot of sensations inside her than anything. "You couldn't have liked it that much. You used to sit on me until I cried uncle."

Matt laughed. "Yeah, you really knew how to piss me off back then. But you were my best friend when we were little."

"Until you left private school and started going to Rochambeau Junior High. Then I was persona non grata."

"Hardly. But you were a girl, and I needed to get in good with the guys."

"And the other girls."

He gave her that pretty grin of his. "Yeah, that too."

As if he'd ever had an ounce of trouble in that department. She remembered his first day in public school, how thrilled she'd been to have him there where they could hang out together—and how jealous she'd been when he'd started paying attention to other girls.

"We go back a long ways, don't we?" Her arms around his neck relaxed a little, until it felt almost natural to be dancing with him like this.

"Yeah. It's kinda nice, isn't it?"

41

Her body was singing and zinging with sparks. "It is, in a way. In other ways, it's not so great."

He looked puzzled. "How do you mean?"

Evie sighed. "Geez, Matt, you aren't that clueless. It was fun while we were kids. I adored you—and then it changed as I got older and realized what boys were for. But it didn't change for you, and that set me up for a lot of angsty nights discussing you endlessly with my friends."

"You discussed me?" He looked puzzled and she wanted to pinch him. Men.

"Of course. It's what girls do. We like a boy and we obsess about it. About what he said, what he did, how he looked at us. Does he like us or not? Things like that. I wanted you to like me as a girl, not as a buddy. And you never did."

"I did." Her heart did a little skip that it shouldn't have so long after the fact. "But I tried not to. I didn't want to mess up what we had."

"We didn't have anything by then. You'd been ignoring me since I got breasts."

His gaze dropped to her chest and she automatically stuck a finger under his chin and tilted his head up again.

His grin was not in the least apologetic. "Hey, you mentioned them. They are magnificent, by the way."

She refused to feel an ounce of pleasure over that comment. "I did indeed, but that wasn't an invitation to ogle. Focus on my eyes, Girard."

"Such pretty eyes. So blue they're almost purple."

Evie rolled said eyes. "Flattery? After all this time? Care to tell me what's up?"

His expression changed, growing quietly serious. "I wish I could." He gave his head a little shake. "I've seen a lot of bad shit in this world, Evie. You're soft and sweet and you smell good."

There was a lump in her throat. "It's just perfume. You should smell me when I've been picking crabmeat out of shells all day. Or after a long shift on the line, standing over a hot grill—"

"Evangeline."

Evie blinked up at him. "What?"

"You gave me one dance. Do we have to talk about crabmeat and grills?"

Heat slid into her cheeks. "No, I suppose not."

He slid his hands to her hips and pulled her tighter against him until she wanted to whimper. "Good. Because I want to remember this the next time I'm on an op."

Evie dropped her gaze from the heated intensity of his. They moved together silently for a few moments. And then she spoke. "I heard you got shot. Did you really?"

"Yes."

Her eyes flew up again and her heart pounded. "Where?"

"A flesh wound in the side, nothing life threatening. Hurt like hell though."

She shook her head. "I can't understand how you ended up in the military. It's not what I thought you'd do."

His eyes glittered. "And I always knew you'd do something with cooking."

She didn't miss that he'd deflected her comment, but she smiled anyway. "How could you know that? It wasn't like I ever cooked a meal for you when we were swinging from trees or sneaking up on Christina with crawdads."

"No, but you talked about food a lot. About the texture of cupcakes, the correct sweet-to-tart ratio of lemonade, and the heat index of your mama's jambalaya. And then you went to work out at Charlie's that summer before my senior year. I brought Jeanine Jackson on a date there, remember?"

Evie had to stifle a groan. "God, how could I forget? I dumped a pitcher of sweet tea down her shirt. But that had nothing to do with cooking."

Matt laughed. "No, it sure didn't. What did she say to you again?"

"I think *you bitch* is about right. Or some variation of that phrase."

"No, I mean before that. Before you 'tripped' and lost control of the tea."

Evie sighed. "She gave me a dirty look and told me not to talk to her boyfriend if I wasn't taking his order."

"Was that it?" His brows drew down as if he were thinking back. "I thought for sure it must have been something worse."

"I didn't like her tone."

Matt snickered. "Sounds about right. You never did back down from a fight."

The song ended then and Evie took a step backward. Matt's grip on her tightened, but then he let her go, his hands dropping to his sides. Evie swallowed. "Thanks for the dance. It was nice."

His gaze was so intense she wanted to look away, but she didn't. "It doesn't have to end here. I'm home for a few days. I want to see you again, Evie."

Her heart ricocheted around her chest. "I don't think it's a good idea."

He shook his head. "You keep saying that to me, *chère*, but your eyes say something different."

She clasped her hands together and took a deep breath. "I've always been weak where you're concerned. But too much time has passed and there's too much drama when you're involved. I've got enough going on in my life without adding you to the mix."

His expression sharpened. "Are you seeing someone?"

She wished she could say yes, wished it were true just long enough to make him go away. And she didn't, because she didn't want him to go away.

Geez, way to be strong, Evie.

"It doesn't matter. Besides, you're leaving in a few days. What would be the point in spending any time together?"

"I think you know the point." His voice was a deep, sexy growl, and she felt an answering throb in her belly and her sex.

Impulsively, she stepped forward and squeezed his hand while she gave him a peck on the cheek. He turned his head and their lips met, but the contact was too brief as she backed away again, her heart hammering in her throat and ears.

"Goodbye, Matt."

Evie turned to go just as the lights in the pavilion snapped out. She stumbled to a halt as the crowd gasped. Scattered headlights illuminated the area, but not enough to see more than a few inches.

A car backfired, and Evie nearly leapt out of her skin. Someone screamed, and then a chorus of screams erupted when the car backfired again. The crowd surged, knocking her off balance. A hand wrapped around her arm and tugged her up against a hard chest.

"We have to get out of here." It was Matt's voice in her ear and she turned her head, prepared to ask him why—until the car backfired again and she realized what was really happening.

That wasn't a car. It was a gun.

FOUR

MATT STOOD IN THE DARKNESS with Evie pressed against his body and listened. She was soft and warm, but he had no time to enjoy the feel of her in his arms. Something was wrong. The power could go out, sure enough, but those had been gunshots in the aftermath.

Probably just some drunken rednecks, but Matt never assumed. He didn't even want to be thinking about work now, but his instincts had jolted into high gear the instant the lights went out. Too many years in HOT had made him into a military machine that kicked into action at the slightest hint of trouble.

Someone might be playing, but they were playing dangerously, shooting a weapon in a crowded area. It was utterly dark—and then a couple of cars popped on their headlights, shining straight at the crowd. Matt swore. The lights weren't helpful so much as blinding.

The gun sounded again, and someone screamed. The crowd started to surge forward.

"Come on." He started to pull Evie toward the woods.

"Where are we going?"

"Away from the crowd."

"Shouldn't we get to a car?"

"We will. But right now, we need to go this way."

Out of habit, he'd assessed the area when he'd first arrived, and he'd kept a mental calculation of landmarks and cover the entire time he'd been here tonight. It was as natural to him as breathing, and just as necessary to his survival. Though his eyes hadn't quite adjusted, he knew the parking lot was a couple hundred yards away even without the headlights for reference.

Too far across open ground to make a run for it, especially when the person on his six was a woman in high-heeled shoes.

Matt reached instinctively for his military-issue nine mil before he remembered it wasn't there. Damn thing was in a locker with all his other gear, far away at Fort Bragg.

Hell, he didn't even have a knife. He should have— every Southern man carried at least a pocketknife—but he didn't. Colonel Mendez had told him to keep out of trouble, so he was keeping out. Besides, this was Rochambeau, not some third world shithole where the latest terrorist scumbag was hiding away.

Yeah, sometimes a crazy Cajun got a little out of hand, which is what he suspected now. Didn't mean it wasn't dangerous though.

Matt started moving again, getting farther from the pavilion. This time when he stopped, he drew Evie up close behind him.

He could feel her trembling but he knew she'd never admit to being afraid. That had never been Evie's style.

"It'll be okay." He spoke over his shoulder. "Trust me."

He scanned the darkness, wishing he had his night-vision goggles. With NVGs, he'd be able to distinguish terrain, see movement. Find this jerk and take him down before anyone got hurt.

But first he needed to get Evie somewhere safe, away from the shots. And then he *would* find this guy and kick the fucker's ass for being so damn stupid. If the cops didn't get here first.

Behind them, the pavilion was in pandemonium. People yelled and screamed, surging toward their cars. Tables scraped against concrete. Bottles shattered. A woman wailed.

A car turned then, the headlights sweeping across the grass. Straight toward their position.

Matt tried to duck out of the path of the beam, but too late.

The gun exploded again, closer and louder this time, and Matt jerked Evie to the ground.

Evie hit the grass with an oomph. "What the—"

Matt clamped his hand over her mouth, pressed his lips to her ear. "Shh."

Miraculously, she stilled. He could see her eyes in the darkness, see how wide and frightened they were. Part of that, he knew, was the way he was acting. But he didn't know what was going on, and he wasn't taking any chances.

What he knew was this: someone was shooting a weapon, unsafely, in a crowd of people. And that someone had to be stopped.

"Stay here." He breathed the words more than said them.

She gripped his arm. "I'd rather not," she whispered.

49

"I think we should go to your car, or I'll see if I can find Julie and Steve."

Disbelief punched him in the gut. His team never argued when he gave an order. *Maybe they should have. Maybe Jim and Marco would still be alive if they had.*

Matt shook off the doubt and despair that internal voice filled him with. He had no time for self-pity. "It's too dangerous. Stay here while I get this guy."

"Let the police take care of it. I'm sure someone called them by now, but we can call again to be sure." Her head dipped as she fumbled with the tiny purse slung across her body. "Just a sec—"

Matt circled her wrist, stopping her. "I need to find him before someone gets hurt." He left *if they haven't been hurt already* unspoken. "I can't do that if you won't cooperate."

Her teeth fastened onto her lower lip as she consider-ed it. "Wouldn't it just be easier to call the police?"

"No."

Her breath left her on an irritated sigh. "Fine, I'll stay. But not for long, Matt. I don't like this at all."

"If I'm not back in ten minutes, head into the trees. Call the cops if they aren't here, and don't stop until you reach the road."

Matt started to go, but then he stopped. Quickly, he dug his fingers into the soft earth, then smeared dirt across his face and down his arms, dimming the reflection his skin would make in the headlights. It wasn't as good as greasepaint, but it would have to do.

Evie squeezed his arm. "Be careful."

He would have laughed if he didn't feel the urgency of finding this sonofabitch. Instead, he kissed her, a quick peck on the lips that surprised her if the way her eyes widened was any indication.

"Please stay here," he added. He was unaccustomed to asking, but she nodded. Then he started up the slope, belly-crawling inch by slow inch.

He sent up a brief prayer that he didn't crawl over a fire-ant mound. No Louisiana native could ever forget the sting of a fire ant, or the knowledge of what a nest of the nasty critters could do. Not a pleasant thought, though he reckoned the parish was pretty good about ant control in a public park.

After he'd crawled about fifty feet, he stopped and dropped his head to the side to make sure Evie was where he'd left her—and his heart lodged in his throat.

Fuck.

Her face was a beacon, her skin reflecting the light from the parking lot even when it wasn't pointed straight at her. He'd taken care of himself, but he hadn't considered her.

Idiot. She'd wound him up so tight he hadn't been thinking straight. He should have rubbed dirt on her, whether she liked it or not. Jesus, he was losing his touch. Maybe it was a good thing the Army was thinking hard about his future. If he couldn't get the most basic things right, how could he go back into the field and be in charge of a team? How could he risk losing anyone else because he screwed up?

He signaled to Evie to put her head down and hoped like hell she understood what he meant. She dropped her head to her arms, but didn't hide her face.

Holy hell. He could go back, but that would waste valuable time. He resumed his crawl, listening for any movement close by. Soon, he reached a picnic table and pulled himself to a crouching position behind it. One glance back at Evie to make sure she was okay.

There was a good hundred feet between them now but he had no trouble finding her. Her face shone, but she was safe.

Then a movement to her left caught his eye. He stared, willing the shape to take form. When it did, his heart slammed into his chest. He'd never get there in time.

"You think Girard is so cool now?"

Evie watched the hand holding the knife. It wasn't pointed at her, but still. The gun, at least, was tucked away in his belt.

"Jimmy, this isn't funny. You need to stop it right now."

"I ain't hurt nobody. I just want to talk to you."

"You were firing a gun," she pointed out. "In the dark. How do you know you didn't hurt anyone?"

It was ninety damn degrees on a steamy Louisiana summer night and her teeth were chattering like she was standing in downtown Chicago, sans clothing, in the middle of January. It infuriated her to be so helpless, but she couldn't stop the chattering no matter how hard she tried.

She didn't really think Jimmy wanted to hurt anyone. But he was just stupid enough and mean enough to do it anyway. He'd been one of the bullies back in high school, one of the guys who picked on those littler or stranger than he was.

Her eyes had grown accustomed to the dark now, and she could see Jimmy blink as he considered her question. "I fired in the air," he said after a minute. "Not *at* anyone."

Evie gritted her teeth. "Bullets come down again." It happened all the time in those countries where people fired weapons in celebration. They aimed automatic rifles high in the air, and the bullets came down in the crowd. Sometimes, people got hurt.

"I fired toward the lake." He said it as if he were proud of that fact.

"Why did you do it at all?"

His jaw thrust out. "Did you know that Girard's daddy bought him into the Rangers?" Jimmy spit on the ground. "I coulda been a soldier, but my knee blew out. Can't pass the physical so they won't let me in."

Evie wanted to choke him at that moment. This was about some pissing contest with Matt? "I'm sorry to hear it. I'm sure you'd have made a fine soldier."

"Damn straight." He waved the knife. "I got the jump on him, didn't I?"

Anger was a slow boil in her belly. "You sure did. Now can I please go?"

"No." His voice was hard and it sent another shiver down her spine.

"You don't want to hurt anyone, Jimmy. You don't want to get in trouble with the law."

He snorted. "I'm not going to hurt you."

"Then put the knife down."

He lifted the hunting knife in his hand. It was serrated

and ugly, the kind of thing a guy used to stab deer or something. Hunting, thank heavens, was something she'd never had a taste for.

Sure, she deboned chickens and cleaned fish and it didn't make her queasy—not a good thing for a chef to be, after all—but hunting and cleaning big game was not her kind of thing.

He slid the knife into the sheath at his side. He hadn't been wearing that earlier, or she would have noticed it for sure. That meant he'd left the party, went to his truck, and got his weapons. And all for the purpose of… what? Getting one over on Matt? Getting even with her?

"There. Satisfied?"

Evie shifted on her feet. She wasn't used to standing in heels and they were starting to hurt. It didn't help that the ground was soft nearer the lake and the spikes kept sticking in the dirt.

"Better, yes."

"You weren't nice to me, Evie." He spoke as if he were lecturing her on manners. "I got you a drink and everything, and you weren't nice."

"I'm sorry." It made her furious to say it, as if he hadn't tried to feel her up, but she didn't suppose now was a good time to point out his boorish behavior.

"You can be nice to me now." His voice was low, suggestive.

Her stomach turned. "How's that?"

"You could kiss me."

Evie's heart knocked against her ribs. Bile rose in her throat. She hadn't been attracted to Jimmy before. The thought of kissing him now was absolutely abhorrent.

"I don't kiss on the first date." She said it primly,

aware of how ridiculous she sounded. "You'll have to ask me out proper and keep your hands to yourself, and we'll go from there."

Not that she'd go out with Jimmy Thibodeaux if hell froze over, but she'd sure like to get away from him now. She didn't like being alone with him. She had no idea where Matt was, but she kept hoping he'd show up with a few other guys and kick Jimmy's ass into next week.

Jimmy snorted. "Hell, Evie, why you gotta play hard to get? Everybody in Rochambeau knows you aren't."

For half a second, she wanted to launch herself at him and slap his stupid face. But that wasn't a good idea, so she stood her ground and let fury wash over her. "Do they, Jimmy? Do they really? First of all, we graduated nine years ago. Second, how many of the guys do you know who actually had sex with me?"

The second she asked, she knew it was the wrong question. It didn't matter that Matt had been the only guy she'd slept with in high school. The others would say she had, even when she hadn't. And Jimmy would have believed it. Hell, he'd probably told them she'd slept with him too.

"A few," Jimmy said, proving her point.

"So just because they said it was true, that makes it so?"

Jimmy's hand drifted to the knife at his side again, and her heart skipped a beat. He didn't unstrap it, but his hand rested on the hilt. "You sure are a sassy bitch, you know that?"

Behind Jimmy, a black shape coalesced from the darkness. Evie couldn't stop from gasping automatically. She'd been hoping someone would show up, but she still wasn't prepared for a sudden movement out of nowhere. Jimmy whirled, the knife whipping out of the sheath.

"Watch out," Evie cried. She didn't know if it was Matt, but she damn sure hoped so.

Everything happened so fast then. The shape rushed at Jimmy and she heard a dull crunch she recognized: bone snapping.

Jimmy screamed, a sound that made the hair on her scalp crawl.

Matt stood behind Jimmy, who doubled over, cradling his arm. He was blubbering like a baby. "I fucking hate you, Girard! I'm gonna sue your ass!"

"Shut the fuck up, you piece of shit," Matt growled. She heard the slide of a gun, and she rushed forward automatically. But Matt ejected the clip and winged it into the lake, and she realized he'd taken the gun from Jimmy.

"You okay?"

Her teeth were still chattering as adrenaline flooded her system. "Yes."

Jimmy was crying and groaning, and she hated the sound of it. Hated everything that had happened. A rush of bile flooded her throat. Nausea followed on its heels. She'd had nothing more than a slice of Mama's apple pie for dinner. It was currently mixing with the swallow of wine cooler and threatening to make a repeat appearance.

Evie pressed her hand to her lips and concentrated on breathing.

"I'm sorry, Evie," Matt said.

She wanted to sock him. And throw her arms around his neck and hold on tight. "I told you it was a bad idea," she said through her fingers.

Matt dragged her into his arms and held her tight. She

could feel his mouth pressed against her hair. The gun dangled from his right hand and a shudder went through her. Jimmy hadn't pulled the gun on her, but he'd had it and it had been loaded. And he'd shot it several times in an effort to scare people.

Bastard.

Matt's fingers glided down her spine, up again. She no longer wanted to punch him. She just wanted to go home and crawl under the covers. Forget that any of this ever happened.

A siren sounded in the distance and was soon joined by two more. "They'll be here in a minute, *chère*, and then we can go." His mouth was against her temple as the Cajun French slipped into his voice like melted wax.

While Jimmy whined and cried, the sound crawled inside her and echoed in her head. She could still hear the dull crunch of bone in that moment when Matt had disarmed him. Her stomach heaved.

"I think I'm going to be sick," Evie choked out. She pushed away from Matt, stumbled blindly—but he was there, holding her up while she lost everything.

Sarah slipped on her tightest pair of jeans and a Juicy Girl tank top, then swiped cherry-red lipstick across her mouth. Then she grabbed her handbag and ran for the front door. Any minute, Kyle Jenkins would be out front in his old Chevy truck, honking the horn and getting impatient if she wasn't ready to jump into the front seat and slide over next to him.

This time, she was ready. Every week when Mama went to bingo, Sarah sneaked out of the house and met Kyle. Her heart beat hard at the illicitness of what she was doing, but she couldn't help it. Kyle was so handsome, so cool. He was twenty-one and worked for his daddy over at the garage, rebuilding transmissions and tuning up cars.

Mama would never let her date a guy like Kyle, which was why she had to sneak out.

Sarah laughed then. God, her best friend Mindy would be so jealous when Sarah showed up tonight with Kyle. Mindy might have the hots for Craig Landry, but he was just a senior.

Kyle could buy beer and daiquiris from the drive-up window. And he was way handsomer than Craig, with dark hair, the kind of muscles a guy got from working hard, and a wicked smile that curled her toes whenever he turned it on her.

A minute later, as if thinking conjured him, Kyle's red truck pulled into the drive. Sarah popped the door and slid inside, right over next to Kyle, who looked her up and down appreciatively before kissing her quickly.

"You sure do look good, baby doll." His breath was minty from the candies he sucked between cigarettes.

"Thanks." Her heart skipped a beat at the look in his eyes. Oh, he made her all tingly inside—but they hadn't gone all the way yet. Maybe tonight, she thought. Maybe.

"Cigarette?" He held out the pack.

"Oh yeah." She took it from him and slid a cylinder from the paper, then put it in her mouth and fired up the lighter. Sucking smoke deep into her lungs, she felt the calming rush of nicotine fill her. *Yeah, baby. Yeah.*

Kyle reversed out of the drive and then they were flying down the road, the radio cranked on high as Alice in Chains belted from the stereo. They made a quick stop at the store for some ice, and then Kyle was turning the truck onto a side road they'd not been down before.

"Is this where the party is tonight?"

"Baby, the party is wherever we are."

Sarah blew smoke into the air and fidgeted with her hair. She had no idea what Kyle had planned, but it was always fun, whatever it was. He'd been in jail a couple of times, but nothing serious. A marijuana charge that hadn't stuck. Destruction of private property. He'd paid for that, however, and the jail time had been waived.

Such a badass. That's why she loved him.

Eventually they pulled into a clearing that was empty of anyone else but them. A tiny feeling of apprehension unwound in Sarah's stomach.

"Where is everyone?"

Kyle put the truck into park and turned to her. "It's just us, baby." His grin was turned up to high tonight. "I thought we could smoke a little weed, drink a little beer, and finally make love."

Fear grabbed hold of her and wouldn't let go. "I'm not sure, Kyle." She wanted to be with him, but she'd had some vague idea it would be way more romantic than this. Not a pickup truck in a field, but a bed, with candles and wine, and maybe even some flowers.

"Why aren't you sure, baby?" Kyle lifted a hand and cupped one of her breasts. Her heart rate shot higher. "We've been together for nearly a month now. Surely that's enough time for you."

"It's a big step. I need more time."

She would do this, she really would, but it had to be right first. She wanted to feel special, not like every other girl Kyle had ever driven out to the woods.

Kyle dropped his hand away. "I've waited longer for you than for any other girl. I'm tired of waiting."

"Just a little more time." She knew she was begging. "I want it to be right."

She tried to kiss him, but Kyle pushed her away. "I'm tired of going home with blue balls every night." He shook his head as he started the truck. "Damn, I knew I shouldn't have dated a virgin. So fucking uptight."

"Then let's go to a motel." It terrified her to say it.

He looked at her in disbelief. "You think I'm made of money?"

"Your house then."

"My mother's home."

Sarah folded her arms over her chest. "I want my first time to be special, Kyle."

Kyle swore. "You think this ain't special? I buy you beer and weed, and I drive your ass all over town. But apparently that's not good enough for you. I'm beginning to think you're using me for the freebies, Sarah."

"That's not true."

He gunned the truck. Sarah didn't know what else to say as he flew back toward the highway. Her heart was hammering in her chest, her throat. She hated fighting, but it seemed like they fought more and more often of late. And usually about this.

Kyle didn't say anything as he pulled into a gas station on the edge of the town limits. He got out to fill the tank—though why he hadn't filled it when they'd stopped for ice she didn't know—slamming the door hard, and Sarah decided to go inside and buy some potato chips before she said something she shouldn't.

She stood in the aisle, deciding between regular and barbecue, then took her choice to the counter and pulled out her money. When she paid and stepped outside, however, Kyle's truck wasn't there. It took her a moment to realize that he'd really left, that he wasn't sitting nearby waiting for her.

Fuck. Now how was she getting home? It was a good three miles, and she couldn't call Mama for a ride. Evie was out at the lake, but that was even farther. She glanced back at the guy sitting behind the counter, arms folded, watching something on a television mounted high above his head. She could ask him to use the phone, but who would she call?

If she had a cell phone of her own, she'd text Mindy. But Mama wouldn't let her have a phone, no matter how she begged. Still, she could ask this guy if she could use his. Then she'd call Mindy and pray she reached her.

Sarah went back inside and asked if she could use the phone. The guy grunted something and shoved an old landline phone at her. Sarah punched in Mindy's number —which, thank God, she knew because she dialed it a lot.

"Come on, Mindy," she muttered. But it went to voice mail. Sarah tried again, just to be sure, but Mindy still didn't answer. She hung up without leaving a message and tried to think of who else she could call. Not Mama. No way in hell.

She would call Evie, because she was pretty sure Evie wouldn't rat her out since she seemed so eager to get Sarah to be nice to her, but she didn't know Evie's number.

Sarah frowned.

God, she was so using this to talk Mama into a cell phone of her own. Not that she could say who it had happened to, but she could use it as an example of why she should have her own phone.

If she didn't want to get caught, her only choice was to walk. She briefly thought about staying at the store and hoping someone she knew would stop, but time was not her friend tonight.

Kyle was just angry. Tomorrow, he'd be calling her up again. She might forgive him, but she might not.

Damn it.

Sarah left the store and started walking down the darkened road. Town was a good mile away, but she wasn't scared. She'd lived here her whole life, and she knew the terrain well. It was dark, with old oaks dripping Spanish moss over the roadway, but the gators were out in the swamp.

Not only that, but it was entirely possible someone she knew would drive by on the way to town. Not Mama, thank God, because the Moose Lodge was the other way.

Sarah swatted a mosquito, cursing and grumbling at the heat and humidity. Oh yes, Mama wouldn't be able to resist this story once she was done with it. Sarah could already see that shiny new phone in her hand. A car rolled up behind her and slowed.

"Hey, you need a ride?"

She didn't look at the guy. "No, thanks."

"It's kinda lonely out here."

"I'm fine." Her heart kicked up, slamming into her chest. How far had she walked? She looked back. The road curved away and the gas station was lost around the bend.

"Maybe you can tell me where I can find someone then."

Sarah kept her arms tight to her body and didn't answer. Damn Kyle for leaving her.

"I'm looking for Evie Baker. Do you know her?"

Sarah ground to a halt. The guy in the Taurus was huge, the arm hanging out the window as big around as her thigh. From inside the car, a woman with a ponytail watched her. Movement from the backseat revealed another man, not as big as this one. The man in the backseat raised his hand to his face. A cigarette glowed red as he sucked on it.

"Why do you want her?"

"She's a friend of mine." It was the woman. Her voice was raspy, like she smoked a lot. "I used to work with her in Florida, at her restaurant."

"What was the name of it?"

"Evangeline's."

Sarah considered that. "So why didn't you call her before you showed up?"

"Tried. She's not answering her cell phone. I'm just passing through and wanted to see her before we go on our way."

Sarah rolled her shoulders. Her cheek throbbed where she'd slapped at the mosquito. Another one buzzed by her ear, a big mother this time. "I might know where she lives."

The woman smiled. "So get in."

"I shouldn't."

"Suit yourself. But if you could just give me her address, I'd appreciate it."

Sarah looked down the road. It was a long way to

walk. The car was inviting. If it was just men, no way would she go with them. But there was a woman. A woman who knew her sister.

Still, she was wary. "It's on Fourth Street. One-ten."

"Thanks. You sure you don't want a ride?"

Sarah looked both ways down the road. There was no traffic tonight. If she kept walking, someone might come along. But they might not, and she was tired of getting bitten by mosquitos.

Besides, this woman knew Evie. Why else would she come to a rinky-dink town like Rochambeau?

"All right," Sarah said. Then she crossed to the car and slipped inside.

FIVE

EVIE SAT IN MATT'S BMW and watched the steady parade of cars roll away from the scene. In spite of the heat, she was cold. She hadn't stopped shaking since Matt had materialized from the darkness and broken Jimmy's arm. Adrenaline still coursed through her system, wreaking havoc on her nerves. Matt had told her it was normal, but she felt so out of control. She felt like she should be able to stop it, but she couldn't.

She flipped down the visor and checked her reflection. She had dark smudges of mascara under her eyes, her hair needed combing, and there were grass and dirt stains on her dress where Matt had dragged her down to the ground. She picked up a napkin from the stack Matt had brought her and poured some bottled water on it. Then she tried to scrub out some of the stains while she waited for him to return.

She'd probably have to buy Julie another dress. Knowing her cousin, this wasn't a Gap dress either. It'd probably cost her a week's worth of tips.

She watched as Matt shook hands with the patrolmen

he was talking to. The driver's door swung open, and he sank down beside her. "You okay?" His gray eyes were sharp as he studied her.

She shrugged, too embarrassed to admit she was still shaking. As if he couldn't see. "I'll be fine. Did you find Julie? Is anyone hurt?"

"Steve took her home already. And yeah, there were some minor injuries. No one got shot, though."

"Bastard," Evie spat. "Stupid bastard."

"Jimmy's always been a bully. Tonight, he took it too far."

"I heard he pulled a knife on Ginny Temple. I should have been more careful."

Matt gripped her chin and forced her to look at him. "It's not your fault. Jimmy's an asshole. And now he's an asshole with a broken arm and a few criminal charges. If it's anybody's fault, it's his."

"He seemed pretty pissed at you."

Matt ran a hand over his face. He'd tried to rinse the dirt away, but there were still streaks of it across his skin. Not that it made him look any less appealing, unfortunately.

"Yeah. He wanted to join the military but he couldn't pass the physical. It drives him crazy that I'm in and he's not. Last time I was here, he picked a fight with me out at Dean's Bar. It's like he's got something to prove."

"Did you break his arm that time too?"

His eyes glittered. "I'm sorry you had to see that."

Evie wrapped her arms around her body. Where had that come from? He'd pretty much just saved her from God only knows what.

"It's okay. I'm not typically squeamish. It's just a

combination of a lot of things in my life right now. And I know you broke his arm because you had to, not because you wanted to."

He laughed low in his throat, a sound that curled through her and made her shiver again. "Believe me, I wanted to."

Matt started the car and reversed out of the parking lot, and Evie turned away from his hard profile to look out the window. It was dark and she couldn't see anything, but she had a sudden need to breathe without him taking up all the air. Of all the places she thought she might be tonight, alone in a car with Matt Girard hadn't been one of them.

"What's a Ranger?" she asked after they'd turned onto the main road. She had no idea what all that military jargon was, but Jimmy had seemed impressed with it.

Matt glanced at her. "A Ranger is a special operations soldier. They parachute behind enemy lines, take the difficult targets, smooth the way for the rest of the Army to follow."

"Jimmy said your daddy bought you in."

Matt laughed. "If only it was that easy. Believe me, I've got the scars to prove I did it on my own."

Evie watched his profile. She hated to think of him with scars. He was beautiful.

And she was ridiculous. She shook her head as if that simple movement would clear him out of it. He'd never really left her thoughts. He'd just been hidden behind a curtain. Now that he was here, the curtain had been peeled back, and she was grappling with his presence in her life all over again.

"Why'd you choose to do something so hard, Matt? You could have done anything." It made no sense to her. If she'd had the advantages he had, she would have made good use of them, not thrown them away getting captured by enemy soldiers.

He glanced over at her again, his eyes gleaming in the darkness. "You think it's crazy?"

"It seems a little odd for someone like you."

He flipped on the turn signal. "Because I'm a Girard, you mean."

She sighed. "If I could have anything I want, I doubt I'd risk my neck jumping out of airplanes."

"Maybe you think I ought to sit on my daddy's porch sipping iced tea all day. Or do nine to five at Girard Oil, pretending I like being a businessman. No, thanks. When I go to work, I know what I do matters."

Her pulse throbbed. "A job doesn't have to be dangerous to matter."

He flashed her a grin. "Maybe I've just got a thrill-seeking personality."

Evie found that she couldn't look away from him. Even with dirt streaking his face, he looked like he belonged in the pages of a celebrity magazine. When he used words like *thrill-seeking*, something inside her turned to putty.

She swallowed. "It's because of your mother, isn't it?"

His hands tightened on the wheel. "What makes you say that? She's been gone a long time, Evie. And I don't think she would approve of what I do any more than you do."

"I didn't say I don't approve." It wasn't that she didn't think it was an important job. She just thought it was odd that Matt had chosen it when he could have been anything he wanted to be. "But when she died... well, I remember what you said to me in the tree that day."

Her throat was tight and her eyes stung. Matt glanced over at her, his jaw as hard as a block of granite. "I was twelve, Evie. Twelve-year-olds don't know what they want out of life."

"You said you'd have given anything to save her. You said you wanted to save people when you grew up—I thought you were going to be a doctor." She laughed, but it didn't contain much humor. "God, even when you got appointed to West Point, I thought you were going to be a military lawyer or something."

He didn't say anything for a long moment. "I would have given anything to save her." His voice was quiet in the darkness. "We needed her. Christina needed her. The old man..." He swallowed. "He's not bad, Evie. He's just self-absorbed. It's always been about *his* feelings, *his* grief, *his* needs. He never really had time for us, and I'd have given anything to bring her back again."

"I don't understand how doing what you do now makes up for any of that."

He made a sound in his throat like a growl. "If I'd known you were going to try to analyze me, I'd have stayed home tonight."

"Maybe you should have."

He glanced over at her. "It doesn't make up for a damn thing. But I do something important and, yeah, people live because I've done my job. Running an oil company would seem pretty meaningless in comparison. And I wasn't about to be a doctor. No patience for the kind of time that takes."

"You'd rather jump out of airplanes and get shot at."

"Something like that." His tone was clipped. "So now that we've had fun with me, what about you? I notice you aren't precisely cooking for a living at the moment. And Christina told me you'd gone to culinary school, so that can't be the problem."

Evie rubbed two fingers along her temple. "I'm surprised you haven't heard all about it yet. I had a restaurant in Florida, but I also had a partner who stole from me. I lost it all."

"I'm sorry."

She sighed. "Yeah, well, lesson learned and all that. Now I wash hair in Mama's salon and send out résumés every week. Something will happen eventually."

"I've noticed life has a way of piling on the shit sometimes."

"I'd like to think I've had all the shit I'm going to get for a while, but with my luck, God only knows."

He laughed. "*Chère*, I so hear you."

Evie turned toward him. The lights from the dash illuminated his features, caressed the bridge of that aristocratic nose, those full lips and firm jaw. He was gorgeous, but that had never been the sole source of her attraction. It didn't hurt, of course, but there was more to it than that.

He'd always made her laugh, and he'd been her friend, and he'd let her see the parts of him that weren't strong. She'd never forget hugging him while he cried in the hollow of that tree. She hadn't quite reached the stage of having a crush on him then, but she figured that was the moment when she'd fallen in love, before she even knew what it meant.

"Folks in town seem to think you're in some kind of trouble. Were you really captured?"

He stared straight ahead. "Yeah, we were captured. People died. It wasn't pretty, but war never is."

"I'm sorry." She wanted to ask what had happened, how he'd gotten away, if he was okay now—but she couldn't seem to find her voice. How did you ask someone how he'd escaped death? How it had felt to wonder if you were going to die?

"It is what it is. But thanks."

The car rolled to a stop at a four-way intersection. He didn't even glance at her as he took a left instead of a right.

"You turned the wrong way."

Mama's house was to the right, and Evie couldn't wait to get back there, stand in the shower for about an hour, and then crawl into bed and pull the covers over her head and try to forget everything about this night.

Well, maybe not everything. Not the part where she'd danced with Matt, even if it had called up all those latent feelings and memories she'd tried to suppress.

"Reynier's Retreat is closer than going to the other side of town. You can clean up a bit before I take you home."

Her heart kicked up. The thought of entering that fabulous antebellum mansion tonight was enough to drown her in shame. "I can't see your family looking like this!"

She'd been inside dozens of times, but an eight-year-old with dirty knees was completely different from a twenty-six-year-old who looked like she'd been rolling in the dirt. Reynier's Retreat was over one hundred and fifty years old, and it'd been in Matt's family all that time. It also looked as if it had come straight out of *Southern Living* magazine. If she ever went inside the grand mansion as an adult, she damn sure didn't want to look like something off the set of a zombie movie.

"Relax. We won't go near the house. I'm in the guest cottage."

Evie shook her head. "I appreciate it, Matt, but there's no reason I can't go home. Mama's playing bingo at the lodge tonight and Sarah—"

Sarah. Hell. What would her sister think if she walked in looking like this? There'd be questions.

Matt turned toward her. "Your little sister?"

Evie swallowed. "She's home tonight." Then she let out a sigh. Sarah might be grumpy and hostile, but she wasn't stupid. "Maybe it is best if I clean up before going home."

Matt nodded. "That's what I thought. It won't take long, I promise. I'll have you home again before anyone misses you."

A few minutes later, Matt pressed a button over the rearview mirror as they turned into the lane to Reynier's Retreat. Two iron scrollwork gates ground open slowly.

The drive to the house was at least half a mile. Oak trees lined the lane, the car's headlights illuminating the Spanish moss that dripped like ragged beards from heavy branches. The main house stood on a low knoll at the end of the drive, gleaming white in the darkness. Light spilled from the windows across the bottom half of the home. Several cars were parked in the circular drive, and several more sat in a cordoned-off area that served as a parking lot. A white-coated attendant sprinted up the stairs as the front door opened. A formally dressed couple emerged onto a sweeping veranda studded with eight fat columns.

Evie looked at the big house with a pang of envy.

72

She'd never attended a fancy party here before, though she did have an invitation to Christina's wedding in a few days. She'd said yes, but she'd been torn about coming. She'd been worried about the wistful memories this place would call up. And about seeing Matt.

"You came to the lake when you could've been here?"

"Boring as hell. I gave it an hour before I left. Chris understands. Besides, it's just an excuse for the senator to glad-hand some of his wealthy constituents." He drove past the house and turned in the opposite direction.

"Your sister seems happy. I haven't met her fiancé yet. I'm not sure many of us have."

Christina Girard had been in Rochambeau for a couple of weeks now, but her fiancé only flew in a few days ago. The couple lived in Washington, D.C., but according to Mama—and the gossip mill—Christina had always had her heart set on marrying at Reynier's Retreat.

"Yeah, Ben's an attorney on the Hill." Matt paused as if considering what else to tell her. "If the senator has anything to say about it, he'll be a congressman in a couple of years."

She thought he sounded annoyed.

"Does that bother you?"

"What? Ben in Congress?" He shot her a look. "No, not really. But I'm not sure it's what Chris wants. The old man wants another politician in the family and he probably won't take no for an answer."

She knew what he didn't say. That his father had wanted *him* to be the one to follow in his footsteps.

"Why did your father never run for Congress him-self?"

Matt laughed. "One word, *chère*. Strippers."

"Oh, geez, I almost forgot." Matt's father had married a succession of ladies who entertained in nightclubs, to put it politely, after his first wife died. It was almost a cliché in some ways, but politicians and strippers were somewhat of a Louisiana tradition. Though it had played just fine up at the Statehouse at one time, it probably wouldn't translate well to Washington.

"The old man has a weakness. He's married four of them since our mother died."

"Four? Wow, a lot happens in ten years."

"Yeah. The second one left him when I was still in high school. The third lasted a couple of years. The fourth will be here forever, I imagine."

"Really?"

Matt nodded. "Misty Lee really loves him, though God knows why."

At that moment, the guest cottage came into view from behind a stand of trees. Having originally been a carriage house, the building sat a good distance away from the main estate. A hundred years ago, the smell of horses would have been too strong for the residence's inhabitants.

Matt parked inside the garage and came around to help her out of the car, though she didn't need it and had climbed out before he could get there.

"What?" She crossed her arms, feeling suddenly self-conscious with the lights of the garage shining down on her and the damp dress that clung to her body.

"I was coming to open the door for you."

Evie smiled. "Aw, that's sweet. You still remember your Junior Cotillion training."

He grinned at her and rubbed a hand over his nape.

"Well, yeah."

The only reason she'd had cotillion training was because she'd begged her mama for it after Matt had to go. They'd learned how to behave like little ladies and gentlemen, and clearly those lessons had stuck. She couldn't remember the last time a man had tried to open a car door for her.

"Since you clearly don't need help out of the car, let's go in." He turned and led her into the house, flipping on lights and setting down his keys as they went. Evie's legs were wobbly, and she shivered anew at the coolness of the house as compared to outside. To think she'd actually wanted air conditioning earlier.

She rubbed her bare upper arms as goose bumps popped up.

"You can use the master bath." Matt flipped on a light switch in the bedroom before continuing across the room. Evie's gaze stumbled over the king-size bed. The covers were twisted, the sheets rumpled. The room smelled faintly masculine, both spicy and woodsy.

Matt turned to her as he reached the bathroom and flipped on the light. Then he frowned. "Are you cold?"

She nodded.

He walked over and put his arms around her and she leaned into his heat as it enveloped her. Though she'd danced with him only an hour ago, it was still astonishing to be against his body like this again. He was solid, warm, and smelled like earth and man.

"You've had a shock." His voice was smooth and calming. "It'll take a little time to process it all, but you'll be fine."

She was already starting to thaw. "I'm sure the

shower will help."

"Yeah." He stepped away and put his hand in the small of her back, propelling her toward the bathroom. "There's a robe on the back of the door. I'll find something you can wear home."

Evie glanced up at him. "I ought to call my mama first. If she hears about what happened—"

"I'll do it for you, *chère*. You'd only upset her with your version."

She blinked. "Version?"

He rubbed her arms, his touch leaving a trail of sensation up and down her skin. "Trust me."

"She's at the Moose Lodge playing bingo." Evie cocked a hip and gave him an even stare. "Don't think I don't know you've been taking control of this situation since the lights went out."

His eyes gleamed as he shrugged. "And I figure the first instant you don't feel like doing something the way I want you to, you'll tell me to go to hell."

"Damn straight."

He grinned. "It's what I love about you, Evie Baker."

Her heart skipped a beat. He was teasing her, but those words slid under her skin and set up a longing she hadn't felt in years. "I'm going to remind you that you said that."

His gaze slipped over her, and heat followed in its wake. "Take your shower, Evie."

She closed the door, her pulse throbbing in her throat and her temples. What the hell? She hadn't seen Matt Girard in ten years, and she was panting over him as if high school and her crush were only yesterday.

Evie lay her forehead against the door and stood there

for a long moment, breathing. So many things had happened tonight, so many feelings pinging around inside her. Matt was just as confusing and compelling as he'd ever been. Maybe more so, considering everything they'd said to each other and the way he'd held her on the dance floor before Jimmy cut the lights.

He'd seemed thoughtful. Even vulnerable in some hidden way she hadn't quite figured out. She wanted to wrap her arms around him and not let go until she knew all his secrets. Until this itching under her skin went away.

Forget it, she told herself. *You aren't going there.*

But damn she wanted to.

She wasn't coming out. Matt looked at his watch and realized it had been nearly forty minutes since Evie had gone into the bathroom. He shoved a hand through his damp hair—he'd gone across the hall to the guest room and taken a quick shower, then changed into fresh clothes that weren't streaked with dirt—and stared at the closed door to the master bath.

He could still hear water running. He stepped up and rapped on the door. "Evie?"

She didn't answer. After a moment's hesitation, he tested the door. It swung open.

"Evie?"

"Go away." Her voice came from the shower enclosure. It sounded smaller and more uncertain than it should.

He told himself that he hadn't seen her in ten years. That he didn't know her the way he once had. That he didn't have the right to push her into talking to him or into coming out of that shower.

And yet he knew something of what she was going through. He understood the crash that came after that kind of adrenaline surge. He understood the self-doubt and the impact of the sudden knowledge of what could have happened. What *might* have happened. She'd witnessed the kind of violence she probably wasn't accustomed to in her everyday life.

And he'd been a part of it when he'd taken Jimmy down.

No, he couldn't walk away. He wouldn't. Matt went over and leaned against the marble vanity. Citrus-scented steam curled overhead and he flipped on the switch for the fan.

He could hear Evie's gasp. "Go away, Matt! I'm not done yet."

In that moment, hearing the uncertainty and plaintive note in her voice, Matt almost wished he'd broken Jimmy's other arm too. "I'm sorry to intrude, *chère*. But I've been through this kind of thing. I know what you're feeling."

"I'm not feeling anything. I'm just taking a shower."

He almost smiled at the underlying current of steel he heard that time. If she could say that to him, in that tone of voice, then maybe she wasn't feeling too badly. He'd been worried about how she would react once the reality of being held captive set in.

The incident hadn't lasted long, and Jimmy hadn't hurt her, but he had threatened her with that knife. And he'd called her a bitch. He'd also fired a weapon repeatedly and dangerously. Evie would have to be super-human—or hardened by combat—not to react to the feelings of powerlessness she'd have felt at the time.

"You've been in there a long time."

She didn't speak at first. "I hadn't noticed."

"Bet the water's only lukewarm by now."

Another long pause. "It's cooler than it was."

"Why don't you come on out then?"

"Why am I acting like this?" Her voice was hard, as if she were angry with herself. "Nothing happened. It's over and no one got hurt. So why can't I stop thinking about it?"

Matt sighed. He didn't have an answer for her. He was still battling his own demons. The only difference was that he'd been trained to deal with it. That and the military psychologists who evaluated him and the team every time they returned from a mission.

Usually, he put everything that happened in the field into a box in his head and left it there. This time, the box wouldn't stay closed. Marco and Jim kept coming back to haunt him. It didn't happen as much anymore, but he still woke up in a cold sweat sometimes, reaching for his weapon and determined to kill every goddamn thing between him and his men.

"It's not every day some idiot waves a knife at you and threatens your safety. You're entitled to get upset about it."

"Maybe so. But I want to be able to do what you did. I want to know what to do if someone ever threatens me again." She sucked in a breath. "You took him down so fast. I didn't even see what you did."

"I'll teach you a couple of moves." He surprised himself with the declaration, especially when he had to be back in North Carolina soon for the hearing that would determine his fate in HOT. Just thinking of the hearing gave him a chill. He didn't know for sure his career was over, but he had to force himself to consider the possibility. Better to be prepared for it than to be blindsided.

Still, he'd manage to show Evie something before he went. He'd teach her a maneuver or two that would give her confidence, then insist she enroll in a self-defense course to learn more.

"Really?"

"Yeah, when I get done with you, the Army will come calling."

"I'm a chef."

"So you'll be a deadly one."

"Cool." Her voice was smaller than he liked, but still strong. Evie had never let anything cow her for long.

"You ready to come out of there?"

After another moment, the water lessened to a trickle and then ceased. Matt reached for a towel and held it over the wall. When he felt a soft tug, he let go. He knew he should leave now and give her some privacy, but the truth was he didn't want to go. He had a burning desire to see her clad in nothing but a towel.

But that was territory he didn't need to explore, he reminded himself. Earlier, he'd wanted to be with her simply because she made him feel oddly grounded and connected again, but now there was more to it. He wanted to see her naked, wanted to lose himself in her for a few hours, but he didn't know what that kind of intimacy would do to her.

Or to him.

She appeared in the door, looking smaller and more vulnerable than when she'd walked in. Her wet hair was slicked to her head, and she'd scrubbed off her makeup. She looked like a little girl, like a woman who needed his strength and his protection. He hadn't seen that look on her face in a long, long time.

A stone settled in his gut. Not since the night he'd taken her virginity. He should have told her to go away, to forget it, but he hadn't been in control of his impulses. Until that night, he'd done a good job of keeping her about twelve years old in his head. Oh, he'd gotten a jolt a few times when he'd looked at her and realized she'd grown out of her tomboy ways, but he'd always managed to put her back into the mental slot he kept her in.

She looked up at him now, twisting the knife in his belly. The towel covered her from breasts to knees, but it wasn't quite enough. There was definite movement in his groin. He turned his back on her, fetched a thick robe from its hook on the door, and handed it to her.

"I'll get some clothes for you," he said, not having managed to complete that task yet. He left her standing there and went into the bedroom, welcoming the blast of cold air conditioning that hit him.

He rummaged through the drawers, found a silk nightgown that was more night than gown. Damn Misty Lee. If it wasn't one thing it was another. Fuzzy pink handcuffs, a variety of lotions and edible panties in the bedside table, and now this. He fingered the lacy cups as the damn thing sent his imagination into hyperspace.

And after the past few months of celibacy, his imagination didn't need any help. He shook his head and dropped the gown.

Yep, that's what happened when your stepmama was a former stripper with a romantic soul. She stocked the place like a brothel. He'd have paid money to see his Great-Aunt Maybelle's reaction the last time she visited. No wonder she'd insisted on staying up at the house this time.

Matt dug out a pair of athletic shorts and a T-shirt from the duffle he'd left open on the stand. The bathroom door was open, so he walked in and set the clothes on the vanity bench.

Evie stood at the mirror, trying to comb out a snarl. "Do you have any scissors?"

He blinked. "You want to cut your hair?"

"Just this," she said, yanking.

"Here." He walked over, took the comb away, and tried to separate the knot with his fingers. "Just like getting a tangle around your reel. Can't sacrifice all that fishing line for one knot, right?"

She rolled her eyes. "Patience was never my strong suit, remember?"

He laughed. "Yeah, you were fun to play with when we were kids, but I seem to remember the fishing never went all that well."

She frowned. "I don't like standing around."

"Or being quiet."

She rolled her eyes. "Matt."

"Hey, it's true. You scared away a lot of fish."

The strands of her hair were damp and smelled like his shampoo. They coiled around his hand, slid through his fingers. He worked slowly, using the comb and his fingers to pry her hair from the knot's grip. The minutes ticked by and the air seemed to thicken. He stared at the top of her head and wondered if it was just him who felt this tightening under his skin.

She fiddled with the ends of the robe's belt, tugging and scrunching. She seemed to be growing impatient—until she looked up and her gaze tangled with his.

Wide violet eyes gazed up at him with raw heat. He felt the blow of that look down to his core. Not impatient then. Needy. A normal reaction to the stress of tonight, but considering how she'd brushed him off only a couple of hours ago, he suddenly felt as if her reaction was wrong somehow.

Not that he didn't want her. He did—hell, he'd thought of little else since he'd seen her in the salon today —but he couldn't take her. Not now. Not like this. Then, it had been a challenge, a sort of goal he'd focused on because it made him feel normal.

Now? Now she was confused and vulnerable, and taking advantage of her feelings was wrong. He wanted her to want him because she couldn't deny the chemistry between them, not because Jimmy Thibodeaux had pulled a knife on her and she was feeling vulnerable and mixed up.

He stared at her for a long minute, his body remembering how it felt to be inside a woman, responding to her against his wishes. She dropped the belt, her hand coming to rest lightly on his chest. Her hand trembled as she spread her fingers, and that single moment of vulnerability almost undid him.

Her hand was warm as she smoothed it across his chest. He burned beneath her touch, ached to have her slip her fingers under the material of his shirt and caress his bare skin. All he had to do was let it happen.

But his conscience had grown a whole damn lot in the last ten years. He swallowed the lump in his throat. "I don't think this is a good idea."

She looked confused. Her gaze focused on her hand, on the smoothing motions she made. It was torture. He continued working the strands of her hair, sliding them a few at a time from the knot. It'd been a long time since he'd gotten laid. A long damn time.

"You said earlier—"

"I know what I said." Christ, this wasn't working. He dropped her hair and grabbed her wrist to halt the torturous motion. "That was before."

She stared up at him with liquid eyes. Any second, he expected her lip to tremble.

It didn't.

She took a deep breath and lightly pushed him away.

"I'm sorry, then." She turned her back to him.

He felt like a jerk. An idiot. "It's a common reaction to be attracted to someone who rescues you." Great, now he sounded like a damn textbook. He didn't want to push her away, but he wanted to do the right thing. Apparently, doing the right thing meant sounding starchy and proper.

She choked on a laugh. Her eyes were bright. "Well hey, thanks for not taking advantage of me." She grabbed the comb and worked the knot methodically, succeeding where before she'd failed. He couldn't help but notice her hands shook.

"I want to." God, did he ever. The irony of the situation wasn't lost on him. Once, she'd offered him her body and he'd practically tripped over his tongue saying yes. Now, however, he was trying to be noble. And aching in all the wrong places because of it. "But I can't. It's not professional."

The comb stilled as she looked up at him. "Professional? Why's it suddenly about being professional? You've propositioned me at least twice tonight, and now you *can't* because it would mean going against some code or something?" She dropped the comb on the vanity, dragging her fingers through the last of the snarl until it came free.

When she tossed her hair over her shoulder, he thought he might drop to his knees and beg her to forget everything he'd just said. His mouth went dry as he imagined her on top, her beautiful hair hanging down in a curtain around him as she leaned forward to kiss him.

Matt shook his head to clear it. He tried hard—damn hard—to remember little Evie Baker, twelve years old, being a pain in the ass. Or sixteen-year-old Evie, disappointed in him because he took what she offered and gave nothing back.

But all he saw was this Evie—beautiful, needy, ready. He wanted to possess her. He had no right, especially since he couldn't offer her anything beyond a few nights.

There were plenty of women in Rochambeau, plenty who'd take him home and break the drought if sex was what he wanted. Plenty he could have a clear conscience about.

"I didn't say it made sense. But I'm trying to do the right thing here."

Her eyes flashed and vulnerable Evie fell away. "You sure are making a lot of assumptions, Matthew Girard. What makes you think I wanted anything besides a kiss?"

He stared at her for a long moment. And then he burst

out laughing. It was definitely the wrong thing to do because she snatched up the comb and winged it at him. He caught it and tossed it onto the vanity.

But he couldn't let that pass. He couldn't let her get away with being disingenuous.

"You and I both know, *chère*, that if I'd done what you wanted, we'd be naked right this minute. Don't act like you expected anything less when we both know it isn't the truth."

"And don't *you* pretend like it's some blasted code making you change your mind either." She slapped the clothes she'd picked up onto the bench again and crossed her arms. "I wouldn't be very attracted to me right now either."

Matt was having trouble keeping up. Okay, so he was clueless. Totally in the dark here. "You think I'm not interested because you took too long in the shower?"

"Oh my God." Her cheeks were slashed with red. She waved a hand at him. "Forget it, Matt. Just go so I can get dressed."

It took him another minute of staring at her, watching her blush spread, before he got it.

Aw damn, now he *had* to kiss her. And he didn't know if he'd survive the experience.

SIX

"JESUS, EVIE." MATT CLOSED THE distance between them. "I can't believe you think I don't want you because you fell apart a little. I've seen grown men lose their lunch, believe me. Hell, I've done it myself."

Embarrassment sizzled through Evie's body. What the hell was wrong with her? Why had she even touched him in the first place?

Because she'd been standing there while he worked the knot free, and she'd been enveloped in his scent and his presence. She'd felt so lost and alone in the shower when she'd started thinking about how helpless she'd been against Jimmy's threats. If Matt hadn't arrived, what might have happened to her? Would Jimmy have raped her? Cut her?

But Matt had talked her out of the shower, and then he'd stood there and calmly worked on the knot in her hair while her heart pounded hard at his nearness. She'd had a sudden, powerful urge to lose herself in his arms and forget all about Jimmy Thibodeaux, David West, and her broken dreams—at least for a little while.

So she'd put her hand on his chest. And she'd liked the feel of all that solid muscle, so she kept touching him. Considering what he'd said to her earlier, she hadn't thought for one moment he would turn her down.

But of course he had. She'd practically gotten sick on his shoes. What man wanted a woman so soon after he'd had to hold her hair and watch her retch? He'd been tough, disabling Jimmy and calmly dealing with the gun and the police, while she'd been a mess of nerves. She'd fallen apart in front of him. Mortifying.

She looked up into eyes that were deadly serious. There wasn't a hint of mockery in them. "You've gotten sick like that before? For no reason?"

"It's not for no reason, Evie." One corner of his mouth crooked in a soft smile. "And yeah, I've gotten sick, though it's been a while. You can't be in my line of work and not see some serious shit. None of us are immune to it. We're human. Now, come here."

He put his arms around her, cupped his palm to the back of her head, and pulled her in close. She closed her eyes and breathed in the clean scent of him. Willed back tears that surprised her with their sudden sting.

She hadn't broken down once, not when David ran off with the payroll—and much more than she'd known about that night—not when the bank called in her loans, not even when she sat stone-faced in that meeting of lawyers and listened to them carve up her dream.

She sucked in a breath that trembled as she put her arms around Matt's waist.

After a long moment, he spoke. "Look at me."

She tilted her head up, meeting heated gray eyes. She suddenly couldn't breathe, couldn't think.

"You're crazy if you think I don't want to kiss you."

He cupped her cheeks in both hands. She closed her eyes as his head dipped, her breath shuddering in her chest as his mouth pressed gently against hers.

It wasn't passionate, this kiss; it wasn't anything other than sweet and comforting. Yet something stirred inside her, that little tingle of excitement, of anticipation. She wanted more, so much more than she should. This was the man who'd started it all, who'd taken what she'd given him and thrown it back in her face as if it were nothing.

And here she stood, ready to lose herself in him one more time. Because there'd always been more between them than just one night. Because they went back a long ways, and she'd loved him as a friend long before she'd ever fallen for him as a man.

And though she wasn't in love with him anymore, they were both adults now and she knew what she was asking for. Earlier, she'd thought she couldn't handle it, that it would be too much—but now she wasn't worried. This time she would take as much as she gave.

Evie wrapped her arms around his waist and fitted herself closer to his body. He groaned then, his hands slipping down over the robe, bunching the fabric at the small of her back as if it were a lifeline and he couldn't let go.

She opened her mouth on a moan and his tongue slipped inside, tangling with hers while her body melted. She ached in a way she hadn't in a very long time. It was thrilling to feel this way when she'd felt numb for so long. She ran her hands up the hard muscles of his chest and over his shoulders. He was so much stronger than he'd been at seventeen. Her blood hummed with electricity.

Fireworks sparked in her belly, her sex.

He pushed her gently away and disappointment crashed through her. "You're making me crazy." His voice was thrillingly low, sending shivers of anticipation along her spine. "But we can't do this—"

"I want to." She really did. To hell with all the reasons she'd told herself she shouldn't do this earlier. Julie had told her she needed to get laid, and maybe her cousin was right. The sparks between her and Matt were combustible—and it had been a long time since she'd felt any combustion with anyone.

She could spend the night in Matt's bed and walk away in the morning without a backward glance. And that was a mighty liberating thought.

He closed his eyes on a groan. "I don't get hostages out of bad places and then sleep with them. It's unprofessional conduct and it's unbecoming an officer in the United States Army. Tomorrow, maybe—"

"God, Matt, just stop fighting it! This isn't the Army and no one paid you to help me. I'm not somebody you've never set eyes on before today." She sucked in a ragged breath. "This is me. Evie. I used to be your best friend, remember? We're adults, we know what we want. You said it yourself."

His eyes searched hers. "But do you really? You didn't seem so eager when we danced earlier. Or in your mama's salon."

"I know. Maybe I was scared of you, scared of everything that happened before and how it made me feel. But I'm sure now. Because I'm not sixteen and I don't feel anything for you now except lust."

One eyebrow lifted. "Lust, huh? So now I'm a piece

of meat?"

"That's right, Matt. You're meat. I want a piece of you."

His laugh was strangled. "Jesus, Evie. I'm serious when I say I missed the hell out of you. I wish I'd realized it years ago."

Her heart did a little skip. "There's no need to sweet-talk me, soldier. I'm already naked under this robe."

"You kill me."

"I'd rather do something else to you."

His grip on her arms was light. She wasn't going to give him a chance to back away. She broke his hold easily enough, flowing into his arms. He didn't protest as she took his face between her hands and pulled his head down for a kiss.

At first, he didn't react. She was ready to break the kiss when he suddenly squeezed her tight.

"I give up," he said hoarsely. "You win, Evie. You win."

And then he kissed her with the kind of heat that curled her toes.

Sarah huddled against the car door, as far from the man who stared at her as she could. She wrapped her arms around her body and tried to make herself smaller. He finished his latest cigarette and flicked it out the window. The air stank of sweat and stale smoke. She had no idea how anyone could stand it. Surely the smell was as bad in the front seat as the back, but no one seemed affected. These people were creepy.

"Can you please just drop me off now?" Sarah said to the woman, though she kept slanting her eyes to the man beside her. They'd driven past the house once, but no one was home and the woman hadn't wanted to stop and wait. Sarah's pleas to be let out were ignored. They'd driven to the cross street and pulled over, waiting for Evie's car.

"Don't you want to party with us?" the woman said. "Hang out until your sister comes home?"

Sarah was really beginning to regret that she'd told them she and Evie were related. "I'm tired. I'll be sure to tell Evie you're looking for her, though."

The woman turned in her seat and speared Sarah with glittering eyes. "Now that, sweetie, is something I'd rather you didn't do."

Sarah clasped her shaking hands between her knees. Something definitely wasn't right here. She should have never gotten in the car with these people. God, please just let her live and she'd never sneak out again. "I won't tell her, I promise."

"No, you won't." The woman turned around again. "Let's go," she said to the big guy driving.

"You wanna go in the house, see what we can shake out?"

The woman huffed. "No, let's go back to the motel and make our guest comfortable. George and I'll return while you watch the girl."

"You planning to keep her now?"

"I don't think we have a choice. We may need her for leverage."

"Do you really think Evie knows where it is?"

"If David gave her something, she'll know. Even if she doesn't know what it is. We could search, but I'd rather not. It'll be easier to get it out of Evie."

"And if she doesn't have it?"

"She has it."

"But if she doesn't?" the man insisted.

"Then she'll get it for us. She'll do anything to save her baby sister."

Sarah wrenched her gaze to the window, trying to hold back the tears that threatened. One escaped. They didn't really know Evie if they thought she'd do anything for Sarah. Evie could care less about her, no matter how she tried to be so nice and attentive now. Let her leave town again, and they'd never hear from her. Just like before.

No, Evie wouldn't do a thing to save her sister. And Sarah wasn't sure what that meant for her right now—except she was pretty certain it was a bad thing.

To hell with his conscience. Matt was ready to sink into Evie Baker and not come up for air for at least ten hours. There was something about being with her, something about kissing her and feeling her soft skin beneath his fingertips that made him feel grounded again. She reminded him of who he was. Of the parts of himself he liked.

With Evie, there was no need for pretense. She'd been his complement since they were children, and he was surprised to find it hadn't changed very much. Oh, they were different, sure. But she still seemed to know him in ways that surprised him.

He'd been so damn restless for the last two months, his mind occupied with thoughts of everything he'd done wrong, but right now he couldn't think beyond getting this woman naked and under him.

Which wasn't going to be difficult, considering she was only wearing a robe.

Her arms were around his neck, her body arched into his as their tongues tangled in a hot, sensual duel. He had his hands on her ass, pulling her against the hardness between his thighs. Soon, he was going to carry her the few steps to the bed and lose himself in the delights of her body. He'd worry about the implications tomorrow.

And then the doorbell rang. *Shit*.

Still, he planned to ignore it.

But it didn't stop, and Evie shifted restlessly in his arms.

"Shouldn't you get that?" She sounded husky and breathless, and a shot of desire throttled through him.

"No." He dipped his head to kiss her again.

Except the bell kept buzzing. It took a minute to penetrate the fog in his brain, but he suddenly knew who it was. What he didn't know was why.

When they were teens, his sister had loved to punch the doorbell the minute he was rounding third base with a girl he'd brought home. It was like she had radar and lived to make his life hell.

But they weren't kids anymore, and if Christina was

here now—during her dinner party, no less—punching the bell with her trademark series of short, sharp dings, then something was up. Something he couldn't ignore.

Matt lifted his head, cursing inwardly six ways to Sunday. Just when he'd shoved his conscience deep, just when he was about to get up close and personal with Evie's delectable body, this happened.

Maybe it was a sign.

Evie gazed up at him with molten-hot eyes he wanted to drown in. "Give me a minute." He kissed her again. "Don't move from this spot."

He left her there and strode to the door, intent on getting rid of his sister as quickly as possible. Perhaps Misty Lee had decided to dance naked on the terrace in front of all the guests, or maybe Aunt Maybelle had finally collapsed in a faint upon finding a giant dildo and a riding crop in her bedroom. With this family, anything was possible.

When he whipped the door open, his sister stood on the step in a pale pink silk gown, one gloved finger poised over the bell. She looked apologetic.

"So you did hear the door." Her smile was teasing.

Matt frowned and shifted his stance to hide the evidence of what he'd been doing. Or about to do. "What's up, Chris?"

She clasped her hands together. "Is Evie Baker in there with you?"

"Yeah, why?"

One eyebrow lifted imperiously. "Are you planning to invite me in?"

"That depends. What do you want?"

"I enjoy teasing you, Matt, but really, this is something you'll want to hear. I promise."

Matt pulled the door wider, sighing. He couldn't get a break. "Fine."

Chris went inside and sank onto the overstuffed couch. "Heavens, my feet are killing me." She slid her feet from the mile-high shoes she was wearing. "I came to tell you Evie's mother called the house. She said you'd called her earlier, but you weren't answering your phone now."

Damn it. He'd left it plugged in on the kitchen island. And then he'd gotten just a little bit distracted.

"I'll call her now." He was feeling annoyed, and it must have shown in his voice because she arched an eyebrow at him. But really, she'd needed to come down to the guesthouse for this?

"You definitely should, but I can tell you what's going on." Chris leaned forward, frowning. "Evie's little sister is missing. She was supposed to be at home this evening, but when Norma returned from bingo, Sarah was gone. She said she checked Sarah's friends, but Sarah's not with any of them. No one's seen her, and the police aren't interested just yet."

Before Matt could respond, Evie walked into the room. His gut clenched. He should have known she wouldn't stay put. But that wasn't what made his belly tighten.

No, it was the sight of her in his too big T-shirt—which she'd knotted at her waist—and shorts. And since she didn't have any other shoes, she was wearing her high heels. He thought his tongue would stick to the roof of his mouth at the sight of those long, long legs.

Chris stood, smiling broadly. "It's great to see you, Evie. I've been intending to get over to the salon, but I've been so busy since arriving."

Evie's wet hair hung in long ropes down her back, and her cosmetic-free face looked so fresh and innocent. She must have known how it looked to Chris, and yet she stood there with all the grace of a debutante at a cotillion.

They shared a quick hug. "Please don't explain. You've been much too busy for visiting!"

Chris frowned. "I know, but I wanted to see everyone. I really had no idea how much work I'd have to do once I moved the wedding to Reynier's Retreat."

"But it'll be worth it all. Reynier's Retreat is the perfect place for a wedding."

Chris beamed. "Thank you. I thought so too." She reached out and squeezed Evie's hand. "I'd so love to catch up, but there's something you need to know." She slanted her gaze toward him. "Do you want to tell her?"

Evie's expression grew suddenly wary as she darted a look between them. "Tell me what?"

"Your mama called," Matt said. "Your sister isn't at home like she's supposed to be."

Evie's brow furrowed. "She must be with a friend."

Matt shook his head. "Doesn't appear to be. But that doesn't mean anything. I think your mama's probably worried because of the shooting at the lake. Anyone with a police scanner has heard it by now."

"But Sarah wasn't there."

"Not that we know of, no."

Evie put a hand to her head. For the barest moment, she looked as if she might crumple and he took a step toward her. But she stiffened her spine and faced them both as if someone had injected her with steel. He should have known that was coming. Evie was never down for long.

"I shouldn't have left her tonight. If I'd just stayed home, none of this would have happened. She could hardly sneak out with me there."

Matt took her by the shoulders and forced her to look him in the eye. Her eyes were haunted, guilty. It made something in his chest tighten. She looked helpless, though he knew she wasn't. But in that moment, she made him think of the women and children he'd seen in the burned-out villages sometimes.

We can't save them all. Colonel Mendez had said that to him more than once after the team returned from the field. But, damn it, Matt wasn't prepared to accept that edict. He would keep trying to save them, every last one, until the Army wouldn't let him anymore.

"There's no point in beating yourself up over what you might have, should have, could have done." He squeezed her shoulders. "What's done is done. Now we need to go and find your sister and get you both home so your mama can stop worrying."

Evie took a deep breath as if she needed to ground herself. "Right. Okay, she probably snuck off to a party somewhere. Or out with a boy."

"Sounds likely. Why don't we call your mother and see what she's done and who she's called?"

"I think I left my purse in your car. My phone is there."

"You can use mine." Matt went and got his phone and handed it to Evie. She dialed her mother, moving across the room toward the windows along the side of the house.

Chris stood and smoothed her skirt. "I better get back to the party now." She shot a glance at Evie before focusing on him. "So are you taking up where you left off?"

"What's that mean?"

Chris gave him a look. "You know what it means. But Matt, be careful."

A current of irritation flared to life inside him. "Careful? What are you talking about?"

"You. You're the same dog you've always been, and Evie's just another woman who can't quite resist your charms. But she's also the one you shouldn't mess with, because you've already done wrong by her once."

Matt felt as if she'd jabbed him in the gut with her spiked heel. "Thanks for the advice, though I don't remember asking for it."

Chris smiled at him. Presumably to soften the blow. "It comes free because you're my brother."

Matt frowned, though hurt swirled deep down. *The same dog you've always been.* "Go tell Ben what to do. He signed on for it. I didn't."

Chris came over and tugged him down to her level. Then she kissed his cheek. "Don't do anything stupid, Mattie."

"Don't call me Mattie," he growled. "And I'm not planning to do anything stupid."

"Says you." Chris slipped out the door and closed it behind her.

Matt turned to find Evie still on the phone, one hand to her temple as she spoke. She looked so vulnerable in his shorts and too-big shirt, and he felt that same protective instinct he always felt when faced with a woman in crisis. It was probably nothing, just a teenager being a teenager, but he could no more walk away before they'd found Sarah and gotten her back home again than he could cease breathing on command. He wasn't wired that way.

When his mother had been dying, he'd felt so helpless and useless. He didn't feel that way anymore, or at least not often. That was a big part of why he did what he did. He felt a sense of accomplishment he'd never felt before. It was dangerous, sure, but the rewards made it worthwhile.

Evie finished the call and turned to him, her eyes full of concern. "Mama's at home in case she shows up there, but my aunt and cousin are out looking for her. I need to get my car so I can help."

Matt shook his head as he took his phone back. "I said I'd help you."

She looked determined. "You've done enough for me tonight, Matt. Maybe you should go back to the party."

He blinked. Did she want him to go? Was she finished with him? "So this is it, huh? Thanks and good night?"

She shrugged and he wanted to kiss her again, make her remember what kind of sparks had been zinging between them just a few minutes ago. "I think I forgot why you were in Rochambeau until Chris showed up. You're missing her party and time with your family."

As if family time in the Girard household had ever been something to look forward to after their mother died.

"I told you before that I already made my appearance. So either I help you, or I'm lying on the couch with a bag of chips and the remote."

She rolled her eyes, and a current of warmth began to filter through him. "You didn't get abs like that eating chips. Or watching TV."

"Maybe I did."

"Well if you did, I want to know the secret." She had both hands on her hips now, and she was smiling. He liked it when she smiled.

Matt grabbed his keys. "Come on, let's go. If you're lucky, I'll tell you the secret while we're searching."

They didn't speak as Matt backed out of the garage and turned the car into the long driveway. Evie was worried, but mostly for Mama. Her mother would be frantic until Sarah came home again. She felt a twinge of anger at her sister, but she pushed it down and concentrated on what she would say when they found Sarah. She wanted to wring the girl's neck, but she wouldn't. That certainly wouldn't make things better between them, would it?

Besides, she shared the blame for this. She should have known Sarah wasn't planning to stay home after everyone was gone. Had she ever stayed put as a teen? On a Saturday? Hell no.

She'd gone to parties with her friends. The same kind of party where she'd walked up to Matt, bold as brass, and asked him to be her first.

If Sarah was out with a boy...

Evie shivered and Matt turned to her. "Cold?"

"Not really. Just a momentary chill."

"You can set your own temperature." He pointed at the controls for the passenger.

Evie pressed the button to increase the heat to her side and they lapsed into silence again. Her skin still tingled from his touch. Her lips felt as if they were on fire. If Christina hadn't rung that bell, she had no doubt they'd be tangled together in his sheets right now. Something she'd wanted badly when she'd been wrapped up in his kiss.

Something she still wanted, if she were honest with herself. But while she'd stood there, waiting for him to come back, she started to panic. She asked herself what she was doing and what she thought would happen if she and Matt had sex. Suddenly, with him not there in the room, she'd lost her nerve. Now, she pushed her hand through her damp hair and wondered if she'd ever get that nerve again. If it was even a good idea.

"Thanks for doing this, Matt."

"It's not a problem, *chère*."

Evie blew out a breath. "This night has definitely not turned out the way I expected it to when Julie dragged me to the lake."

Matt chuckled. "No, I imagine not." He glanced over at her. "Do you have any idea where Sarah likes to hang out? Who her friends are?"

Evie closed her eyes. She'd been home a month and, no, she didn't know any of that. Why didn't she? She should have known everything about her sister's life. But she didn't have the first clue. What did that say about her?

"I don't really know," she said softly. "Sarah and I aren't all that close."

"I'm sorry."

"It's my fault." Evie twisted her fingers together in her lap. "I was so determined to shake off the dust of this town that I hardly ever came back. In almost eight years,

I've been home twice."

He was quiet for a moment. "Rochambeau is the kind of place that gets under your skin. You're never quite free of it."

"That's certainly true." She stifled a bitter laugh. "And here I am, back again, dying to get out as soon as I can."

"Is it still so bad?"

Evie shrugged. She'd been asking herself that question for the past month. Was Rochambeau all that bad, or was it just the way *she* felt whenever she was here? No one treated her badly. No one seemed to care about anything that had happened in the past. Oh, that wouldn't stop them from gossiping over something juicy—her and Matt together again after the Night That Changed Everything—but they weren't malicious or vindictive about it.

"Honestly, I don't know. I just know there are a lot of memories here, and not all of them good."

His hands flexed on the wheel. "Was it really that bad? After I left?"

She swung her head toward him. He was in profile to her, his handsome face so strong and beautiful. But his jaw was tight. She had an urge to reach out and run her fingers along his skin, to see him soften, even if only for a moment. She'd sensed such pain in him tonight.

He wasn't the same cocky bastard he'd been in high school. She wanted to know what had happened to him. And yet she knew he wasn't going to share it with her. Matt had always kept his secrets close.

"We keep coming back to this, don't we?"

He glanced at her and then back at the road. "Yeah, I suppose we do."

"I could lie and tell you it was nothing. And maybe it was, in retrospect. But not then. Then, I wasn't prepared for the teasing and bullying."

He swore. "Jesus, I'm sorry. If I could go back and kick my own ass, I'd do it."

She shrugged. "It made me stronger in the end."

"You were always strong."

She gave him a sad smile. "No, I was just good at pretending."

"I don't believe that, Evie. You never let anything stop you back then."

"Maybe I was just too scared to give up."

"Sometimes that's all it takes. There have been days —missions—when giving up would have been easier. But fear of the unknown stops you, and then you come out on the other side."

"I suppose it's a part of what made me who I am today. It wasn't a picnic, Matt, but I'm not still crying myself to sleep over it at night."

His throat worked as he swallowed. "You cried yourself to sleep?"

"I was sixteen. Of course I did. But not forever. These days, I never cry myself to sleep. I just deal."

He frowned. "I'm sorry you lost your restaurant."

"Thanks. But I'll start again. Eventually. I lost my business, my life savings, a bit of my pride—but I'm determined to fight until things get better."

Because she would fling herself at the brick wall again and again until she finally scaled it. She wasn't the kind of girl who gave up. She liked that about herself.

Matt shook his head. "I should have never touched you, Evie."

She laughed. "Matt, you were seventeen! What kind of seventeen-year-old boy is going to turn down sex when it's offered?"

He pushed a hand through his hair and shot her a self-deprecating grin. "Yeah, not likely, is it?"

"Especially not a boy like you. Rich, spoiled, entitled."

"Damn, you know how to jab a guy when he's down." He was smiling at her, but she knew it bothered him.

"If I'd been in your place, I'd have done the same thing. I don't really blame you anymore, you know. It takes two, and I was definitely a participant."

"If I could change it, I would."

She reached over and squeezed his arm. His skin was warm, and a tingle slid over her. "I know."

He glanced over at her one more time. "Now please tell me there's not a secret baby stashed away somewhere."

Evie stifled a groan. She'd heard that rumor. It had started a couple of years after she'd left Rochambeau, but so far as she'd known, Matt had never heard it. Clearly, she'd been wrong.

"Oh God no! Believe me, if I'd gotten pregnant, you'd have known. My mama would have marched out to Reynier's Retreat and demanded that your daddy haul your ass back to Rochambeau."

He laughed. "Yeah, and he'd have probably done it too. Nobody crosses Norma Breaux."

Evie put her face in her hands. "Sometimes, this town. I had no idea you'd heard that one."

"I figured if it had been true, things would have

happened as you said." He shrugged. And then he looked somber again. "I'm glad we didn't make a baby, Evie. I don't think either of us was prepared to deal with that back then."

"Definitely not. Can you imagine? We'd have a nine-year-old right now."

He looked… sad, she thought. Or maybe troubled. "My life is not conducive to raising children."

"Is that why you've never married?"

He sighed. "It's kind of hard to maintain a relationship doing what I do. Most women think twice before getting involved with a guy like me."

Evie shook her head. "I still don't get why you do it, but okay. Who am I to judge? If I'd done what I was supposed to do, I'd have stayed in Rochambeau and found a guy to settle down with."

"But you aren't the settling down type?"

"Oh, I think I probably am. Just not yet." She toyed with the edge of the shorts she wore. "I still have to figure my own life out. See if I can accomplish my dreams without always running into a roadblock of my own making."

"We all make mistakes, Evie. I wouldn't be too hard on yourself for them. Could you have honestly known your partner was going to steal from you?"

She'd asked herself that before. Many times. "I like to think I might have realized it before he stole the payroll, but he was really good at what he did. He was patient too. I didn't let him handle the money for months, but his advice was so damn good. I could see the profits coming in and after a while it just made sense to let him handle it. I looked at the books, but there was nothing wrong."

"Two sets of books then."

"Yes. I'd just like to get to that point in my life where the mistakes I make don't have quite so many consequences. For now, I'm back in Rochambeau and trying to figure out how I can escape again."

"You'll figure it out, I'm sure. And just remember, it could always be worse."

"I'm not sure how." She sounded glum and she knew it.

He turned the car onto a dirt road and put his foot on the brake. And then he looked at her steadily, the harsh planes and angles of his face stark in the dimly lit interior. "When you make a mistake, no one dies. Nothing on this earth will make that kind of mistake better, I assure you."

Evie swallowed back the lump in her throat. Matt was a soldier, the kind of man who lived with life-and-death decisions on a regular basis. How could she have forgotten that for even a moment? She suddenly felt petty and small. As if he knew what she was thinking, he reached out and ran his fingers along her cheek.

"You've made mistakes, and you have every right to regret them. But don't let them own you, Evie. Don't let them be more important than they are."

Before she could say a word, he flashed her that famous smile again. "Now come on, let's go cruise the make-out spots and see if we can track down your sister."

He turned back to driving, but Evie couldn't seem to drag her eyes away from him. He was definitely not the same boy he'd been ten years ago. She'd had a crush on that boy—that popular, gorgeous, unattainable boy.

But the man before her now was terrifying in ways that boy hadn't been. The man was empathetic, authentic —and far more appealing than the boy had ever been.

Evie fixed her eyes on the dirt track in front of the headlights, her heart thrumming a little bit faster than it had before. He might be appealing, but she had to remember that Matthew Girard was just as unattainable as ever.

And far more dangerous.

SEVEN

THEY SPENT OVER AN HOUR searching all the popular spots where teens hung out. The kids weren't happy to see them, but a wad of cash waved under a few noses—thanks to Matt—made them more talkative. Still, the only thing Evie knew about Sarah at the end of it was that she was going out with a guy named Kyle Jenkins.

But Kyle had been seen only a half hour before and Sarah wasn't with him. According to Mindy, Kyle had been pretty pissed off when he'd blown through their little group earlier. When Mindy asked where Sarah was, Kyle said they'd had a fight and he didn't know or care.

Mindy had no idea where Kyle had dropped Sarah off, but it wasn't with her. And it clearly wasn't at home either. Or hadn't been in the last couple of hours.

"Why don't you call your mother," Matt said as they drove away from the farmer's field where Mindy and her friends claimed they were only drinking sodas and smoking cigarettes.

As if. She'd been sixteen once. She knew what they were doing.

"If she had a falling out with this Kyle guy, maybe she's home by now," Matt continued.

"I will. But we can't leave those kids like that." Evie turned to peer out the back window at the gathering of cars. "They have beer for sure. And who knows what else."

Ten years ago, she'd have been doing the same thing and thinking it was perfectly acceptable. But get a little older, get a little more righteous. It wasn't acceptable and she couldn't pretend it didn't worry her.

"We won't. I'll call the RPD and have them send a cruiser out."

While Matt made a quick call to the police, Evie punched in her mama's number and waited as it rang and rang. When it clicked over to the answering machine, Evie hung up with a growl of frustration.

"No answer. Mama probably went out on her own. Or maybe Sarah called her from the convenience store."

That was one place they hadn't gone yet. The store was also a popular hangout for teens, who gathered in the parking lot in their cars. They listened to their radios, danced, and did whatever kids did. She'd spent many nights in that parking lot when she'd been a teen. The owner, Mr. Landry, said he'd rather have them there than out in a field somewhere. It worked for the ones who couldn't get someone to buy them any alcohol.

"So we'll check it out. Then we'll head for your house. Keep trying."

Evie's phone blared suddenly. It startled her so much that she fumbled it. "Shit!" She scrambled to pick it up before it went to voice mail.

She punched the call button without looking at the

display. "Mama?"

"Hey, baby."

Evie's heart throttled up as she nearly dropped the phone again. She clutched it tight and wished she could reach through the other end. If she could, she'd choke the bastard. "David? What the hell do you want?"

"Aw, is that any way to greet me, honey?"

Heat rolled inside her. Angry heat. He'd disappeared from her life months ago. She'd spent weeks imagining him behind bars, forced to listen while she told him how much she hated him and what a prick he was. She'd wasted enough breath on him in those imaginary conversations that she had no desire to repeat any of it now.

"Unless you plan to tell me you've brought my money back, I don't want to hear anything you have to say. A lot of people didn't get paid that night you disappeared. You stole from all of us, asshole."

"Maybe you better listen anyway." David's voice shifted, becoming low and menacing. "If you want to live, that is."

An arrow of fear sliced through her. Followed by a wave of fury. "You dare call me and threaten me after what you did? You think I believe you? You lied to me, stole my money, and ruined my business. No way in hell do I believe anything you say."

David swore. "Yeah, yeah, I get it. You hate me. But listen, damn it, I'm not kidding. I need your help or we're both dead. And maybe your mother and sister too. How about them, huh?"

Evie forced herself to breathe normally. Beside her, Matt was still, and she realized he'd pulled over to the side of the road. She glanced at him. He watched her with a single-minded focus that was almost unnerving.

"What do you want from me?"

"I need to talk to you."

"You are talking to me."

"No, I need to see you. It's too dangerous to explain over the phone. Can you meet me?"

Evie trembled with fury. A cold shot of fear for Sarah traveled into the depths of her stomach and wouldn't go away. Where was her sister?

She pressed a hand to her forehead. She didn't want to do this, she really didn't. Not right now. But what choice did she have? If she hung up on him, which she was sorely tempted to do, and he wasn't kidding—then what? "Where and when?"

"How about at your mother's house? You can come out on the porch and talk to me. I'll see you in half an hour."

"Wait—" He hung up and she dropped the phone into her lap. *Shit.* It was bad enough that he knew where her mother lived—that he was even close enough to be there in half an hour—but what was all that crap about lives in jeopardy? She had nothing left to steal. Nothing to give him. He'd drained her and he knew it. Even if his ties to organized crime were real—and the police had no evidence they were—what did it have to do with her?

"You want to tell me what that was about?"

She met Matt's gaze. He was angry, but in control. Such fine control. Control she'd almost broken earlier. She shivered just thinking about it.

"I told you about my ex-partner. That was him." She shook her head. Her hand curled into a fist in her lap. "Why now?"

"What did he want?"

"He…He's in town. He wants to meet me. He says—" She swallowed hard.

"Says what, Evie?"

"He said he needs my help or something bad could happen."

Matt's voice was firm, commanding. "Tell me everything he said."

She hesitated for a moment—but after everything that had happened tonight, she needed someone to share this with. And she could think of no better person than Matt. She told him everything David had said and how much money he'd drained her of before he'd fled—but she left out the part about organized crime. She simply couldn't voice it without feeling sick. Besides, there'd been no evidence, only speculation.

Matt's jaw was tight. "Anyone who stole over a hundred grand from you, skipped town, then calls you and wants to talk doesn't have a friendly session of chitchat in mind. He must think you have more to give him."

Evie nervously tapped her fingers against the armrest. "I don't see where I have a choice except to meet him. Mama and Sarah could be there now and I damn sure don't want them letting David into the house. I have to get home before he arrives."

Matt popped the Beemer into gear. "Then I'm meeting this guy with you. If he's desperate, he'll come anyway. And if he's trying to get you alone for something, he'll skip out and try again. At the least, we'll know his intentions by how he behaves. We'll hit the convenience store and gas station on the way, in case Sarah's there."

Guilt reared its ugly head again. "This isn't your

problem, Matt. You came home for a wedding, not to bail me out of trouble all night."

He flashed her a meaningful look. "Not up for negotiation. I'm going."

Something didn't feel right. Matt had learned over the course of three years as a covert operator to trust his gut. The one time he'd ignored it, the one time he'd convinced himself he had to be wrong, the shit had hit the fan in a spectacular way. Hell, he'd made mistakes tonight that pissed him off, but they were somehow smaller and less important than the feeling rolling through him right now.

Ignore this one, his instincts told him, *and you'll be on permanent leave. And so will the woman sitting beside you.*

Sarah hadn't been seen in town. She hadn't stopped at the convenience store to call her mother, hadn't popped up at Charlie's Diner on the bayou. Nothing else was open this late, other than the quick mart and gas station about a mile out of town. They didn't have time to hit that one yet, but they would as soon as they got this meeting over with.

Still, even if she'd been there, she wasn't anymore. Of that he was certain. Sarah could have gone to a friend's house, but it wasn't likely, since her best friend was in a field with most of the kids they hung out with.

Chief Laurent had no doubt sent a cruiser out there by now, and the teens were dumping their beer and scattering like cockroaches—the ones who passed the sobriety tests, that is. He remembered doing the same thing at their age, and he'd been lucky it hadn't killed him.

He'd gotten falling-down drunk more than once back then, too. And he'd certainly puked up his guts enough times after a night of partying. Moderation had not been a word in his vocabulary.

It's also why he didn't drink anymore.

He quit for good when he was recruited for HOT. He needed a clear head and a fit body, and alcohol did him no favors in either department. Some of the other guys could handle it just fine—drink that one beer and stop—but not him. No, if he cracked open a beer, he'd want the whole six-pack.

"That's odd." Evie was sitting forward, peering out the window as he turned into the driveway. She'd been tense since her ex-partner had called, but this was a whole new level of anxiety.

"What's odd?"

"The exterior lights are out."

"How many are there?"

"The porch light and two floods. And Mama's usually obsessive about turning them on when it gets dark. No way would they all be out, even if one blew."

The feeling in his gut went from a simmer to a boil. A flash of red reflectors at the rear of the house indicated a car sitting back there.

"Is that your mama's car?"

"Yes." The word sounded pinched, as if she had trouble getting it out.

And he could guess why. She didn't have to remind him she'd been calling her mother regularly for the past fifteen minutes. Or that no one had answered the phone.

Matt braked and put the car into park. "I need you to stay here." He reached for the knife he'd clipped to his belt before they'd left Reynier's Retreat. Once unarmed tonight was enough.

"No way, not this time. We did it your way the last time and look what happened."

He crushed his exasperation, carefully blanked his mind to everything except the job ahead. She was right, but he didn't have time to argue with her. "I'll be back in ten and you can come out then."

"No." She grasped his arm and held it hard. "This is my family, Matt. I'm not sitting here waiting for you to return. It didn't do a damn bit of good before, and I won't do it again."

Her eyes glittered in the dash lights and her jaw perched at a stubborn angle. He wanted to shake her. And kiss her.

Yeah, arguing with this woman was useless. He got the feeling she'd go *through* him if he didn't let her go with him. The next best thing he could do was make sure she stayed safe.

"When you exit the car, wait for me to come around to your side. We go together."

Her hand dropped away, grasping the door handle. "Fine."

Matt reached across her, popped open the glove compartment, and grabbed the small flashlight inside. When he got to her side of the car, she was waiting. He hadn't been sure she would. He tucked her behind him and listened to the night sounds. Crickets and cicadas sang loud and strong, and an owl hooted in the trees. A good sign, though not foolproof.

He felt his way through the darkness without use of the flashlight—he'd shoved it into his waistband just in case he needed it—keeping an ear cocked for any noise that didn't jibe with the sounds of a summer night.

Evie followed close behind, grasping his T-shirt for guidance. He led her around the back of the house, flicked on the flashlight, and swept it over the area. Her mother's little pickup looked normal enough. No open doors, no broken glass.

He turned and put his mouth against Evie's ear, inhaling the clean scent of her hair as he spoke. "Wait here for a second while I check the back door."

She nodded and he left her standing beside the truck while he worked his way up the wooden stairs. The door was locked. He considered picking the lock and slipping inside, but discarded the idea for two reasons. One, Evie would follow. Two, though the situation seemed odd, there was every chance her mother was inside asleep. With his luck, if he startled her, he'd either end up dead from a shotgun blast or she'd have a heart attack and keel over.

He wasn't taking the chance. He returned to Evie and made for the other side of the house. When he came to the main power meter, he stopped and lifted the flap.

Sonofabitch.

The circuit breakers were off. Not a good sign at all. If he flipped them on, he'd lose any chance he had for surprise. On the other hand, whoever had turned the power off would have seen the headlights when Matt turned into the drive. Assuming the guy was still here.

And Matt couldn't keep slinking around looking for the perpetrator when he had Evie tagging along.

He had no other choice. He flipped the breaker switch and the front of the house lit up like someone ignited a bonfire. There were no other noises, no footsteps or slamming doors or, thank God, gunfire.

Matt glanced at Evie. She worried her lower lip with her teeth. "Somebody shut it off, didn't they?"

"Yeah," he admitted.

"Is it safe to go in?"

"I don't know." That was the truth. "I need to go alone."

She studied him, her brow creasing. "I know. Do you want me to stay here, or is there a better place?"

He admired her more in that moment than he ever had. She was worried, maybe even scared, but when push came to shove, she accepted that he would be better off operating alone. Smart woman.

"Stay here and I'll come for you when it's clear." He'd rather she was in the car, but he'd have to take her back around the house to get her there. Better to do what needed to be done and hope for the best.

Still, he wasn't quite at ease with the situation. Norma Breaux's car was here and the lights were out. To his mind, that didn't bode well. If she'd been robbed, if she'd been hurt—well, he'd rather find that out alone.

He stayed close to the side of the house, moving as silently as he could until he reached the front. He studied the area for a long moment and then took the steps up to the porch when he felt it was safe.

Once he reached the top, he jerked to a stop. There was a body near the front door, but it wasn't Norma's. Matt padded over and hunkered down beside the lifeless form. Male, about thirty, slightly overweight. Blond hair, goatee, pasty skin. Blue sweatshirt, jeans.

A pool of blood congealed beneath the body, which lay facedown, head turned to the left. A carving knife lay off to the side, the eight-inch blade bloody. The handle appeared clean, though.

If this were an op, Matt would go through the guy's pockets, find some identification. But here, he couldn't touch anything. He was taking a risk entering the house, but he had to do it. He had to know if Evie's mother and sister were in there, and if they were alive. Yeah, he'd fuck up the crime scene a little bit by going in, but he couldn't go back out there and tell Evie there was a dead guy—probably her ex-partner—and give her no information about her family.

Colonel Mendez would have Matt's skin if he learned about this. Best to make sure he didn't hear about it then. Though how in the hell that was happening, Matt wasn't certain. Mendez had an uncanny sense of trouble on the brew. So uncanny that Matt almost expected his phone to start buzzing in his pocket at any second.

Matt gave the body a wide berth as he worked his way over to the front door. He stuck his hand into the tail of his T-shirt to turn the knob and the door swung open on squeaky hinges.

A lamp was on in the living room, illuminating yellow walls, wood floors, and an entertainment center against the far wall. The television was off. Two chairs flanked the cabinet and a couch faced the television, its back to the door. Matt glanced over the room as he headed for the rear of the house.

He stopped short when he saw the body sprawled in front of the couch.

Norma Breaux was on her stomach, one hand to her side, the other bent beneath her. Matt crossed the distance in two steps and knelt beside her. Her pulse was strong. He let out a breath, surprised at how his heart kicked up at the sight of Evie's mother lying so still.

This kind of thing didn't usually get to him. It was all part of the business. But this was home, goddammit. This kind of violence wasn't supposed to happen here. Yeah, good old boys got drunk and had fights—or shot off weapons and took hostages, apparently—but murder? It wasn't right.

Matt didn't move her while he did a quick check for any injuries. When he was satisfied she hadn't been shot or stabbed, he snatched up the phone on the end table and placed a call to 911. In the minutes left to him before the emergency vehicles would arrive, he cased the rest of the small house.

There was no sign of Sarah, and no evidence of a struggle. If the girl had been here, she'd either left willingly before any of this happened, or she'd been marched out at gunpoint. But he'd bet his next paycheck Sarah hadn't been here. Call it instinct or whatever, but he couldn't shake the feeling.

He slipped out the front door and ground to a halt. Evie stood on the porch, her eyes wide as saucers as she stared at the body.

"It's David. H…He grew a goatee, but—" She covered her mouth and turned away.

Matt came around and led her back down the steps. "I thought you were going to wait."

Her wild gaze landed on his face. "You took so long I thought something happened. I was coming to help."

Matt closed his eyes. Saints preserve him from women who thought he couldn't take care of himself.

He hadn't been gone long at all. But she'd probably stood there alone, the night sounds and the eeriness of the situation working on her mind, until she convinced herself she had to investigate. Had to *save* him, God help him.

He could tell by watching her face when the shock started to wear off and a different reality slammed into her. Matt gripped her arms hard, held her to him when she tried to wrench away.

"Mama," she cried.

"She's okay, Evie."

She twisted like a tiger. "Let me go. I have to see her!"

"It's a crime scene, *chère*. You can't go in, but I promise you she's okay. I promise you, Evie."

A sob wracked her body, the first he'd heard out of her tonight, and it damn near tore him up. She'd been through a lot, but it was fear for her mama that finally wrenched the tears from her.

She gripped his biceps in her hands, her forehead dropping to his chest as she lost the control she'd been holding on to so tightly.

She screamed and cried and he soothed her in Cajun French, like his mama used to do when he'd had a nightmare. When he realized what he was doing, he switched to English. Evie's mama was a Breaux, but Evie didn't speak French. He knew that because he used to make her mad when they were kids by talking to her in a language she couldn't understand.

"If she's not okay, you can shoot me, yeah *ma petite*?" The cadence of the bayou was still thick on his tongue, and he couldn't control it just yet. He never could when he let emotion get the best of him. Which was damn rare. "I swear to you on my mama's grave she gonna be fine, yeah."

The sound of sirens split the night and Matt gave a silent thank-you. The quicker the police and EMTs got here, the quicker Evie would know he spoke the truth. He wrapped his arms around her and held on tight as her sobs lessened along with her grip.

The first patrol car rocketed into the driveway, followed by two others. The ambulance shot between them and skidded to a halt behind the Beemer.

Doors popped open in almost perfect unison. Uniforms poured from the vehicles and spread around the scene. Matt pulled Evie away from the steps and waited for the officer in charge to start pelting him with questions.

It was gonna be one long-ass night.

EIGHT

EVIE HUDDLED ON A CHAIR in a small metal room at the police station. How long had it been since she'd been escorted to this room? Two hours? Three?

She couldn't remember. She'd tried dozing, but she was too wired to sleep—in spite of being so damn tired she could barely keep her head up. And she was cold.

She hadn't seen Matt since the police arrived at her mother's house. He'd left her sitting in the back seat of a patrol car while he went to talk to someone. She didn't know if he was here too, if he was in another room, or if he'd gone home and disappeared beneath a mountain of soft covers. If she were him, she'd probably opt for the covers.

Especially after the way she'd bawled all over him. God.

She closed her eyes, seeing again the body on her mother's porch. The blood that looked more like motor oil because it was in shadow. She'd never seen a dead person before. Obviously, Matt had. How did he deal with it, with the knowledge of what death looked like?

It made her shiver, and she had to fight the urge to retch.

David was dead. She still couldn't believe it, especially since she'd been talking to him on the phone only a few minutes before. She replayed their conversation, but got nothing new out of it. He'd said his life—and by extension hers and her family's—was in danger. But from whom? And why?

And Mama. Oh God, Mama. Evie swallowed against a fresh wave of tears. Mama had a broken wrist from where she'd fallen on her arm. Evie had learned from one of the officers on the scene that, aside from the break, her mother would be okay. Though Mama had been knocked out, her respiration and heart rate were normal and that was a good sign.

Evie wanted to go to the hospital with Mama, but the police chief arrived and denied the request. So here she was, waiting for something that didn't seem to be all that pressing since no one had arrived to talk to her yet. She had no idea what was happening with Mama now. Matt promised to find out for her, but surely he'd gone home by now. As soon as she got out of here, no matter what time it was, she was going to the hospital.

And then there was Sarah. A thread of panic wound through Evie's belly and squeezed her throat tight. Where was her little sister? Matt didn't seem to think she'd been there when David had been killed, but how could he be sure?

Evie's head was so heavy. She hadn't been sleeping all that well lately, and she'd been up since around three a.m., when she'd finally given up on sleep and gotten out of bed. Add in a full day at the salon, the evening at the lake, and everything since, and she was feeling pretty worn out.

She laid her head on the table, clasped her hands in her lap, and closed her eyes. If she could turn back the clock on this day, what would she have done differently? If she'd been in the house, she'd probably be in the hospital with Mama right now.

Unless whoever had killed David decided to kill her too. Evie shivered.

"Can you ID the victim, Miss Baker?"

Evie snapped upright. Two men stood inside the room. She hadn't even heard the door open.

She blinked. She didn't know these guys at all. The Rochambeau PD had grown a bit since she'd last lived here, and they'd apparently hired officers who weren't native to the town. It was disconcerting. Or maybe it was just one more thing to add to an already disturbing evening.

The one in a yellow polo shirt perched on the edge of the desk and bent toward her. The gold badge clipped to his belt disappeared into his spare tire when he leaned over. "You okay?"

Evie threaded a hand through her hair and nodded. "It's been a long day."

The man gave a snort of laughter. "Yes indeed, I'd say so, young lady. I'm Detective Odell. This here is Detective Proctor. We'd like to ask you a few questions." He twisted to the side and flipped open a folder he must have laid on the table. "Can you tell me the victim's name, Miss Baker?"

"David. David West."

"And how did you know the deceased?"

"He was my ex-partner."

"And your lover?"

Evie cleared her throat. "Yes, occasionally."

"For how long?"

"He was my partner for six months, but I knew him for nearly a year. We were a couple, if you could call it that, for only two months."

"Why did he come here tonight?"

"I don't know. I haven't heard from him since he stole my restaurant payroll about five months ago. He called and asked to meet, but when we got there... Well, he was..." She closed her eyes and swallowed. "Dead."

Detective Odell crossed his arms. "Seems as if you've had one very busy night. First Jimmy Thibodeaux and now this little incident."

A cold finger of dread slid over her at his use of the word *incident*. He made it sound like she'd tripped and skinned her knee. "I'm sorry, but can you tell me what this is about? I've told you all I know. And I'm sure Matt Girard said pretty much the same thing. We've been together since we left the lake earlier."

"West stole your money, right?"

Evie looked at Detective Proctor. It was the first time he'd spoken. "Yes. I just said so."

"Ran your business into the ground?"

She should be surprised they'd found that out so fast. Instead, she was just weary and ready to be done with it. "Yes, I lost my restaurant because David stole my money and I couldn't pay the bills."

"Did that make you angry?"

"Of course." The instant she said it, she wished she could call it back. It was the truth, but the way they now

126

looked at her…

"Angry enough to kill him?"

Evie sat up straight. "And what would be the point in that, Detective? It's not like I'd get my restaurant back, now is it?"

Odell smiled again. "Sorry, Evangeline—can I call you Evangeline?"

"Evie."

"Evie, then. We're trying to figure out what happened out there at your mama's house. Detective Proctor's just doing his job."

"I didn't kill him. I didn't even know he was in town until he called me. You can check my phone records, and you can verify where I was when you talk to Matt Girard."

"Girard's a trained soldier, Evie." Detective Proctor didn't look up from the file he suddenly seemed so intent on. "He disarmed a gunman bare-handed. He's capable of violence. Maybe if he thought you were in danger again…"

Anger and frustration boiled inside her at the implication. "Today's the first time in ten years I've seen Matt. And Jimmy was holding me at knifepoint. If Matt hadn't acted, who knows what Jimmy might have done." Evie shook her head. "Matt had no reason to do anything to David. He was dead when we got there."

Proctor's mouth opened, but the door swinging behind them made both detectives turn around. A man in a plaid shirt cocked his head. The detectives huddled with him for a minute, Odell straightening first.

"Well, Evie, guess we're done here for now. Why don't you go get some sleep, huh?"

Evie scraped herself to her feet. "That's it?"

Odell smiled. "For now. You weren't planning to leave town or anything, right?"

As if she had anywhere to go. "No."

"Good." Odell's smile didn't reach his eyes. "We just need a bit of time to sort this out, is all."

So friendly, as if they hadn't insinuated she might have killed David. Or that Matt might have.

"What about my sister?" She'd reported Sarah missing when she'd given her statement earlier. The officer taking the statement hadn't seemed especially concerned.

Odell consulted his folder. "Sarah Jean Savoie, right? We're keeping an eye out for her, but she's probably just gone to a friend's house." He smiled again. "I'm sure you'll hear from her soon."

Her throat was tight. "What if someone took her? Whoever hit my mama and killed David is still out there."

She fought to keep the frustration from her tone, the utter helplessness. Her fists clenched at her sides as she squeezed back another round of tears.

Odell put a hand on her shoulder. "We're working on it. Don't worry."

Evie couldn't help but worry. Still, she trudged out the door and followed the uniformed officer who led her silently down the hall and out into a small waiting area. Matt looked up as she emerged. He was leaning against one wall, knee bent, foot and hands flat against the plaster, his expression hard enough to pulverize diamonds.

Evie swallowed, both grateful to see him and apprehensive at the same time. She'd certainly gotten him into a mess tonight, hadn't she? First Jimmy and now David. He had to be regretting the impulse to help her by now, regardless of their past or how obligated he felt. Whatever he'd done when they were teenagers didn't warrant this kind of hassle, she was sure.

"You waited."

"Yeah."

"Did you find out anything about my mama?"

He nodded. "They've operated to repair the damage. She's in recovery now, but they'll move her to a room soon."

"I need to go see her."

"I figured as much."

They walked out of the police station together. Matt opened the passenger door for her. His expression was carefully blank, as if he was fighting some emotion and trying not to show it. When he settled into the driver's seat, he turned to her.

"Do you want to explain?" His blank expression was now dark.

She felt as if someone had let the air out of her tires. "Explain what, Matt? I'm too tired to guess, so just hit me with it, 'kay?"

He leaned back against the seat, shoving a hand through his hair. "Start with the part about organized crime."

So he'd found that out. She was too tired to be surprised. She spread her hands, looking at her nails as if she could find the answer there. "I don't know anything about organized crime. There was some speculation by the Tampa police that David was involved in something, but they never told me what. And before you tell me I should have asked, stop and think about it for a second."

He watched her evenly.

"I don't have your connections and no one was about

to tell me just because I wanted to know. It was over, the restaurant was gone, and I wasn't looking back."

"All right."

"That's it? Just all right? After you glared at me for the past five minutes? God, I'm sick of people jumping to conclusions about me."

He blew out a breath. "Look, I just had my ass chewed out by my commanding officer, and I had to wake Mrs. Doucet—" He glanced at the dash clock. "—at nearly one in the morning to lean on the Rochambeau PD."

"You got me out of there just now?" She'd been so relieved to be let go she hadn't stopped to consider that the whispered conversation was anything more than police talk. Now she got it. The guy who came in had been telling the detectives to lay off. Because Matt had unleashed a Girard-family lawyer on their asses. If not for that, she'd still be there. Still tired and confused and scared. And saying God only knows what just to get Odell and Proctor to let her go.

Matt looked fierce. "Yeah, *mon ange*, I did. You didn't kill the guy."

"I think they believe we did it together."

He snorted. "They wanted to scare you, Evie. They've got no proof. And Mrs. Doucet is the best attorney money can buy. She looks like somebody's idea of a grandmother who knits socks, but she's a tiger. I'm not worried."

Evie chewed her lip. "I am. I'm worried about Mama and Sarah, and I'm worried that whoever killed David isn't finished here."

Matt touched her hand. Her nerve endings stood at attention, acknowledging him in a way that continually surprised her. In spite of her fear and frustration and exhaustion, he seemed to have the power to make her body sit up and say howdy. It was disconcerting as hell. And intriguing too.

His eyes searched hers. "One thing at a time, Evie. Let's get to the hospital; then you need to get some sleep."

When Matt had told her he wasn't worried, he wasn't telling the truth. He set Evie's suitcase in the guest room at the carriage house and turned to her. She hadn't spoken since leaving the hospital.

When they left the PD, she insisted on going to see her mother. He didn't bother trying to talk her out of it. Wouldn't have done any good anyway.

After they checked on her mother, she followed along bleary-eyed when they'd been allowed to collect her clothes from the house.

It'd been too late to call her cousin for a place to stay, so Matt had talked her into returning to Reynier's Retreat with him. It hadn't taken much convincing. The plantation wasn't a military compound, but other than open access on the bayou, it had enough security to alert them to anyone who decided to pay an unscheduled visit.

Evie hadn't mentioned Sarah lately, but he knew she hadn't forgotten. She was operating on autopilot, processing only what she needed to function in the immediate present. He recognized the signs because it was second nature out in the field. Hostile Operations Team members

LYNN RAYE HARRIS

counted on each other to perform under extreme duress. Their lives depended on it.

But Evie wasn't trained and she was perilously close to a crash. It'd been a hard day for her. She was tired, stressed, and ready to collapse. He glanced at the bedside clock. It was nearly four a.m., and by Evie's account of the previous day, she'd not slept in about twenty-four hours.

"I'll be down the hall," he told her, breaking the silence. As much as he'd like to spend the night between the sheets with her, there was too much to do. He needed to call Kevin MacDonald. His teammate was probably sleeping or drinking—or fucking—but Kev would move mountains to get the information Matt needed.

And if he wanted to find Sarah, protect Evie, and catch a killer, he needed all the help he could get. Especially since he'd been ordered—before he ever left Fort Bragg—to keep a low profile. Colonel Mendez was not a happy camper at the moment.

Matt resisted the urge to rub his ass just to make sure it was still there. How Mendez got word so fast about what was happening in Rochambeau, he had no idea. But he'd known it would happen. Truth was, he'd expected more time to operate before incurring the wrath of Mendez.

But the man's sense for trouble was unerring. Matt's phone had started buzzing within minutes of the police's arrival at Norma Breaux's house.

Nothing for it now, no matter what his commanding officer said. Matt couldn't stand idly by and let Evie become the target of a killer. Would *not* stand by. Not that he knew she was a target, but it wasn't looking good at the moment. David West had wanted something from Evie. And someone else wanted it too. Matt prayed they'd gotten it—except Sarah was still missing, and while that didn't have to be connected, he wouldn't stop thinking about the possibility that it could be until they found her.

Matt gritted his teeth. No, he would not stand by and watch from the sidelines, no matter what his CO preferred. He hadn't been able to save Jim and Marco, but he wasn't going to let Evie down. Not this time. He'd suffer the consequences once she and her family were safe.

Evie's bloodshot eyes focused on him. "Thanks for everything tonight."

"It's what I do." And yet it was more than that, at least where she was concerned. She'd been in his life since he was seven years old. He felt responsible, even if he hadn't always done the best job of taking care of her.

"Lucky for me then." She seemed a little stunned, like someone who'd just been told her house got blown away in a tornado and there was nothing left, not even a nail.

"Why don't you get some sleep, huh?" He squeezed her arm and then headed for the door.

"Wait." Her voice was soft. "Could you stay? Just for a little while."

Christ. He knew what the answer had to be and yet he dreaded it at the same time. His self-control was usually unbreakable. It had to be, to do what he did. But tonight, he wasn't so sure about his ability to maintain it. If anyone could get under his skin, it was Evie. He wasn't quite sure why that was, but she'd been stunning him with her ability to do so since the moment he'd seen her in her mama's salon today. He told himself it was because she made him remember more innocent times, more carefree times, but the truth was he didn't really know the reason.

She simply got behind his walls. But, looking at her

wide violet eyes, he couldn't say no. He understood her need for company right now. Sometimes you just wanted another breathing human being to share space with. Didn't have to say anything, just had to know someone was there if you needed them.

"As long as you want, Evie."

She gave him a shaky smile, then disappeared into the bathroom. When she returned several minutes later, she was still wearing his shirt, unknotted now. She'd removed her bra and the athletic shorts and he could see, as he held back the covers, the curve of her ass beneath the hem of his shirt when she climbed into the bed.

Holy shit.

He pulled the covers up to her chin and congratulated himself on his ability to do so while the blood was rapidly draining from his brain. "It's been a hell of a day, huh?"

She settled into the pillows, her eyes closing. Her hair, that silky black hair that his fingers itched to touch again, puddled against the sheets. "It's been memorable."

Matt laughed. "An understatement, *chère.*"

"It's the only way to keep it from taking over." She rolled her head back and forth on the pillow. "If I think about it, think about—" She swallowed hard, and he knew she was fighting tears.

"It's okay, Evie."

She nodded, and a tear slipped free. He reached out and caught it, his fingers brushing the silky skin of her cheek. What would it be like to have the right to touch her whenever he wanted?

He swallowed. "You should sleep." And he should get the hell out of here before he did something stupid. Like wrap a length of her hair around his fist and bury his nose in it. Just a few hours ago, they'd been close to exploring each other again. But that was then. This was now, and she was tired, stressed, and thinking of so many things besides sex.

She blinked up at him, her eyes shimmering. "I wish I could."

Matt sat beside her on the edge of the bed, facing her. He knew what he was supposed to say, but it bothered him he had to say it to her in the first place. Evie shouldn't be dealing with this. It wasn't right. It wasn't what her world was supposed to be about. That was his world.

"It's not easy seeing a dead body. It's even harder when it was someone you knew."

She closed her eyes. "I can't figure out what he wanted. I keep going over it in my head, and I just don't know."

"Don't be so hard on yourself. The guy called you after months of no contact with a cryptic message. How could you possibly know what he wanted?"

Matt reached for the light switch and flipped it off. It'd be dawn soon, but the plantation shutters would keep out much of the light while she slept. He kicked off his shoes and lay on top of the covers beside her. If the room was dark, maybe she'd fall asleep quickly and he could go call Kev.

She turned into him, her hand coming to rest on his chest. He felt as if she'd zapped him with static electricity. Not to mention his jeans were getting too damn tight. "Poor Matt. Bet you wish you'd never asked me for that dance."

He chuckled, trying to concentrate on anything but the way her hand felt on his shirt. "It does seem to be the turning point of my evening."

But he didn't really mind that part. Returning from combat and trying to readjust to a normal life—for the brief amount of time he usually had a normal life—was never easy. Slipping into combat mode this evening was not only normal, it was also a relief. When had it become so routine to him? When had he come to desire the singularity of focus that combat mode required?

My God, if he really got kicked off the team, what in the hell would he do with his life? Put on a suit and work at Girard Oil?

The thought was enough to make him shudder. He had the engineering degree—the old man had pretty much insisted on it, in fact—but no way did he want to sit behind a desk and read business reports and P&L statements on a daily basis. He simply couldn't see himself functioning in that kind of life.

It was meaningless. It didn't help people. It didn't make a difference. Hell, if only he'd had the temperament to be a doctor. But he didn't, and he didn't want to be. He wanted to do what he did, which was to help the people who needed it when getting help could mean the difference between life and death.

The idea he might not get to do that anymore terrified him. But, if that happened, maybe he'd hire on as a mercenary in some dark, dank, disturbed country in need of highly skilled muscle. It's what made him feel useful, alive.

The only thing that filled the emptiness for a time.

Matt blinked. Emptiness? Why was that the word that came to mind? And why did he suddenly want to deny it?

"I'm really sorry I dragged you into this." Evie's

breath tickled his cheek, pulled him back from the precipice of his thoughts.

"I'm not."

"I can't believe this kind of thing is what you do every day."

"Just another day at the office."

He said it jokingly, but the truth was he needed this job. Though, right now, he was thinking he needed something else more. When he was with Evie, he felt like he'd come home. He told himself there was any number of reasons for that, and none of them would last beyond the moment they had sex. It was fascination and history and chemistry all rolled into one. Feed it, and the intensity would ease.

Because he'd been fascinated with women before, and the fascination always faded after they had sex. It was just the way it worked for him. And he didn't believe Evie would be any different in the long run, despite their history.

Evie was soft where she curled against him, her sweet scent soothing. Her fingers slid up his jaw, stroked beneath his ear. He lay there quietly while his cock hardened painfully. For once in his life, he just wanted to slip into the moment and forget everything. Forget the planning and calculating, forget the necessity to think beyond this moment, forget what lay out there waiting to pounce from the shadows.

In a moment of supreme weakness, Matt lowered his mouth to hers. She didn't pull away in surprise but simply met his kiss by opening her mouth and inviting him inside. He should have known Evie wouldn't behave as he expected her to.

He knew where this would lead if he wasn't careful, yet he couldn't stop himself from leaning into the kiss, from demanding more. She tasted so sweet and felt so good pressed up against him. She made him forget everything but her.

She didn't stop giving, didn't stop tangling her tongue with his, though he expected it at every turn.

He pulled back when he found himself reaching for the covers, intending to expose her lovely skin to his hands and mouth. This was Evie Baker, not some woman he'd never see again. They had history—lots of history. And she wasn't thinking straight right now. Neither of them was.

"I shouldn't have done that." His voice sounded thick.

"What? Kissed me? I liked it."

"It's not right, Evie. Not after everything."

She burrowed against his neck, her mouth next to his ear. "Are we going there again? Because I could really use a good lay right now. I need to stop thinking and *do* something."

Matt bit back a groan. "I'll find the Monopoly board. We can play."

Her voice was a whisper that sent a shiver down his spine. "The only playing I want to do is with you."

"Evie." He was trying here, really trying. He was downright frigging heroic, a real martyr for the cause.

"What's the problem, Matt?"

"You aren't thinking straight. It's been a stressful night. And believe me, as much as I want this, I don't want you regretting it tomorrow—let alone immediately after."

She sighed, her breath blowing softly against his neck. "I can't promise I won't regret it. I have no idea. But

I know I need this. I need you. It feels right *right now*. That's all I have to go on."

"You need sleep." His body ached. His cock strained against his jeans.

"I can't sleep, Matt. Not until you make me come."
Jesus H. Christ.

"You've had a hard night, Evie. If you still want this tomorrow, then we'll see."

She sighed and rolled away. "You're right. It has been a hard night. I've seen things I never thought I would. A knife in my face, a dead body, my mama in the hospital."

"I want to, Evie. Desperately. But there's too much history between us, and I won't take advantage of you again."

She pushed herself up on an elbow. "It's just sex, Matt. Do you really think I'm that emotionally fragile that I can't separate the past from the present? Or that I believe for one second this time will turn out like the last time? Yes, we'll go our separate ways. I know that. I don't have starry-eyed dreams of love and marriage, you know."

His gut clenched. Of course he'd been worried about that. "If you were any other woman…"

"What? You wouldn't care about the whole starry-eyed love and marriage thing? Don't you think you've left a trail of broken hearts, killer?"

He reached out and ran his fingers along her jaw. "Maybe. But they weren't you."

She turned her cheek into his hand. "I want this, Matt. I feel cold and lonely, and I just want that feeling to go away for a while."

Matt closed his eyes. Jesus, she was killing him. And

he couldn't deny her, not when it was something he wanted too. Not when it felt like she'd reached inside him and pulled out everything he was feeling too. "All right."

"All right?"

He slid the covers down her body. "I can't say no, Evie. I should, but I can't."

There was a long moment where neither of them moved. And then it all began to happen at once, as if they'd opened the floodgates to a very swollen river. He had every intention of going slowly, but it wasn't happening that way. It was as if once his guard was down he had no control over anything.

They came together urgently, their mouths tangling, hands groping. Matt rolled her beneath him, assaulting her mouth anew while his heart pounded and his skin sizzled with heat. She moaned softly, sliding her tongue against his and going for his button-fly.

He gasped when she got her hand beneath his pants and squeezed his dick. Too much of that and he'd be a goner.

He tried to angle away, but she got her fingers around him, stroked him. The resulting sensation streaked through his body like a lightning bolt.

"Your shirt," he said in an effort to slow the crisis building deep inside him, "want it off."

She stopped touching him as he pulled the shirt up and over her head. Just the respite he needed to rein in this consuming fire for a moment.

"Yours too." Her fingers tangled in the material, tugging upward. He lifted away and yanked the shirt off for her, tossing it over the side of the bed. "Wow," she said, and he trembled as her fingers slid over his bare chest.

It was dark in the room, but not so dark as he thought it would be. He'd forgotten the full moon that slanted in between the blinds. He could see her beautiful body, the moonlight limning her full breasts. He put his hands on her, filling them.

He didn't miss the shudder that rolled through her. His thumbs slid across erect nipples and she gasped. "You're beautiful, Evie. If I didn't tell you that before, I meant to."

"So are you." Her mouth landed on his pec and he hissed in a breath.

"Oh no, you don't." His voice was rough, choked.

He shifted, lowered his head, and sucked a nipple into his mouth. She gasped, her fingers tangling in his hair.

"Matt."

"I know."

He nibbled and sucked while she squirmed, while his body tightened. He moved to the other nipple and back again while she made the most exquisite purring sounds of pleasure. God knows he'd been excited before—but right now he felt like he'd die if he didn't get to complete this. If he didn't thrust into her hard and deep and soon.

His whole body coiled like a tension spring. He was going to explode. Just frigging explode.

"Matt." He lifted his head at the rawness of her voice. "I want you inside me."

He didn't need to be told a second time. It was happening so fast, but now, *right now*, he was burning up and she was the only thing that could cool this flame.

She slid her hands along his abdomen, his hips, shoving his jeans down until he took over and kicked them the rest of the way off. He came back to her on hands and knees, licking a trail up her thighs until he could press his lips to her panties and feel her soft curls beneath the thin silk.

She whimpered, her hands in his hair again, and he pulled the damp fabric down over her long legs until he could toss them aside and push her thighs open.

He'd done this to her once before, but he hadn't been nearly as skilled back then. This time, he knew exactly what to do to drive her insane.

He slid his thumbs into her slick folds and pushed them aside. He didn't waste any time blowing on her sensitive flesh or teasing her with a lot of circling. He simply ran his tongue around her swollen clit and then sucked it between his lips.

She groaned, pushed her hips toward his face, and gasped his name. He didn't want her coming too fast, so he backed off, ran his tongue the length of her while she whimpered.

"Oh God," she cried out when he sucked her clit between his lips again. Her hips flexed toward him as he flicked his tongue over her faster and faster. She bucked, her body moving, tensing.

He knew the instant she came. Her orgasm slammed her back into the pillows, her body arching toward him until she was spent, until she collapsed beneath him, her breath coming out in little panting gasps.

If he were a good man, a decent man, he'd pull the covers up and tuck her in, tell her to sleep now. He'd give her time to rest, time to be certain no-strings sex was what she wanted.

He was anything but good.

NINE

EVIE WAS BONELESS. SHE HADN'T had an orgasm that good in, well, maybe ever. No, probably she had—she just couldn't remember it at the moment.

After an explosion like that, she should be satisfied, ready for sleep. But she wasn't. She was still hot and achy, desperate to feel his body merging into hers. And she hoped like hell he didn't have some crazy idea about being noble. So help her God, if he tried to tuck her in with a chaste kiss and retreat to his own bed, she'd scream.

Yes, she felt reckless, exhilarated, and edgy, and she wasn't ready to stop feeling any of those things yet.

She hadn't come over here tonight expecting to have sex with Matt. After everything else that had happened, it hadn't been high on her list of priorities. Until she'd climbed into bed and he'd sat down beside her. He was so intuitive, so caring about what she'd been through. She'd felt a rush of longing as she lay in the dark with him near. And she'd wanted more.

Now she prepared for him to back away, to try to put the brakes on—but he tugged open a drawer beside the bed and fished around in it. She didn't know what else was in there, but she prayed there was a condom and Matt was looking for it. The unseen contents scattered onto the floor, hitting the wood with thuds and pings.

Definitely a good sign if he was that focused.

Thank God.

And then he levered away from her, paper ripping. A moment later he was back, the head of his cock pushing at her entrance as he held himself above her. If her nerve endings weren't on fire, she'd have sighed with relief.

She ran her hands up his arms and over his shoulders, glorying in the feel of hot skin and hard muscle as she lifted her hips and wrapped her legs around him. She put her hand on his chest, felt the reckless rush of his heart, and had to blink back sudden tears.

He was every bit as affected by the churning emotion between them as she was.

"Tell me you're still okay with this." He sounded hoarse and uncertain as she pulled his head down to kiss him.

She needed—*needed*—to feel him inside her. It was the only thing that made any sense right now.

"Please, Matt. Don't you dare stop. Don't you dare get some stupid idea about nobility."

His laugh was rusty. "I left nobility in the dust a few miles back. But I'll stop if you want me to."

She arched into him. "Hell no."

Matt slid into her slowly, his cock stretching her, preparing her. It'd been so long since she'd had sex that she knew his penetration was going to burn. She hadn't told him that, but still he was careful with her, treating her as delicately as if this were their first time. That made her heart leap in ways it definitely shouldn't.

"Are you all right?" He wasn't fully inside her yet and she moved restlessly against him.

"I will be when you stop playing around."

He slid home, his growl of satisfaction melting into a groan. He was perfectly still except for the pulse-beat of his thick erection. "I think I'm going to die."

Evie sucked in a breath. "Don't you dare."

He lowered his mouth to hers and captured her lips in a quick, sizzling kiss. And then he moved.

Sensation streaked through her, curled her toes, and stole her breath.

My God, she didn't remember it being like this with him. With *anyone*. This amazing sensation as he pulled out and slid back in, each thrust stronger than the last.

"God, Evie." His voice strained with the control he placed on himself. Matt had always been supremely controlled, even as a child. He was a thinker, a planner. He could delay gratification forever.

She didn't want that right now. She wanted to dissolve his control, wanted him as wild as she felt. Wanted that recklessness of his heartbeat to spill over into everything he did with her.

"Don't hold back, Matt."

He looked at her in surprise, and she pulled him down until she could capture his mouth again, gloried in the raw edge of his passion when his tongue met hers. This was nothing like what they'd experienced together as teenagers. That had been passionate and thrilling and, for her, a little bit soul-destroying.

Now, however, they were on equal footing. He kissed her back, his body driving hers relentlessly toward another completion. Still, he was in control. She could feel it, and she gave up trying to make him lose his restraint. Instead, she lost herself to the insanity of the moment. To the implosion dragging her inward, concentrating all her energy on the pressure of his body inside hers.

When the moment came, it sucked her breath away. Drained her. She wrenched her mouth away from his and gasped his name.

When the crisis had passed, he turned her head with his fingers and kissed her so sweetly she shuddered. He was still deep inside her. Still hard.

"You okay?"

"I will be."

His laugh was half-strangled as he rocked his hips into her. "That's one of us."

Evie put her palm on his cheek. "Let yourself go, Matt. It's okay. You don't always need to be in control."

"What makes you think I can't let myself go? Maybe I was making sure you got there first."

She traced her fingers over his lips. "You forget that I know you."

Shadows seemed to stretch across his expression then. "People change, Evie."

"Not the essentials."

He swore. And then he moved. He went slowly at first, building the fire between them again. Evie tried to concentrate on him, tried to divine when he was close to climaxing as he began to move faster, but instead she got caught up in the vortex of her own pleasure. Another climax slammed into her and left her gasping and clench-ing around him. A moment later, he ground his hips into her, a groan breaking from his throat as he shuddered deep

146

inside her.

His breath was hot against her neck, unsteady for several moments. And then he rolled onto his back, one arm over his eyes, the tempo of his breathing evening out as he lay quiet.

She started to drift, her body languorous, her mind still emptied out by the intensity of the moment. It was so much better than ten years ago. Maybe Julie had been right. Maybe she'd really needed to get laid. Evie sighed as she turned into him and slid an arm across his heated skin.

"Evie?"

"Hmm?"

"I can't give you anything more than this."

His words stole into her languor, jolting her. Angering her too. "I don't remember asking for anything more." She pushed away and propped herself on an elbow. "Is this the speech you usually trot out? I bet it makes the ladies melt."

He swore softly. "Look, I'm not trying to insult you. But this night—" His breath released on a heavy sigh. "It's been intense. Adrenaline can mix a person up, make you think things are more important than they are."

Evie flopped onto her back, hurt and fury twisting inside her. It had been so perfect, so wonderful, and he'd gone and ruined it. "I'm tired, Matt. I don't care about your half-baked theories, okay? It was just sex. I'm not planning a wedding, and I'm insulted you would think so."

"I have no idea what you're thinking. I just wanted you to know. After the last time—"

"I'm not sixteen anymore. I'm perfectly capable of meaningless sex, okay? So get over yourself, for God's sake."

A moment later, he climbed from the bed. She could hear the sound of him getting dressed. Hot tears gathered behind her eyelids. Damn it.

"Go to sleep, Evie. I've got some calls to make."

She wanted to scream. Instead, she swallowed all the hot emotions she was feeling. "Fine."

He started to walk out, but then he stopped. "I'm sorry." His voice was soft, yet it carried to her across the room. Evie turned on her side and punched the pillow. She didn't bother answering.

What the hell just happened in that bed with Evie? Matt prowled into the living room, punching in Kev's speed-dial number on his phone. He should have never touched her, never given in to the urge pounding through his veins. Now he was all jumpy and more keyed up than when he'd begun. So much for sex curing what ailed him.

He should have known better. This was Evie he was talking about, not some woman he'd met in a bar. Not that he usually had one-night stands with bar pickups, but it would certainly be easier than having sex with the one woman in this world he actually cared about—besides his sister, of course.

Damn, but he'd screwed that up six ways to Sunday. He should go back in there, talk to her—

"Yo, Richie Rich, whassup?" Kev's voice was gritty

with sleep. Not out fucking some waitress then. Matt was kind of surprised, but then they'd had a helluva tour in the sandbox this last time. Sometimes it messed with your head and you just wanted to be left alone. He didn't know if that was the case with Kev or not—though Kev had seemed more introspective since they'd lost Marco and Jim—and Matt didn't have time to find out.

"I need a favor, Big Mac."

"Name it."

Matt raked a hand through his hair. "The shit's hitting the fan down here, dude. So before you agree, you need to know it's not gonna be kosher, okay? Mendez will have your ass if he hears of it."

He could almost hear Kev shrug. "Shoot."

Matt grinned in spite of himself. He knew Kev would have his back no matter what, but he had to give him a way out. After the last mission, he wouldn't blame anyone who didn't want to fly into the face of trouble with him.

He gave Kev a rundown of everything that had happened since he'd started that fateful dance with Evie a few hours ago. His second in command whistled softly.

"Mendez is plenty pissed already."

"Yeah, I know."

Matt wasn't too surprised Kev knew about the ass-chewing. When Matt lost his job, which was becoming more likely by the hour if it wasn't already a done deal, Kev would be breaking in a new team commander.

"If you want to refuse, I understand. Hell, if I wasn't on this side of it, I'd order you not to do it."

Kev snorted. "You know I'll give you whatever you need."

"It could mean both our asses. You think about it

first."

"I already did."

Matt sank onto the couch and grabbed the remote, turning on CNN International and hitting mute. Man, he loved these guys. He felt more at home with his team than he ever had with his own family. Not that he didn't love Chris. He did and he'd do anything for her. But the old man, well, the guy had never been full of warm fuzzies to say the least.

Matt and the senator didn't see eye to eye on anything. Never really had.

"I need all the stuff you can give me about David West. I want to know every place he's been in the last five years, his jobs, his favorite color, and even how he likes his eggs."

"Hoo-ah, sir. Anything else?"

Matt gazed down the darkened hallway and thought of the woman he'd left in his bed. A wave of need washed over him. He pushed it away, focusing on his job. Forewarned was forearmed. He'd learned the hard way and he was never getting caught off guard again.

Organized crime ties. That's what she hadn't told him earlier when she'd told him about David West. Not that he thought Evie was involved, but he knew from experience you couldn't be too careful.

"Yeah. Get me everything you can on Evangeline Marie Baker, too."

When Evie woke, Matt wasn't there. The room was dark. Though she could see light between the shutters, she had no idea what time it was. She lay there, thinking. Confusion swirled in her brain, along with anger, fear, and a sense of helplessness. Not all those feelings were tied to Matt, of course.

She turned her head to look at his side of the bed. The covers were rumpled, but his pillow appeared untouched. And wouldn't she have known if he'd slipped back into bed with her after his calls? She'd intended to wait up, but she'd fallen fast asleep almost the instant he left her alone.

She reached across the bed and ran her hand over what was supposed to be his side. He hadn't come back. He'd spent the night in another room. After what had happened between them, she wasn't quite sure how that made her feel.

No, she wasn't setting up house, dammit. She didn't expect a wedding, God forbid. But she did expect something approximating normal. She'd never had a one-night stand, other than the first time she'd slept with Matt, and she certainly hadn't expected one now. Or, even if it was a one-time deal, she hadn't expected they'd act like this— like awkward strangers who didn't know how to behave.

Damn him and his rotten nobility anyway.

She stumbled into the bathroom and turned on the shower. The sooner she was ready, the sooner she could get out of here, go see Mama, and find out where Sarah was. Ten minutes later, she rummaged through the suitcase Matt had left in the room last night and found something to wear.

"You need anything?"

Evie stopped in the act of sliding on a pair of Capri

pants and nearly fell over in the process. Matt stood in the doorway, watching her. Her heart began a fast tattoo against her ribcage.

"Do you mind?"

He was leaning against the frame, arms crossed over that impressive chest. "You're kidding, right? I saw a lot more than your underwear last night. Or did you forget already?"

Serve him right if she said yeah, it was plenty forgettable. But they both knew it wasn't. "Just because we had sex doesn't mean you get a free peep show whenever you like."

"Does for me. You just let me know, *chère*, and I'll strip for you any time you want."

"And here I thought you were a one-and-done kind of guy." She said it softly, but she didn't miss the guilty look that crossed his features.

"Sometimes."

Evie stood there with her pants halfway up, wearing nothing but panties and a bra, and stared at him. "Where were you last night?"

He speared her with a heated look, his eyes glittering hot. "I had work to do. And you needed to sleep."

"I was sleeping."

"But you might not have been if I'd joined you."

He let that hang in the air between them. Evie swallowed hard. "Can't keep your hands off me, Girard?" She said it jokingly, but the intensity of his look didn't change.

"It's a distinct possibility, especially if we're naked and in bed together." Matt crossed the room while she stood immobile, her heart thrumming, her body heating.

She wanted him to touch her, wanted him to take her in his arms and—

He walked past her and opened the shutters. Disappointment welled up inside her as bright sunlight streamed into the room and seared her eyeballs.

"Get dressed, Evie. We've got things to do."

How could she forget, even for a moment? But she had. Evie yanked the pants on and zipped them up before pulling a stretchy T-shirt over her bra. "How late is it?"

"It's only eight. I've got coffee made if you want some."

She followed him into the kitchen and stopped to gape. She hadn't made it into this part of the house last night. It had been remodeled in the last few years and this was not the kitchen she remembered when she'd been a kid. This kitchen was a chef's dream. A gleaming stainless Thermidor stove sat beneath a stone French hood, while miles of marble counters beckoned her to roll dough, chop veggies, and create recipes. There was a prep sink in the center island and a pot filler over the stove.

If she could ever afford such a thing, this was her idea of kitchen heaven in a home.

Matt glanced up at her as he poured coffee in a mug. "You like the kitchen, I take it?"

She took the cup from him. "What's not to like?"

He looked around the room and shrugged. "It's nice, but a bit overdone for a guesthouse, don't you think?"

A pint of half and half sat on the island along with a sugar bowl. Evie fixed her coffee and took a sip. Pricey stuff if her taste buds were any expert. And they were.

"Who cares? It's gorgeous. If you could possibly talk your dad into renting it out cheap, I'd consider staying in

Rochambeau indefinitely."

Matt grinned. "I doubt that. On both counts."

Evie sighed as the coffee began to hit all the right receptors in her brain. No, she really didn't want to stay in Rochambeau permanently. And, right now, she had far more pressing things to consider.

"If you could take me to Julie's house, I'd like to get my car." She'd left it there last night before they'd gone to the lake. She'd planned to drive herself, but then Julie had pretty much insisted they ride together—most likely because she knew Evie would have ducked out the first second she could have managed it. Since Julie's house was closer to the lake than Mama's, Evie had followed Julie to her house before she'd ditched her car.

"No problem." Matt looked all broody and sexy as he sipped his coffee, and she found herself thinking about his body thrusting into hers. Her breath shortened, her heart flipping in her chest. What a ride it had been, the heat and skin, the passion.

And she wanted him again with a fierceness that shocked her. She bit back a heavy sigh before she made a fool of herself over him again.

"I, um, I should call Julie and see if Sarah might have turned up there." Nothing like forcing her mind back on track. Her body, however, had other ideas. Desire bloomed in her core, flushing her skin with heat. Her sex throbbed with want.

Oh, but once hadn't been nearly enough.

Matt looked at her as if he knew what was going on inside her head, his gray eyes narrowing, an answering heat flaring in them that made her want to go over to where he stood and wrap herself around him.

His words, however, dowsed the heat.

"She's not there, Evie."

Her stomach sank. "How do you know?"

He set a plate in front of her. A bagel slathered with cream cheese lay on it.

"Eat and we'll talk."

She would have argued about his bossiness, but her stomach decided to growl at that precise moment. She took a bite and chewed. Waited. She had the feeling Matt was assessing her, the way he stared hard, his expression giving nothing away. She finished half the bagel before he said anything.

"It's possible she's at a friend's house, or even with the guy Mindy told us about. They weren't together when Mindy saw him, but that doesn't mean they didn't hook up after."

Evie's heart pounded. "You think she's with him now?"

"Could be. I'm looking into it." He sighed and put both hands on the counter. "There's something else, Evie. Kyle Jenkins has a criminal record."

She dropped the bagel she'd just picked up. "Oh my God, I have to find her. Mindy said they were *fighting*. What if he hurt her?"

"Wait a minute." Matt reached for her, clamping an iron hand around her wrist before she could take off. "His record is for petty stuff—blowing up pipe bombs in his yard, larceny, loitering, shoplifting, stuff like that."

"And that's supposed to make me feel better?" She swallowed against the dread curling in her throat. God, if she'd been here in Rochambeau longer than a month, or at least visited more often, checked in on Sarah and tried to make sure everything was okay with her, maybe her little sister wouldn't have gotten tangled up with a jerk like Kyle Jenkins.

They'd be closer and Sarah might have confided in her instead of being so openly hostile.

"Yes, it is. The guy doesn't have a record of violent acts against other people. That's a good thing."

Evie was furious. And scared. "Maybe he's crossed that line now. They were fighting."

"And they might be making up. She might be scared to go home because she's afraid she'll be in trouble."

Evie didn't like to think of Sarah making up with some guy the way Matt was suggesting, but if the girl had been out all night with the jerk, that's probably exactly what was going on. And she had to consider it.

"How do you know all this?" No matter what kind of shark Mrs. Doucet was, she didn't think Detectives Odell and Proctor had opened up the police files for Matt just because he'd asked.

He shrugged. "It's my business to know these kinds of things. I've got guys checking, but neither your sister nor Jenkins has been seen since last night. It's possible they're together."

"What are the police doing about it?"

"Their resources are engaged with the murder investigation. This is peripheral." Matt looked grave. "There's something else."

Evie didn't think her stomach could sink any lower. But it did. What more could there be? "Tell me."

"Jenkins is twenty-one."

Evie's jaw went slack. A twenty-one-year-old man was dating her sister? Her *baby* sister? She wanted to find this Kyle Jenkins and strangle him herself. "So a sixteen-year-old girl with a grown man doesn't faze the police?"

"If they had more people, yeah."

Evie stared at him, her chest heaving. "Doesn't it bother *you*?"

He slapped the counter hard enough to make her jump. "Fuck yeah, it bothers me. But there's a lot about what happened last night that's bothering me."

Evie felt a shiver slide down her spine. She thought of David's body lying on the porch, of the blood that looked like oil. He'd looked different than when she'd last seen him—the goatee, a bit more weight than he'd had before—so that for the briefest of moments as she'd stood there, she'd entertained a ridiculous hope it wasn't him, that it was some stranger who looked like him.

But what kind of stranger would be dead on her mother's porch after she'd had a call from David not more than a few minutes before? Hell yes, there was plenty about last night to be bothered about.

She lifted her chin. "You can back out at any time if you don't like it." And she meant it too. Except that she had no idea how she'd proceed without him.

His eyes flashed. "That's not happening, Evie. It's far too late for that now. Besides, you're in deeper than you think."

She wiped her damp palms on her pants and looked at him across the width of the island. Morning sunlight shafted through the windows, illuminating the white marble of the island. Matt stood in a nimbus of light. He looked handsome, fierce, and so sexy it hurt.

"And what's that supposed to mean?"

His eyes were hard. "It means the organized crime

connection is no longer a theory. David West worked for Ryan Rivera. Have you ever heard of him?"

The coffee in her stomach was making her queasy. "Should I have?"

"Not necessarily. He's West Coast, but he's been moving east for a while. Loans, numbers, money laundering, drugs—you name it, he's probably doing it. And he doesn't do it alone. West was one of his guys."

Evie felt as if her knees were made of water. If she hadn't been sitting, she'd have sunk into a boneless puddle on the floor.

"I didn't know." Her voice was little more than a whisper.

"You weren't supposed to."

She closed her eyes and tried to process it all. David had blown into her restaurant one day, tousled from the surf and cheekily handsome. He'd flirted with all the women on staff. And then he'd kept coming back. Eventually he'd started talking about the business, offering advice.

What he'd told her to do worked. She'd hired him after checking out his impeccable references.

"He was an accountant." She speared a hand through her hair and tossed the long strands over her shoulder. "He had such great ideas for the restaurant, and I needed the financial advice. I started everything on a shoestring, and it was often month-to-month as we struggled to make ends meet. But when David came along…" She shrugged. "The restaurant boomed. He really seemed to know what he was doing. I was looking at paying off my loans early—and then it all ended."

"I'm sorry, Evie. And I'm sure West did know what

he was doing. He also had an influx of cash from Rivera, I guarantee it. They were washing the money through your business."

The betrayal felt as fresh as that night when she'd realized he'd taken the payroll and wasn't coming back. "But why me? Why my restaurant? It was just a little bistro near the beach, nothing big and fancy. Nothing with a huge cash flow when David came to me."

"They didn't want to draw attention to what they were doing. And I'm sure Rivera planned an expansion once he'd gotten a toehold there. You were the toehold."

"Obviously, it didn't go as planned. David robbed me blind."

"And not on his boss's orders, I'm guessing."

"So is that why he was killed?"

Matt looked grave. "Probably."

As she processed all this new information, she started to get mad. Waves of fury flooded her system, made her want to punch something. Instead, she smacked her palms against the counter. "Damn him! He brought that shit here. To my life, my family's life. My friends! He didn't care how it touched me, Mama, or Sarah. He only wanted to use me again."

"I think you're right about that." Matt's tone was soothing, as if he knew she was on the brink. "But I think it's more than that too."

Her throat hurt from suppressing the urge to scream. "What do you mean, more?"

"Think, Evie. Why would he come here? Why would he risk it unless there was a big payoff for him? He didn't want your protection. And he certainly didn't want any money since he knew you didn't have any."

Evie blinked. "What kind of payoff could there be in just talking to me?"

Matt leaned toward her, his eyes gleaming. "I think you have something, Evie. Something West wanted very badly. Did he give you anything before he left? Leave anything behind?"

Confusion swirled in her brain. "Why would he give me anything? He stole everything I had. He knew he was planning to do it, so I'd be a poor person to entrust with something once he had."

Matt shrugged, but she didn't kid herself he was feeling casual about this idea. "He wouldn't have been overt about it. But you do have something. He wouldn't have come otherwise. It has to be something small, some- thing easily carried. Something you would overlook."

Evie frowned as she ran through the last few days with David. He'd seemed stressed. And they hadn't been sleeping together at all. Not that she'd minded that part. They'd only hooked up a few times in the two months they dated, and while it had been pleasant enough, there weren't any real sparks.

"I don't think so…" And then she stopped. Thought about packing her car for the trip back to Rochambeau. The things she'd piled into it. A small cherry box slid to the front of her memory. "Wait, there was one thing. He forgot an old humidor he said was his dad's. He kept it in his office. But there was nothing in it except a few cigars."

Matt's gaze sharpened. "Do you still have it?"

She nodded. "I tossed everything in my car when I left. I don't know why I kept it." Except that the box was pretty and she'd thought it might be worth a few dollars if she needed to sell some stuff.

"Where is it now?"

Evie felt the heat of embarrassment roll through her.

"It's still in the car." She'd never gotten around to unpacking because she kept hoping to leave again. Kept hoping she'd get that call from somewhere asking her to come work in a great kitchen.

So pitiful.

"We need to go get it. It could be important."

"You really think the humidor has something to do with this?"

He shrugged as he dug his keys from his pocket. "We won't know until we take it apart."

She grabbed her purse and they walked out and got into the car. Matt was backing out of the garage when his phone buzzed. He snapped it up. "Girard... What? You're kidding? Yeah, we're on the way."

"What is it?" Evie's gut was churning when he tossed the phone down again.

The look he gave her was indefinable. "Kyle Jenkins has been detained."

TEN

BRIANNA SWEENEY HATED SMALL TOWNS. She was also developing a severe dislike for the South. It was hotter than hell, for one. Louisiana was muggy, the mosquitoes came in supersize, and she couldn't make sense of the food. She'd bartended at Evangeline's, and she'd even tried the jambalaya and gumbo, but this thing about boiling itty-bitty lobsters—crawfish—with potatoes, lemons, and corn on the cob was just too weird.

Julian ripped the tail off a red bug-looking thing and sucked on the head before peeling the shell away from the tail meat.

"That shit stinks," she said, sucking on her cigarette.

"So don't eat it."

"I wasn't planning to." She gazed out over the water. They'd stopped and grabbed lunch at a roadside stand about twenty miles from Rochambeau. She didn't like being so far from the town, especially after last night, but you couldn't disappear in the damn place. Old ladies stared at you. Men nodded and said howdy—or something like that. She couldn't understand half of what anyone said in South Louisiana. They were speaking English, sometimes, but it wasn't any English she'd ever heard. It sounded thick to her ears, had a different rhythm entirely, and she often found herself trying to work out the words while people smiled and nodded like she was an idiot.

She felt like an amoeba under a microscope in this town, and she didn't like the blatant loss of anonymity. And now, shit—

"What're we gonna do with the girl?"

She narrowed her gaze on the man dripping bug juice from his chin. How had she ever lost her head enough to screw this guy? He was a big hunk of masculinity, muscular and full of stamina, but he was the male equivalent of a bubble-headed blonde. So long as he didn't talk, she'd been able to ignore his deficiencies. She was fast losing patience. The sex was good, but not that damn good.

"We're going to trade her for the information, just like I said before." About a million times before.

"What about George?"

"What about him? Nothing we can do now." George had fucked up and there was nothing for it now. He was gone and they had to work without him. Which they damn well would do without issue.

"Rivera call yet?"

"Yeah. He wants us to finish the job."

"So we finish it then."

Yeah, shit-for-brains, we finish it. Brianna forced smoke from her nostrils. God, how had she ever gotten herself into this mess? And how could she ever get out? Working for Rivera wasn't exactly a walk in the park. She was tired and getting more worried by the day that she'd be the one to take the hit the next time. If she could deliver what Rivera wanted and walk away, she'd consider herself lucky.

But they'd never let her out.

David West—now that guy had balls, that's for sure. He stole all that money—not only from Evie Baker's place it turned out—and stashed it in offshore accounts. Then he systematically collected as much dirt on Rivera as he could and built a database.

Too bad he'd been stupid enough to leave everything where they could find it in New Orleans. Everything except one last puzzle piece, which was the source of her freaking headache now. Rivera didn't know what it was, but he knew West had something else that contained all that evidence. And she wasn't leaving here without it.

If only she knew what to do with the information once they'd gotten it, and how to access that money, she might have been tempted to keep the computer instead of shipping it off so fast. She could be on an island some-where, sipping a tropical drink. David had once told her the same damn thing when he'd tried to recruit her into his schemes. She hadn't believed a word of it, or maybe she'd have warned Rivera.

Then again, maybe not.

"We need to find a place to stay," she said, making a decision. Last night's little fuck up made it necessary to lie low for a while, and staying in town wasn't going to cut it.

Julian wiped his chin and fingers. "We got a place."

"We can't stay in the motel any longer. We need to check out. And then we need a base of operations. This job could take a couple more days."

"Where you planning to go?"

She motioned toward the bayou. "In there. I saw an advertisement for fishing cabins on the bulletin board at the general store." She stubbed out her cigarette in the metal ashtray. "We'll get a cabin and stash the girl there, then make contact with Evie. Once she knows we aren't playing around, she'll give us what we need."

Kyle Jenkins stammered and sputtered and swore he hadn't seen Sarah since he'd left her at the gas station outside of town. Matt had glared at the guy with his best elite-soldier stare, but the story never changed.

"You believe him?"

They were exiting the sheriff's office where Kyle had been detained for questioning in a complaint lodged by a neighbor of his mother's. Evie looked as if she could chew nails. They'd come straight here after Kev's call, hoping to find out where Sarah was. Matt had had to sweet-talk the deputy into letting them in. Having Evie along didn't hurt. She was pretty damn pleasing to the eye, especially when she smiled and flirted the way she had with Deputy Boudreaux.

She was also pretty damn pleasing in other ways. Matt shoved thoughts of a naked Evie out of his head—no mean feat—and concentrated on what was happening right now.

He knew what she wanted to hear—that he thought Kyle was lying and they'd find Sarah in his mama's trailer, playing Suzy Homemaker or something—but he couldn't do it.

"He hasn't seen her since last night."

They were on the sidewalk in front of the jail. She put a hand on the brick wall to steady herself. "How can you be sure? How do you know this tough guy stuff works?"

He'd broken much stronger men than Kyle Jenkins—though of course he'd been able to use other methods of persuasion while doing so. Kyle was a pussy who disintegrated beneath a strong look and the threat of future violence. He knew the type well.

"I've been doing this for a while, *chère*. Believe me, he hasn't seen her."

Evie grabbed onto him, facing him squarely, her chin inching up, her lip just the barest line away from quivering. So why did he want to kiss her? Why did he want to wrap her in his arms and make this all go away?

"What do you think happened to her? I have to know, Matt. I have to. I can't face my mama without having something to tell her."

Sonofabitch, the hard part. He'd been expecting it. And he still didn't know how to ease the blow. So he just said it. "I think someone took her."

Her eyes filled with tears. Behind the tears was the kind of pain that kicked him in the gut. He wanted to make it better, but he was having a hard time doing so. He felt almost as desperate as when he'd been twelve and couldn't make his mother better again. It was disconcerting, and he worked hard to focus. He had to concentrate on the here and now, not on how his past and her past were all tangled and twisted and how he felt responsible for her now.

How he wanted to make everything right because he

wanted her to smile again.

She sucked in a breath. "You said last night—"

"I was wrong. It didn't happen at your mama's house, but someone has her. It might not be related to the murder, but it'd be a damn amazing coincidence if it wasn't."

"We have to tell the police."

He touched her cheek with the back of his finger and caught the single tear she dared to let spill free. "Tell them what, *chère*? That I have a feeling?"

"Why not? She's still missing. They'd have to listen to me now." Her eyes shimmered. All he wanted to do, all in the world he could think about, was lowering his mouth to hers and stealing whatever he could take. Taking away the heartache and pain for however long he could manage it.

"We need something more than that. They have your report from last night, and they're questioning her friends. But they won't issue an Amber Alert without something more concrete."

"Why not? She's missing for God's sake!"

"Teenagers run away, Evie. They do things they shouldn't. If the police put out an alert for every teen who disappeared for a few hours, no one would take it seriously ever again. There's a definite protocol to follow before issuing one."

Her fingers dug into his bicep. "But we won't sit and wait for them to figure this out, right? You're going to do something, right? Call those men in black of yours?"

He put his arm around her, pulled her close, and propelled them back to where he'd parked the car on the street. "I'll do everything possible to get her back."

She pulled him up short, looked at him with violet

167

eyes full of both trust and uncertainty. "Have you ever failed a mission?"

He looked her dead in the eye as his gut twisted into a knot. "No. Never."

They had to get the humidor. They'd been sidetracked with the visit to the jail, and now they were on their way to see Mama. But as soon as that was over, as soon as she'd faced her mama and told her that Sarah was missing, they were going to Julie's house and retrieving her car.

Evie nibbled her lip, her insides twisting and mixing like a spinning top as they took the elevator to the second floor of William Girard Medical Center. They couldn't go to the police. Not yet anyway. She had no friends there, that was for sure. They thought she'd killed David.

Rochambeau was a small town. Murder was unheard of, unless it was a couple of fisherman fighting over traps out in the bayou. That had happened last year. Eighty-year-old Dancy Lafevre shot and killed a man a third his age for poaching his crawdad traps. It took the police ten days, two helicopters, and a team of dogs to bring him out of the swamp.

Murder in Rochambeau tended to be homegrown. And she had a hell of a motive, no doubt about it.

"You never showed me how to defend myself." It was a long stretch from what she'd been thinking about, which was getting the humidor and checking on Mama, but looking at Matt, she couldn't help but think about badassery. Right now, she wished she were a badass too.

Matt's aviator sunglasses hid his eyes. He hadn't taken them off when they'd come inside, and it certainly added to his appeal. The man was a walking advertisement for testosterone. A white T-shirt stretched over his chest. He'd crossed his arms and tucked his hands into his armpits. He looked like nothing less than a huge, menacing guard dog.

A sexy guard dog she'd like to strip were circumstances less urgent.

"Give me your hand."

"How is that supposed to teach me anything?"

His mouth twisted in a frown. "You'll find out if you give me your hand."

She thrust her hand out, trying her best to ignore the frisson of heat that tingled under her skin when he took it in his.

"Curl your fingers like this." He pulled her closer to him and placed her hand midway down his forearm. "Now, if anyone ever grabs you and you get the chance, you dig in right here."

He pushed her fingers into his arm. All she felt was hard bone and taut muscle.

She shook her head. Either he was funning with her or she wasn't doing it right. "I don't get it."

He pulled the glasses off and shoved them into his waistband. Then he picked up her arm in the same place. When he squeezed, she yelped. A sharp pain shot down her arm, up to her shoulder, and through her body. It was like hitting your funny bone, though worse somehow.

"Sorry, but I need you to understand." He took her

hand again, wrapped it around his forearm. "If some guy grabs you, do it hard, Evie, like your life depends on it. There's a lot of muscle in a strong man to go through."

He nodded, his gray gaze deeply serious, and she squeezed. Not like her life depended on it, but hard nonetheless.

And watched pain flare in his eyes.

"More."

She complied, digging in harder, and he dropped to his knees.

She let go with a gasp. "Oh my God, did I hurt you?"

He shook his arm out and climbed to his feet. "Hell yes, but that's the idea. Now if you get that hold on someone, don't let go. Take him to his knees and keep him there. Kick him, do whatever you can to incapacitate him."

Evie shivered. She'd had no idea such a thing was possible. "Okay."

He pressed two fingers behind her ear, at the base of her jaw. "This is another point. Push hard."

His hand dropped away.

"That's it? Just dig my fingers into those places?" She'd at least expected a karate chop maneuver or something.

"The body has sensitive pressure points. Those are only two of them, but they'll do the job."

"What if the guy has a gun?"

He shook his head. "No, there are other techniques for that. Just remember these as a good way to take down somebody who grabs you, okay?"

Evie nodded. Holy crap, she'd have never guessed she could incapacitate a big guy like him with nothing more than her fingers. It was empowering. And she never wanted to have to do it for real.

The elevator came to a stop and she took a deep breath. She had to face Mama and she had to tell her Sarah was still missing. How would she get through it? Sarah was the baby, the little girl who'd come along almost at the point when Mama thought she'd never have another child. In some ways, Evie felt like an outsider. It was self-imposed, certainly, but she felt it just the same. She'd chosen to leave Rochambeau.

And now she had to inform her mother that Sarah hadn't come home and she had no idea where to find her little sister.

"Evie."

She looked up at Matt and realized he was blurry. She turned her head, wiping the corners of her eyes.

Matt swore and punched the button to close the elevator door. Then he pressed her against the wall, anchoring her with his body. A finger beneath her chin tilted her head up. A second later, he covered her mouth with his.

Evie gasped as warmth and sensation flooded her. She clutched his shoulders, slowly wrapping her arms around his neck. His tongue dipped inside and drew her into a luscious stroking that filled her with heat and need.

He leaned into her, leaving no doubt he was aroused and ready to take this moment as far as she wanted to go. A second later, he broke the kiss and lay his forehead against hers. His breathing was unsteady.

"You can do this, Evangeline. I'll be with you all the way."

Evie shivered, in spite of the heat between them. "I know I can," she said softly. "And thanks."

Matt had planned to hang outside the room while Evie spoke with her mother, but she took his hand and led him inside. Norma Breaux lay in bed, propped up, watching television. She brightened considerably when her daughter arrived, though pain lined her face. Her broken wrist was splinted around a metal contraption that held the bones together, and she moved her arm gingerly.

"Sugar!"

"Mama." Evie went over and hugged her tight. Norma held on, stroking Evie's hair with her good hand. Matt averted his eyes and rocked on the balls of his feet. His mother had died so long ago he rarely thought of what it must be like to still have one. He'd missed her badly when he was twelve. Hell, he'd missed her every time he wanted affection, a human touch that was reassuring and comforting. The senator had been gone far too often to be more than a distant and somewhat frightening authority figure.

The stripper-wives were studies in neuroses. Misty Lee, his current stepmama who was actually four years his junior, wasn't like the others. If the old man had married a woman like her when Matt was a kid, he might have had a normal home life. Or normal enough, considering Misty Lee's unabashed embrace of human sexuality. She'd have been the mother who thought it perfectly normal to buy him a prostitute the instant he showed an interest in sex.

"Hello, Matt." Evie's mother was smiling at him like

she always did. Inside, his heart twisted. She had no idea what was coming, and he hated that they had to tell her.

"Mrs. Breaux."

She turned back to Evie. "Where's Sarah?"

Evie sat on the edge of the bed, holding her mother's hand. "The doctor says you had a bad fall, but your wrist will heal nicely. Do you remember what happened?"

Norma sighed, momentarily derailed. "I don't know. The police asked me the same thing earlier, but all I remember is calling Reynier's Retreat looking for you. And then I woke up here."

Normal reaction to being knocked out. It happened in the field sometimes. Trauma to the head was tricky. Victims often couldn't remember the events leading up to the incident even when they remembered everything that happened only hours before.

"They said there was a murder," she continued. "A man."

"Yes. He was my ex-partner."

"But who would do such a thing?"

Evie stroked her mother's arm with her free hand. "I don't know, Mama. David was a part of some things I didn't know about."

Norma seemed to process that information. "Where's Sarah?" She sounded more strident this time as if she knew she'd been derailed and it wasn't happening again. "I called you because she wasn't home."

"Yes, that's right." Evie took her mother's hand in both of hers. "Matt and I went looking for her. She was with a boy."

An understatement, but Norma Breaux didn't need any extra stress heaped on top of what Evie was about to give her.

"Is she at home now?"

Evie looked fierce and determined. She was holding it together well. Strong as ever, his Evie. In spite of the ugliness of the situation, he was filled with a sense of belonging just being here with her. He didn't have to explain himself to Evie. She glanced up at him as if she could feel him looking at her. Understanding passed between them, and she fixed her gaze on her mother again.

"No, Mama. The house is a crime scene. We can't stay there yet."

Norma looked perplexed. But then her chest started to rise and fall a little bit faster as her face screwed up in concentration.

Matt's alarm levels started rising like high tide in the Gulf. Norma wasn't going to take the news well. He knew Evie had considered lying to her, telling her Sarah was with a friend. But her mother would insist on speaking to her youngest child and the whole thing would unravel. Evie knew she had to tell the truth, no matter how difficult.

He shot Evie another look, tilting his head toward the door. She nodded.

He slipped out to find a nurse or a doctor. He made it to the nurse's station right before a wail came from the room he'd just vacated. His first instinct was to run back, to help Evie.

He told the desk nurse what was happening and asked if she could help.

The woman frowned as she got to her feet. "There's nothing I can give her after a head injury. But I can give her some pain medication. That might help her sleep."

Matt followed her back to the room. Evie was holding

her mother, tears streaming down her face as Norma sobbed against her.

"It's not right... It's not right," Norma said in a choked voice. "Something's wrong. Something's happened to her."

The nurse hurried over and helped ease Norma back on the pillows.

"Ms. Breaux, let's get you your pain meds now. Can you swallow those for me?"

It took a couple of minutes, but somehow she got Norma to take the pills and sip some water. Norma continued to cry while Evie rubbed her good arm.

"We'll find her." Evie sounded determined. "I promise we'll find her."

Matt slipped out of the room again, feeling like he was intruding on something he shouldn't. He found a chair in the hall and sat, elbows on the plastic arms, fingers steepled beneath his chin. Somehow, he had to find Sarah. He always detached himself enough to think coldly, to get the job done. This time it was more difficult, and he knew it had to be because of what had happened out in the field—the deaths of his men still weighed heavily on him.

But Evie depended on him. And Sarah's life might depend on him getting this right. He wouldn't allow a child to die when he had the capability of preventing it. No matter how much trouble it got him in with Mendez and the board.

A long while later, Evie emerged from her mother's room looking pale and tired. She managed a small smile when she saw him. It sent a sharp pain right to his heart. Matt went and put his arm around her, pulling her in close. She looked up at him with such faith shining in her tear-stained eyes it made his gut twist. She believed he would find her sister. Believed he would bring Sarah home alive.

He prayed to God it was true.

The contents of Evie's sad life were arrayed on the garage floor of the carriage house. She surveyed the mess, feeling a myriad of sensations crashing through her. My God, she'd kept a corkscrew. A flipping *corkscrew*. As if she couldn't buy another one when she got settled wherever she ended up.

She thought of Mama, of the way she'd fallen apart when Evie told her Sarah was missing for real. Evie hated telling her mother her baby was missing. She hadn't said a word about Matt's suspicions and she hadn't said the part that terrified her—that maybe Sarah was already dead. And if so, it was Evie's fault. Evie's fault for letting David into her life, for trusting him with her business. No, she hadn't known anything was wrong—but maybe she should have.

She dumped the contents of another box. How had she crammed so much crap into her old VW convertible? Matt looked up from where he was systematically going through a different box.

"You okay?"

"Yes." She scattered linens—monogrammed napkins, given to her by Mama when she'd gone off to start her own business after graduating from culinary school—

across the floor. The garage door was open and a steady parade of delivery vehicles came and went with supplies for the wedding. She wondered what was on the reception menu because she needed to think about something normal for a second.

It didn't last, however.

"I don't think you'll find a humidor under those, Evie."

Probably not, but she was stressed and angry—being destructive seemed to help, if only temporarily. She upended the box and tossed the empty cardboard aside.

Matt frowned. "We need to focus, *chère*. Time's not our friend right now."

"I know." She shoved herself to her feet and grabbed another box. "But I'm beginning to wonder if I kept it after all."

"We'll worry about that later. Let's get through these boxes first."

He was right, but she couldn't shake a strong sense of futility. At twenty-six years of age, this was all her life held? A car full of random junk?

Matt must think her pathetic. A girl from the wrong side of town who, ten years later, still had nothing to her name. Why couldn't she succeed at anything she did?

She set the box down and sank to the floor beside it. "Why haven't we heard from whoever murdered David? How do we know they even have Sarah?"

"We don't." He sounded so calm. "But we have to operate based on the simplest assumption. Sarah's missing, no one has seen her, and someone knocked your mother over the head and killed your ex-partner. It's all related."

"Then why haven't they called and demanded the

humidor?"

"Maybe they don't know that's what they want. Or maybe it's not what they're after."

Evie set a stack of cooking magazines on the floor beside her. "You're kind of irritating, you know that?"

"I've heard."

She let out a sigh and rubbed her hands over her face. "I'm scared, Matt," she admitted. "And I don't like it."

He shoved aside the box he'd just finished and climbed to his feet. A second later, he was pulling her up and into his arms, holding her tight. She laid her head on his chest, twisted the fingers of one hand into his T-shirt, and breathed deep. He smelled faintly of laundry detergent, warm skin, and a scent she associated solely with him.

Why couldn't this have been normal between them? Why couldn't they have danced and flirted and maybe got here anyway? Oh sure, she'd been plenty furious with him after ten years—but they could have worked through that without all this other shit.

"This isn't what you're used to dealing with. Of course you're scared."

"What do your men in black say?"

She felt his lips press against her hair. "Kev's got the Kid working on it. We know it's Rivera's men, but that's all."

"You've done this before." Certainty flooded her. He was confident, assured, methodical. Too much so to be the kind of guy who simply jumped out of airplanes and helicopters and had some buddies with insider access to files.

"Yeah."

She leaned back and looked up at him. Her heart did

that little flutter thing it always seemed to do when he was near. "You're more than an Army Ranger. You're one of those SEALS or something."

Matt's finger slid along her jaw. He rubbed her earlobe gently between his thumb and forefinger. Then he grinned. "I can neither confirm nor deny. Besides that, SEALS are Navy. I'm not in the Navy."

"Whatever. The Army has that kind of thing too. Green Berets or Delta Force or something."

He nodded. "They do."

"And you're one of them."

"Can't answer that."

Evie rolled her eyes. "You could tell me but you'd have to kill me?"

He laughed low in his throat, the sound so sexy it sent a shiver skimming. "I can neither confirm nor deny, *chère*."

"I'm sensing a theme, here." How did he make her feel so fluttery inside when everything was falling apart around her? Her world was filled with uncertainty and fear and he could still make her laugh. Still make her ache with need at his proximity.

His fingers slid into her hair. "If we didn't need to keep looking, I'd like to rock your world right about now."

"And I'd like to let you." She put her hand on his arm, reveling in the heat and muscle. They couldn't stop searching for that humidor, couldn't stop thinking about Sarah. She knew it as well as he did, but still she wished for a few stolen minutes where life was normal again.

He dipped his head, kissed her softly. In spite of everything, her heartbeat quickened. Her body vibrated with energy. The vibrating grew stronger, more insistent.

179

Matt stopped kissing her and straightened.

"Is that your phone?"

Shit. She forgot she'd shoved her phone into her pants pocket in case Aunt Betsy or Julie called to tell her how Mama was doing. They'd promised not to leave Mama alone until Evie could return with good news. She dug it out quickly and hit the button.

A picture flashed on her screen. Her legs buckled.

ELEVEN

SARAH'S HEAD HURT LIKE A BITCH. Her eyes were swollen from crying, and one temple throbbed mercilessly. She'd asked the woman—Brianna—for aspirin. She hadn't gotten any.

The big guy, Julian, sprawled on a chair. His attention was focused on a game he was playing on his smartphone.

"Aw, fuck," he said for the fiftieth time that afternoon.

Sarah shifted on the musty bed. They'd cuffed one of her hands to the iron headboard and she hated to move or to call attention to herself because he looked at her like he might want to come over and hit her. Or worse.

The handcuffs rattled with her movements. She shot a look at Julian, praying he wouldn't notice her. His gaze flicked up, then back down to his phone as a musical chime indicated it was time to play again.

The door swung open and Brianna came back in. She'd been spending a lot of time outside since they'd come into the swamp. It was too much to hope a gator would get her. The other guy, the smoker from last night,

181

was nowhere to be seen.

Sarah rolled a stiff shoulder. They'd stuffed her in a big duffel bag, dropped her into a motorboat, and brought her out here. She knew where she was—any local would—though she'd been surprised when she realized where they were. When the motor fired up, she'd been convinced they were planning to dump her in the swamp.

She'd figured Evie hadn't given them what they wanted or wouldn't give it to them. Why would she? Sarah hadn't exactly been pleasant to her. Not that she deserved it after the way she'd gone off and never called.

Either way, Sarah knew she was dead. She cried until they'd dumped her in the cabin. Then Julian grabbed her by the hair and held her head steady while Brianna took a picture with her phone.

Neither one of them had paid much attention to her since.

"You hear anything yet?" Julian asked.

"Signal's bad out here. It comes and goes."

Sarah could have told the stupid bitch that.

"What's the plan?"

"We wait." Brianna picked up a pack of cigarettes and tapped one loose. "God, I hate this place. You smell that?"

Sarah didn't smell anything except the usual scents of mud and rotting vegetation that filled the swamp. But then again, those odors would probably stink to an outsider. To Sarah, it was just another whiff of home.

"What? I don't smell anything."

Brianna sniffed. "The air. It smells dead."

Julian shrugged and went back to his game. Brianna lit up her cigarette and took a long drag. "Dead," she said

182

thoughtfully, watching Julian.

Matt stood on the screened-in veranda and gazed out at the muddy bayou. "All right," he said into the phone. "Let me know if you come up with anything."

He hung up and let out a deep breath. Evie was holding up well, considering someone had sent her a picture of her sister that clearly indicated the kid had been beat up a bit. He'd immediately forwarded it to Kev, but so far Kev couldn't get a lock on where it had been sent from. The person who took it wasn't entirely stupid. Sarah looked as if she was lying on wood of some kind, but it was too grainy to tell. The tips of someone's fingers were in the shot. Someone who'd been holding Sarah still.

The accompanying message said not to contact the police. No big surprise. What Sarah's captors wanted was for Evie to acknowledge the message—done by return text—and wait for further instructions. Presumably to hand over the information they wanted—except Matt still didn't know what that was. The picture came twenty minutes ago, and he'd been on the phone since. He needed to get back to the garage and find that humidor. Surely, West had hidden something in it. Something that Ryan Rivera wanted to get his hands on pretty badly. Matt hoped like hell Evie still had the damn thing.

Because he sure as fuck didn't know what he'd have to cook up if she didn't. He'd figure that out when he came to it. *One frigging thing at a time.*

"I found it."

Matt swung around. Evie stood in the doorway, a wooden box in her hands. Her eyes were glassy, as if she'd been drinking too much. He spent a moment letting his gaze wander over her. It surprised him every time he saw her, the way she managed to send a flash of heat through him. Last night hadn't been enough. He wanted more of her—more sex, more talk, and more time to figure how why she made him feel this way, as if his skin was too tight until she walked into the room. Then it was a different kind of tightness—inside him—that usually took hold.

He silently cursed David West, Ryan Rivera, and this whole fucking situation. If not for them, he could have spent several days making love to this woman before he had to return to North Carolina and face a panel of military officers.

As if anything with Evie Baker could be that easy. Matt ignored the voice and walked toward her.

"I thought you were lying down." He'd carried her to the bed when she'd crumpled and told her to rest. She'd been through a lot and still hadn't had enough sleep, which made him fear another crash might be imminent. An hour or two of sleep would do her a world of good.

"I got up again." She thrust the humidor toward him. "Do your thing, secret agent man."

Matt took the burled-wood box from her. "I'm just a soldier."

Thank God she'd found it, even if he'd have preferred she sleep a while first.

"Whatever you say."

He turned it in his hands, looking closely for any signs of tampering. He speared her with a look. "Think you can lie down for a few minutes now?"

She stared back at him, never flinching. "No."

He'd always loved her spirit, the way she knew her own mind. But now, for some damn reason, it made her irresistible to him. She filled an emptiness he hadn't known needed filling. He wanted to kiss her senseless. Wanted to strip her naked, spread her out beneath him, and take his fill of her.

Goddamn, it wasn't going to happen though. And maybe that was for the best. He wasn't precisely happy-ever-after material. He was too fucked up, his future too uncertain. Not that she wanted that from him. She'd made it clear enough last night.

"Come on. I need to get some tools out of the garage."

When he'd gotten what he needed, he led her back to the kitchen island and told her to sit on one of the barstools. Then he got to work.

An hour later, the humidor disassembled, the cigars dissected and laid into neat piles of tobacco and wrappers, Matt was as puzzled as he'd ever been.

"There's nothing here." He straightened and rubbed the ache in his neck. There were no hidden compartments, no hollowed-out spots, no suspicious seams. If David West had hidden something, it wasn't here.

Evie leaned on the bar, her chin resting on her fists. "Are you sure?"

"Yes."

"What were you looking for?"

"A flash media device, a list, a key card—" He swept

his hand over the mess. "Something with information on it."

"We should call the police, give them the picture."

"They'll kill her, Evie." He sounded brutal, but he didn't care. He needed her to understand. She flinched and he reached out, squeezing her arm. "I'm sorry, but these guys are professionals. You get a cop involved, and they'll make sure Sarah disappears for good. This is the only chance we have to get her back."

"But we don't know what they want!"

He raked a hand through his hair. "It's here. Some-where. I just need time to find it."

The doorbell rang and Evie jumped. Her eyes were wide.

Matt glanced at his watch. "Shit." The series of short dings continued until he strode over and answered the door.

"Are you coming to the rehearsal or not, big boy?" Chris peeked around him. "Hi, Evie."

"Hey, Chris."

Holy Christ. "I'm sorry. I got busy."

"We're starting in five minutes. Don't worry about changing." She eyed his jeans and T-shirt. "We're keeping it casual tonight. Bring Evie along if you want."

He stared at his sister, at the happy expression on her face, and felt like an asshole for wanting to back out. But he couldn't. He couldn't hurt her like that when her wedding was in two days.

He could use the time to think. Since the wedding would be in the gardens up at the main house, it wasn't like he had to go far for the rehearsal. If he had an epiphany, he could be back to the carriage house in two minutes. "Can you wait for me a second?"

"Sure." She stepped into the yard and fiddled with a fat pink rose blooming on one of the bushes.

Matt turned back to Evie, who'd come to join them at the door. "I have to go do this, and while you can come with me if you want, I'd prefer you get some sleep. Can I trust you to do that?"

She had that determined look he knew so well. "I think I'd rather stay here. But what if they call?"

"I'm not expecting it for a couple of hours yet, but if they do, call me. Don't do anything without me, Evie."

"I won't—but why do you think they'll wait so long?"

"Because it'll be getting dark then." He leaned down and kissed her. "No matter what anyone says, no matter what they threaten, you call me. I'm two hundred yards away. Got that?"

She nodded. "I'm not stupid. I know you're my best chance."

He couldn't say why those words wrapped around his heart and squeezed, but they did. She called out to Chris, who came back and spoke with her for a few seconds. He wasn't sure if Evie realized her hand was on his arm or not.

Chris watched them with interest, her gaze darting between them. He could tell by the gleam in her eye she thought there was something going on between him and Evie.

And wasn't there?

"Go," Evie said. "I'll take a nap."

"Don't leave the house."

"Matt." She dragged his name out.

"Yeah, got it." He joined Chris, who hooked her arm in his as they started up the path to the main house. His mind strayed to Evie and the problem of what David West could've left behind. Several silent minutes went by before Chris spoke.

"I've always liked her."

Matt's attention snapped to his sister. "Forget it. I'm leaving in a few days. She's just a friend."

She tsked. "I can tell when two people are interested in each other. Besides, long-distance relationships *can* work. There's e-mail, webcams—"

"You know my life isn't the kind any woman wants to share."

"You don't know until you try."

"Yeah, I do. If Ben left in the middle of the night with two hours' notice and couldn't tell you where he was going or how long he'd be gone—" Not to mention whether he'd ever come back again, though no way in hell was Matt putting that thought in his sister's head. "—would you marry him?"

Chris scrunched up her nose, clearly peeved at being derailed. "Probably not."

"Exactly." He'd made his peace with that a long time ago. Marriage and family life weren't for him. He was too focused on what he did, and not ready to give it up.

But what if you have to? What if Mendez and the board make that choice for you?

Matt firmed his jaw. He'd deal with it when the time came.

Brianna walked around outside the cabin, fishing for a signal. It would have been easier if she wasn't constantly looking at the ground to make sure she wasn't about to step on a snake, stumble over a gator, or drop into quicksand.

She swatted at something that buzzed past her head and stifled a shriek. Goddamn swamp! Why had she thought coming out here would be a good idea? She shot a glance at the cabin. Inside, Julian was playing that stupid game, totally engrossed. There was nothing else to do and she was getting jumpy. And the smell. God, what kind of people built cabins in the middle of a swamp?

All around her, tall cypresses rose out of the murky water, creating a canopy over her head that filtered sunlight in tiny drops. Spanish moss hung in long hanks, swaying with the passage of the occasional breeze that came through. Julian had told her when they were motoring in here that the deafening sound coming from every dark corner of the place was made by frogs.

Ugh. She spent ten years living in the country when she was a kid and she never wanted to go back. This assignment was a frigging nightmare.

"Yesss," she said when the bars on her phone appeared. Quickly, she punched in a number. He picked up on the second ring.

"Does this mean the answer's yes?" a male voice said.

"I'm still thinking." Her heart was suddenly doing the

flamenco against her ribs. "What are my guarantees?"

He laughed. "There are none, baby."

"How do I know this isn't a ruse? That you won't double-cross me?"

"Shouldn't I be asking you that question?" His voice was cool, alluring. She'd always thought so.

He was trying to shake her up. Still, the implication stung.

"I do what's best for me," she said. "That's all it is."

"Then give me an answer. Nothing's changed since the last time we discussed this."

"I could get it first. I have the girl."

"You don't know what you're looking for. I do."

"Evie knows."

"I wouldn't count on it. Yes or no, Brianna?"

"I'm thinking."

The line went dead. Brianna swore. A second later, the phone rang again. She answered, triumphant. "You need me for this, don't you?"

"It's why I sent you," Ryan Rivera said, his voice as full of menace as ever. "And what the fuck are you doing answering the phone like that? Looking for a fucking pat on the head?"

Brianna swallowed her heart. Jesus-freaking-Christ. Her pulse refused to slow down and her head got swimmy. She leaned against the side of the cabin and breathed deep. "No, sir. Sorry, sir. I was just, uh, talking to Julian."

Rivera grunted. "Where are you with this? Have you made contact with the Baker girl yet?"

Brianna blinked. "Um, yes, sir. Soon she'll turn over the info in exchange for her sister. We're waiting until it's dark."

He sighed patiently. It was never a good sign. A second later, as if to confirm it, he got mean. "Listen carefully, Brianna, because I'm not very happy with you at the moment. Get your fucking ass in gear and get me that information pronto. Then you need to make sure there are no witnesses, understand? Don't leave a mess behind."

Brianna resisted the urge to stammer. She didn't mind killing Evie and her sister, but she didn't think it was going to be all that easy. "Evie has help, sir. A military commando of some sort."

This morning, the whole damn town had been alive with talk of Evie Baker and Matt Girard, a high school relationship gone wrong, and the way he'd saved her from a bully out at the lake last night. She wasn't too concerned about him—he was as vulnerable to a bullet as anybody— but it added extra work to an already difficult job. Especially when she didn't know precisely what the hell they were after yet. West had left the information with Evie Baker—but Brianna still didn't know what form it took. And she was beginning to worry Evie didn't either.

Rivera wasn't concerned about any of it, of course. He just expected results.

"If he gets in the way, kill him too."

Misty Lee had done wonders with the gardens. They'd always been beautiful, green, lush, and required an army of gardeners, but Misty Lee had gone in with a vision and made changes that turned Reynier's Retreat into the envy of the Rochambeau Garden Club. Long sweeping lawns were planted with a variety of blooming flowers, ornamental grasses, and shrubs. Matt wouldn't have noticed something as mundane as landscaping, but the transformation still stunned him each time he came out here since arriving two days ago. Who'd have thought his stepmama had it in her?

No wonder Chris had decided to get married at Reynier's Retreat instead of in a church. Workers were busy placing chairs, the florist fiddled with vines on the trellis, and the minister directed a run-through of the actual ceremony that managed to drag on at least an hour longer than Matt anticipated. Evie hadn't called, and he didn't bother trying her because he hoped she was sleeping. She wasn't stupid, and she wouldn't leave the grounds without telling him. Of that he was certain.

Misty Lee sidled up to him, a Pomeranian tucked in one arm—and smashed up against her considerable assets —and batted her eyelashes. "You look bored, Matthew, honey."

"Not at all, Mother, dear."

Misty Lee giggled. She loved it when he called her mother for some silly reason. Anyone observing the two of them would probably think she was flirting, but then Misty Lee flirted with everyone. It was as natural to her as breathing.

"Are you staying for dinner?"

"I can't."

She frowned. "Your daddy would love to see you, Matt. He said just this morning that he's hardly talked to you since you got back."

Somehow, Matt doubted the senator had put it quite like that. The man was too busy playing the elder statesman to notice he hadn't talked to his son more than ten minutes total in two days. But he would notice if it appeared Matt wasn't playing the role of dutiful child.

When he'd been little, the senator had always been about appearances. They'd been an ideal-looking family, even if the picture hadn't been reality.

And then his mother died, and the picture crumbled. Matt and Christina spent their childhoods with nannies and shockingly tacky stepmamas while their father spent his time getting people to vote for him—a task made more difficult by the stripper wives, but then Matt pretty much figured his father had counted on that. It was as if he'd wanted to self-destruct but couldn't quite manage it.

Matt ground his teeth. If the senator was thinking about him now, there had to be a reason for it other than a sudden urge to be a father.

No doubt he was wondering if Matt was ready to leave the military and take his place at Girard Oil yet. That was a refrain Matt had heard before, and one he didn't need to listen to right now.

"There's plenty of time." He said it smoothly, evenly—though it was a lie. In a few short days, he was leaving again.

And that didn't bother him in the least. He'd never known what to say to his father. Any conversation between them always degenerated quickly. The old man didn't like that he'd joined the military, and Matt didn't like that his father had spent the best part of their childhood away from him and his sister.

They were never going to see things the same way.

Not only that, but Matt also had his own secrets to keep. There were things he'd done when he was a reckless teenager who resented his father that still caused him more shame than he liked to think about.

There were things you did not do, lines you did not cross. And he'd crossed them long ago. There was no point in pretending things would ever be normal after all these years.

Misty Lee was about to say something else when one of the caterers approached to ask a question. "Well I know I saw that dish in the sideboard just this morning." She stood there frowning for a moment and then excused herself to rush off to find some ancient piece of family silver.

The minister called for yet another run-through of the ceremony. As soon as Matt walked up the aisle with his assigned bridesmaid—a blushing young woman from Shreveport who slanted him heated glances and giggled nervously—he ducked out and sat down. Another five minutes and he was leaving. They'd already done this five times, and he was done.

Besides, the sun was slipping behind the horizon, and it would soon be dark. Sarah's kidnappers would make their move then. It was easier to hide and they were less likely to be seen when they met with Evie.

And with him. He wasn't letting her go by herself, no matter what they wanted.

The senator caught his eye from where he stood with Chris at the end of the center aisle. His father looked unpleased. Whether it was with him or someone else, Matt didn't really care.

Since leaving home ten years ago, Matt had seen

more of this world than his father could ever hope to imagine. Where once the old man had scared him half-silly, now Beauregard James Matthew Girard the Third was like a toothless old lion in Matt's mind. Frightening at first, a nuisance maybe, but ultimately without the teeth to back up the threat.

The military had done that for him. Taught him what was really scary in the world. And taught him how to defeat those fears.

But if the board convening to discuss his fate next week decided he was no good for the U.S. Army after all, he'd find himself back in Rochambeau a whole lot sooner than planned. Provided he didn't end up spending time in Fort Leavenworth military prison for gross negligence or for posing a threat to national security.

And if he had to return to Rochambeau even for a little while, he knew the conversation about his future at Girard Oil would heat up to a boil.

His gut churned at the thought. He couldn't even begin to express how trapped that idea made him feel. He'd spent too many years living life on the edge to suddenly do something normal. Except, a little voice told him, normal was what a woman like Evie would want.

He didn't bother wondering where that thought came from. It was simply what she did to him, he was discovering.

By the time the latest rehearsal was over, the shadows were stretching across the gardens. Matt stood. No way in hell was he staying for another one of these damn things.

Chris caught him as he was striding down the aisle. "Leaving so soon?"

Matt put his arm around her and hugged her. "Yeah, I

have things to do tonight."

She arched an eyebrow. "Do these things involve a pretty girl named Evie?"

He smiled. "They might."

Her expression grew serious. "Don't hurt her, Matt."

"What makes you think I'd do that?"

She shrugged. "You said you weren't settling down. And in case you didn't know it, she's pretty much always had a crush on you."

Old guilt bubbled to the surface. And pleasure, too. He liked the idea that Evie might still have feelings for him. "I appreciate the concern, but we're adults now, Chris. We know what we're doing."

"All right, but—"

A loud crack echoed from the darkening bayou.

"Damn rednecks." Chris glowered. "They better not come around shooting birds tomorrow night when the reception's going on."

Cold fear sliced down Matt's spine. It could be Cajuns out hunting in the bayou, but there were other possibilities as well. Possibilities he couldn't ignore.

"I gotta run." He gave his sister a hasty kiss on the cheek and strolled down the center aisle, whistling as if he hadn't a care in the world.

But once he passed out of sight of the gardens, he broke into a run.

TWELVE

EVIE WAS GONE. MATT BLAZED through the rooms, methodically checking for signs of her, but she wasn't anywhere. Two cakes sat on the counter and the house smelled like chocolate. The front door had been locked, but the back door was open.

Fear turned his gut to ice. He sprinted for the safe he knew his father kept behind the Early American landscape in the study. He whipped the painting away and turned the dial. The combination hadn't changed in years and he was counting on that still being the case. After the third click, he wrenched open the door and reached for the pistol that'd always been inside.

The safe was empty. Fine time for the old man to remove it.

Matt swore again and took off for the back veranda. He'd have to make do with a knife and years of intensive combat training. A litany of all his fuck ups ran through his brain.

He should have left the rehearsal sooner. He should-n't have trusted that she would be fine, no matter that she was tough and smart. He should have protected her.

He slipped into the backyard, scanning the bayou in either direction. If a boat had passed by, it wasn't recent. There was no wake, no disturbance to indicate anyone had been here. His next option was to head for town and see if he could get a lead on her. Whoever had taken her couldn't have gotten far, whether by boat or car.

And someone had to have taken her. Evie wouldn't have left without telling him. He was certain of it. He had to get it together and think like the machine he'd been trained to be.

Or he could lose her for good.

Matt bounded up the steps and back into the house, pulling up short when he stepped over the threshold.

Evie looked up from where she was sitting at the island and shot him a weak smile. "They haven't called yet. I'm getting worried."

She twirled her phone on the marble counter, lines of sadness and worry bracketing her mouth.

Matt crossed the distance in two strides and crushed his mouth down on hers. She gasped, clutching him. Heat and want spiraled deep in his belly and made him long to strip her and lay her out on the marble island while he took his fill of her. His dick started to harden and he let her go abruptly, struggling to find his center. *Focus, goddamn you.*

She looked stunned. And aroused. Her pink lips glistened. Her chest rose and fell a little faster than usual, her skin flushing. God, he wanted to taste her. All of her. One night wasn't nearly enough.

"What was that about?" She sounded as breathless as he felt.

"Where have you been?" He was proud of how calm he sounded.

"In the garage. I was cleaning up the mess we made."

The garage. Shit. He hadn't looked in there. *And why not?* Another indication he was losing his touch. When he hadn't found her in the house, he'd panicked. The garage had been the furthest thing from his mind.

"Did you hear anything? Any noise?"

She frowned. "No. Did something happen?"

Matt shoved a hand through his hair. "No, nothing." He'd heard gunshots. Chris heard them too. Maybe it was someone shooting birds, like she said. Or hunting gators, though it was out of season. Anything was possible around here. He wasn't going to mention it to Evie and spook her, though.

"Why haven't they called?" Frustration was evident in her voice. "It makes no sense. Unless they've hurt Sarah."

Matt shook his head. "I'm not sure, but we can't think like that. Sarah is their leverage to get what they want. Hurting her would be foolish."

At that moment, the phone vibrated across the marble. Evie gasped and looked up at him. Matt nodded.

She grabbed it, her expression collapsing. "It's another text message."

"What does it say?"

She scrolled down, and he found himself wishing she had a smartphone so she could see the messages easier. "Oh my God, it's them. Charlie's. Ten P.M. Bring the files." She met his gaze. "Files?"

Matt swore. "It's what I thought. We're looking for flash memory—a thumb drive or a media card—or even a key card."

She looked perplexed. "I don't have a thumb drive or a flash memory card. All the key cards I had went with the restaurant, and they were turned over with everything else. I don't even have a computer anymore. I had to hock it for gas money."

Matt didn't like the sound of that, but then he figured West probably wouldn't have put the files somewhere as obvious as her computer. Too much danger she'd discover them. "He must have left something, Evie. Or at least they think he did. Do you have a camera? Maybe he put the info on the media card that goes there."

She looked crestfallen. "Even if he did, I lost the camera a couple of months ago. I left it on a table in a restaurant, and when I went back, it was gone. It wasn't a good camera, so I figured I'd just have to buy a new one."

Shit. "But David would've thought you have the card, so maybe that's the answer."

"So what do we do now?"

He stared over her head, thinking. "We need a media card. I'll get Billy to build a mock-up of files we can download onto a blank. It might buy us enough time to get Sarah."

"Who's Billy?"

He'd called Billy by his team name earlier. "The Kid. He's a whiz with computers. He can make a file complicated enough to look real. It must be accounting files or business records for Rivera's illegal activities that've got the guy so worked up. Billy can incorporate enough real information to fool our kidnappers... for a short while at least."

Or so he hoped. If Rivera's people traveled with a

computer expert in the group, it wouldn't work. If Rivera had simply sent enforcers, that was another story. Then Matt had a good chance of pulling it off.

"Where do we get a blank card?"

"I'm hoping there's one up at the house. The computer's there anyway, so if we're lucky this'll be a quick trip." He glanced at his watch. "It's nearly eight thirty, so we have a little time."

"And if you can't find one?"

"We'll have to go shopping."

Evie's smile was more genuine this time. "You're really amazing, you know that?"

Her hand settled on his arm, stroked his skin, and left a wash of sensation trailing in its wake.

"I'm just doing my job, Evie."

"No." Her eyes were shining. "It's more than that." He started to protest, started to stop her before she confessed she'd convinced herself he was in love with her and happy-ever-after was right around the corner, but what she said wasn't anything remotely like he expected. "You care about people, Matt. You can't let anyone suffer if you think you can change it."

His chest felt tight. "It's what I've been trained to do. You'd do the same thing if you were me."

"No, I don't think I would." She seemed troubled, but she looked away and he thought he might have imagined it.

"Let's get up to the house." He squeezed her hand to reassure her. "We've got work to do."

She snapped him a salute. "Aye, aye, Captain."

Matt laughed.

Sarah sucked back tears. It didn't help. Crying only made her head hurt worse. But the cabin was dark and she was scared. The sounds of the swamp were deafening. Frogs, whippoorwills, and cicadas, among other things, sang night songs that penetrated the paper-thin walls.

Brianna and Julian had left over an hour ago. They hadn't said where they were going, when they'd be back, or even turned on a light. And, aside from a fast-food burger earlier, they hadn't fed her in hours.

She wasn't cold, but she was cramped and hungry. And her freaking head hurt like it'd never hurt before. She screamed, just in case a fisherman was out there in another cabin. Or passing by. Someone could be frog gigging or night fishing. The swamp at night was no big deal to some of these old Cajuns who'd lived in it their whole lives. It wasn't Sarah's favorite place to be, but at least she was inside four walls. No gator was climbing the steps and opening the door to come eat her.

She yanked the cuff against the iron headboard as if she could somehow free herself by sheer strength alone. She knew she couldn't. The only thing she accomplished was rubbing her wrist raw. Her skin felt wet and sticky as something oozed down to her elbow. She realized with a jolt that she'd made herself bleed. What kind of night creature might smell the blood and come to get her out here?

Sarah strained her ears against the noise, finally heard

the faint sputter of a motor coming closer. She had to save her breath in order to yell when the boat was passing in front of the cabin. She waited, her heart pounding so hard she thought she'd have a heart attack. The throbbing in her head kept time with her heart and her empty stomach churned.

The boat drew closer and the motor cut. Fresh tears welled up. It was Brianna and Julian returning then, not a fisherman. A few moments later, she heard voices. Male and female. Then the door swung open and light from a lantern flooded the cabin. Sarah blinked as the pale beam stabbed into her irises.

"So that's her then?" The man who spoke was someone new. She couldn't see him behind the lantern light but he didn't sound like Julian or the other guy from last night.

Brianna sounded smug. "Yep. We picked her up hitchhiking."

Sarah's tongue burned with the urge to contradict the woman, but she kept her mouth shut. She hadn't been hitchhiking at all. She'd been walking into town and she'd been dumb enough to get into the car because Brianna claimed to know Evie.

"Stroke of luck," the man said. "Amazing. And your luck's just gotten better now that you're working with me."

"I'm counting on you. You better not fuck this up or we're both dead."

The man laughed. "You can hardly turn back now, can you, doll? You made your choice."

"Don't make me regret it."

"You won't. Soon as we get those files, we'll be safe. And rich."

"Then let's go get them."

The light disappeared behind the closed door. Sarah shifted until she was lying on her side with her arm stretched above her head. She was tired of crying, tired of yelling, tired of hurting. The motor fired up and sputtered into the night.

"We better get back to the guesthouse." Matt logged off the computer and popped the media card out of the slot.

Evie got to her feet and waited for him to shut everything down. They had files to trade, though she didn't know how they were going to fool the kidnappers into believing this was the information they wanted. How would anyone verify it? And when would they be satisfied enough to turn Sarah over?

Matt said they had to take it one problem at a time. He seemed to have a plan, but she didn't know what it entailed beyond getting to Charlie's and making contact with these guys.

She followed him through the house. She'd always loved Reynier's Retreat. Timeworn oak floors and soaring fifteen-foot walls, decorated in plaster friezes, were all original to the house. Priceless works of art decorated the walls. Antique couches dressed in pale silk perched on top of intricate oriental carpets. A grand piano, made of burled walnut, sat in one corner of the front parlor.

A lush painting of the latest Mrs. Girard hung over the fireplace. Misty Lee had impossibly large breasts and the skinniest waist Evie had ever seen. She was draped in a flowing fabric that clung to her many curves and left little to the imagination. No doubt this was the sexiest painting ever to grace the mansion's antebellum walls.

The polished Japanese secretary desk pulled Evie up short. It hadn't been here when she'd been a kid. She touched it with a finger, traced one of the Asian scenes painted on its surface. Family photos decorated the open desk. There was one of Matt in his uniform. He looked much younger, and she realized it must be a photo from his days at West Point.

He drew up between the ten-foot-high pocket doors and waited. "Misty Lee has done a great job with the decor, huh? She kept all the original pieces, but she's put her stamp on it."

Evie remembered the old house had always been elegant. But it had also been a bit more sedate back when Matt's mother had been alive. Probably because she was sick for so long.

"It's an amazing house. Always has been."

She'd spent her childhood in a twelve-hundred-square-foot cottage in what was then the poorer section of town. Since the neighborhood was declared historic a few years ago, several new people had moved in and renovated their properties. Mama had followed the trend, and now her home was a cute bungalow with all the modern conveniences and a gorgeous plot of land. But nothing in Rochambeau compared to Reynier's Retreat.

His expression clouded. "Yeah, I guess it is."

He looked sad and Evie walked over to touch his arm.

"What's wrong?"

"After my mother died, it didn't seem the same." He let his gaze travel the room. "I love what Misty Lee has done. I even wish my mama could see it. I think she'd approve."

"I'm sorry she died, Matt. You know that."

"Yeah. It was long ago, though." He shrugged. "I think I'll always feel like I missed out on something, but I'm fine now."

She wasn't quite sure she believed him. He said it too quickly, too casually. She did not doubt he was over the grief that had gone with losing his mother at such a young age. But the pain? She didn't think that was something that ever quite went away. There was always a hole you couldn't fill.

He took a deep breath as if he were pushing his feelings into a box and looked at his watch. "We need to get going."

They slipped out onto the sweeping veranda and down the stairs. Evie could hear laughter and voices raised in conversation coming from the side of the house. It must be the rehearsal party.

A party Matt was missing for her.

"We'll head straight for Charlie's." He sounded so calm and focused; she took comfort in it. "You go in and sit at a table and I'll scout the perimeter."

Evie strode by his side through the darkness, her pulse pounding at the thought of what she had to do. She could *not* screw this up. Sarah might not have been able to count on her for the past ten years, but Evie wasn't failing her sister now. She'd die first. "How will they know where to find me?"

"They know who you are, Evie. They'll be watching for you."

They were almost to the guesthouse when Matt stopped. He threw his arm out in front of her, drawing her up short.

"What is it?"

"I'm not sure. Something." He listened for a few moments, his eyes scanning the darkness around them, before he motioned her forward again. She followed him up the steps.

Pain shot through her as she was knocked against the wall. The full length of Matt's body pinned her tight. He'd thrown her sideways and pressed his back to her front, covering her, but she didn't know why. Her cheek mashed against his broad back and she drew in a deep breath, preparing to tell him to give her some room. The rumble of his voice sounded in her ears, but it took her a second to make it out.

"Someone's been inside. Soon as I move, you lie flat on the ground, hear me?"

She squeaked out an affirmative that seemed to satisfy him and then the pressure of his body was gone. Evie dropped to her stomach on the whitewashed boards of the porch. Blood pounded in her ears, her heart racing along like an Olympic skier on a slalom run.

Matt hadn't been gone more than a minute when a crack rang out in the night air. Evie's stomach dropped to her toes. She bolted up out of pure instinct. No way in hell was she lying here when Matt could have been shot.

The sound echoed from the rear yard and Evie took off, hugging the side of the house as she went. The yard was dark as pitch and she stumbled to a stop. Her night vision was good, but something big and black seemed to swallow the yard whole at a certain point.

The bayou.

Before she could get her bearings again, a motor roared to life. Seconds later, the whine of it was shooting down the bayou, rapidly moving away between the cypress trees. The acrid scent of diesel fuel hung in the air.

"I thought I told you to stay put." Matt's voice cracked like a whip in her ear and she jumped sideways, colliding with him.

"Don't do that," she hissed as strong arms caught her close and steadied her. Her heart hammered like crazy, the blood rushing loud in her ears. "I heard a gunshot and I thought you might need help."

He let out a half-strangled sound, grabbed her hand, and squeezed. "Get up to Reynier's Retreat and stay there until I come for you."

"I'm going with you, Matt. We have to be at Charlie's in half an hour."

"Evie—"

"No." She pressed her trembling fingers to his lips. "I'll stay in the rear, I'll get down when you tell me, and I won't do anything stupid, but I *am* going with you. It'll waste too much time if you have to come back and get me."

He was still for a moment and she knew he was trying to figure out how to get around the facts. But then he swore and grabbed her hand. "Sonofabitch, I hate it when you're right. Let's go."

THIRTEEN

WHAT HAD SHE GOTTEN HERSELF INTO? Evie gulped as Matt pulled her down the dock. She could do this. She *could*.

He jumped into the small pirogue tied up at the end of the dock and tried to crank the motor. The sharp scent of carbon filled the air. Her blood turned to ice, her chest constricting until she had to work to get air into her lungs. *No, no, no.*

She dug deep for her courage. It had been years since she and Julie capsized their canoe in the bayou. Years since she'd sputtered and coughed and thought she was going to die because she wasn't a very good swimmer. The long, ugly water moccasin had slid across the water toward her, and Evie couldn't even scream because she couldn't stay afloat.

If not for the guys who'd come along in their fishing boat just then, she'd still be at the bottom of the swamp.

Yet she knew Matt wouldn't let anything happen to her. She trusted him. He wouldn't capsize the pirogue, and he wouldn't make her swim in the dark, dank bayou with snakes and gators.

"Get in." He glanced at her before turning back to the motor and trying again to crank it.

She swallowed hard, forcing her feet to move until she stood at the edge of the dock. Slowly, so bonelessly she didn't even feel herself do it, she slipped down to sit on the wood planking.

Good, very good.

Now put a foot into the pirogue. She stretched her right foot out, touched her toe to the narrow canoe bottom. Her whole body shook with the effort. Matt didn't seem to notice. He was still bent over the motor, trying to get it started.

He didn't know about her and Julie and the canoe because it was the summer before his senior year and they hadn't been hanging out anymore. He'd been preoccupied with other things then. And it had been years since they'd gone swimming together—or what passed for swimming for her. Standing in the shallows and watching him cut through the water like a fish.

He'd never dunked her—or at least not after the first time when she'd screamed and cried and tattled on him for it.

"Fuck, they've ripped out the fuel line."

Evie wilted—until another thought occurred to her: what if he wanted to pole the thing into the bayou?

Pirogues were extremely narrow, flat-bottomed boats that could move through shallow water, which made them popular in the marshes and swamps. They didn't need motors, though fishermen often added them for increased maneuverability and speed. But there wasn't much sense in chasing after someone in a motorboat when your own motor was shot. Or so she hoped.

"What do we do now?" She wanted to sound brave and strong even when her mind was gibbering at her in cold terror. If Matt didn't think they needed a motor to follow whoever fired that shot, they'd soon be gliding through murky water in the dark and she'd be fighting just to keep conscious.

"Try something else."

Relief made her light-headed.

He sprang from the boat and helped her to her feet, seemingly oblivious to the fear that had nearly paralyzed her. "We have to get to Charlie's. Whoever was here didn't get what they were looking for, so we need to move on."

"How can you be certain?"

"Because he didn't get into the garage, and that's where all your things are. The door was still locked."

It amazed her that he'd had the presence of mind to check, but of course he would have done so. Matt was a precision machine in many respects. His mind worked in ways hers didn't, and she thought only part of that was thanks to his training.

They hurried up to the house and slipped through the unlocked back door. He didn't turn on the light. She didn't need to ask why not. They could both see better in the dark now, and there was no sense in becoming a giant backlit target for whoever had taken that shot, just in case they turned around and decided to try again.

"Stay on my six, Evie. Don't stray."

"Your what?"

"Right behind me."

When he reached the door to the garage, she felt his

arm stretch upward and heard his fingers running along the jamb. He must have been satisfied with what he found, because he opened the door and pulled her into the garage. He reached to his right and a flashlight flicked on. A quick sweep of the light across the room and then he was crossing to the Beemer.

"Stand here." He dropped to his stomach, the light arcing beneath the car. A handful of minutes later, he was on his feet again, opening the passenger door for her.

"I left my purse inside." She felt ridiculous for saying so.

He laughed softly, surprising her. "So I won't ask you to drive, okay?"

He came around to the driver's side and popped the hood. She couldn't see what he did, but he fished around in the engine compartment for a couple of minutes before slamming the hood down and jumping behind the wheel. Then he was turning the key and pressing the remote. The garage door ticked upward and Matt gunned the car in reverse before the door reached the top of the track. Evie grabbed the handle over the door as they slipped underneath and Matt whipped the wheel around. The tires spun for a second before finding purchase; then they shot down the driveway.

"What were you checking for back there?" The oaks sped by in a blur, and her heart clawed its way into her throat.

Matt didn't even spare her a glance. "Explosives."

Explosives?

He swung the car into a sharp turn and she instinctively threw a hand up to brace against the center console even though the seat belt locked her in place.

212

Her neck was stiff from clenching it. "Do you have to drive like a maniac?"

"The only place that boat could be going is Charlie's. It's the first place on the bayou where someone could leave a car. I don't know why they came to Reynier's Retreat, or what they thought they'd find, but I want to be waiting for them when they arrive, if at all possible."

Though they were already going at what seemed like light speed, he shifted one final time and the car responded with a throaty growl, leaping forward to burn up the asphalt.

Evie stifled a groan and closed her eyes. "Look, I don't care if we beat them or not, I just want to live through this."

"Relax. I know what I'm doing. If it makes you feel any better, I've done this hundreds of times. It's part of the training."

"Training for what? The Indy 500?" Okay, so her voice was a little high-pitched there.

"Escape and evasion." He shot her a look. "Nobody said this'd be easy. In fact, it'll probably get worse before we're through."

Great. "So long as we get Sarah back alive, I'll do what I have to do to make it through."

"You're interesting, you know that?"

The compliment warmed her. "I appreciate it, but I'd trade interesting for mundane and boring right now."

"Boring can be nice too."

She doubted he could do boring. "I don't know how you do this all the time."

"You do what you have to do."

"But you didn't have to—that's the point."

He whipped the car into another sharp turn, then straightened it out. "And you didn't have to leave home to be a chef, did you?"

"There was nothing for me here." Except Mama and Sarah, and God what she'd give to have them both safe and well and for none of this to have ever happened.

"That's *my* point."

She didn't have an answer for that. Before today, she hadn't understood how anyone could come from the kind of wealth and privilege he did, could have a beautiful home like Reynier's Retreat and a job as an oil executive waiting for him, and could choose instead to drive getaway cars, deflect bullets, and rescue little sisters.

But she was damn glad he did.

Julian was fucking pissed. She'd ditched him. The bitch had ditched him here on the dock at this joint called Charlie's Diner over an hour ago. She'd claimed she had something to do, that Rivera had a last-minute task for her. If Julian liked his balls any less, he'd call Rivera and find out if the cunt was telling the truth.

As it was, he'd sit here at a corner table, eating fried oysters and sipping a beer, and wait. She swore she'd be back before Evie Baker arrived. That she'd be here to meet with Evie while he scouted out the woman's military escort—oh yeah, they knew the guy would come with her—and that she'd let him take the prick out if he got in the way.

Fucking military asshole. Thought he was one badass motherfucker, no doubt. Well, Julian had spent a tour in the Marines. Wasn't no motherfucker badder than a former Marine motherfucker. *Former* Marine, not ex. Once a Marine, always a Marine.

Semper fi.

This was a busy place. He watched the doors open and close so many times he stopped paying complete attention. A band played Zydeco at one end of the rustic room, and people twirled on the dance floor. The place was a diner, but unlike any diner he was used to. The building sat on pylons over the water, and a dock stretched out into the bayou. Boats tied up, people coming and going from them in a steady stream.

The door to the dock opened and Brianna rushed in, her blond hair messy and wild. She smoothed it quickly as she strode toward him.

"Where the fuck you been? It's almost time."

She yanked out a chair and sat down. "I'm here now, aren't I? Stop whining."

Whining. If Rivera ordered him to shoot her between the eyes tomorrow, Julian would do it without a shred of remorse.

"I need you to get back to the cabin," Brianna said before he could ask her how she planned to follow Rivera's orders and take care of Evie Baker after they'd gotten the goods.

Julian stared at her. "What? What's this shit? That wasn't the plan, Bree."

"I'm changing the plan. Get back there and watch the girl."

"You better tell me what's going on." He narrowed his eyes at her, pouring every ounce of meanness he had into his glare. If she was fucking with him, he'd whack her in a heartbeat.

"Evie's not going to give me what she's got without some proof her sister's alive. You need to be there so I can call."

"You couldn't think of this earlier?"

Brianna shrugged. "I did think of it, but it took me longer than I thought to get back." She glanced at her watch. "You've got about ten minutes. Better hurry."

Julian's gut churned. He shoved the chair back and got to his feet, glaring down at her. "You can pay for the food. When this is over, I'm talking to Rivera about you."

"You do that, Julian. Boat's wedged into a spot between two cuddy cabins toward the end."

"How do you plan on getting back later?"

"I don't. You'll bring the girl out. I'll let you know."

"Fuck," Julian said, then strode through the doors and down the broad wooden planks. He found the motorboat, jumped into it, and cranked the engine before turning to untie the anchor rope. "What do you want?"

A man had appeared out of nowhere and stared down at him from the dock above.

"Let's make a deal," the guy said, stepping closer. That's when Julian noticed the gun.

Charlie's was on the southern end of town, about ten minutes away from Reynier's Retreat. It took Matt less than five to make the trip. Evie was amazed they didn't get pulled over before they got there. The answer to why not, however, sat in the jammed parking lot. Three of the town's six police cars were parked side by side.

Evie swallowed and shot a glance at Matt.

"It'll be okay." He sounded calm and cool. It gave her confidence, though not much.

She just hoped he was right. David's body had been found less than twenty-four hours ago and the police were under pressure to find the killer. And since they wanted to believe the killer was Evie, in spite of her corroborated alibi, they weren't going to be all that nice when she strolled in.

She wasn't surprised the police were here. In fact, most of the town wound up at the popular restaurant some time or another during the week. Nobody could resist the lure of Charlie Boudreaux's cooking.

Seeing the place always brought back memories. How many hot summer nights had she spent at Charlie's with her friends? She'd waitressed the summer before her junior year, fetching iced tea and soda for the customers along with mile-high po' boys and steaming bowls of gumbo. Charlie had been the first person to nurture her cooking talent, to teach her when to add a pinch of seasoning or a dollop of sauce. And he'd taught her how to make a creamy roux, which came in darn handy when she was mastering French sauces under the tutelage of Monsieur Bertrand.

Charlie'd been happy when she'd gotten accepted to culinary school, but baffled too. He didn't understand why anybody needed to go to school to learn how to cook. *Dat crazy, ma chère. Wat you want to do dat fo? You know how to cook, yeah.*

When she'd come back to town a month ago, she'd driven past on the way to Mama's beauty parlor and been surprised to see that the once Pepto-Bismol clapboard siding had faded to a dusty pink over the last few years. Now, in the dark, it looked almost white. The boxy building sat on stilts over the water, and a ramp sloped up to the door.

Folks congregated on the ramp, laughing and talking, some smoking cigarettes, while they either took a break from the action inside or waited for a table to open up.

Light spilled from the windows, lighting the first row of cars, while inside a local band jammed. She could feel its swinging beat, even in the car with the windows rolled up and the AC going. Charlie's was a diner, a family place, though they served beer and wine as well. No one mistook Charlie's for a rough and tumble bar. There were always strangers among the regulars, folks who'd read about the place in a guidebook or heard about it from friends who'd passed through.

Matt slipped the BMW into a parking spot near the end of a row and shut off the engine. He glanced toward the dock and the boats tied up there. "I think, even if we beat our mystery guest, it's probably too crowded here tonight to catch whoever it was. Instead, we're gonna concentrate on the meeting and see what we can't find out that way. You ready for this?"

Evie nodded. "Absolutely."

"I'm going to poke around outside, see if our mystery visitor has made it yet. You go in and wait for someone to make contact."

"What if they try to force me to leave with them?"

"I won't let it happen."

"I admit I don't understand this. Why do they want to meet in such a public place? And how will we know they really have Sarah?"

"They knew you wouldn't go anywhere more remote, so they want to make sure you have the files." He handed her the media card. "Don't give it to them yet. Make them tell you how they see the exchange happening, and don't agree to anything that isn't within the town limits. Anywhere open and well-lit is good—a parking lot, for instance. Tell them you want to speak to Sarah and make sure she's okay before you agree to anything."

"All right."

"They'll be hoping you're dumb enough to hand over the information with only a promise in return, so don't be surprised if they suggest it, or even demand it, before agreeing to let you speak to Sarah."

Evie snorted. "That's not happening."

Matt flashed a smile. "Yeah, I'd say they aren't actually acquainted with you or they'd know better." He leaned forward and kissed her. "There's at least three cops in there—and I'll be watching carefully—so don't worry."

Evie got out of the car and marched up the ramp. It took a tad longer than she'd like since she had to stop and speak to everyone she knew. People made sympathetic noises about Jimmy, about her mother, and her dead partner. Evie thanked them all, said she didn't have the faintest idea what was going on, and kept moving until she reached the doors and finally got inside.

Don't worry, Matt had said. Right. Evie scanned the

crowded restaurant and wished her stomach wasn't doing flip turns. The second she walked inside, her mouth started watering for a bowl of Charlie's jambalaya. Except she couldn't keep any food down right now.

Her gaze snagged on a woman at the back. The wild blond hair and shape of the nose were familiar. It had to be an old classmate, but who hadn't she seen out at the lake last night? Before she could figure it out, the woman ducked through the rear door.

"Well, bless my soul if it isn't little Evie Baker! Been worried about you, sugar."

Evie spun to find a pint-size woman smiling up at her. "Trish!" Evie hugged Charlie's wife, who was always ready with a smile and a warm word. "I'm fine, really, but thanks for worrying."

Trish frowned. "Heard your mama had a nasty fall, sugar. And what about that man, hmm? Can you believe it? Who do you think killed him?"

"I wish I knew." It wasn't the first time tonight Evie had said it.

Trish talked a mile a minute and hardly waited for her questions to be answered before zooming ahead. "I heard he was your ex-boyfriend and he stole a lot of money from you."

Evie nodded. She'd been hoping to keep the circumstances of her return to Rochambeau secret, but of course that was all finished once David showed up and got himself killed. It was bad enough to feel like a failure to yourself. To have everyone else know you were a failure was a different story altogether.

And yet that was nothing compared to the fact David was dead. She may have hated him for what he'd done to her dreams, but there'd been a time when she'd liked him. When he'd made her laugh.

"Yes, he stole from me. I don't know why he was here, though."

Trish swatted her with a napkin. "Probably wanted to beg your forgiveness. Just look at you. You've grown into quite the lovely thing, haven't you?" She popped her hands on her ample hips. "So what's it gonna be tonight? Meeting anyone? How about that handsome Matt Girard, hmm?"

Evie's face was hot. Great, now she was blushing over Matt Girard. "I'm expecting someone to come talk to me about a job."

A lie, but at least it would explain why she was talking to a stranger. She just hoped Trish didn't question why someone would come to Rochambeau to interview her.

As hoped, Trish sailed right on by that little snag. "Oh honey, you could always come work here. Charlie would love to have you."

Evie's smile was genuine. There were a lot of good people in Rochambeau. Times like this, she felt guilty for wanting to escape. "I'll think about it."

"You do that. Now let's get you a place to sit, *chère*." Trish hurried her to a table and plopped down a menu and a basket of corn fritters she'd acquired along the way. "I'm rushed off my tootsies tonight. But you be sure to come back and say hello to Charlie before you leave. He's always happy to see you."

Evie promised she'd do just that. When Trish walked away, she scanned the crowd again. She recognized a few faces, though no one who felt it their immediate duty to come over and talk to her. Missy Sue waved and motioned her over. Evie pointed at the seat in front of her, indicating she was waiting for someone, and shrugged. Missy Sue nodded and mouthed, "Later then."

Evie glanced at the table of cops. They hadn't yet noticed her, and for that she was thankful. She pretended to study the menu—as if she didn't already know it by heart since Charlie hadn't changed it in twenty years—and watched the doors for newcomers. There were a few people she didn't recognize, but no one paid any attention to her beyond a glance and a whispered conversation here and there. No doubt they all knew about David's murder and were speculating whether or not she could be a stone-cold killer.

Evie recognized a man moving through the crowd and suppressed a groan. Oh God, not now. Detective Proctor sighted her and changed course. She set the menu down very carefully and composed a smile for him.

"Heard your mama's doing well," he said.

"Yes, thank you."

"You hear from that sister of yours yet?"

Evie's heart thudded into her throat. Wouldn't it be good to have the police on their side? Cops had resources they could mobilize in a heartbeat to find Sarah. But the people who had Sarah were professional killers, as Matt said, and they wouldn't hesitate to follow through on their threats if the police got involved. And Matt's resources seemed to be pretty good if the work they'd done on the media card was any indication.

Evie swallowed. "Um, yes. She went to a friend's house."

He nodded, his expression somewhat smug. "Thought

222

so."

Anger flashed through her in spite of the fact she should be relieved they weren't digging any deeper. "Weren't you supposed to be questioning her friends? Making sure she wasn't missing?"

"Twenty-five years' experience tells me she went somewhere to pout after the fight with her boyfriend. I don't have the leisure time to chase after a teenager in a snit when there's a murderer on the loose."

His look was pointed. Evie picked up the menu again, fiddling with it. "Then don't let me keep you from finding that person, Detective Proctor."

He tapped the back of the empty chair facing her. "Don't worry, Miss Baker, you won't."

When he walked away, Evie resisted the urge to drop her head into her hands. She drew in a deep breath. This was *insane*. She was a chef—a broke, unemployed chef—waiting to meet with ruthless mob thugs in a public restaurant while the police sat fifteen feet away and didn't have a clue. It was almost too ridiculous to be real. If not for that picture of Sarah, she wouldn't believe it was.

Her phone chimed and she answered without checking the display. She already knew what it would say: *unknown.*

"Meet me on the dock." A woman's voice, ten minutes early.

"I'd rather not. Come inside."

"Too crowded. The police don't boost my confidence any. You wouldn't have been dumb enough to tell them, would you?"

"No! Charlie's is a popular spot in Rochambeau. Everyone comes here."

"Outside, Evie."

Something in the woman's voice as she said Evie's name registered in the recesses of her brain and dredged up a memory. "Brianna Sweeney?"

"Aren't you clever? Now get out here." The phone went dead.

Evie's temples throbbed. Brianna? Her bartender? The woman had worked at Evangeline's for about four months. Bree'd had a boyfriend—Julian, a big, muscular dude who looked mean enough to eat a helping of railroad spikes for breakfast. The two of them had left shortly after David, but she hadn't thought anything of it at the time. Staff always came and went in the restaurant business. Besides, she'd lost several servers in the days after David stole the payroll.

Yet it now looked as if Brianna was more than she'd seemed.

Evie punched in Matt's number. A second later, he answered.

"They want me to come out on the dock."

"Go ahead, I've got your six. Don't go any farther than the first landing."

Evie rose as nonchalantly as possible under the circumstances. When she reached the door, she glanced at the cops' table. Detective Proctor's hard stare was pinned on her. She pushed the door open and walked across the wooden decking. A quick scan didn't reveal Matt anywhere. Since she didn't want to look obvious in her search for him, she focused on the long dock. A woman with blond hair waited twenty feet on the other side of the first landing, the glow of her cigarette like a homing beacon.

"You got it?" Brianna asked when Evie was within

earshot.

"Yes." Evie took the media card from her jeans pocket and held it in her palm before dropping it inside again. "Where's my sister?"

"She's fine."

"When will you let her go?"

"Soon as I confirm." Brianna took out her phone.

Bitterness coated Evie's tongue with acid. This woman had worked for her. Shared breathing space on a daily basis for four months. Worse, Evie'd kind of liked her. She had a funny streak, a keen sense of irony. She must be laughing her ass off at this turn of events.

"I don't understand, Bree. How'd you get tangled up in this? I thought you were honest." She couldn't help the words that spilled forth, the anger.

Brianna flicked the cigarette butt into the bayou. "It's not personal, okay? It's just a job."

"A job that involves hurting people. *Killing* people. Did you kill David, or did someone else do it?"

Brianna laughed. "Oh God, you'd be surprised, sweetheart. But no, it wasn't me." A second later, she had the phone to her ear. "A media card. No? Thanks."

Evie's heart felt as if it would leap from her chest as Brianna slid her phone into her pocket with a scowl. "Nice try, but that's not what I want." She reached behind her and Evie stumbled back, envisioning a gun.

"Relax," Brianna said. "Got a card for you from your sister."

She handed Evie a thick white envelope, then strode past her toward the restaurant.

"Wait! What about Sarah?"

"Get what I need," she shot back. "I'll be in touch."

FOURTEEN

EVIE WAS ONLY IMMOBILIZED FOR a second. Then she sprang into action, deciding to follow Brianna. Since the only way to the parking lot was through the restaurant, maybe she could catch up with the other woman as she threaded her way through the tables and demand more information. Or maybe she could at least see how Brianna left the premises. Was someone waiting for her? What was she driving?

Evie yanked open the door, nearly colliding with a man as she rushed inside. He steadied her. When she looked up, her heart dropped into her toes. His dark eyes were alight with interest.

"The devil on your heels, Evie?"

She focused on his bulbous nose and decided he must like his liquor pretty well considering the redness of it. "Not at all, detective."

"What's that?" He gestured a stubby finger toward the envelope.

"Just a card from a friend."

"You didn't have it when you went outside."

Evie dropped the hand holding the envelope to her side. "No, I didn't. If you'll excuse me, I need to get back to my table."

His eyes narrowed as he studied her. "You know what I think?"

She almost didn't answer him, but she was frustrated at losing Brianna and pissed this guy was so smug in his opinions that he couldn't consider alternatives. "Yeah, you think I killed David because I was angry with him. And you're wrong. Instead of looking for the real killer, you're focusing on me while he's getting away." Or she. No matter what Brianna said, Evie had to consider that she was perfectly capable of murder.

Where was Matt? She hoped he'd seen her with Brianna and was following the woman right now. Maybe he'd call, telling her he'd found the place they were keeping Sarah.

"No, that's not what I'm thinking at the moment," he said patiently as if she were a child and he was explaining a very simple concept. "I'm thinking you're hiding something."

She resisted the urge to clutch the envelope to her chest and looked him square in the eye. "I think you're reaching for excuses."

"Let's assume you didn't kill David West. You're still tied to this somehow. And that's what I want to figure out—how *you* fit in."

"Hey, *chère*, sorry I took so long." Matt seemed to appear out of nowhere. He put his arm around her. "Detective, you bothering my girl?"

My girl. She loved the way that sounded. She wanted to melt into his warmth but settled for leaning into him just

227

enough to prolong the delicious contact.

Proctor looked annoyed. "Just chatting a bit."

"Hope you're finished then."

"For now."

"Good. See you around." Matt ushered her through the restaurant and out the front door. Brianna was nowhere to be seen. The crowd out front had scattered somewhat. No one looked at them twice as they hurried down the sloping plank ramp to the parking lot. Matt didn't say anything until they reached the car and stood beside it.

"Open it, Evie."

She ripped the envelope. Inside was a musical birthday card. She pulled the flap open, unsure what she'd find. There was nothing inside, no writing, no instructions. She tugged the card open farther to hear the music. Maybe that was the clue.

Except it wasn't music. It was Sarah's voice. "Evie, help me, I want to go home. Don't let them kill me. Don't call the police."

Hot tears filled Evie's eyes as Sarah's voice broke on the last word. Sick assholes!

Matt closed the distance between them, his arms going around her, squeezing as he held her close. "I'm sorry, *chère*."

"How could anyone do that? Poor Sarah's scared out of her mind." She sucked in a breath, trying not to cry. "It's all my fault."

"It's not your fault."

"If I'd been satisfied living here, if I'd never left Rochambeau, never dreamed there were bigger things—"

"It doesn't work like that, Evie, and you know it. You left because you had dreams. There's nothing wrong with that. And even if you'd stayed, you couldn't keep her safe. You can't keep anyone safe forever." He spoke with the conviction of someone who knew.

"Did you see Brianna?"

"Yeah. You know her?"

Evie pushed away from him, swiping her eyes. "She was my bartender, but I guess she was a bit more than that. Another person put in place by Rivera."

Matt looked frustrated. "I couldn't get close enough to bug her vehicle before she left. But she's driving a Chrysler sedan. Dark, blue or black maybe."

"We're back where we started, aren't we?" Hopelessness threatened to close around her throat and choke her.

"We've got the card, Evie."

"I don't see how that'll help."

He took it from her and ripped it at the seams. A small device dropped into his hand. "This is a flash media device, just like that media card. The recording is digital, so it's pretty pure. We'll load it onto the computer and send it to my guys for analysis. If we're lucky, they can isolate the background, maybe narrow down the area where your sister's being held."

She stared at him, awestruck. "This is just like one of those military techno movies, you know that? I thought they made all that stuff up."

"Not all of it."

"Next you'll tell me Elvis is alive and living in Mexico or something."

"Tahiti, actually."

Evie laughed through her tears. How did he do it? How did he make her laugh even when she was falling apart on the inside and shaking from fear? She wasn't sure, but thank God for it.

"Wait a minute," she said as he opened the car door for her. "You never asked me what happened out there when I met Brianna."

"Didn't need to." He grinned. "I saw the whole thing and heard most of it."

"But you weren't on the dock."

"No, I wasn't."

His gaze strayed up and she turned to follow it. "The roof? You were on the roof?"

"Best place to watch from. I could hear her, but not you since your back was to me."

"What if she'd pulled a gun on me, forced me into a boat?"

"I told you I wouldn't let that happen."

She decided not to ask him how he planned to get off the roof and thwart an abduction in the space of only a few seconds. It had to be twenty feet from the roof to the dock. Evie shook her head. There were some things she was probably better off not knowing.

"Let's get back to Reynier's Retreat, *chère*. If luck's on our side, we'll have this file analyzed before Brianna calls you again."

A new awareness was dawning. "We're not going to find David's files, are we?"

"Probably not. Someone knows what form they take, but they aren't sharing the information. With anyone."

"Maybe that's who was in the guesthouse when we returned, the person who knows what to look for."

She saw respect in his eyes as he nodded. It made her feel warm inside. "Yeah, that's what I think. He knows where you're staying and thought you might have the information with you. It also means he knew we'd left, which means he was watching from the bayou. He waited, in case we returned, then broke in when he deemed it safe."

"But if it was the person on the other end of the phone, he didn't get what he wanted."

"No, but he's convinced you have it... and I think he may be right."

"Mendez is asking questions, Richie."

Matt rubbed one shoulder. He was just a little stiff after pulling himself onto that slippery corrugated roof. Not that it wasn't something he was unaccustomed to doing, but sometimes his muscles protested anyway. Especially when he had a months-old gunshot wound on his side that still throbbed from time to time.

"What'd you tell him?"

"Nothing yet." Kevin MacDonald grunted. "The Kid's on board though. He knows our asses will be in a sling, but he doesn't give a good goddamn. Hawk said he'd be glad to come shoot somebody for you."

In spite of everything, Matt laughed. Hawk could blow a flea off a dog at three kilometers without hurting the dog. "Yeah, if I need someone shot, I'll call. Look, this one's more difficult, but I need you to trace a Chrysler." He gave the make and model and the possible colors. "It's probably a rental. See if you can find any cars fitting that description that have been rented in New Orleans or Baton Rouge lately. Look for a Brianna Sweeney on the rental, but don't limit it to that name. We'll expand the search if nothing appears in either of those places."

"How big you want to go?"

"These people are from California, though Sweeney was a bartender in Florida for a few months. I doubt they drove from California, so I'm thinking they must have flown in and rented it at the airport. If they'd driven from Florida, they'd have found an opportunity to intercept Evie before now."

And didn't that thought just give him a shiver? No matter how tough and resourceful Evie was, she'd have been unprepared for an ambush on the road. They could have killed her. Probably *would* have killed her to get what they wanted.

"So we'll check the airport rental counters first. It's too bad about the cell phone."

"Yeah, but maybe this digital recording will yield something." The phone Brianna and her accomplices used to communicate with Evie was a dead end. An unregistered burner that couldn't be traced. But maybe there was another way to learn something about these people. A long shot but worth a try.

"Hey, can you check David West's phone? Find out who he made calls to before he came to Rochambeau." West called Evie from phone registered to him. If he'd been in contact with his killers, and they'd been using burners, it wouldn't matter. But maybe, just maybe, there'd be something in the log Matt could make sense of. Matt didn't know why the guy wasn't using a burner too, but maybe he'd been too arrogant or cocky—or too careless—to be more careful.

"Yeah, can do. Anything else?"

Matt swallowed the lump in his throat. God, was he getting sentimental in his old age or what? After everything that had happened, these guys would still risk their asses for him without a second thought. He felt like he didn't deserve that kind of loyalty, and yet not one of them had ever pointed blame at him for what had happened to Jim and Marco. They were men, not boys, and they all knew what they'd signed on to do. Death was a constant companion in their line of work.

Matt knew it, and he knew Jim and Marco went out doing something they loved—but that didn't stop him from feeling he should have called off the mission when he'd known in his gut that it was compromised.

"Not yet," he said. "Keep me posted."

"Hoo-ah. I'll let you know if I find anything."

"Kev," he said before the other man could hang up.

"Yes, sir?"

"Thanks."

There was silence on the other end of the line for a moment. "You'd do the same for me. For any of us. We all know it."

Evie sat at the kitchen island, stirring up a batch of chocolate buttercream frosting. She was going to frost these cakes she'd just baked if it was the last sane thing she did. Because there'd been plenty of insane moments over the last few hours and she just wanted to feel normal, at least for a little while. So long as she did something she knew how to do, she didn't feel so helpless while they waited for Brianna to call back.

Matt looked up from the laptop he'd borrowed from his sister. She didn't know what he'd been doing, but he'd been silent since he'd ended his phone call with his team- mate. When they'd first returned to the house, he'd check- ed it thoroughly, creeping off to do his military thing before coming back to tell her all was clear. He'd also procured a pistol, presumably when he'd gotten the laptop. It lay beside the computer along with a box of bullets. She'd been trying not to focus on it.

"You planning to beat that bowl to death?"

"Thinking about it."

"It's only been twenty minutes."

Evie gave the frosting a vicious twist with her spoon. "Why doesn't she just call and tell me what she wants?"

"Because she doesn't know what she's looking for. She's arguing with whomever she called on the dock. And this guy—or gal—isn't being cooperative. My professional opinion."

"But they're supposed to be working together to get David's files. Ryan Rivera wants them badly enough to kill for them, so why wouldn't someone tell Brianna what she's supposed to be looking for?"

Matt leaned back on the bar chair. "I don't think it's Rivera. If he knew, he'd send her after it. No, this is someone else, someone who doesn't fully trust Brianna. Someone who wants the files pretty badly but doesn't want to negotiate for them in person. Did David have any other friends? Any girlfriends? Someone he could have told about what he'd done?"

"Not that I'm aware." Evie gave the frosting another twist. "I can't recall anyone he spoke to a lot or any strange calls. But I was running a restaurant, Matt. I was worried about menus, supplies, training my employees— things like that. I suppose he could have been selling Girl Scout cookies from the trunk of his car and I probably wouldn't have realized it."

"Girl Scout cookies?" Matt grinned at her.

Evie stopped whipping the frosting and yanked a cake toward her. "I hate to think about anything worse, so allow me my fantasy, okay?"

Not to mention she was still angry with herself for not figuring out what David had been up to sooner. Didn't matter how good he was or how well he hid his tracks, she just felt like she should have known he wasn't the nice guy he pretended to be.

"Sure." His sudden smile could've melted an ice cube. "But tell me what other kind of fantasies you think about."

A tendril of heat uncoiled in her belly. She found herself thinking about licking chocolate frosting off his tight abs, about him moving deep inside her again. She wanted to forget everything and lose herself with Matt for an hour or so.

But she couldn't. Not when so much was at stake. Not when she needed to have her mind in a different place, needed to be prepared to deal with a killer.

"I can't, Matt. Later, when this is over—"

"I know." He got to his feet, stretched. "Can't blame me for trying."

"No." She spread a dollop of frosting across the top of a cake, searched for a way out of the awkwardness she suddenly felt. "I'm sorry I'm keeping you away from your family. But if you weren't here, I don't know how I'd deal with this."

"It's okay. Chris is busy with the wedding preparations and the senator and I don't have a lot to say to each other."

Evie smoothed the frosting methodically. "He isn't interested in what you do in the military?"

"No."

She stopped. "Does he mind what you do?"

"Yeah, he does. But it's not his choice."

"It's dangerous, isn't it?" She'd known, especially as the evening went on and she'd listened to his conversations with his teammate, but she hadn't wanted to really think about it. If she were honest with herself, she'd known it from the moment he'd disarmed Jimmy Thibodeaux and broke his arm. "You do dangerous things."

He pushed both hands over his head and laced them together behind his neck. His breath let out on a long sigh. "I go to some pretty bad places. There's always a chance I won't come back."

Evie nearly dropped the spatula. A twist of dark emotion grabbed her heart and wouldn't let go. "Won't come back? As in ever?" She couldn't say *dead*. She couldn't think it.

"Precisely."

Horror gripped her by the throat and squeezed. How could he? How could he risk himself that way? And yet he'd been shot. She knew it because she'd seen the red and puckered scar on his torso. And the smaller scars that marred his perfect skin in places. "Why would you do that? Why would someone like you do that?"

The look he gave her was gently mocking. "You think people born into privilege shouldn't serve their country since they have the means to do other things? Should it only be the poor or disadvantaged who risk their lives?"

"I didn't mean that." Her heart ached.

"Yes, you did."

Okay, probably she did. But it was unfathomable. If she'd had his background, his money and access, she wouldn't be in this predicament right now. She'd have never listened to a jerk like David, never got entangled in anything remotely dangerous. She'd be running a chain of Evangeline's, flying from city to city to oversee her business, spending time in a test kitchen making up new recipes. Life would be so good.

Or would it?

Did money really make anyone happy? Clearly, it didn't make Matt happy. He'd always been restless. The summer he'd been fourteen, he'd stolen his daddy's car and talked her into going on a joyride with him. They'd gone to Baton Rouge and back, and no one ever figured out they were missing. Because he'd had a plan.

She'd never stopped to think about it then, but she knew looking back that he'd always had that daredevil streak. And it suddenly made more sense than she would have liked that he risked his life in the military.

"I would have made different choices if I had your resources." She frosted the cake a bit more viciously than necessary. "I'm sorry if that offends you, but I refuse to believe there isn't a better way to contribute to society, if that's what you want to do."

His expression grew hard. Hidden pain flared in his eyes. She wanted to go over and put her arms around him, but she knew he wouldn't welcome it. Not right now. She'd crossed a line and he was angry with her for it. It wouldn't be the first time. She'd pissed him off plenty when they were kids.

Except this wasn't an issue for kids. It was serious, frightening, and she hadn't yet figured out how to reconcile it in her head.

"I wouldn't change what I'm doing for anyone." He said it coolly, and her head snapped up to meet his gaze. There was steel in those eyes.

She got the hint. Not that she'd expected there was a future with him, but it might be nice if it were at least a possibility if it was something they both wanted. Clearly, Matt didn't even want to think about it.

Well, dammit, neither did she. She had things to do, and Matt didn't figure into any of them. "It must be a lonely life."

"Sometimes."

She moved the spatula against the cake more gently, smoothing the thick frosting while her heart skipped. She hated the idea of him in some foreign country, dying, and her never knowing about it until it was too late. They'd spent the last ten years not being in touch, but now that they were, she knew the love she'd always felt—and by that she meant the love of a friend for another friend—had never disappeared.

You didn't stop loving someone you'd been attached to for so much of your life, even when you'd had a falling out. You always grieved the friendship lost. And now that she had him in her life again, she didn't want to lose that connection.

He reached for her hand and grasped it gently in his until she looked up at him again. "I'm sorry, Evie."

She shrugged, though she felt anything but light-hearted. "For what? You don't have to explain yourself or apologize. I was out of line."

"No, but it came as a shock to you. I shouldn't have told you that what I do is dangerous."

She laughed. It wasn't a humorous sound. "I think I already knew that, Matt. It's kinda obvious to someone who saw you in action last night, and then again just now at Charlie's."

"Chris doesn't know. I'd rather she didn't."

Evie swallowed the lump in her throat. "She won't hear it from me. But you were captured, Matt. She knows that."

"Yeah, but I'm back now. She has no idea that kind of thing could happen every time I go out with my team."

"And your father?"

He looked down at the counter for a long moment. "I don't think he'd care either way."

She squeezed his hand. "I think he would."

"You're a sweetheart, Evie. Always have been. But the senator and I don't get along very well. I think you know that."

They both knew what he was talking about. The time shortly before his mother had died when the senator had come out into the garden and railed at him for tracking dirt through the house. Evie had cringed on the garden seat where she'd been playing and pretended not to hear. That was the first time she'd realized that Matt's life wasn't perfect.

After that, there were many times when Matt had been red-faced and sullen. Usually, after an hour or so, he was himself again. After his mother had died, Evie's trips to Reynier's Retreat became more infrequent. He had come to her then. Until, one day, he noticed other girls and hadn't come anymore.

She set the spatula down and licked chocolate from her thumb. Then she reached up and skimmed her fingers over his cheek. "I do know. And you'll just have to forgive me for caring what happens to you, okay? I won't tell Chris, but I also won't stop worrying about you either."

He caught her fingers and sucked the tips into his mouth while she felt the sensual tug all the way down to her sex. "I don't deserve your worry, Evie. I betrayed our friendship."

She sighed. "Maybe we both did. I shouldn't have asked you to be my first. That was the first step over the line."

He growled and pulled her toward him until she was standing between his legs. "I'm glad I was your first. I just wish I'd taken more care with your heart."

His mouth fitted over hers and she melted into him. They kissed for a long minute, but then a phone rang and she jumped away from him, scrambling for the phone she'd laid on the island. But it wasn't her phone ringing.

Matt put his phone to his ear, his voice clipped as he spoke. "Yeah."

She watched his face as surprise crossed his features. "What? You're kidding... You got a vector on that? ... Holy fuck, yeah." He cradled the phone against his shoulder, checked the safety on the gun before stuffing it into his waistband. Then he grabbed the bullets and motioned for her to follow. "All right, let me know if there's any change. … I'm on my way."

"What is it?"

"Someone just made a call from David West's cell phone."

Evie gaped at him. "How is that possible? Didn't the police get his phone last night?"

"Apparently not. Kev's got a lock on the location, so we need to get moving."

"Where are we going?" she asked as they hurried out to the garage and slipped into the car.

Matt gunned the engine to life. "Your mother's house."

FIFTEEN

"IS THIS LEGAL?" EVIE ASKED as the trees whipped by for the second time that night.

"Speeding? Only if we don't get caught."

"I meant the military tracking civilians. It seems, well, questionable."

"Are you complaining?"

"Of course not! I'm just amazed, is all."

"That it can be done or that we're doing it now?"

"Both I guess. How'd you get your bosses to let you do something like this? It's not like we're on a military operation."

He shot her a glance. "Who said I asked permission?"

Her blood thickened in her veins and her breath shortened. "I don't understand how it's possible in the first place. Don't you need to be on the phone with someone to track them?"

He shook his head. "Not these days. All cell phones are equipped with GPS trackers—it's how emergency personnel find you if you call 911 and don't know where you are. We're using the same principle to track West's phone. Someone has it and they're using it. Good for us, bad for them."

"It could always be one of the cops, right? Maybe they just found it—"

"They've been done with the crime scene investigation since this afternoon. Whoever it is, it's not the police."

Evie tried to digest this information. Someone had David's phone and was making calls from it. Someone who'd taken it from him after they killed him. If that wasn't creepy, she didn't know what was. "What if your boss finds out? What then?"

"Believe me, I sincerely hope he doesn't. I imagine my stay at Fort Leavenworth will be of some duration."

Her heart felt as if it had slipped into her toes. "Leavenworth?"

"It's a military prison."

"My God, Matt, I know what it is. You can't be serious!"

"Dead serious, *chère*."

"You can't do this." She was trembling from fear and adrenaline. She needed him, needed his expertise, and yet he was risking his entire career to help her. She felt distinctly unworthy in that moment. And grateful too. "It's not worth the risk for you."

"It is for Sarah."

Evie pressed a hand to her mouth as she stared at the neighborhood lights blurring by. How could he risk such a thing? He could've turned this over to the police—surely they could do these things legally and find Sarah's kidnappers without alerting anyone. Without endangering Sarah.

But he hadn't. He was risking everything—his life,

his future, his career—to help her find Sarah and bring her home safe. Insanely, she didn't want him to do it. Didn't want him to take such a chance. And yet she needed him to. But she cared too much—

"Evie, look at me."

Matt's handsome face was in profile, his concentration on the road as he shifted the car into one of those killer turns of his. She barely registered the sliding, braking, leveling action as she instinctively braced herself for it.

He shot her a glance. "I chose to do this, okay? If I go to prison, it's not your fault. It's the culmination of several things. I make my choices in full understanding and acceptance of the consequences. Got that?"

Her lip trembled. "Yes. But Matt, if this is because of what happened in high school—"

"It's not." His voice was strong and firm. "This is what I do, Evie. I rescue people. And I can't stand by and let something happen to Sarah when I'm capable of doing something about it. I'll deal with the consequences later. For now, your sister is what matters."

She felt like she was going to cry, and that was the last thing she needed to be doing right now. She didn't speak for the rest of the ride as she tried to keep a lid on her emotions. Soon, they approached her mother's street and Matt slowed. He switched off the headlights as he made the turn and then brought the car to a stop about thirty yards from the driveway. She could see flashes of the white clapboard house between the trees. Everything seemed still and quiet. No lights winked from the windows, no cars passed by, though a truck was parked near the Landrys' driveway facing toward the BMW. There was no one inside.

"I want you to stay here," Matt said. "It's safer."

"But, what if—"

"Evie." He sounded grave. "Trust me on this. I know what I'm doing."

"I'm not really thrilled about sitting out here alone."

"Get into the driver's seat and keep the engine idling. Don't unlock the doors for anyone but me. If anyone tries to get in, gun it. Don't think twice, don't worry about running someone over or wrecking this car, just go. I'll meet you at Charlie's. If you haven't heard from me in an hour, call Kev MacDonald. Give me your cell phone."

She handed it to him. "Matt—"

"I'm not arguing about it." He punched in a number, handed it back to her. "It's saved under your speed dial. Hit three and Kev will answer."

She grabbed his arm, panic flaring inside her belly. "This isn't what I thought was going to happen."

"You promised me earlier tonight that you'd stay put when I told you to."

Damn him for remembering that right now. She sucked in a breath. It all seemed so much more intense now that she knew he risked death on a regular basis. Not that it hadn't already been intense, but it was somehow worse knowing that. "I'm not waiting an hour. Fifteen minutes. If you aren't back then, I'm driving up to the house."

"Jesus God." He wiped a hand over his hair and down his face. "Why can't you just cooperate? You have any idea what would happen to one of the guys if they dis-obeyed a direct order from me?"

She firmed her jaw. No way could she blindly do

what he told her. Not when he was risking so much. "If I *was* one of the guys, you'd be taking me with you. So forget it. Fifteen minutes, and I'm coming up that driveway."

"Thirty minutes. B and E takes time."

"Twenty. Not a second more."

He sat there, just looking at her. If he thought she was going to be intimidated by his Mr. Bad Ass Military Man act, he was wrong. There was too much at stake. His life, for instance. If anything happened to him, she didn't know what she'd do. He didn't have to do this, didn't have to help her. But he was, and because of it she found the strength to return his hard stare until he got that she meant business.

Finally, when she didn't back off, he nodded. "Twenty."

He reached for the gun he'd tucked into the side pocket of the door and lifted the handle.

"Wait," Evie said, her heart hammering.

He turned back to her and she leaned forward, curled her palm around his neck, and pressed her mouth to his. She kissed him with all the heat and fire, all the frustration, that was boiling inside her. He grinned at her when she pulled back.

"I'm looking forward to a whole lot more of that when I get back, Evangeline."

When he got back. *When* not *if.*

"As much as you want."

His grin still managed to be wicked in spite of the gravity of the situation. "Remember that. Showtime, Evie." His door ghosted open and he melted into the night.

Evie straddled the gearshift and maneuvered over to

the driver's seat. It took her a few moments of reaching around to finally locate the buttons to slide the seat forward. If she had to make a getaway now, she'd be in a lot of trouble since her feet didn't even touch the pedals. The seat motored slowly forward until she felt comforttable. She adjusted the mirrors, checked the dash clock. He'd been gone three minutes.

Seventeen to go. Oh God. How did he do this kind of thing on a regular basis?

She peered into the darkness, tried to discern any movement. He'd disappeared too quickly for her to follow his progress. He could be anywhere out there. She checked the mirrors and craned her head around to see if someone was sneaking up behind the car. She dropped a hand to the gearshift, ready for anything. She felt vaguely like she had her junior year when she and some friends toilet-papered the principal's house at one in the morning. Exhilarated, frightened, and wanting it to be over with all at once.

Yeah, she was ready for anything.

Anything except the huge flash that lit up the sky.

The explosion was similar to a flash-bang, all bright light and deafening kaboom. Matt was in the process of slipping from the giant magnolia in the side yard to a moss-draped oak about ten feet farther on when the house exploded. The shockwave knocked him on his ass with the force of a heavyweight punch. Only hard-won experience allowed him to tuck his head and twist to the side as the force lifted him off the ground.

He landed hard, his elbow and shoulder driving into the earth. The wind got knocked out of him and the heat of the blast felt like it was sucking any remaining air he may have had out of his lungs. He knew he had to get away from the flaming debris as fast as possible.

If hot ash didn't burn a hole in him, whoever'd set the charge could find him. Not that he knew anyone was looking, but it wasn't a chance he wanted to take. He shoved away the pain and forced his good arm forward, dug his fingers into the grass and dirt, and pulled, his legs remembering to propel him at the last possible second when his muscles were screaming, and he was sure his body wasn't going to move.

One-armed, he pulled himself back by degrees into the cover of the trees. He'd find a place to hole up until his head stopped spinning, then make his way to Charlie's. He'd told Evie to go there because the place was so public. He figured she'd be safe if she stayed until he could get to her. He could've sent her back to Reynier's Retreat, but no telling what might be waiting for her there.

Somehow, he managed to get his legs beneath him. Levered upward, a tree trunk at his back. The world spun. He dragged in a breath, then another. Pushed farther up until he was standing. His legs shook beneath him, threatening to drop him again.

He refused to let it happen.

He had to get out of here, had to find Evie. Had to protect her.

The sound of tires crunching on gravel and bleached clamshells reached him through the ringing in his ears. He flattened against the tree and made himself a part of the trunk. The car was coming fast, gravel spitting and plinking against the sheet metal. Brakes locked up and the car skidded to a halt. A door opened.

"Matt?"

Fucking A.

His heart plummeted to his feet at the same time a swell of adrenaline pumped through his veins. He had to get her out of here. Someone could grab her and take her away from him.

Hurt her.

Though it hurt like a sonofabitch, he stumbled away from the trunk, swaying unsteadily in the glowing light of the fire eating the house.

Evie was backlit by the flame, her body in shadow. He couldn't tell whether she was looking at him or at the house.

"I told you to go," he croaked into the thick air.

She spun around and gasped. And then he found himself wrapped up in a bear hug, her lips raining kisses onto his cheek, his jaw, his lips.

He grasped her, spreading his fingers along the small of her back. He wanted to hold her, just hold her.

The kisses felt so good, so sweet. Nothing like what usually happened on an op. He turned his mouth into hers and said against her lips, "Have to go. Now."

She shifted his weight until he was leaning on her, then hauled him around to the passenger side of the car until he could fall inside. "Get in," he said when she tried to fuss and help him get settled.

She ran around the car and hopped in, shifting into reverse. Gears ground together, then smoothed out when she found the groove.

"Where… going?" He spoke through the soup in his mind when she pointed the car opposite of the direction they'd come.

She shot him an incredulous look. "The hospital."

Matt grabbed her arm. "Marina."

Evie shifted the car and shook her head emphatically. "No way. You're hurt. I'm taking you to the hospital."

"Not hurt. Stunned. It'll pass."

"Yeah, well, I'll feel better when a doctor tells me that."

She glanced up, frowned, and stepped on the gas.

"Evie—"

"No." The car leapt forward with a short burst of speed. "We're doing it my way this time." She glanced up again. "Uh oh."

"What?"

"I think we're being followed."

"Cop?"

"I don't think so. Wouldn't they have tried to pull us over by now?"

Matt blinked against the fuzziness crowding his head. It would go away, he knew, but it was going to take time. Time they didn't have.

But she was right. The police wouldn't waste time following them. They'd turn on the lights and make them pull over. If someone was pursuing them, it was a sure bet it was someone they didn't *want* coming after them.

Helluva time for it. He couldn't take the wheel, couldn't drive.

He swallowed a wave of dizziness and made himself turn around to look at their pursuer.

"Take a left at Robbins." First, he had to determine if they were really being followed or if this was just a coincidence. But what kind of person drove past a flaming house in the dark and didn't stop to look? Especially in Rochambeau where everyone knew everyone else?

Evie didn't signal, even though he forgot to tell her not to. She waited until they were almost upon Robbins Road when she slammed on the brake and whipped the car left.

The headlights behind them slid sideways for a second, then straightened out, aiming toward them once more.

"Hit the gas," Matt ordered.

Evie complied, and the car shot forward. The car behind them did the same.

He knew they needed to do something, a sequence of somethings in fact, but it wouldn't quite come to him.

Think of a route.

Yes, that was part of it.

Turns, stops, slides.

Right. He knew intimately what a car could do, how to push it to its limits, how to make it do things that seemed, if only briefly, to defy gravity. But he wasn't the one driving.

"Whatever you do," he said, concentrating on the words, "don't panic."

She laughed without humor. "Easy for you to say." She glanced up. "I think we need to get to the police station. He won't follow us there."

"No. He'll try to force you off the road before that."

"Robbins crosses Old Oak Road. If we make a right there, it'll take us straight to the PD."

There was a reason not to take Old Oak, but he couldn't remember what it was. Something stuck in his mind, something he couldn't pull up from the depths where it was buried.

"No."

"If you have a better idea, then tell me." Her voice was sharp, demanding.

He couldn't think. He lifted a hand to his head, pressing against his temples. Sweat beaded on his skin. He needed time.

The one thing they didn't have.

"Matt?"

"No." He wasn't sure what he was saying no to, in fact, but she didn't seem troubled by any doubt.

"Right." She pressed the gas pedal. He leaned his head back on the seat and closed his eyes. A few seconds later she said, "Hang on."

The car shifted sideways as the seat belt grabbed on and held him tightly against the leather. She swerved hard, the car bumping crazily as they slid across the road and into the grass on the left shoulder. The engine whined and the tires spun as she crammed her foot against the pedal. The sickening smell of burning rubber filled the interior.

"Ease up." He wasn't sure if he'd spoken aloud until the car began to move as she backed off the gas a bit. "Where'd he go?"

She got the car pointed toward town and they picked up speed.

"Still behind us. He overshot the turn, but I see headlights again."

She'd actually widened the distance between them, though not by much. Still, he was impressed she'd managed it. For an amateur, it wasn't half-bad driving. If she could keep the distance, they'd make it. There were no more turns to negotiate since Old Oak went straight past the station.

There were no lights out here on the back roads, no oncoming cars, nothing but the sweep of the xenon lights in front of the BMW. A rabbit darted off the road up ahead and Matt cast a glance at Evie. She gripped the wheel hard, concentrating on the asphalt in front of her. He had the feeling she'd run over anything that got in their way, and that was a good thing at this point. No time for squeamishness if another rabbit crossed too close to avoid.

"Holy crap." Her voice was soft at first, then louder. "Holy crap!"

Matt whipped his gaze back to the road and reeled when his head turned faster than his eyes could focus, then steeled himself against the stab of a headache.

"What is it?" He was subtly aware she'd backed off the gas.

"The bridge is out."

Fuck. The thing he couldn't remember. The fact that this small country bridge over an insignificant creek was often washed out. That there'd been a thunderstorm and flash flooding only last week, according to Chris. That it was a good bet the bridge was out.

He could jump it. If he was driving, he could do it. Wouldn't be the first time he'd had to do something like this.

But he wasn't driving. And he didn't think he could talk her through it. It wasn't safe, and it wasn't something to attempt for the first time. They could end up in the creek, sitting ducks for the guy behind them. The impact would stun them, stun him even worse, and he didn't think he needed a new concussion on top of another one.

"Don't slack off," he said automatically when the car slowed even more.

"What the hell do you expect me to do? Jump it?"

"No." His mushy brain drew up every ounce of strength he had and channeled it into thought. "We're going to turn, Evie. A one-eighty. You with me?"

"Tell me what to do."

"You've done power slides, right?" Every kid in the parish had locked up the brakes and slid to a sideways stop on gravel roads. It was considered fun when he was growing up.

"Not since high school."

"It works similar, okay." A pain stabbed him behind the right eye. "But we're not going to use the emergency brake. Instead, when I tell you, I want you to brake enough to shift down to second and turn the wheel hard left. It's important to shift and turn at the same time. No brake at that point, okay?"

"Matt—"

"You can do it, Evie. The car will slide around until we're going the opposite direction. Don't hit the brake, or we'll stop somewhere short of the turn. We'll lose valuable time trying to get going again. Soon as we stop, shift down and hammer it."

"Okay."

"First, we gotta let him catch up a bit. But don't let him get too close to the rear bumper. He'll try to pit you."

"Pit?"

"He'll tap the bumper and send you out of control. Don't let it happen."

Her chin dipped down in a firm nod. "Got it."

Matt focused on the road, on the signs indicating the bridge was out. Five hundred feet to go. He glanced around and saw the car behind them gaining. He watched the road ahead, making the calculations, not sure if his brain was functioning right or if he was off. But he didn't have the luxury of double-checking himself.

He was a member of HOT for God's sake. He'd had enough training he could make this turn with his eyes closed. Now he just had to trust that he could count it off right for Evie.

Another glance behind them revealed a truck, not a car. Two people inside, it looked like, except the headlights were high enough as they got closer that the beam shot into his eyes, intensifying the pain in his head so that he wasn't really sure what he'd seen.

"Ten, nine, eight," he said, counting it out, giving her warning. "Brake and shift," he said, finishing the count. She hit it hard, the engine roaring with the sudden change. "Turn it now!"

The back end of the car swung hard right, pivoting beneath them even as the entire car slid through the turn. Tires squealed against asphalt, rubber smoking through the vents and grabbing him by the throat. His head felt like cotton candy, fluffy and ungrounded, and he was grateful for the belt wedging him into the seat as the bile rose in his throat.

The BMW snapped to a stop as the taillights of the truck flew past the driver's side.

He meant to tell her to go, but he couldn't get the words out. He'd used every bit of energy he had dredging up the last few minutes of conversation from his psyche.

He could only stare at her face, seemingly paler in the dash lights. She lifted a shaking hand and choked out something that sounded like *holy shit*. And then she was springing into action, her hand falling to the gearshift as the wheels squealed and the car sprang forward.

"I think they went into the ditch," she finally said, shoving the hair from her face with a hand that still shook. "But I don't know."

"Marina." He forced the word out, past the thickness settling once more in his head.

"What about the police? Maybe we should get them involved now. Maybe they have Sarah in that truck and we can get her back if they're in the ditch—"

"Marina. Go."

He thought for sure she was about to argue, and he dreaded it since he couldn't imagine holding out against the verbal onslaught that would very persuasively convince him they needed to go to the police or the hospital. He'd find himself saying yes even though he knew he shouldn't agree. Sarah's life—and Evie's—depended on him figuring this out, and he couldn't do that if he was explaining to Chief Laurent how he happened to be near the house when it exploded. Because that's all the cops would be interested in right now, guaran-damn-tee it.

Evie gave him a look that tore his heart from his chest and turned him inside out at the same time. It was a look of anger, concern, and more tenderness than he'd ever remembered seeing in any one person in his life. It struck him at that moment how very like him she was in some ways. And how very much he liked that about her.

"I'm trusting you," she said. "Don't make me regret it."

SIXTEEN

THE ADRENALINE RUSH WAS SEEPING away, leaving Evie tired, shaky, and yet oddly awake at the same time. Matt didn't say anything more as she navigated the car across town. She didn't want to go to the marina. It seemed contrary to all common sense, yet Matt had talked her through the kind of daredevil driving that only an hour ago she'd have sworn she couldn't do without a whole lot of practice and nerves of steel. For that alone, she'd give him the benefit of the doubt.

But only for so long.

She kept a wary check on the rearview mirror, but no headlights seemed to be following. There was a car here and there, but nothing consistent, and nothing gaining fast. She still couldn't believe what had happened. One minute she was waiting, jumpy as a cat, and the next there was an explosion. She hadn't even thought twice about what to do. She'd gunned the car up the drive, panicked that Matt was in the middle of the blast. When she saw the house with one side of it blown away, her insides melted. She hadn't thought Matt would answer her, but she'd gotten out of the car and called for him anyway.

When he'd spoken, she'd never been so relieved in her life. She glanced over at him, her heart twisting at the sight of his head lying back against the seat, his eyes closed, his brows drawn low in pain. She'd give him time to explain, but if she didn't like the plan, she comforted herself with the idea she could summon an ambulance with a quick phone call.

The marina entrance was up ahead on the right. She took the turn and slowly drove through the lot, winding back toward the dock where the Girards kept their boat. She drove past a row of whitewashed buildings. The lake stretched out dark as spilled paint to the right before another set of buildings sprang up to block the view.

"Inside there." Matt pointed to a low building with a large double door that faced the road.

"I remember." She pulled the car in front of the white clapboard structure, the headlights focusing on a rusted chain stretching from one handle to the other. A shiny padlock dangled in the middle of the entrance. "It's locked."

The passenger door slipped open. She turned as Matt stuck a leg out. Gravel crunched beneath his boot. He folded back against the seat like a popped balloon.

"Matt—"

"I'm fine."

"I don't think—"

He pulled himself from the car, surprisingly agile compared to a moment ago, and her speech died in her throat. He took something from the knife case on his belt and bent down to fiddle with the lock. A minute later, it popped free. Then he threw the doors wide and Evie drove inside.

She brought the car to a halt and let out a breath before turning off the engine and getting out to join Matt. He'd closed the entry behind them and was hunkered down in front of a long table that sat against one wall. Evie stumbled forward, calling herself ten kinds of a fool for listening to him in the first place. She should have taken him to the hospital, no matter what he said.

When she would have dropped to her knees and wrapped her arms around him, she ground to a heart-pounding halt. Matt glanced at her over his shoulder. He had one long arm stretched beneath the table. Slowly, he ran his hand back and forth beneath the surface.

And then he stopped and smiled. "Found it."

"Found what?"

He levered himself upward. In his left hand was a key.

"I put this here when I was sixteen. Figured the old man would have found it by now."

"You hid a key to your dad's boat?" She felt slightly hurt that she hadn't known that, but by the time he was sixteen, they hadn't been hanging out together anymore. He'd had a jealous girlfriend and they'd grown apart.

He gave her a grin. "Party boy, remember?"

"So we're hiding on the boat for a while?" Because she really didn't want to consider the alternative—that he intended to take the Girard yacht out into the pitch-dark night.

"We're going out."

Evie swallowed a bubble of panic. After everything else, she couldn't just jump on his daddy's yacht and sail off into the lake like her childhood home hadn't recently exploded. What the hell were they doing here? They should be at the hospital making sure Matt wasn't injured worse than he thought.

"Come on." He turned away from her and headed toward a door at the back of the garage.

"I'm not comfortable with this, Matt."

He threw a look over his shoulder.

Evie's resolve strengthened. "I've pretty much done everything so far without complaint, but I want to know what you think we're going to accomplish out there."

He turned around, hands on hips. "Without complaint?"

"Without *much* complaint," she amended, ignoring his smirk. She gestured toward the water, praying he didn't read anything more into it than a determination to know what was going on. And her concern really *was* about the best choice for the situation and not her fear of being on the water.

"Why is this better than going to the police with all we know? Or to the hospital? My God, Matt, someone blew up my mother's house! What more can we do? I'm scared to death for Sarah, and I know they told us not to contact the police, but no one's called us back and someone just tried to kill us."

"Listen." He came to stand in front of her. She had to tilt her head up to look at him and realized for the first time that soot darkened his cheekbones and forehead. That his pupils were dilated. "We can't stop now."

Her heart ached with the need to touch him, to draw him to her and hold him until the world faded away. He touched her cheek, and she turned into his hand, feeling his fingers skim along her jawbone and behind her ear.

Sensation streaked to her fingertips, then down into her toes. Desire tugged at her.

"You're hurt," she said softly.

"It's a concussion. A mild one. This isn't my first time." He let out a sigh when she gave in to the urge to touch him in return. "Evie, I don't trust anyone right now. And I don't know what's going on or how many of them there are, so I want us out on that lake, maybe even hidden in the bayou. I want time to take some Tylenol, rest, and think. I also want to talk to Kev. If Brianna calls you, we'll decide what's next. But for now, this is best. Trust me."

Unshed tears clogged her throat. She hated that he was hurting. Hated that he was probably right. "This is all so new to me, Matt. I'm a chef, not a secret agent. I don't want to go out there and have something happen to you because I should have taken you to the hospital instead of blindly following orders."

He dipped his lips to hers, a brief caress that sent a shiver through her. "Trust me. All I need is Tylenol. Unless you've got some in your pocket, *Candyland* has a whole medicine chest full. And you have yet to blindly follow orders, believe me."

Evie clutched him. "Promise that if you feel worse, you'll tell me. That you'll agree to come back in and go to the doctor."

"I don't have a death wish. I promise we'll come back if I don't feel better."

She swallowed. "Let's go then."

God, he was about to take her out on the lake. In the dark. But at least it'd be on board a thirty-six-foot Carver and not in a tiny pirogue. She could handle that.

Right.

No, dammit, she *would* handle it. She'd just spun an über-expensive sports car into a one-eighty at sixty miles an hour, so what was a little night boating compared to that? She'd been fine with boats until she and Julie had turned theirs over and nearly drowned. This boat was *not* going to turn over.

"I hope you don't expect me to drive," she grumbled to his back. The thought of ramming a several-hundred-thousand-dollar yacht—give or take a few bucks—into a cypress tree somewhere was just a little too much to contemplate.

"I can manage." He stopped and unlocked a door that spilled them onto the dock. A few steps away, the gleaming white Carver rocked gently against the pylons.

Matt climbed on board first, then turned and held out his hand for her. It was an easy step from the dock to the boat, but he must have sensed something of her hesitation. She stared at the small gap between the boat and the solid pier she stood on before raising her gaze to Matt's face. He smiled.

"I won't let anything happen to you, Evie. You're safe with me."

She put her hand in his and stepped lightly onto the deck. Matt squeezed her to him for a quick second, and then turned toward the narrow steps that led up to the command bridge.

"You can go inside if you want. I'll get us out a ways before coming below."

"No, I'm coming up." No way was she letting him out of her sight just yet. He seemed better, steadier on his feet, and he was talking in more complete sentences than before. She climbed up the steps behind him. He started the yacht while she took the seat beside his.

The boat eased backward from the slip as she gazed toward the shore. The marina was hopping tonight, as was usual for a Friday. Folks partied on a houseboat a few slips away, strains of rock music and laughter drifting onto the night air. In spite of the drama of last night—my God, was it really only last night?—a group of people were up at the pavilion, sitting at the tables, hovering by the grills, and generally doing what folks always did at Rochambeau Lake.

"We're going to be noticed. You can't take a boat this big out, even in the dark, and not be," she said, gazing at Matt's profile, the strong lines of his chin and nose. He was so stubborn and so determined. Very much the Matt she'd always known.

He glanced at her. "It's a chance we have to take. We're still better off if we're somewhere hard to track, and unless these guys are local, they can't know this water like I do. We'll be fine once we're away from here."

They rode in silence as the lights of the marina receded into the background. A cool breeze ruffled her hair. It wasn't so bad out here after all. The yacht was big enough she didn't feel confined or like she was mere inches from being plunged into the water. She refused to think about sinking. Boats didn't sink without good reason.

Senator Girard's yacht was not going to sink, dammit.

"Did you get into the house?" she asked, tucking a strand of hair behind her ear. She figured there hadn't been enough time, but anything was possible with him.

"No. It blew before I got there."

"So you didn't see anyone who could have been using David's phone."

"No."

"None of this makes any sense to me. Why would they blow up the house?"

"To hide evidence."

Evie turned sideways to stare at him. A horrible thought began to take shape in her head. "To hide a body, you mean."

"It's possible, but it's not a terribly good way to go about it. Hell, far better to take a body out in the bayou and feed it to the gators."

"What then?"

"I wish I knew. But it was a stupid thing to do. It could also be competitors."

"Someone else after the files?"

"It's possible."

She didn't want to contemplate the possibility of another person, or persons, after David's files. Brianna had Sarah and that's what Evie cared most about. She had to get Sarah back, but every minute that went by without a call leached a little more hope away.

She'd brought death and destruction to Rochambeau when she'd come back home. She might have her issues with this town, but the plain fact was that she loved it anyway. And she was pissed that someone was defiling it.

They glided through the water for about half an hour before Matt cut the engine and dropped anchor. She couldn't tell where he'd taken them, but she followed him down the ladder and into the interior of the yacht. She'd never been on this yacht before.

She stopped in the doorway, her foot on the first stair. "Wow. Impressive."

Cherry surfaces gleamed everywhere she looked—the

cabinets, the table, the shelves, a built-in area with a flat-panel television, and all the trim throughout. Granite counters, a small wine refrigerator, stainless sink, micro-wave, fridge, and a small electric cooktop filled the kitchen area. The floors were cherry too, and the banquette running along one wall was leather. So was the booth with table opposite. There was a window above the banquette and puck lights inset into the ceiling. At the end of the room, a door led into a bedroom containing what looked like a queen-sized bed.

Evie took the steps down to join Matt. He stood in the kitchen, opened a cabinet, and pulled out a First Aid kit. "You've never been on board before?"

Evie crossed her arms. "No. I think you were dating Belle Landry when your dad bought this, and we both know how she felt about me."

He flashed her a pained smile. "Yeah, sorry about that."

He opened a bottle he'd found in the kit and shook four tablets into his hand. After he popped them into his mouth, he opened the gleaming fridge and grabbed a bottle of water. He chased the pills with a swig, then came over and flopped onto the banquette. He leaned back, his eyes closing briefly.

She sat at the table, sighing as she sank into the cushion. It'd been a long couple of days. And they weren't done yet.

"So you were never on board *Candyland*." He rolled his head from side to side, taking in the glossy interior. "She's a beauty, just like her namesake."

"Stepmama number two, right?"

He'd spoken with an edge of bitterness, but she knew

better than to expect she'd get to the root of it. One thing about Matt Girard—he was about as open as a padlocked chest when he wanted to keep his secrets close.

He snorted and took another swig of water. "Yeah. Lucky number two."

Evie's brow furrowed as she contemplated him. She'd known his mother's death had been hard on him, and she'd known he resented the first woman his father had married afterward. But they hadn't really talked about it. The senator had remarried within the year, and Matt had been bitter about it. She hadn't blamed him at all.

By the time Senator Girard had married his second Playboy Bunny wannabe wife, Matt didn't like to talk about it and she hadn't known how he felt anymore. Now, looking at him, she realized it was no wonder he'd played the womanizing jock so well in school—he'd had a fine example in his own father.

"So why didn't your father rename the boat when they divorced? It must be kind of difficult bringing new wives here and having to explain the name."

Matt laughed softly. "First of all, it's bad luck to rename a boat. And second, the old man doesn't much care about sparing feelings, *chère*. Neither did Candy, for that matter."

"You didn't like her much, huh?"

The look he gave her was unguarded, full of emotion. It shocked her, considering how good he usually was at shuttering the things he felt. It made her curious and strangely uncomfortable at the same time.

"What the hell." He said it more to himself than to her. He speared her with a look that pinned her in place. His eyes gleamed bright in his soot-darkened face. Bright and hard as diamonds. "I thought I loved her."

Evie's heart thudded painfully. "You mean—?"

"Yeah." He swallowed the rest of the water. "I'd just turned sixteen. Candy was twenty-two. She thought it'd be a nice revenge on the old man, I think. Either that or she got off on the idea of screwing us both. Didn't matter though because I thought it was true love. Planned to run away together."

Evie swallowed. She had no idea. "What happened?"

Matt shrugged. "He gave her a divorce settlement that made her happy, so she left. Told me to grow up and get over it."

"My God, what a rotten thing to do to a kid. You were only sixteen."

He was looking at her intently. "No worse than what I did to you."

Evie went over and sat beside him, threading her fingers through his. "No, Matt, it's much worse. She was an adult. She took advantage of your feelings for her and your inexperience."

She'd been so jealous of Belle and all the other girls he'd paid attention to back then. Little had she known.

His thumb traced a circle on the underside of her wrist. "I know. Though believe me, sleeping with a stripper was pretty much a fantasy come true at that age."

Heat flared beneath her skin. She cleared her throat, trying to focus. "Did your father know?"

"I'm not sure, but I doubt it. I don't think the old man could have kept it to himself had he known. I can't imagine why she didn't tell him. It would have been just like her to set us against each other. I guess she figured we didn't need any help in that department."

"I'm sorry you don't get along with him, Matt. I wish there was something I could say or do to make it right."

He smiled. "You can't, but I appreciate the sentiment."

She sucked in a breath, willing her roiling feelings to subside. "But that's pretty normal, really. Not to get along with a parent, I mean."

"Probably. Except I don't think we've spoken more than two paragraphs in ten years. To say he was disappointed in my career choice is putting it mildly."

"Have you even tried? Talking, I mean."

His thumb stopped its lazy circuit on her skin. The pain she saw on his face wasn't just from the headache. He finally succeeded in shuttering the emotion roiling behind his gray eyes and she could have kicked herself for pushing him. "My head's about to split open, *chère*. Why don't we worry about our more immediate problems, yeah?"

Evie nodded. She couldn't imagine what kind of hell it must have been for him to think he loved a woman who was his stepmama, a woman who was older and more sophisticated than any Rochambeau High girl could have been. Maybe it was guilt that kept him from talking to his father. Or maybe they just didn't like each other, like Matt said. It could happen, though she couldn't imagine not talking to Mama or Sarah for ten years.

True, she'd practically run away from this town the minute she was old enough, and she didn't come back very often, but she did call. But she couldn't deny that everything that had happened in the last twenty-four hours was her fault. If she hadn't taken up with David and been oblivious to his sticky fingers, her mama's house would be intact and she'd be back in Tampa. Maybe Evangeline's would have failed anyway, but at least it would have been her own failure.

She'd never know. But if she were still in Tampa, she would not be sitting across from this man, aching for him so much it hurt and knowing this thing between them was never going anywhere.

Oh God, she was right back in it, wasn't she? Wanting him just as much as she ever did when she'd been sixteen and star struck. Matt Girard was a good man, a decent man. He'd risked his life and career, risked jail time, to help her.

Because Sarah, a girl he didn't even know, was in danger. He didn't have to do this. He could have washed his hands of the whole thing the minute she'd gotten the news that Sarah was missing. Instead, he'd offered to help—and he hadn't stopped helping since. Anyone else would have walked away by now.

Not Matt. She admired him so much in that moment. And she really, really wanted to press her mouth to his and show him how grateful she was for what he'd become.

She wasn't going to do it, of course. Evie bit the inside of her lip. She was so sunk. She liked Matt, really liked him, and she wanted to spend time with him. Time making love, talking, and doing all the things couples did.

She wanted a relationship with him, and she didn't quite know what that said about her right now.

But when this was all over, when Sarah was safe and Christina's wedding was done, Matt was leaving Rochambeau. He was going back to his shadowy military world of secret operations. A world he loved. A world that put him at risk every time he went to work.

The truth was that she might not ever see him again. And that thought pierced her like a dagger to the chest.

His fingers grasped hers across the table. "This stuff that's happened isn't your fault." The little pain in her heart intensified. "We can't ever know what people will do, what lengths they'll go to. Don't blame yourself for coming home again, Evie."

She sniffed. "How did you know that's what I was thinking?"

His grin slid into her heart and made her warm. "Call it a hunch."

"I know you're right. We can't ever know what makes someone tick. But I still wish I'd made better choices."

He squeezed her hand. "We make the best choices we can with the information we have. Did West tell you he was a criminal? Did he present you with a plan that mentioned Ryan Rivera or tell you he was going to steal all your money?"

"Of course not. But it's not that simple. I should have been more cautious."

Matt leaned forward. "Evie, you aren't omniscient. West was a pro at what he did. Accept that things happen and move on."

"Is that what you usually do?"

His eyes clouded, but then he nodded firmly. "Absolutely." He let go of her hand and pulled himself upright as he reached for the phone he'd clipped to his belt. "Better call Kev and see if they got anything yet."

"Nothing on the recording, huh?" Matt's head was throbbing less, and he'd managed to shove the aches and pains of slamming into the ground from his mind as much as possible. Man, a nice long soak in a hot tub with the jets on high—and Evie naked beside him—would be so heavenly right about now.

"Just typical night sounds in the analysis. Frogs, crickets, birds—that kind of thing. Something that sounds like a splash, but that's it."

"Could be a gator." Which means they had Sarah near the bayou. But that hardly narrowed things down.

"I might have been able to analyze it more extensively, but Mendez came in. I had to back out of the program pretty quick."

Matt pushed a hand through his hair. "Jesus, Kev. You better stop now. Don't do anything else for me, okay? Wipe the files and forget any of this happened."

Kev swore. "Christ, Richie, we used military assets to track a civvie for you. You think I'm backing out now?"

"I could order you to cease."

"Just like you ordered me to help, right? Forget it. Sir," he added, emphasizing the difference in their ranks as if to say, this time, it didn't matter to him in the least. Matt didn't bother arguing. It was no use when Big Mac made up his mind to do something. If this were an official op, yeah, his second-in-command would obey orders. But not now. Matt didn't know whether to feel grateful or guilty.

Right now, he was opting for grateful. He needed the help and he was damn glad to get it.

"You got anything on that car yet?"

"Glad you see it my way. Nothing rented to a Brianna Sweeney, but several dark Chryslers from at least five airports in the region. Kid's working on narrowing that down. West's phone hasn't been used again."

"Can we tap the GPS positioners on the rentals?"

"Kid wants to narrow it down before we do. Less of a signature."

"Got it." The smaller their electronic signature, the better. If this were a sanctioned op, it wouldn't matter. Since HOT was operating under the radar, they had to be damn careful. Hell, he'd gone so far over the line he didn't even know where the damn thing was anymore. And he didn't regret it. He would *not* let Sarah die at the hands of those maniacs just because it was against the rules—hell, the law—to use HOT assets for personal reasons. He'd pay for it later, gladly, so long as Evie's sister was alive and well.

And so long as Evie was out of danger permanently. He could go back to whatever life he had so long as he knew she was safe. If he had to give up his life on the team, it didn't seem quite as soul-crushing a prospect as it had only hours ago. Because there was life after HOT, even if he'd never quite thought so.

There was Evie. There was this thing between them. And maybe a whole lot of steamy nights where he lost himself in her arms, provided he were free to return to Rochambeau. There were worse things he could do. Even if it gave him a twinge of regret to imagine his life without HOT, it wasn't the completely empty prospect he'd always thought it would be.

Matt finished up the call, then sat back and closed his eyes to think. He needed to turn on the marine radio, listen to the police chatter, and see what was going on with the house explosion—but he wasn't ready just yet.

Jee-zus, he still couldn't believe they were sitting here, on Rochambeau Lake, alive and contemplating their next move. Not because he didn't fully expect to be able to take care of himself with a contract killer on his tail—in a way, he was a contract killer too, except his targets were usually terrorists—but with a concussion, and a chef in charge of the getaway car, he was simply amazed they were here at all.

She'd done some mighty fine driving back there. Except for a few moments on the dock, he'd barely divined even a hint of panic in her. She was calm and cool-headed under pressure, though he'd definitely noted the effects of adrenaline in her shaky hands on the steering wheel. It was to be expected, yet she'd liked it too. Oh, not at first, certainly. But after, when they'd driven away, she'd been happy with herself, even if she couldn't quite admit it.

Evie Baker was an adrenaline junkie in her own way, even if she didn't know it.

She'd been calm about Candy though. Calm and understanding. What the hell was he doing spilling his guts like that? He'd never told anyone about Candy. Man, just get him a spot on fucking *Dr. Phil* or something. He'd be mighty entertaining, wouldn't he?

He rubbed the side of his head. The hammers in his temples had subsided to a dull thudding and he didn't feel dizzy when he turned. *Progress*. He'd hate to have to make a quick getaway right now, but soon enough he'd be back to normal.

Or normal enough anyway.

He got up and flipped on the radio. Evie smiled at him, the corners of her mouth barely lifting. She was tired, operating only on adrenaline again. He wasn't sure how much more she could endure. Which was another reason he'd wanted to take *Candyland* out. He could leave her on the boat, secure in the knowledge she'd be safe, while he went after Brianna Sweeney and her comrades. He didn't plan to tell her about that part until he had to.

"...a late-model BMW, silver, possibly with two people. A Ford F-150, red, reported stolen, last seen heading north on Lake Avenue..."

"They're talking about us, aren't they?" Evie leaned against the counter, staring at the radio as if it would be the one to answer her question. "Whoever was behind us stole the truck they were in."

"Yeah." Finding the Chrysler probably wouldn't do them a bit of good now, but he decided not to stop Kev from tracing it.

"Detective Proctor will be thrilled once he figures out who was in the BMW."

"If we're lucky, it'll take them a while to find the car. They'll connect it with me pretty quickly, but the senator will make them jump through hoops before he admits I have it."

"Why would he do that?" She looked genuinely puzzled.

"He'll be trying to decide how embarrassing it could be for the family, and he'll get Mrs. Doucet on it ASAP. They won't make a statement while they consider all the possibilities." And just wait until Colonel Mendez learned about it. The nails were pounding the coffin closed on Matt's career faster than he could knock them back out again.

"What about the people who saw us leave the marina?"

He didn't bother to lie. "A bit more problematic. Still, it'll take the police some time to mobilize the cavalry. In the meantime, we need to go into the bayou."

"Will this thing make it?"

"The channel's deep enough if you know where to go. We only need to get under the cypresses and turn off the lights."

"And then what? We can't sit out here all night."

"No."

She flipped absently through a rack of CDs sitting on the counter, her frustration evident in the way the cases clacked together. The old man hadn't quite made the shift to MP3s yet. Hell, he probably didn't even have an iPod. Suddenly, Evie's hand stilled above the next case in line.

"What is it?"

She looked like a movie on pause. Then she snatched a case from the rack and opened it, took the CD from the holder and turned it over in her hands. "Is it possible to put information on a pre-recorded CD? Like a band's CD?"

"No."

She looked crestfallen, so he tried to explain.

"The information is burned onto a polycarbonate surface. You'd need a rewriteable CD with a phase-change alloy surface in order to make any additional changes to it."

Violet eyes stared back at him for a moment. She

flipped the case over, studied it. Two spots of color appeared in her pale cheeks as she turned something around in her head.

"David liked music. He got me into the Red Hot Chili Peppers. I have a CD of theirs he gave me, greatest hits I think. He had them on his iPod, but he liked to have the CD too. Said the music was purer or some such thing. There are a few other bands he liked as well. I have all the CDs he gave me, Matt. What if he put one of those media cards into one of the cases?"

SEVENTEEN

"THIS IS RIDICULOUS." EVIE WATCHED as Matt stood on the stern and shed his clothes. He'd jolted into gear the second she'd told him about the CDs. It was like someone had flipped a switch on a Christmas tree and all the lights popped on the way his face had lit up. "Let's take our chances driving. We can get back to Reynier's Retreat and get the CDs from my car in less than twenty minutes."

"We can't risk it, Evie. The cops are looking for the Beemer, and you have no idea who was in that truck or where they've gone. They could be at the marina now, talking to people and learning we took the boat."

"Then at least *drive* this thing back to the marina to get a smaller one."

She still couldn't fathom that he planned to swim the distance. In alligator-infested water. Naked—or nearly naked anyway. Evie wrapped her arms around her middle and shivered. Made snakes look like a breeze.

"I already told you," he said patiently while he stood there in his underwear and sent her pulse revving, "we're too visible in this boat and it's too big to take up the bayou to Reynier's Retreat. We need a smaller one."

Evie forced herself not to let her gaze drift. She kept her eyes locked on his.

"So you're going to waltz up in your underwear and ask someone to give you a key?" Though she had to admit if it were a female he talked to looking like that, he'd likely get offered a whole lot more than a key. The thought did not amuse her in the least.

He grinned. "No, I'm going to swim up and borrow what we need."

"Borrow? You're planning to hotwire a boat?"

"Something like that. I'll take it back later, don't worry."

"Isn't it a long way to the marina?" She could see the lights winking in the distance since he'd moved the yacht closer. But still. It had to be at least a mile.

He put his hands on her shoulders. "*Chère*, I usually swim five times this distance in full gear. This is easy, believe me."

"I bet you don't usually swim that far with a concussion or into a sea of evil lizards looking for a meal."

His mouth crooked again. "Don't bet on it. Besides, the gators prefer the bayou to the lake. I'll be back before you know it."

"Promise?" She couldn't keep the worry from cracking her voice.

He hugged her close to his big warm body. She took the opportunity to run her palms over his muscular back. God, what she wouldn't give for this to never have happened: for Sarah to be safe and happy at home, even if she was still being a brat. If Sarah was safe, Evie could spend the next forty-eight hours or so entwined with Matt. And that was a far more pleasing prospect than watching him lower himself into the water and leave her behind as he risked his life for Sarah.

"See what you do to me." His voice was a soft growl as his cock stirred against her belly. "I'm coming back, Evie. I haven't finished with you yet."

Yet. Still, so long as he came back, she didn't care. She'd take what she could get.

He turned away from her and took a leaping dive off the side of the boat so quickly her heart pounded with fear and excitement. She hurried to the edge, trying to find him in the black water below. She couldn't see him, but the smooth sound of his strokes cutting through water drifted back to her. She strained her ears listening for him until long after he'd disappeared.

The night had turned oppressively sticky. Frogs rumbled in the waters and bugs the size of bombers buzzed by her ears. She went below and found a can of bug repellent, then doused herself in it. She couldn't wait down here for Matt to return. She needed to be topside, listening for any sounds of him. She went back and sat on the bench seat at the rear of the yacht. The bugs strafed her, whining loudly as they passed, but they didn't stick around to bite.

She couldn't imagine what Matt was going through. She refused to even think about gators. She could only pray he was right about them liking the bayou better.

Who'd have ever thought the richest kid in town would turn into a hero who'd stop at nothing to get the bad guys? Matt had been the golden boy, the one whose future was so bright it seemed to laser through any difficulty or pain. She'd wanted what he had, even when she'd known it wasn't perfect. She'd been too young and naïve to realize that his fights with his father were indicative of something more, or that he hadn't bounced back from his mother's death the way she'd thought.

Of course he'd been a lonely, angry kid. Even with money.

Evie's hands curled around the railing. How would she manage living in Rochambeau without him when he left again? He'd said he'd missed her—and she'd missed him too. He was a part of her childhood, a part of her adolescence. And yes, a part of all the trauma and pain of being a teenager.

Regardless of anything else between them, he'd been important to her from the moment he'd first walked into her life when she'd been six. The knowledge that, once he left again, he'd be somewhere foreign, fighting and maybe dying for his country, made her frantic and angry all at once. She wanted him to stop doing that. She wanted him to have a reason to want to stay right here.

She wanted him to want *her*.

Evie closed her eyes tight. That wasn't going to work and she knew it. Matt had his own life and she had hers. They had chemistry, but that wasn't enough to make life-altering decisions.

And she knew that Matt wasn't going to give up his job as a military badass. He loved it too much.

When he'd been gone for half an hour, she seriously started to consider firing this big puppy up and driving it to shore, no matter if she plowed into a tree or ran aground or sank it in the channel. Anything was better than sitting, waiting and wondering and getting more and more scared for Matt as the night dragged endlessly on.

"Screw it," she finally said, heading for the command bridge. She had one step to go when the sputter of a small outboard engine cut the night.

Evie squeezed the warm metal railing beneath her sweaty hand, listening for any indication it was Matt. The engine drew closer, until she could hear the water softly soughing away beneath the hull of a craft.

Finally, the motor cut back. Water sloshed against the *Candyland*. It had to be Matt. He was going to tie up and come aboard.

But what if it wasn't? What if they'd caught him? What if they were coming for her?

She slipped down the stairs, wishing like hell she'd thought to carry the gun Matt had left below. Did she have time to get it?

"Evie?" The sound of her name reached her and she sagged in relief.

"Here." She went to peer over the side of the yacht. Matt sat in a tiny aluminum boat at the rear of the *Candyland*. Thankfully, he was alone.

"Catch." She caught the rope he threw and held the small boat against the bigger one while he pulled himself onto the rear platform. He took the rope and made a quick knot around one of the cleats, mooring the little boat securely.

"I was beginning to think you decided to go without me," Evie said as he stood on the deck beside her and reached for the towel she'd brought up for him. He wasn't very wet after riding back, but he rubbed the terrycloth over himself anyway.

"I did. But it took longer to find this boat than I thought it would." He finished toweling off and yanked his dark T-shirt over his head. "I figured if I didn't come back, you'd try to come after me in this monster."

"Damn straight. And I'm angry you were planning to go without me, by the way. Just so you know."

He finished buttoning his jeans and clipped his phone to the waistband. Then he grinned. "I know it. But I thought of a better idea anyway and this one involves you."

She crossed her arms. "I'm not sure that makes it better, but I'm listening."

"I'll take us as far into the bayou as this'll go. You can wait while I go downriver in the other boat."

Evie wanted to stay on the bigger boat, no doubt about it. But she couldn't endure this kind of uncertainty again. She couldn't drive herself nuts with regrets and *what ifs*. She'd just have to face her fear, suck it up, and get on board that wafer of a fishing boat. It was the only way to know he was safe. And to help him if he needed it. "I'm going."

He scrutinized her. Just when she thought he was about to order her to stay behind, he shrugged. "Suit yourself, Evie. But don't say I didn't warn you."

Sarah woke up when someone banged open the door and flipped on a light. She tried to stretch her cramped limbs and bit back a wince. Her stomach growled loudly and her head throbbed—less painfully than before, but still badly enough that she knew the migraine could come back full force if she wasn't careful. She needed food, caffeine, and ibuprofen. None of which she was likely to get.

"Get up, kid." Brianna tossed a warmly scented bag down beside her. Sarah sat up and ripped into the food with her free hand. Brianna popped open a soda and set it down. Sarah gulped half of it at once.

"Slow down or you'll make yourself sick."

Sarah slowed only marginally, figuring the bitch was probably right.

"You should have fed her hours ago." It was a man's voice. The man from earlier tonight. She squinted at him. He was good-looking, sort of familiar in a way.

Sarah swallowed a mouthful of burger. "You look like that other guy, the one who smelled like smoke all the time." She winced when she realized she'd spoken aloud. What if he was mean? Would he come hit her?

"First cousins. You're observant."

"Too observant," Brianna grumbled.

Sarah's heart dropped to her toes. She didn't like the way Brianna said that, the way the woman chewed on the inside of her cheek like she was thinking about something.

"Doesn't matter, Bree. In a couple of hours, we'll be out of here."

Brianna whirled away and gathered some things into a bag. "You better be right. It won't take Rivera long to send in reinforcements. We need to be long gone from this place."

"Let the kid finish her food. We have enough time for that."

Brianna stopped what she was doing and glared at the man. "We had an agreement."

"Still do."

"So what are we after? Evie either doesn't have a clue, or she tried to pull one over on me with that media card. If I have to call her back, I need to know what it is. I'm tired of these games."

The man simply looked at her. "Relax."

Brianna exploded. "How can you tell me to relax? Our lives are at stake here, and you promised me we'd be safe. If you'd just tell me what we want instead of casing those houses and chasing after Evie and her boyfriend like some kind of stunt driver, I could get her to bring it to me. You nearly got us killed back there."

The man's expression grew black. "We're doing it my way. If you don't like it, you can leave."

"Yeah, so you can put a bullet in my back or stab me? No, thanks."

Oddly enough, his glare turned into a grin. "I could have already done that, so stop bitching. We'll be out of this town before dawn. You'll be sipping a margarita on the beach by this time tomorrow."

It was too dark to see much of anything, but Matt knew Evie was white-knuckled right about now. They'd left the *Candyland* behind an hour ago and begun their journey downriver to Reynier's Retreat. It wasn't that it was a long distance, but the boat he'd *borrowed* was small and only had a twenty-five-horsepower motor. He'd wanted something bigger, but the opportunity for this one presented itself and he had to take it. There'd been too many people at the marina tonight, partying on that houseboat or grilling at the pavilion, and he'd been a man in underwear lurking around the boats.

Yeah, like that wasn't going to get him noticed.

So he'd taken the small fishing boat, knowing Evie would hate the very idea of getting on the thing—though she'd tried to hide it from him—and crawled his way back to where he'd left her. He hadn't really expected she would come with him. He hadn't argued with her, figuring by the time they anchored at the mouth of the bayou and he prepared to climb down into the small craft, she'd chicken out.

If that didn't do it, then she *had* to chicken out when she made the descent and stepped foot onto the rocking aluminum. He didn't know why she was afraid of boats, but he knew that she was. She'd nearly wet herself trying to climb into the pirogue earlier.

But she hadn't chickened out when push came to shove. She shook, that much he knew because he'd steadied her as she transferred from one to the other boat, but she'd steadfastly refused to wait on the yacht for him to return. One of these days, he was gonna have to ask her what about boats terrified her so much. He knew he'd taken her out in a pirogue when they were kids, but that had been a long time ago.

She turned around to look at him, her fingers clutching the edge of the johnboat.

"Almost there," he said. He'd told her not to speak unnecessarily since their voices would carry on the still air. She'd taken him so seriously that she hadn't spoken at all. "Are you all right?"

She'd faced straight ahead again. She glanced over her shoulder and nodded once.

He hoped like hell that Brianna Sweeney hadn't gotten to the CDs yet. Maybe the guy who knew what to look for had finally caved. And maybe they'd taken the opportunity while Matt and Evie disappeared from the radar to go back to the guesthouse and try the search again. Obviously, whoever'd been there before got interrupted before he could finish.

Matt wanted to know what was in the files. They had to point to accounts where West stashed money, he was certain, and yet his gut told him there had to be something else to it. Something Rivera wanted even more than he wanted money.

Until Matt found the files and decoded them, he couldn't verify what that was. He slewed the tiller to the right as they entered the final turn.

The bayou at night was a fascinating place. He knew this water like he knew his own skin. When he was younger, before his mother died, he'd spent time on the bayou with his great-uncle Remy. It was Remy who taught him where to look for gator nests so he could spy on the creatures, how to tell the weather by the way the leaves on the trees looked, and how to fish for bass the size of his arm. Remy'd also given him a deep appreciation for the uniqueness of the Louisiana wetlands, their fragility and beauty, and the necessity for preserving them.

Something twisted inside him. Regret? He loved this place, and yet he'd blown out of here at the first opportunity and left the conservation and preservation to others. Matt didn't think he'd actually been on the bayou since he'd left home ten years ago. That he could still navigate it in the dark ought to come as a surprise, and yet he'd have expected nothing less.

Rochambeau—the lake, the bayou, the town—and Reynier's Retreat were in his blood. Would always be in his blood, no matter how far he went or how long he stayed away. He understood why Evie disliked it, why she wanted to get away. Hell, he'd done the same thing.

But he'd always, on some level, pictured himself returning. It might be in a coffin, though he definitely hoped not.

At that moment, exactly when he'd expected it, the ghostly white form of Reynier's Retreat appeared in the darkness. What must his ancestors have thought when they returned from the fighting and saw their beautiful mansion intact, unharmed by the destructive force of a war that had ruined so much in its path? Did their bodies sizzle with a primal recognition the way his did?

Light spilled from her leaded glass windows onto the lawn, illuminating the colonnade fanning from the back of the house. A faint burst of laughter drifted to his ears and he realized someone was still in the garden.

Of course they were. The rehearsal dinner had been tonight. The dinner was over hours ago, but some of the guests had lingered to enjoy the setting. It might be hot, but Misty Lee had no doubt had fans brought out and set up on the perimeter so people could enjoy an *al fresco* meal. Not only that, but no mosquito would dare to crash Misty Lee's party. Whoever was out there was having a great time and probably had no plans to leave anytime soon. He just hoped no one decided to go wandering down toward the guesthouse because he didn't want to end up

287

immobilizing the wrong person.

Worse, he didn't want to incur Chris's wrath if he accidentally punched, say, Ben's brother instead of one of the bad guys. *Dieu*, no.

As the estate loomed closer, Matt seriously consider-ed anchoring the little boat in the channel and swimming to shore, just in case anyone was waiting in the guesthouse for them to return. He hadn't seen any signs of recent boat traffic, so he didn't think anyone had come by water. And though it was more difficult for unauthorized people to enter the estate by road, it wasn't impossible. Not with the wedding in two days. Caterers, florists, guests, wedding participants—a whole host of people had passed through those gates today.

Their opponents could be hiding their boat against the shore somewhere, concealed by vegetation, waiting for Matt and Evie to return. It was a gamble to wait, though, and unless there was a whole platoon of men out there, it was a poor use of resources. The bad guys had no idea *how* Matt and Evie would return, or even *if* they would do so.

No, Matt was driving straight to the dock and tying up. If someone was waiting on the water, he couldn't leave Evie behind and put her in danger. If someone were already here, at the house, then he'd deal with that compli-cation when he came to it.

He stood up as they approached the low wooden dock. The pirogue sat where they'd left it, dead in the water. He shifted the tiller slightly, brought the aluminum boat alongside the dock, and tossed a rope around one of the thick pylons. He made quick work of tying up, then hopped onto the dock and turned to help Evie.

She stumbled when her feet hit the solid structure,

knocking heavily against him.

"Careful." He brushed a kiss across her forehead. It was disconcerting, he knew, to go from the rocking motion of being on the water to suddenly standing on land. He'd done it a thousand times, though, both as a kid growing up on the bayou and as a Special Forces soldier inserting into hostile territory by whatever body of water happened to be convenient to the target. It was as easy for him as breathing.

She leaned against him for a moment, her hands pressing into his chest, her fingertips burning through his T-shirt and into his skin. What he wouldn't give to take her into the house and straight to the bedroom, to make love to her until he had to go board that plane for North Carolina.

Why'd all hell have to break loose the minute he found her again?

"Stay on my six," he said, nuzzling the hair at her ear and breathing deeply the sweet scent of her. "You remember what that is, right?"

"It's your ass."

He bit back a chuckle.

"Yeah, that's right. You watch my ass and I'll watch yours. That's how a team operates, got it?"

"So we're a team, huh?"

"We're a team."

"Then let's go get 'em."

"Easy, tiger. We're going through the back door, but only after we've set up a perimeter."

"Lead on, Superman."

Matt bit back another laugh. "It's Richie Rich, actually."

"What?"

"My team name. Richie Rich."

He saw the flash of her teeth in the darkness. "Of course it is."

Matt couldn't resist the impulse to touch his mouth to hers. A jolt of need shot to his groin, but he ignored it, concentrating instead on the amazing sensation of feeling her hot tongue against his. He broke the kiss sooner than he wanted.

She got behind him, shadowed him up to the side of the house. He stationed her behind the AC unit, told her to stay put and watch for anyone coming up from the bayou or through the backyard.

"Can you whistle?"

"Yes."

"Loud?"

"Loud enough."

"Then if you see anyone before I get back, whistle. But only if they aren't close enough to make your position right away. Soon as you whistle, head toward the front of the house. When the coast is clear, run for the main house but stick to the woods. Here."

She took the knife he held out, her eyes growing wide as she met his. "Matt, I—"

"Use it if you have to. Don't be squeamish, Evie. They won't be."

She nodded, her eyes still huge, and he squeezed her shoulder quickly before slipping toward the front of the house. As he moved, he drew the .45 he'd taken from the main house. He had to case the place and make sure no one was inside before going for the garage and her car. He didn't want to be here any longer than necessary. His plan was to get the discs, Chris's laptop, and get back to the *Candyland*. The senator had satellite Internet on the yacht—just in case he had a desperate need to follow the market while enjoying a leisurely afternoon with his wife —so transmitting any files wouldn't be a problem.

The other option was to get up to the main house and check out the discs there, but it was too dangerous. If someone was watching the house, he didn't want to put his family in danger from an assault. Not to mention the likelihood of a police visit to ask questions about the explosion.

No, it would take a little more time, but going back to the yacht was the best option. He came to the front edge of the house, hunkered down in the bushes, and studied the area. There were no cars down here, no movement of any kind. He eased from behind the bushes and skirted the front perimeter, keeping the house at his right.

It took a few minutes to make sure the entire peri-meter was clear; then he was back at Evie's side, urging her to follow him to the rear of the house. They crept up onto the porch and took up stations on either side of the door. Matt took the small flashlight from his pocket and held it in his right hand, directly above the gun in his left. He'd love to have some breaching explosives right about now, maybe a flash-bang to toss into the room, but all he had was the element of surprise and his training.

He'd warned Evie not to be startled, instructed her to wait here until he gave her the all clear. He met her gaze now and she nodded. *Go for it.*

What happened next occurred in a sequence so ingrained in him he didn't have to consider the steps before acting. One minute he was standing outside, the next he was in, gun in front of him, flashlight sweeping into the corners of the room, blinding anyone who looked directly at him. It also put him in silhouette, making it harder for someone to target him. Add in the surprise of a bursting door, and you were guaranteed a disoriented criminal, at least for a few seconds. With a flash-bang, the disorientation would be complete.

He quickly went through the house the same way and then returned to the door.

"It's clear."

"Thank God for that." Evie let the knife droop in her hand. "I think I prefer being a chef to a secret agent."

"But if the chef thing doesn't work out, you have a career to fall back on," he teased.

"That's okay. I'd rather be Mama's shampoo girl if it came down to it."

"Come on." He led the way to the garage. Evie hurried to her car and yanked open the passenger door. She rifled through the side pockets, pulled out papers and a candy bar wrapper. Next, she opened the glove compartment. She came up with three discs, all of which she tossed into the pile.

"Are there any in the player?" It was an older car that had been fitted with an aftermarket disc player which sat on the floor beneath her passenger seat.

"Yes." She slid the door to the changer open and took out the cartridge. Six discs fell into the pile. "We have to go through the boxes," she said, looking at him apologetic- ally. "The cases for these are in there. There should be other discs too."

"We'll have to do it quickly." Matt grabbed a box, upending it on the garage floor. They didn't have time for preamble, and Evie didn't protest. She picked up another box and turned it upside down, scattering books and papers across the floor.

Matt located two CDs. He grabbed another box. Fifteen excruciating minutes later, all her stuff was scattered across the third bay again. But they had a pile of CDs, including one of the Red Hot Chili Peppers.

"Is that all of them?"

"Has to be. We've been through everything."

"Then we gotta boogie." The tension to escape the garage and get back to the yacht began beating a drum in his head. They gathered up the CD cases, stuffed them in a small box, and went back through the house. Matt took a moment to grab some cheese and fruit from the fridge, snagged the laptop and cord off the counter, and led the way back to the dock.

They were gliding down the bayou away from Reynier's Retreat when Evie's phone rang. She glanced at the display and then looked up at him. He couldn't see her face well in the darkness, but her agitation was evident.

"It's David's number."

EIGHTEEN

BRIANNA UNLOCKED THE HANDCUFF FROM the iron headboard and made Sarah stand. Her legs were shaky and stiff, but she felt better after eating the hamburger and fries. The man had gone outside to talk on his cell phone. His voice drifted through the open door.

"Yeah, babe, it's me... I know you're surprised... No, I didn't blow anything up, it was probably Rivera's guys... My cousin, George... Yeah, strong family resemblance..."

"I gotta pee," Sarah said.

"Tough. We're going."

"I'll piss in the boat if you don't let me go."

Brianna scowled. "Get in there and don't waste time." She gestured toward the bathroom.

Sarah hurried inside, thankful Brianna hadn't cuffed her wrists together yet, and yanked down her pants to squat over the toilet. She could still hear the guy talking through the cracked window as she concentrated. Her bladder had been abused so long it didn't want to let go.

"I need you to bring it to me... What do you mean

you don't have it?"

He sounded like he was going to pop a blood vessel or something.

"Go get it then. And call me once you have it... Why? Because I can help you get your sister back, that's why... Just fucking call me, you got it? And don't think of pulling any funny shit with that tough military guy you got salivating after you, okay? Yeah, I'll be waiting."

A second later, she heard footsteps on the stairs. "What're we waiting for, Bree?"

"She had to take a piss."

Sarah jumped as the door rattled on its hinges. Her bladder chose that moment to release.

"You better hurry it up, little girl, or you'll be gator bait."

"Almost done," she said, her voice hoarse. God, had it ever felt so good to pee? Warm liquid flooded out of her until she was empty. She reached for the toilet paper, thanked God there was a little left, then finished up and thought about escape. There was no use trying to slip through the window—it was too small and there was nowhere to go if she did get through. Only if she could make it to the boat first would she stand a chance. Since she couldn't, since she felt weaker than a newborn baby, and since she was sick and tired of all this shit anyway, she opened the door and rejoined Brianna and the new guy.

They hustled her outside and into an airboat, sans duffel this time.

"What're we doing with her anyway?" Brianna said. "Hauling her around is too much trouble."

"We may need her. We'll stick her in the trunk of your car. If we need her, she's there. If not, it'll be awhile before anyone finds her."

"Why not just leave her in the swamp and be done with it?"

Sarah's heart thudded. She had no doubt what Brianna meant.

"Did you hear anything I said? We might need her."

"And when we get what we want?"

He made a slicing motion across his neck that would have been comical if he weren't serious. "Then we take care of them all."

When they got back to the yacht, Evie scrambled on board and let Matt hand up the box of CDs and the food. He joined her before cutting the aluminum boat adrift. There just wasn't enough time to return it, and they needed to move quickly. The small craft would float into the swamp and maybe get stuck in the marsh grass or the duckweed. The owner would be able to retrieve it, if he could find it.

"I'll make sure whoever owns it gets the boat back, Evie," Matt said as if sensing the direction of her thoughts. "Or I'll buy a new one."

"I suppose that's the last thing I should be thinking about. But you're right, I was."

She'd been focusing on mundane things since the phone call for the simple fact she still couldn't believe David was alive and well. He claimed the body was his first cousin, George, who also worked for Rivera. And he admitted he'd been at the house and switched ID when he found his cousin's body. He said he wanted the police to think he was dead because it would make leaving the country easier. She wasn't sure she bought that excuse, but whatever.

He also claimed to be able to help her get Sarah back. He hadn't bothered to explain how.

Evie followed Matt below. He set the box of CDs on the table and rifled through it.

"Red Hot Chili Peppers?" He held it up for her inspection.

"That's what he said." She hadn't admitted to having the CD when David told her what he wanted. Something stopped her. Was it the right thing to do? It'd felt like it at the time, but now she wasn't so sure. What if she'd said yes? She might be on her way to retrieving Sarah right now. Instead, she was sitting on the Girard yacht anchored at the mouth of the bayou and waiting for Matt to examine the CD case for evidence of hidden information.

He opened the case and took the disc out. Carefully, he pried the case apart and spread the contents across the table. He looked at the band information folder, then took out a penlight and ran it over all the surfaces.

"Well?"

Matt shook his head. "Unless this guy knows something I don't about information storage, I'm not seeing anything. Shit." He snapped off the light and picked up the disc, running his fingers around the edge. Then he turned the disc over. His smile was immediate. "The tricky bastard."

"What?"

He turned the back of the disc toward her. "See the bluish color? It's rewritable. The label is a copy. He used labeling software to duplicate the original so you wouldn't notice he'd switched it out. You said you bought it new, right?"

"Yes. But it has the music on it. I played it not too long ago."

He held it up at eye level and studied the label. "He probably copied the disc, then added his information to it. It's a good job on the label. Not noticeable unless you study it closely."

And she'd never noticed the switch, just like she'd never noticed that a dead body that looked like David wasn't actually the man she'd once shared a bed with. My God, how obtuse did she have to be?

"Evie."

"What?"

Matt took her hand, pulled her over until she could sit on his lap. He nestled her between his strong thighs. His fingers threaded into the hair that had fallen forward over her breasts. He twisted a lock around his index finger, lifting it to his nose. Then he tugged her down and kissed her. Softly, so softly. She felt his body stirring even though the kiss wasn't very sexual. It wasn't meant to be sexual. He was comforting her, giving her his strength, telling her it was okay. And he was doing it all with his lips and tongue. She moaned into his mouth and sank into the deliciousness of a kiss with this man she could love.

Tears sprang to her eyes and a sob caught in her throat. She wrenched her mouth away as it burst from her. He hugged her to him, his strong arms encircling her, cradling her against his broad chest.

She didn't want to feel anything for him, and yet she couldn't help it. She *could* love him. Hell, she was more than halfway there already. Damn him for being so decent and unselfish.

"How many times have you ever seen a dead body?"

He'd misunderstood, of course, and she was grateful for it. "Once," she managed, gulping in air and forcing the tears into the void. She would *not* cry. Not now, not here, and not over him.

"It was dark, even with the porch light, and there was a lot of blood. You saw what you were meant to see, Evie. The guy looked enough like David to pass for him if you didn't study him. You seemed surprised he had a goatee."

"He was heavier too, but I figured he put on weight the last couple of months."

"It's not your fault, okay? You saw a dead man who looked like David. You didn't spend time looking at him. It was a natural conclusion to make and the fact he had David's ID on him confirmed it for the police."

"Brianna knew he wasn't dead." She remembered what Bree had said on the docks—*you'd be surprised*—but she hadn't understood it at the time. "And she still hasn't called. Do you think David got to her? Maybe he killed her. Maybe he hid her body in my mother's house before blowing it up."

David hadn't admitted to setting the explosion. He'd said he was inside the house looking for the disc when someone else arrived and he had to get out. He also said he hadn't chased them afterward. She could imagine a lot of things from him, but she couldn't imagine him killing anyone. She'd been wrong about him once before, though.

Wrong enough that she would never believe a word

he said again.

Matt shrugged. "It could mean a lot of things. But we better get to work figuring out what's on this disc if we want to find out." He kissed her again, then sighed in frustration. "Damn, I'd like to be inside you right now. Just ten minutes, that's all I need." He blew out another breath. "But we can't."

"When this is over." She pushed away and stood up to slide into the seat across the table. "You're mine for twenty-four hours."

She thought maybe a flash of regret flickered in his eyes, but she wasn't sure.

"You're on. We aren't getting out of bed except to eat. And even then, I think we're gonna do it naked." He set the laptop on the table and powered it up, then slid the disc into the drive. His fingers clicked across the keys. "Yep, here it is. Along with your songs, there's a compressed file." A frown creased his face. "Password protected, of course. Any idea?"

"Try 'lying snake.' Kidding," she said when Matt looked up at her. "I'm not sure. Maybe his birthday." She rattled off the date, miffed on at least one level she could still remember it.

"Nope."

She suggested a couple more things—his mother's name, Helen, and his favorite drink, absinthe—both of which came up negative. Oddly, she began to realize she hadn't really known that much about him. He liked to surf, so they tried various "surfer dude" combos. She didn't know if he had a sister, a favorite color, or even a favorite food. Strange, considering she was a chef and cooking was her business. She'd never thought to ask David what he liked to eat. He ate the food in the restaurant, but she'd never known if he had a favorite.

"You're thinking too hard about something," Matt said, jerking her back to the present.

"Sorry." She leaned her cheek against one palm. "I was just thinking that I didn't know him very well for a guy I dated for two months."

"I'm sure he didn't want you to know him. He told you what he thought you wanted to hear."

"You're sweet, but I think I tend to have lousy taste in men. It's an inherited trait."

Matt grinned. "Thanks, *chère*, I appreciate the compliment."

"You aren't lousy, but you aren't good for me either." She smiled when she delivered it, yet she meant it too.

"Why's that?" He looked genuinely puzzled.

"Because you aren't available. You're already married to your job. Nothing and no one comes before that, I think."

"Yeah." He looked troubled, but then the look passed and determination took its place.

"See," she said brightly, "I'm cursed with the family gene."

"You'll find the right person. It just takes time."

"I'm sure you're right." Her throat ached. "Everything worth having takes time."

She heard him tapping on the keys again. "I need to get this file to Kev. We won't figure it out by trying different combos of stuff. The Kid can crack it for us."

He picked up his phone and punched a button. She was grateful for these guys even if she never got to thank them personally.

"Got another file for the Kid," Matt said after the preliminaries were finished. "An encrypted data file. This is the info we were looking for, Big Mac. I need this as fast as he can get it done, top priority. I'll owe him one, believe me."

A minute later, he finished the call and then got to his feet. "We need to move. We can't sit in one place too long."

"Do you really think anyone is looking for us?" Who could be out there trolling the lake for the Girard yacht? The police, maybe, but not if their hands were still full with what had happened at the house earlier. She pictured it again, one wall blown away—in the kitchen, of course— and the flames eating at the rest of the structure. All of her childhood memories were gone with that blast. The pictures, the ridiculous things she'd saved—the movie ticket stub from her first date, the candy wrapper from the bar Matt gave her in class once when she was in her full-blown crush mode. She'd saved so much silly stuff, never bothered to toss it out or take it with her when she left, and now it was all gone. Everything, ruined.

"We can't take a chance, Evie. We don't know how many people are looking for us, or how long it'll take them to figure out the yacht's gone." He glanced at his watch. "We've been out for nearly two hours now. Someone's noticed, believe me."

"Where are we going?"

He paused in the doorway to the rear deck. "I'm taking a different finger of the bayou, a deeper one, where we can get into the cypresses and wait. Hopefully, we'll hear something from Kev soon."

"When was the last time you took this thing into the

302

bayou?"

"Years ago." He held up a hand to stop her protest. "I know it's changed, that the hurricanes have silted the bottom, but we only need a few feet. We'll be okay."

He disappeared through the door and scrambled up the ladder. Evie laid her head on her arms while he fired up the engines. She hoped he was right about the depth because if he drove this beast into the bottom, they'd be sitting ducks.

"Goddammit," Brianna swore, throwing something that hit the deck with a clink.

"You aren't helping any, you know that?" The guy she called David looked angry.

Sarah wanted to laugh it was so damn funny, but she didn't want to call attention to herself. What if they decided to toss her into the bayou after all? The gators were out. They'd already seen the glow of eyes lurking above the surface when David turned the spotlight on to figure out where they were in relation to land.

They weren't, of course. The swamp stretched around them, nothing but cypresses, Spanish moss, and duckweed as far as the eye could see. The mosquitoes were murder. Sarah hunkered into a ball. She couldn't cross her arms against her body because of the handcuffs, so she shook her arms as much as she could to drive the bloodthirsty things away. It didn't really work and she could feel the welts rising. Her skin itched like crazy, but there was nothing she could do about it.

Her only consolation was that her two idiot companions were as miserable as she was. The boat drifted silently, the motor having died several minutes ago. It was probably the fuel pump, but she wasn't telling them. Not that it'd do a bit of good anyway if they didn't have a spare on board.

"Why'd you have to switch to this anyway? The motor boat worked perfectly well."

"Airboats are faster, and they can cross land," David said.

Idiot. They *could* ride across land, but you'd damn well better know what you were doing. Airboats didn't have brakes and idiots shouldn't be at the tiller. He'd rented it or stolen it, no doubt from Bubba Boudreaux's. Probably watched a movie or something and thought it'd be a breeze, *ha-ha*, to operate. If these two didn't kill her on purpose, they'd probably all end up dead out of sheer stupidity.

"This one doesn't seem to be faster, Einstein. In fact, I'd say it's dead. So now what the fuck are we supposed to do? Wait for someone to rescue us?"

"You know, I'm beginning to regret this deal." His voice was a hard growl.

Brianna didn't seem to care. "Yeah, well you need me now, so don't get any funny ideas. Ouch!" She slapped herself to dislodge a mosquito. "Where are the paddles?"

"Give me a few minutes. I'll figure this out."

"Fine, you play mechanic, I'm finding them."

David didn't say anything else while Brianna flipped open compartments.

"Here they are. Thank God." She pulled two paddles from the storage locker under the deck and tossed one at Sarah. "Make yourself useful, kid."

Sarah struggled to position herself at the side of the boat and dipped the paddle into the dark water. She thought about dropping it accidentally on purpose but rapidly discarded the idea because Brianna would probably make her go in after it.

Still, she wasn't in any hurry to paddle quickly or well. They inched forward at a snail's pace while mosquitoes ate her alive and her muscles screamed. She began to think that falling in and drowning would be preferable to even a single second more of this torture.

Kevin MacDonald rocked back in his chair and rubbed his eyes. The strain of sleepless nights was beginning to burn deep, but he couldn't seem to stop them. He couldn't quit thinking about that last mission. Matt was going to take the heat for the whole damn thing, but he shouldn't have to. It wasn't his fault. Wartime was different. Things happened. Things you weren't always prepared for.

A fifteen-year-old traitor wasn't something any of them were prepared for. Not that the kid had a choice, probably, but the information passing through him had been reliable before. It wasn't Matt's fault it was a setup this time. Wasn't his fault he wanted to save the kid and his family and ended up losing two of their own instead.

Marco and Jim were gone. Kev slid a hand through his hair. He'd liked Jim well enough, but Marco had probably been his best friend in the world. They'd gone through Hell Week together when they were trying out for the Special Forces, and they'd been best buddies since.

Kev tried not to think about that last day when the tangos had taken Marco and Jim away and made an example of them. He would have given anything to save them both. Marco had a wife, for fuck's sake. Lucky San Ramos wasn't answering the phone these days. Hadn't answered his calls since they'd returned, and he'd tried to make sure she was okay and to tell her he was sorry.

When he went around to Marco and Lucky's place that one time, no one was there. A For Sale sign tilted crookedly in the yard, the only indication Lucky still owned the place. He'd tried a couple of times, but she was never home.

At another terminal, Billy Blake's fingers flew over his keyboard while he worked at cracking the password. Kev didn't know too much about it, but he knew it was only a matter of time. The Kid had programs that cracked passwords with amazing speed. They'd been at this one only a few minutes because they'd had to badge back into the building, pass through several layers of security, and get to their desks. Kev glanced at his watch. Nearly four a.m. now. Colonel Mendez wouldn't be in for another two hours at least.

Kev picked up the phone and dialed by rote. The answering machine kicked on, spooking him as usual. Marco's voice sounded so alive as he announced they weren't available so please leave a message. He started to hang up, but when the beep sounded, he tossed a glance at Billy and lowered his voice.

"Hi, Lucky," he said. "I, uh, hope you're okay. Let me know if you need anything, okay? I'm really sorry. Um, call me if—"

If what, fuckhead?

What could he possibly say that would ease her pain? Jesus God. Kev stabbed the disconnect button and dropped the phone onto the desk. His gut roiled. It was unfair as hell that Marco was gone. And there was nothing he could do about it, nothing he could say to ease Lucky's pain or his own guilt.

Billy grunted and Kev spun in his chair. "You got anything yet, dude?"

"Close, but no. I thought I had it for a sec. I've got the hashing done, but it's still trying to work out the plaintext word from the hash."

"Yeah, whatever you say."

Billy turned to grin at him. "It's easy, B. Just load the program and let it go to town. Hey, you okay, man?"

Kev pinched the bridge of his nose and yawned. "Yeah, just got a lot on my mind."

"You talk to the psych yet?"

The military psychiatrist they were all required to talk to after returning from a mission. He'd meant to. Had to if he ever wanted to go on another mission. "No, not yet. Next week."

"You talk to Lucky at all?"

"No."

"Man, it was a bad trip this time. Fucked us all up. Wish we could have been here for the funeral, though. She'd have appreciated it, don't you think?"

Kev ignored the question. "We're going to lose our team leader over this."

It was the first time any of them had voiced it aloud, though they'd certainly all thought it. Hell, and if they got caught doing what they were doing right now, they'd find themselves at Fort Leavenworth along with Matt. And Kev just damn well didn't care. If he could do anything to save Matt Girard's ass, he'd do it. If he could take the fall for the guy, he'd do it. If he had to go down with his team leader, he would.

Billy tapped a key, then folded his arms. "I hate to see Richie go, you know? I'd follow him anywhere."

"We *have* followed him anywhere, man. We're still following."

"Yeah, guess so. Damn," Billy said, thudding his fist on the desk. "Almost had it."

"Almost had what, sergeant?"

Kev closed his eyes for only a second before rocketing to his feet and snapping a salute. Beside him, Billy did the same. Colonel Mendez eyed them both, his gaze flinty. The Colonel was imposing in his Army Combat uniform, even though his nose wasn't quite even with Kev's chin. At the moment, he looked about ten feet tall and angrier than a wet cat.

"You, sit down," he barked at Billy. "And you, start talking right this instant or I'll make you wish I had just put your balls in a vise by the time I'm done with you."

NINETEEN

MATT DROPPED ANCHOR IN A narrow cove and headed below. Evie's head was on the table and a soft snore escaped her. He flicked off the light over her head and pressed eject on the laptop. He put the CD back in the case and went over to rummage through the cabinets. When he found what he was looking for, he ripped off a long strip and pressed it to the case. Then he bent down and taped the CD beneath the cabinet and behind the sink, as far and as high as he could go to make it disappear. A glance at Evie told him she was still sleeping. He ripped off another piece of duct tape and secured the package.

It probably wasn't necessary, but too many years as a covert operator wouldn't allow him to do only what was necessary. He went the extra mile because he had to, because it was as ingrained in him by now as putting on his pants in the morning. There was something about doing this, something about helping Evie, that made him think, even if he never went into the field with HOT again, he'd be all right.

Of course Leavenworth was still hanging over his

head, but he tried not to think too deeply about that prospect.

He returned to the desk and tapped a few keys on the laptop, wiping any record of the transmission to Kev. Then he took the box with the rest of the CDs and stashed them in a cabinet in the bedroom.

Evie stirred when he returned. Her hair was mussed, her cheek red where she'd been lying on her arm. She blinked. "Have we stopped?"

"We're anchored. I assume you didn't get any calls?"

She reached for her phone, checked the display. "No, nothing. What could've happened to Brianna? It's been about five hours or so, hasn't it?"

"Yeah, it's three a.m."

Evie pushed a hand through her hair, trying to straighten it. "No wonder I'm tired." She looked as if she just remembered something. "Isn't your sister's wedding today?"

"Tomorrow, actually. We have time."

She frowned. "I hope you're right. If you miss it, she'll hate me forever."

"I'm not missing it. Neither are you."

In spite of everything, she smiled. He loved the way her mouth lifted at the corners in a smile he liked to think was only for him. When he thought about her smiling at David West like that, or worse, thought of her naked with the guy, he wanted to punch something.

"I'd like to be there for Chris. She asked so many people in town, you know. She didn't have to do that."

"I want you to go with me."

One eyebrow rose. "Are you asking me on a date, Matthew Girard?"

"I am. What do you say, want to go?"

"I'll think about it." She looked away, leaned back against the wall. Oddly, he felt disappointed.

"What happened to that twenty-four hour pass you were planning to give me? The one where I keep you in bed and don't let you out until every last hour has passed?"

She sighed. "It was a nice thought, Matt, but maybe it's best if we don't explore this any further."

He couldn't believe it. Couldn't frigging believe she was blowing him off. And yet he should have expected it. *Can't have things both ways, dude.* "Is this because of what I said earlier?"

"You said a lot of things earlier."

"About the job coming first." He didn't know why he'd said it, considering he might not have a job.

She met his gaze then. Her expression was a mixture of sadness and resignation. "You didn't say it, I did. You just agreed." She sighed. "You broke my heart once before. I think I'd like to keep it intact this time."

Pain twisted inside him. "I didn't know I broke your heart."

"You should have."

He nodded. "Yeah, I should have. I was young and stupid." She'd been his friend for so long—his best friend at a time when he needed her—and then they'd drifted apart as he'd gotten involved with his friends at Rochambeau High. He'd known, on a level he hadn't been willing to admit, how she felt about him. And he'd been so dangerously close to feeling something similar that he'd pushed her out of his life as hard as he could.

"You said you'd missed me. I missed you too." She sighed. "It almost feels like we've never been apart in some ways."

"Butch and Sundance ride again."

She laughed. "Yes, but apparently with real danger and mayhem this time." She sobered. "But we're adults now, and you've made it pretty clear that your job is your priority. So maybe we should keep being friends, now that we've found each other again, and leave it at that."

He swallowed his disappointment. "All right."

What else could he say? But he didn't like it, didn't like the thought of not kissing her silky skin again, of not tasting her and driving her crazy with his tongue on her most sensitive flesh. Of not losing himself inside her and forgetting who and where he was, even if only for a few moments. Because she meant something to him, and she made him feel something more than the emptiness he usually felt. He would never forget his guilt over Marco and Jim, but she made him feel like it was bearable somehow. Like there was something redeeming about him after all. She wasn't obligated to care for him by family bonds —but she did anyway.

Goddamn it.

She reached for his hand, squeezed. "Thanks for understanding."

But he didn't understand, not really. He had a dark urge to haul her into the bedroom and thrust hard into her. To thrust until she recanted every word she'd just said. Until she begged him never to leave.

"I *am* leaving my job." His throat was thick with the words. But the second they were out, he felt better somehow.

She looked confused. "Why? I thought you loved what you did."

"I do. But I may not have a choice. Probably don't have a choice. And not because of this, Evie."

"Because of what happened when you were captured."

He gave a brief nod. "It's not by choice."

He couldn't believe he'd admitted that, but somehow it felt right telling her. She gazed up at him with big, sad eyes. He slid into the seat across from her and she reached for his hand. He let her take it and squeezed back when she squeezed in reassurance.

"Our last mission went wrong. I trusted someone I shouldn't and we were led into an ambush. Two of my men died, and the rest of us spent a hellish ten days in captivity before we managed to get free. I don't think any of us believed we were ever coming back." He sucked in another breath. "I'll probably be relieved next week. I have to return for a hearing, but I think it's simply a formality. If I'm relieved, my military career is over. They'll assign me to a desk for the rest of my commitment. If I'm lucky," he added.

She frowned. "I'm sorry, Matt. I know you love your job, and I know you would never have done anything you thought would hurt your team or those you were sent to rescue."

"They blame me. I can't fault them for it. Kev was wary, my gut was telling me it was wrong, and my head wouldn't listen."

Surprise etched her features. "I don't know how you can say they blame you. You told me earlier that what you're doing to help me is against the rules, and yet it's not just you. Without your team behind you, we'd have been in big trouble hours ago. They've helped us get this far, and they did it because you asked."

She was right, and yet that'd been weighing on him too. "Kev's following me down a path that will only lead to ruin if he's caught. I hate asking him, and yet I have no choice."

Evie's smile was bittersweet. "You had a choice. But you're just wired to assist people who need you. You can't help it."

"Anyone but you and we wouldn't be sitting here right now."

It was the truth. He felt responsible for her, and not just because of his stupid last act before he'd left town. He'd always felt responsible for her, from the moment she'd looked up at him with her freckles and pigtails and followed him wherever he led her. She'd trusted him and worshiped him and he'd loved her for it.

Maybe he still loved her for it. His insides twisted tight. She'd been the only person to ever take him for what he was, to see beneath the surface and adore him anyway.

But that was long ago, and you couldn't love someone because of what you'd meant to each other when you were children. It didn't work that way.

"Yes, you would." Her faith in him was steadfast and it made him want to drop his head onto his arms and weep. She reached out and touched his temple, and he thought he would dissolve at that simple touch. "How's your head?"

"Better. In fact," he said, glancing at his watch to cover his emotional turmoil, "it's time for another shot of Tylenol."

"I'll get it," she said when he started to move. She pushed herself up and went over to the cabinet where the First Aid kit was located. She brought back the pills and a bottle of water from the fridge.

Matt shook two pills into his hand and cracked open the water, gulping both.

"Why don't you lie down in the bedroom for a while? You could probably use a nap."

He shook his head. "No can do. It won't take the Kid long, and then we'll need to make our next move."

She looked concerned. "So lie down until then."

He was adamant. "No. I'll lean back here." His eyes were heavy and gritty. He was accustomed to it in the field, yet he wasn't necessarily accustomed to the soft cushioning of a three-hundred-thousand-dollar yacht beneath his ass while he waited for the order to go. It would be easy to doze. Too easy. He jerked himself out of that dreamlike state of pre-sleep and set the alarm on his phone for fifteen minutes. "Fifteen minutes and then we'll decide what to do next if we haven't heard back from my team."

She didn't look very happy about it, but she shrugged. "You're the boss."

A gut feeling woke Matt with a start, his pulse hammering in his ears as he reached for the .45. Evie wasn't at the table, and he had no idea how long he'd slept. He grabbed his phone and checked the alarm. It was off, and right now he didn't know whether he'd done it in his sleep or she'd done it instead.

And he didn't have time to worry about it.

He shoved to his feet and lurched toward the stairs. He'd heard something. Or thought he heard something. A cry? He emerged into the predawn darkness, his eyes focusing on Evie standing at the stern, her hands gripping the rail.

A sound in the water shot a spike of adrenaline through his system. Before he could do anything about it, someone spoke.

"You get him right now, Evie. You pull anything, I'll blow your sister's brains out, you got that? I want to see that sonofabitch standing beside you with his hands on his head."

Evie turned to call for him, the words dying as her gaze met his. She looked scared and hopeful all at once. Goddammit, there was nothing he could do. He knew it in that instant, that one look. He couldn't see them, but he knew there was a man and he had a gun held to Sarah. If Matt stalled for time, tried to slip into the water and come around behind them, the guy'd kill somebody. Maybe Sarah, maybe Evie.

Maybe both.

He couldn't let that happen. He slipped the gun beneath his T-shirt at the small of his back and stepped forward, hands on head. An airboat bobbed to the rear of the yacht. A man and two women stood there, staring up at them. How had he missed the sound of an airboat engine roaring up in the night? It wasn't exactly quiet.

The man had an arm around the neck of one of the women and what looked like a .357 at her temple. The sky was just beginning to lighten, but it was hard to mistake the silhouette of a weapon like that. Jesus Christ, if he shot her there'd be nothing left for the paramedics to retrieve. It was a big, brawny weapon and destructive as hell.

"Glad you could join us, Rambo. Bree, get up there and frisk them both."

The woman from the docks earlier climbed on board and leveled a 9 mil at his heart. "Drop it, handsome."

"Drop what? My pants?" Okay, so he was fucking pissed. Amateurs, both of them, and they'd gotten the jump on him. He shouldn't have closed his eyes for a second. A major fucking mistake.

"Another time," she said with a smirk. "I meant the gun."

"I'm not armed." And if he could get his hands on her, she wouldn't be either. She just needed to come a little closer.

She wasn't buying it and she wasn't moving. "Sure you are. One-handed, you get it and drop it on the deck. You try anything, I'll blow you into next week."

"Thanks for the offer, but you aren't my type."

She grabbed Evie by the arm and pressed the pistol to her jaw. Evie's eyes went wide, stark terror reflected in their depths.

He was fucked.

Matt slowly dropped one hand, reached behind his back, lifted the gun, and tossed it on the deck.

"Kick it here."

He did. Brianna let Evie go and shoved her toward him. Matt caught her as she stumbled.

"I'm sorry. I shouldn't have turned your alarm off. But you were so tired, and—"

"Too late for apologies, Evie." His voice was hard because he was focused on the job, on getting out of this with all three of them alive.

She recoiled, but he couldn't take time to reassure her right now. He needed his mind in a different place. The kind of place where he wasn't constantly thinking about what he'd do if someone shot her, if she died tonight and he couldn't save her. He couldn't risk even a moment of tenderness if it knocked him off his game.

Brianna had snatched his pistol off the deck and held hers on them both while Sarah and the man climbed on board. The man shoved Sarah forward and she fell. Evie went down on her knees, grabbed on, and hugged Sarah tight. The girl broke down, sobbing.

"I'm sorry, Evie, sorry I went with them—" Her voice dissolved in wracking sobs.

"Sweetie, it's okay. Shh, shh. Did they hurt you? How did you get this black eye?"

The girl didn't answer, and Evie stopped asking and just held her close, rubbing her back while she cried. Matt's resolve hardened. If he got his hands on this guy for even a second, he'd break his fucking neck.

"How sweet. Now where's my disc? You've had plenty of time to get it, babe."

Matt swore silently as realization struck. *This* man was David West. Hell, Matt didn't need a hearing at all. It was obvious he wasn't any good anymore. If he couldn't avoid letting a couple of amateur thugs take him by surprise, he didn't need to be in charge of an elite team like HOT.

Matt stared hard at Evie, willing her to look at him. If she admitted they had the disc, this was the end of the line. He could feel it in his bones. This guy was desperate, and desperation bred recklessness. If they handed over the disc, David and Brianna weren't going gently into that good night. West would shoot all three of them and drop them in the bayou for the gators to dispose of.

Evie lifted her head. Even in the dim light, Matt recognized the signs of fury taking root in her. Her expression was hard, her limbs shaking as she pulled her sister up and wrapped her in her arms.

God, she was something else. Brave and beautiful, yet vulnerable too. She was everything good that he'd never thought he deserved. When had he realized how empty his life was without her in it? He wanted more, but he didn't know how that would ever happen.

Even if they got through this, how could he ask her to be a part of his life when he didn't yet know what that life would be?

Evie didn't even glance at him. Her voice was cool when she spoke. "I don't have it yet."

"Where is it?"

"Reynier's Retreat." Her voice was so smooth, as if she weren't lying through her teeth. "We were waiting for morning when we could see better to navigate the bayou."

Matt shouldn't have been stunned. But he was. She lied so well, so beautifully, like this bastard didn't bother her at all. And yet now he had no doubt she knew their lives were on the line. He wanted to wrap her in his arms and protect her. And he wanted to tell her how damn proud he was of her. He knew, right now, if he never got another thing out of life except one more night with her, that would be enough for him.

David looked up at the sky. "Well it's damn near morning, isn't it? Bree, you know how to drive this thing, right?"

"Better'n you, Gilligan."

Matt perked up. Trouble in paradise? Anything that might work to his advantage, no matter how small, was worth thinking about.

"Then let's go." David ignored the smartass remark. "The plantation is up the next tributary, right?"

"Yeah," Matt answered. No sense lying about it. If Brianna bottomed the boat out in the channel, it might give Matt a chance to take down David. The senator'd be pissed off if his boat got ruined, but that was the last thing Matt cared about at the moment.

"Let's hustle, Bree." Brianna shot David a hard glare but climbed the steps to the command bridge without complaint. A second later, the engines hummed to life.

West slapped at a mosquito, then motioned with his gun. "Get inside. You, pretty boy, hands on head. You try anything, I'll shoot first and ask questions later, got it?"

"Come on," Evie said to Sarah, pulling her forward.

"Let her go down first," David said. "You come here."

Evie didn't hesitate, though Matt's heart suddenly leapt into his throat. She went to David, who leveled the gun at her chest and gave Matt a hard stare. "Now, try anything, Rambo, and I'm shooting your sweetheart. Move."

Matt ducked into the cabin, hands still laced over his skull. Sarah had already stumbled down the steps and collapsed in a heap on the banquette. Rage slammed through him at the sight of her under the bright lights. Her shirt was torn and she was covered in bloody welts. Dried blood snaked down the white skin of her right forearm to her elbow. The right wrist was raw beneath the cuffs and her left eye was swollen, the skin beneath it turning purple.

Evie came next with David right behind her. Matt stood in the middle of the cabin, imagining all the ways in which he'd take delight in slamming this asshole's head against a wall. West was a good six inches shorter than Matt's six-two and his build was slighter. Matt had no concerns he'd lose a fight with this guy.

When Evie saw her sister beneath the cabin lights, she let out a cry. Then she turned to David, who still held the gun on her, fists clenched at her sides. "You get those cuffs off her right now."

"I don't take orders from you anymore, sweetcakes. Sit down and shut the fuck up."

"She's a kid, for God's sake. If you want to cuff someone, cuff me."

David's eyes narrowed. Matt could almost hear the wheels grinding and he knew he wasn't going to like it one bit. "Better yet, why don't you put them on Rambo for me."

Fuck.

"Give me the key." Evie held her hand out, waiting. It was too much to hope she'd know how to cuff him without actually cuffing him.

David produced a key and dropped it in her palm. Evie went over and unlocked Sarah, her face white with compressed fury. Sarah wrapped her freed arms around herself and kept crying.

When Evie looked at him, he thought she might crack. She blamed herself. He could see it in her face. She'd added the commandeering of the yacht and getting him handcuffed to her list of personal sins.

The yacht accelerated at that moment, knocking Evie off balance enough that she fell against him. The contact electrified him, solidified his resolve to get them out of this mess. Some way, somehow, he was making love to her again at least once before he died. No way was it ending here. He set her away from him and stuck his wrists out, hoping David wouldn't tell her to cuff him behind.

With shaking hands, she wrapped one cuff around his wrist and snapped it closed. He watched the top of her head and willed her to look up at him. She did, her eyes watery with unshed tears. So much sorrow contained in those depths. All he wanted to do was stand here and drown in her eyes.

"It's okay," he said softly. "Go ahead."

She reached for his other wrist.

"Behind his back, Evie."

She snapped the cuff in place quickly and whirled away from him. "What's it matter? He's still cuffed. You want his hands behind his back, you do it yourself."

David simply glared at her. "You're a pain in the ass, you know that?"

"And you're a liar and a thief."

Dear God. Matt's insides threatened to melt. She was baiting a guy who would just as soon shoot her as look at her. He didn't need this, didn't need to worry about her safety when it was imperative he be ready to take this guy down when the opportunity arose.

"Sticks and stones, babe." David edged over to the table and opened the laptop with one hand.

"So what happened," Evie threw out. "Did you lose your computer, Ace?"

David looked up and pressed the power button. "If I didn't need you to get that disc, I might have to dump you over the side, you know that?" He jerked his head toward Matt. "Did you tell him you can't swim? That you'd rather wait tables naked than stick a toe in the water?"

Evie crossed her arms and didn't say anything. She simply glared. Matt already knew she wasn't a good swimmer, so he didn't know why she seemed embarrassed about it.

"Doesn't matter," he said. "I still think she's got more balls than you."

David's gaze slewed over. "Maybe I should shoot you now. Can't imagine why I need *you* for anything."

Matt didn't bother answering. The guy was simply baiting him. West wasn't ready to eliminate anyone, plain and simple. He was a calculating bastard. He was the kind of guy who didn't make a move without being certain he'd gone to the next level of the game. He wouldn't kill any of them while he thought he might need one of them for something.

It wasn't much consolation, but it was something.

The laptop chimed, indicating the operating system was online. West pressed a few keys, no doubt bringing up the e-mail program. Matt wasn't worried he'd find any-thing there. A couple of minutes later, he'd obviously decided the computer was a dead end. He slapped it closed and hitched a leg on the table.

Evie sank onto the banquette as Brianna Sweeney jacked the speed up another level. Sarah put her head in Evie's lap and held on to her waist while Evie smoothed her hair.

"Why'd you do it?" Evie said. "If you'd have asked me for the damn CD, I'd have given it to you. You didn't have to do any of this. You didn't have to hurt a kid."

"It wasn't me. Talk to Bree up there about your sister."

"Why didn't you just tell me what you wanted when you called?"

"Believe me, if you'd shown up at your mother's before Bree and the boys did, I'd have gotten the disc and left."

"So it's Brianna's fault, huh?" Evie shook her head. "I guess she's forcing you to threaten us now too."

"It's not personal."

"What do you plan to do with us once you have the CD?"

David shrugged. "Won't need you then. You'll be free to go."

Like hell they would. Matt didn't look over at Evie, didn't want to scare her, but there was no way this guy was letting them go. He'd gone too far, done too much, to risk it. One man was already dead, and Matt would lay odds that West had been the one holding the knife, family be damned. The choice of weapon had been symbolic, as if he were planning to eviscerate someone who used knives regularly.

A chef, perhaps.

Matt suppressed the shiver that threatened and focused on how he was going to get free and stop this asshole. Whatever was in those files was beyond important to David and he'd do anything to retrieve them. Time was running out for him. The odor of desperation surrounded him like a blanket.

Matt's phone buzzed insistently, vibrating the table. Sonofabitch, he'd left it there when he'd gone outside looking for Evie. David watched the phone with interest.

He jerked his head at Matt. "Get over here and answer it. You say anything about what's going on here, anything that sounds like a code, and I'll kill you where you stand."

He got up and backed away from the table, the gun pointed at Matt's chest. Matt moved slowly, half hoping Kev would give up if he took long enough but knowing his teammate wouldn't. He was across the cabin in two strides, his gaze on David. He rolled his shoulders, aching to take this guy down. He could do it. Handcuffed, he could still do it. Something of his thoughts must have telegraphed to West because the dude backed up another step, the move automatic. He looked annoyed, like he'd admitted something he didn't want Matt to know.

Yeah, motherfucker, I intimidate you, don't I? Get close enough and I'll show you why you should be afraid...

"On speaker," David said as Matt slowly reached for the phone.

He pressed the talk button, leaving the phone where it lay on the table. "Girard."

"You ain't gonna believe what's on this disc, Richie—"

"Put the report on my desk, Sergeant."

There was a long pause on the other end. "Yes, sir," Kev said. "Copy."

TWENTY

KEV LOOKED UP FROM WHERE he was sitting at his desk, met Mendez's eyes, and stated what was obvious to them all. "The mission's compromised, sir."

Mendez rubbed a hand over his salty high-and-tight haircut. "Goddamn, this gets more and more interesting, doesn't it?"

Kev didn't think the colonel wanted an answer, so he didn't offer one. Something was wrong and they all knew it. When Mendez snuck up on them earlier, he'd been one pissed off dude. A pissed colonel was never a good thing for a soldier's health and Kev had been envisioning a pretty grim future.

But then Billy's program cracked the code and the files opened like an accordion out of control. This David West had enough dirt on mob boss Ryan Rivera and his connections to send a whole lot of people to jail for a very long time. The information on that disc could effectively dismantle one of the major organized crime operations on the West Coast, put a damper on East Coast activities, and stop the flow of drugs from at least one source.

The colonel cussed a blue streak but understood the significance. He'd authorized them to give Matt the information and advise him to exfiltrate the situation immediately.

Now Mendez lit up the room with words Kev wasn't sure he'd ever heard. The colonel could swear in six languages, and Kev had no doubt that's what was going on.

Billy Blake sat at his desk with his fingers poised over his keyboard, eyes wide. Jack Hunter leaned against the doorjamb, cool as a cucumber. His blond surfer-boy looks gave absolutely no hint to the lethal skill lurking beneath the surface. His superior abilities with a 50-caliber sniper rifle were legendary in the spec ops community. The guy'd taken out two terrorists on board a yacht from a little under two miles away—an unofficial record since the United States couldn't admit involvement in the incident— and then gone in and rescued the dizzy American pop star who'd been stupid enough to think her Greek industrialist boyfriend was really just a Greek industrialist. Hawk hadn't been quite right since that encounter, quieter and more introspective maybe, but then none of them had been in the right frame of mind since the last op.

They were a matched fucking set, weren't they? God pity the woman who tangled with one of them.

Kev forced his mind back to the issue at hand. He could do something about his team leader's current predicament. All he needed was the go from Mendez.

"Shit," the colonel said. "I'm gonna fucking fry for this."

Kev let out a relieved breath. Jack's tense stance eased, and Billy's fingers started to fly even before the CO gave the order. Mendez was on board, consequences be damned.

"Enable the satellite tracking on his phone," Mendez said. "Let's find out where these bastards are. Soon as we got it, call in the locals. No time to get a team down there."

"Hoo-ah, sir," they said in unison.

Kev just hoped Matt was in a position to stay alive a little while longer. They needed time to track him. Not much, true, but sometimes even a minute was too long when lives were on the line.

Evie let out the breath she'd been holding when Matt disconnected the call. Sarah held her so tight it broke her heart. Just a couple of days ago she'd been a typical teenager who didn't much cotton to a prodigal big sister. And now the kid clung to her like Evie was her salvation. It wasn't right.

A couple of steps away, David gripped the gun in a white-knuckled fist. Matt stood beside the table, his cuffed hands resting in front of his body. And yet he looked anything but helpless. David sensed it too, if his grip was any indication.

She lowered her gaze to Sarah's dark head and continued smoothing her sister's hair. Pain exploded in Evie's scalp as David wrapped a fist in her hair and yanked her off the banquette. She cried out as her hip smacked hard against the cabin floor. Her eyes smarted with tears. Sarah wailed, reaching for her. Somehow, Matt was there, preventing Sarah from latching onto Evie as David tugged her back toward the steps leading up to the deck. She scrambled to keep up with him, to keep him from ripping her hair out or killing her in his rage.

When David stopped moving, Evie felt the cold press of metal to her temple. She closed her eyes, then snapped them open again to meet Matt's icy stare. If she was about to die, the very last thing she wanted to see was his face. It didn't matter that he'd gone into badass mode, that his expression was carefully blank of emotion, or that she could have meant about as much to him as what he'd had for dinner for all the concern he showed.

"Where the fuck is that disc?" David demanded.

"What makes you think I have it?" Matt's voice was ice.

The gun dug into her head. "If you don't hand it over, I'll kill her."

Matt shrugged. "You'll kill her anyway. And me and the girl along with her."

"Maybe, but I don't see where you have a choice. Not if you want her to stay alive for more than the next five minutes."

Matt managed to look menacing enough that the pressure of the gun eased up slightly. He tilted his chin toward the table where his phone lay. "You heard him. They've cracked the code. You kill us and you're gonna have the meanest motherfucking Special Forces team the military ever created tracking your ass." If anything, his voice grew harder, colder. "I've spent a lot of miserable hours in some of the worst shitholes this world has to offer with those guys. If you think we don't know ways you've never thought of to kill a man, you aren't as smart as you seem. What they do to you will make a mob hit look like a pleasant death."

The flat, dead look in Matt's eyes made her heart ache. What had he been through that could leach the life out of him like that? She wanted to hold him, to disappear with him. She focused on him and tried to shut out David and the reality of the gun barrel against her skin.

I love you. The words popped into her head, and she knew they were true. It was a stunning realization. And a sobering one. She wanted to say the words, wanted him to know, and yet she couldn't endanger him. Couldn't put any thought in his head that pulled him out of the zone. Somehow, she knew that instinctively.

David let go of her hair, put his arm around her waist, and jerked her against him. The gun dropped, reappeared beneath her chin. He dragged her up the steps. She stumbled, grabbing his arm with one hand to steady herself. The movement dredged up a memory.

"Get it," David said, "or so help me God I'm throwing her to the alligators."

Matt eased backward toward the galley. He jerked his head in the direction of the sink. "I have to reach under there."

David moved his head so it was behind hers, making himself less of a target. Hot breath fanned her neck. He was nothing like the man she'd once known and that saddened her as much as it angered her. "If you come out of there with anything besides a CD, you've signed Evie's death warrant."

From the vantage point of the steps, she could see as Matt stooped and slowly stretched his arms into the cabinet. He fumbled for a second and then something ripped, excruciatingly slow. Tape, she realized. He must have done that while she slept.

Slowly, he stood, the disc in his hand. David trembled. The pressure of metal against her skin wavered as he sagged against her momentarily. Her breath ripped into her chest like a dagger. She had one chance. *One*. She could do it, could stop him right now.

She *had* to do it. It was up to her to save them all.

She willed her fingers to move. What had Matt shown her? The nerve right below the elbow, inside of the arm, against the bone. *Squeeze hard*. Mess it up, and he'd blow her head off. Lightning fast, she dug her fingers into his arm, praying she had the right spot.

David swore, his grip tightening on her as the gun shifted away. The sound as it went off was deafening. She felt the hot breeze of the bullet, the concussion of the explosion against her skin, but she didn't let go. Matt yelled at her as he shielded Sarah, but the blood pounded so hard in her ears she couldn't focus on what he said. He'd covered Sarah's small body with his bigger one, and he looked murderous.

Evie ignored him, dug harder, felt the instant her fingertips slid between muscle. She squeezed for all she was worth. David's breath rushed out and he dropped the gun at the same time he began to fall to his knees. She spun away as he fell, kept up the pressure, and aimed a foot at his crotch.

She only landed a glancing blow, her foot hitting his thigh instead. He grunted. She had balled up her fist and was about to smash him in the face when the boat lurched hard forward. She lost her grip as she was thrown backward on the rebound. She sailed over David's head and onto the deck, landing in a tangled mess of arms, legs, and pain. The rear deck slammed into her, knocking the breath from her body. She was thrown up and against the rear wall until she found herself doubled at the waist, hanging over the side with the water a couple of feet beneath her head.

Somehow she managed to claw her way back onto the deck, sliding down the wall until her ass hit the floor. Evie drew in a painful breath and wheezed to get air into her lungs. The yacht listed starboard. She launched herself forward and struggled on hands and knees toward the cabin, her vision wavering as hot liquid burned into her eyes.

She wiped her face, her hand coming away red. *Oh God, had she been shot?*

She struggled not to panic and to coolly assess her body for injuries. She touched her head again, finding it tender. A cut on her scalp. They bled like a bitch. She wasn't dying; she wasn't shot. Relief flooded her.

Where was Sarah? And Matt?

She groped toward the cabin. Sarah was sitting on the floor, pushing her hair from her face.

"Are you hurt?" Evie asked.

"No." She lifted a shaking hand, dropped it again. "I hit the wall, but I'm okay."

"Where's Matt?"

"I don't know. He grabbed the other guy and when I looked up again, they were gone."

Evie spun away. A glance up to the command bridge revealed Brianna slumped against the seat. First things first. Evie scrambled up the steps, her heart pumping, her stomach aching. She had to get to the other woman before she regained her senses and got her gun.

Evie rocketed to the top, then stumbled to a halt. One side of Brianna's head was smashed in, blood and brain matter sprayed over the console. Evie swallowed a sob and spun away.

God, she'd never wish that on anyone. Poor Bree. Whatever her sins, she shouldn't have died like that. Evie went to the railing, breathing deeply, trying not to lose the little bit of food she had in her stomach.

A movement in the water caught her attention.

David's blond hair and Matt's darker head disappeared beneath the surface.

No!

David bobbed back up, his head and shoulders above the water. He seemed to be pushing on something, pushing down.

Drowning Matt.

Oh God, no! She spun around, searching for the gun, anything she could use, but it was gone. There was nothing. Evie took a sobbing breath, her arms and legs trembling as she stared at the brackish water far below. There were things in there, nasty things, things that bit and stung and killed.

Matt.

But, oh God, she loved him and she wasn't going to let David take him away from her too.

Evie shot down the stairs and jumped onto the edge of the listing boat, balancing her body in that one last second before she committed herself to what she was about to do. All she had to do was launch herself as far as she could and try to land on top of David and pull him away. She could do it.

She *had* to do it. She had no choice.

Dark, dank water yawned beneath her. The sky was brighter now, but the bayou was still murky. There could be a snake. A gator. Certain death lurked beneath that surface. She couldn't *swim*. Not like that. Not after diving into the murk.

But if she didn't jump, certain death would claim Matt. David was still above the water and Matt wasn't.

Evie bent her legs and sprung into thin air. She was suspended there for what seemed like forever, falling in slow motion. She reached out, stretched her arms as far as she could, and grasped David's shoulders as she came down hard on the water. The impact hurt like hell, knocking the air out of her for the second time and stinging her skin with the power of millions of tiny needles.

But she refused to let go. She scissored her legs, got them beneath her and then around David's waist, dragging him backward with all her weight. It didn't take much effort, or it happened so fast it seemed like it didn't take any effort; then they were falling under with David on top of her.

Panic clawed at her with icy fingers, but she held on and held her breath until she thought she was going to pop. She couldn't see a thing, but David fought her, twisting, pulling, and trying to get his head above water. He snatched at her hair, jerked hard until his fingers slipped through the slippery strands, then tried to twist again. He got sideways enough to get a hand around her neck, then squeezed hard while she resisted the urge to cry out. She'd gulp black water if she did. Just when she thought it was over, when her lungs couldn't hold it another minute, air burst into her chest.

First, she wondered what had happened to David. He was gone, as if he'd vaporized into nothing. Second, she realized she was standing up, that her feet were on the bottom and her head and shoulders were above water. She hadn't been in deep water at all. She could have stood up at any time.

But, oh God, where was Matt? Her heart tattooed her ribs as she spun in both directions, looking for him.

A dark shape moved near *Candyland's* ladder. Matt propped a boneless David against the ladder and turned. A shaky breath rattled out of her and his scowl gave way to a smile.

"I think I've got another concussion," he said.

She laughed, but it came out sounding like a sob. She fought her way through almost five feet of water, half swimming and half running, and wrapped her arms around his neck and held on tight. Her heart pounded so hard she couldn't hear a thing he said.

And then she realized it wasn't her heart, but a helicopter. She tilted her head back as the police helicopter passed over them. Instructions issued from a loudspeaker, but she wasn't listening. She was clinging to Matt, loving the feel of his warm wet body against hers, and thanking God he was still alive.

"I thought I'd lost you," she said, her cheek against his chest.

He squeezed her. "You didn't."

Evie closed her eyes. *Not yet* remained unspoken.

Detectives Proctor and Odell sat across from Evie and Matt at a table in a room far more comfortable than the one she'd been shown to last night—or was that the night before? She was so tired she couldn't remember which day was which, or when this nightmare had begun.

Now, thankfully, it was over. Or mostly over.

With both hands, Evie lifted the cup of coffee she'd been given, inhaled the fragrant steam, and sipped. Who'd have ever thought office supply store coffee could taste so good?

Beside her, Matt recounted everything that'd happened since they'd left her mother's ruined house earlier. Evie interjected comments as necessary, but mostly she left it to Matt. It was up to him to decide how much to reveal about the military's involvement, so she kept quiet and savored the weak coffee. Best damn coffee she'd ever had.

Proctor took notes, tight-lipped, but Odell was friendly and effusive.

"It'll take time to ID the body, but it seems as if the deceased is actually a George Allen Larson. His mother and David West's mother are identical twins. Larson was a year older than his cousin."

"We still don't know who killed Larson," Proctor added. "West claims it was the dead woman."

Odell cut in. "But we know that West, Larson, and Brianna Sweeney all worked for Ryan Rivera's California operation. There was another guy too, a Julian Fletcher.

We found his body this morning near Charlie's Diner. He was shot with a three fifty-seven."

"West's gun," Matt said.

"Yes, though we have yet to run ballistics on it."

"What about the house?"

Odell shot a look at his partner. "Unrelated, in fact. Kyle Jenkins was feeling a bit upset over his falling out with Sarah Savoie, so he decided to try one of his home-made bombs in the yard. Except when he got there and realized no one was home, he thought it'd be more fun to set it off inside. For good measure, he turned on the gas. While he was setting the explosion, someone, presumably West, stole his truck."

"I hope you plan to keep him locked up for a while," Evie said sternly, meaning Kyle.

Odell's gaze settled on her. He had no trouble figuring out who she meant. "We surely do. Judge Hunt set bail at fifty thousand dollars, so Jenkins won't be getting out anytime soon."

"What about my sister? She's underage, and he was buying her beer. And God knows what else."

Odell looked sympathetic. "Not much we can do about that, really. The only crime he's committed that we can prove is setting the pipe bomb."

Evie gritted her teeth. She knew it would have to be enough, but she was still pissed off that Kyle Jenkins had left her sister in the middle of nowhere after they'd fought. If not for that, Sarah might have never come into contact with Brianna and her thugs. On the other hand, if she'd been at home as she was supposed to be, who knows what could have happened if either Brianna or David had shown up there when she was alone.

Thankfully, Sarah was going to be okay. The EMTs had already taken her to the hospital to be checked out. She'd be reunited with Mama, and she'd give her statement to the police when the doctors were through with her.

And then Evie was going to hug her tight and not let go for at least an hour.

The detectives talked a few more minutes and then left Matt and Evie to write out their official statements. As soon as the door closed, Matt took the coffee from her hand and set it on the table. Next, he pulled her into his lap and crushed his mouth down on hers.

Evie threaded her fingers into his hair and kissed him for all she was worth. They hadn't been alone since the ordeal on the yacht. When she was gasping for breath and Matt's erection pressed insistently into her bottom, she broke the kiss with one hand laid against his chest.

"If you ever, ever do anything like that again," he growled.

"Like what?" She'd jumped into the water to save him, the stupid man. Not that he'd needed saving apparently. Going under was part of the strategy, according to him. He'd had his cuffed hands on David the entire time. David hadn't been pushing down; he'd been trying to get away.

"I told you never to do that to a guy with a gun. It was the wrong maneuver to use."

Evie pushed upright in his arms. "Well I don't think it was. I stopped him, didn't I?"

"Plowing into an underwater stump stopped him. He could have killed you."

"He was on the way down when Bree wrecked the yacht."

"Jesus, Evie, you scared the hell out me. When that

fucking *cannon* went off—holy shit." He shook his head and twisted a lock of her hair around his finger.

"Hmm, it was a bit loud." And she had a powder burn on one arm where the gun had been so close when it fired.

His laugh was strangled. "Damn, that's an understatement." He squeezed her to him, nuzzling her ear. Shivers streaked across her skin.

"What now, Matt?" She was breathless, aching for him, dying to tell him about all these crazy feelings inside her, and confused all at once.

His gray gaze met hers. "I know what you said earlier, but I want to go back to Reynier's Retreat and spend the next twenty-four hours in bed together."

She hooked a finger in the sleeve of his T-shirt, fiddling with the material. She wanted to say yes. Planned to say yes. Anything to be with him. Anything…

"I'm not sure I can," she said softly. "I have to go to the hospital, have to figure out where Mama and Sarah and I are going to stay now—"

"You can all stay in the guesthouse. I'll clear it with Misty Lee, but you need a place and it's furnished. I'll be gone day after tomorrow."

Evie forced herself to smile. "Yes, I know."

His eyes were suddenly flat, haunted. Confused.

"I told you before that I can't give you anything." He pressed a fist to his chest, his voice coming out low and soft. "There's not much in here, but whatever I have is yours. Except that I can't ask you to be a part of this life yet. I don't know what's going to happen or what the consequences are—"

"I don't care about that. I care about you."

His beautiful eyes were so serious. "I care about you

339

too." He ran a knuckle against her cheek. "Now is all I have, Evie. Right now. You'll understand after I'm gone."

Evie disentangled herself and slipped back into her chair, her eyes stinging and throat aching. There were things happening here that she wasn't quite ready for. "Now's not the time to talk about this. We need to write our statements."

"I'm trying not to be a jerk about this." He raked a hand through his hair and rested his forehead in his palm, letting out a frustrated sigh. "Fuck, this is why I don't get involved." He raised his head. "I'm pretty sure I'm not the kind of guy who can make you happy, Evie. I want to be, but I don't know that I can."

"Isn't that for me to decide?"

His throat worked as he swallowed. "You just had a taste of my life. If by some miracle I don't end up booted out of the Army, do you want more of that? Do you want to wonder about where I am and what I'm doing?"

She dropped her gaze to the cold table. What would it be like to always worry about him? To not know if he was coming back? To be unable to help him?

"And if you get kicked out? What then?"

His mouth tightened. "Right now, right here. This is all I have to give you, Evie. I'm being honest. I can't think about the future just yet."

Her heart felt like glass. And she had to protect it. This time, she had to keep it from shattering. "Then maybe we should say goodbye now. Because I can't be with you and know it's going nowhere."

He stared at her for a long, tense moment.

"Très bien, chère, très bien." He picked up the pen and started to write.

TWENTY-ONE

MATT WORE SUNGLASSES FOR THE wedding. The doctor told him he needed to stay inside and rest, but he was one of Ben's groomsmen and he had to be there. Christina looked happier than he'd ever seen her. Her hands shook as she took the ring from her maid of honor and slipped it onto Ben's finger. For a moment, he imagined himself in her place with a woman who smiled, cried, and held up her hand for the ring he would slip—

Shit no. He shook his head and took a deep breath. No way. He couldn't. Even if he was done in HOT, he didn't know what the future held; he couldn't involve Evie in his life until he did. Was he supposed to ask her to wait for him? How could he do that to her?

And if by some miracle he went back to the team, then what? He knew what it cost the guys who were married. He'd served with them before, saw the pain and agony in their faces every time the C-130 lifted off. They loved the job too much to quit and their families too much not to.

Pure fucking hell. Maybe it was best she'd walked

away, though he still felt a pinch in his chest where his heart ached. She'd left him, and it was the right thing to do.

But he was fucking miserable.

Magnolias and jasmine perfumed the air, wrapping around his senses and making him think of a different kind of perfume, the one he associated with Evie. Citrus and spice, flowers and woman. How would he ever breathe normally again?

He lifted his gaze, trying to shift focus. Beyond the garden, the water of the bayou sparkled with the red fire of the setting sun. Hard to believe that only a day ago he'd been on the verge of dying out there.

The senator had been remarkably nonplussed about the wrecking of his yacht. He'd already called in a firm to raise her out of the bayou and transport her to dry dock for repairs. The stump had torn a hole in her bow and she'd gotten waterlogged. Thankfully, the damage was mostly limited to the hull. Matt expected the old man to blow a gasket, but he'd simply clamped Matt's shoulder and squeezed briefly. Matt still wasn't sure what that meant, but it didn't seem to be a hostile gesture. In fact, it was probably the friendliest overture he'd had from his father in years.

He hadn't seen Evie since yesterday morning. After she'd had the cut over her eye taped by the EMTs, they'd spent a couple of hours at the police station. He'd thought they would leave together, but he'd fucked that up beyond repair by trying to be truthful with her. She'd written her statement in silence, then left him sitting there alone calling himself six kinds of a jackass and wondering how to get her back, even if only for a moment.

The vows wrapped up and the wedding guests adjourned to a different part of the garden for the reception. People came up to him, congratulated him, and asked all kinds of questions about his profession and if he usually did this kind of thing for the military. He gave the standard vague answers, his head lightly pulsing with a headache brought on by not one, but two blows to the skull within a few hours' time. It was a miracle the headache wasn't worse. Hell, it was a miracle he was upright and had the power of speech.

He'd gone after West the instant the boat crashed. He'd realized what was happening immediately, braced himself for it, and grabbed the guy as he came hurtling toward him. They ended up on the deck when they were thrown forward and West scrambled outside as Matt tried to catch him. Matt flipped West into the water and followed, hell-bent on squeezing the life out of the motherfucker. He was about to do just that when David was forcibly ripped from his grasp.

God, she'd scared the shit out of him. Again.

Evie, thinking to save him—his ridiculous, brave, beautiful chef. His best friend in the world. She'd battled her greatest fear and leapt in after him. He should be ecstatic. He should be loving her silly right about now, stroking into her while they both shuddered and gasped and came.

Yeah, but he'd fucked that up pretty good, hadn't he? He'd never get that chance again.

"Hey there, Richie," a soft voice said, and he turned to the right, seeing her leaning against a column a few feet away on the wraparound veranda, her body encased from breast to knee in a silky navy dress. He excused himself from one of the senator's donors who was holding court with a bevy of ladies and gentlemen and made his way to her.

"I didn't think I'd see you again."

She shrugged one gorgeous shoulder. "I had this wedding invitation, you see." The strapless dress fit her like a glove, sending his imagination into overdrive. How could any woman have so many lush curves packed into one small dress? Her breasts jiggled when she moved and sent an arrow of need straight to his groin.

"I'm sorry about earlier. I didn't mean to hurt you."

"I know."

Her black hair was pulled back, away from her face, and piled on top of her head in some concoction that had him concentrating on the slim column of her neck. Damn, he wanted to bite her there. And other places too.

"I didn't expect you'd come, after everything."

She straightened and smoothed the fabric even though it didn't need it. "I didn't plan to. But I couldn't disappoint your sister."

"Is that the only reason?"

She shrugged again.

"If you're here now—if you don't walk away right this minute—you know what's going to happen, right?" His voice sounded rough. Blood surged into his veins, his cock, drowning him in a current of need and want.

"I've resigned myself to it, yes."

He hesitated. "What's that mean, Evie? Because I don't want to hurt you. Honest to God, I don't."

She closed the distance between them, slid a finger down the lapel of his tux, and fiddled with his top button. "I guess it means I've decided to accept your terms."

He couldn't stop himself from drawing her into his arms. She was warm, vibrant, and alive. A woman he cared about. A woman he wanted more than he could remember ever wanting anyone.

He dipped his head to place a kiss on the corner of her mouth. She sighed, turning until her mouth connected with his. His cock throbbed as her tongue slipped against his. She tasted like chocolate, happiness, and all the things he'd ever wanted. A bright light flashed, the work of a photographer. He didn't care.

"I want you," he growled against her throat. "But I'll let you go if it's what you want."

"It's not what I want at all."

He kissed her again, oblivious to any attention they might draw. Before he lost his mind, he lifted his head and scanned the garden. One or two people looked away quickly, but mostly they were concentrating on Chris and Ben and having a good time.

"You want to get out of here?" He prayed the answer was yes.

She smiled up at him. "Oh yeah."

He wrapped an arm around her waist and propelled her into the house. He thought about finding a closet, a bathroom, any secluded spot he could, and burying himself inside her until the world went away.

But he kept going, straight through the house to the front porch, down the steps, and up to a waiting limo. She looked at him quizzically and he shrugged. "I'm in a hurry."

He pulled a fifty from his wallet and told the driver it was his if he'd take them to the guesthouse. The man looked at him strangely, then nodded and climbed in the front to start the car. Two minutes later, Matt fumbled with the key to the front door. He wanted her so frigging bad he couldn't perform a simple task like opening a door. She placed her hand on his and guided the key into the lock. The door slipped open. He turned to her and had the oddest sensation in his chest.

God, he loved her. He'd always loved her, but he'd been too stupid to see it. She made him feel alive, whole, and he needed her so much. But he couldn't tell her those things because it wasn't fair to her. He couldn't drag her into his life until he knew what it was going to be.

He swept her into his arms and across the threshold. When he kicked the door closed and set her down, her fingers tore at his bow tie.

She started on the shirt studs, but he grasped the edges and yanked so the studs went flying.

Her hands splayed over his chest; then she was yanking his T-shirt up and out of his trousers, pressing her hot mouth to his abdomen. He threw his head back, groaning.

"Evie—"

Her quick fingers slid his zipper down. Somehow, he found the side zipper of her dress and tugged it until her breasts sprang free. Her nipples pebbled. He was dying to suck them, dying to make her squirm beneath him. Before he could act on those thoughts, she shoved his shirt and jacket off his shoulders, trapping him with one hand twisted into the fabric. He could get free, of course, but it was damn exciting to watch her take control. To be at her mercy.

"I have to be in you." His voice sounded strange to his own ears.

"All in good time." She let go of the jacket as she

dropped to her knees in front of him, all gorgeous, tempting woman. Her moist lips parted. "Don't you want this?"

Matt closed his eyes as his head fell back. Want it, hell. He'd die if he didn't get it.

She freed his cock from his pants and stroked it until electricity zinged from his scalp to his toes. When her lips parted and she took him inside that gorgeous, lush mouth, he thought he'd come undone in half a second.

It was lust, but it was more than that. So much more. He felt this woman in his blood, his bones. He felt incredible when she was with him. Couldn't imagine another woman doing this to him.

Her tongue swirled around him, flattened against the underside of his aching cock, and tickled the tip until he was gripping her head and gasping. He couldn't let her finish it, couldn't let it be over so damn fast, and yet he wanted nothing more than to thrust between her lips and give himself up to the nirvana.

She made the decision for him. She grabbed his ass with both hands, held him hard against her while she sucked him. He couldn't have stopped the crisis if he tried. His hands threaded into her hair, held her gently yet firmly. If she wanted to stop, she could.

But she didn't.

Her mouth and tongue were magic, lashing him forward until he was like a speeding train incapable of stopping. He'd wanted to come inside her, and yet he thrust into her willing mouth one last time—and lost his everloving mind.

When she'd drained him, he shuddered and groaned and felt like he was falling into a bottomless crevasse the pleasure was so intense. His knees gave way until he was on the floor at eye-level with her.

"Holy shit." Those were the only words he could manage.

What was she doing here? For a second, as Evie stared into Matt's glazed eyes, panic twisted her stomach into a knot. She'd spent the last day and night with Mama and Sarah, getting them all settled at Aunt Betsy's. There'd been calls to the insurance company, another visit from the police, a steady parade of friends and neighbors bearing food and small gifts.

She hadn't planned to see him again. It was simply easier to let him walk away before the vise around her heart squeezed tighter.

But she couldn't do it. She'd realized as she sat there listening politely while yet another person dropped off a casserole and talked about dead bodies and kidnapping that she wanted these next few hours with Matt, no matter what happened at the end of them.

She planned to enjoy every last minute of them, too. She ran her fingers along his jaw and shivered when he repeated the motion. They were kneeling on the floor, facing each other, touching with nothing but fingertips to faces. It was heartbreaking and beautiful, and tears gather-ed in the corners of her eyes.

He caught one as it escaped, rubbed it between his fingers, and then gathered her to him. He pressed her back on the oriental carpet, stretched out beside her, and kissed her so tenderly it made her heart ache.

"I want to make love to you, but I think I'm about to fall asleep. You slayed me just now."

Evie laughed. It'd been an exhausting couple of days for them both. "Why don't we just lay here for a while then?"

She watched the rise and fall of his chest as he settled beside her, then turned and curled herself into him. It felt so right, just lying here with him like this. They were still half-dressed when they fell into a doze in the middle of the living room floor.

When she woke sometime later, night had fallen and the house was dark. Matt was still beside her, his hot skin sizzling into her where they touched. She moved gingerly, trying not to wake him, but he lifted onto an elbow beside her. His fingers ghosted along her collarbone.

"You awake?"

"Yes."

"Me too." His hips flexed. He was hard and ready, and brightness flared inside her as his lips found hers and stole her breath away. She knew this time he was taking control. He was no longer pliable, no longer content to allow her to take the lead.

He stroked her skin with tender fingers until she thought she'd die if he didn't touch her where she most wanted to be touched. She gripped his muscular shoulders and clung to him as he kissed her. Her body throbbed with need. All she wanted was for him to strip her dress away and join his body to hers.

He pushed away from her, his breathing as unsteady as her own. "We're going to need a bed for all the things I have in mind tonight."

He got up and helped her to her feet. They hurried down the hall to the master bedroom; then he was deftly removing her dress the rest of the way and sliding her undergarments from her sensitized skin.

He pushed her back onto the bed, her butt on the edge, and dropped between her legs. There was no mistaking what came next. She was already so hot for him that he seemed to know better than to waste any time. He lowered his head and touched his tongue to her clit, then sucked it between his lips while he inserted two fingers inside her.

Oh God, she was going to die. Her body clenched around his fingers. She wanted more. More than just his fingers and tongue. She wanted him inside her, stroking hard, driving her over the edge.

But he wouldn't give it to her. He was going to torture her with this, same as she'd done to him earlier. The pressure of his fingers increased, the tempo growing faster, while he manipulated her with his hot tongue. She came hard, gasping his name.

Before the tremors ceased, he'd pushed her higher on the bed and settled between her legs. He was inside her with one long stroke, right where she wanted him to be.

"It's amazing with you." He withdrew and slid into her again, shuddering so hard she felt the movement in her core. "It always has been."

She laughed brokenly. "This is only our third time together. Like this, I mean. You inside me."

"I know. And I stand by the statement."

She felt a tear slip down her cheek. "Matt—"

She wanted to let the words out, wanted to tell him how she felt, but she couldn't place that burden on him.

Not when he only wanted now.

"I know."

"You have no idea what I was going to say."

He kissed her. "No, but I know it anyway."

Whatever she might have answered was lost when he rocked into her harder and faster, suddenly losing the control he'd always enforced on himself. Their bodies slammed together in a desperate rhythm, rising and falling, straining as if it were the last time, slipping across the bed as the need consumed them both.

Her climax took her to dizzying heights before dropping her in a long undulation of pleasure so deep it stole her breath. Matt followed, grinding into her one last time. "Evie," he said as he found his release. "Oh God, Evie."

He hovered over her, his weight on his elbows, his hips gently rocking against her. He was still deliciously hard.

Hot tears spilled down her cheeks, surprising her with their suddenness. She turned her head away, hoping Matt wouldn't notice the wet trail in the dim moonlight stretching across their sweat-dampened bodies.

"Don't cry, Evie," he whispered. So much for that thought.

"I can't help it."

It was too hard to keep it bottled up when she was so desperately in love and knew she would lose him in the morning. She'd thought she could do this, could spend this time with him and accept what he offered. She'd been mistaken.

He silenced her tears with a kiss. "I'll come back whenever I can."

Evie pressed her fingers to his lips to stop the words

351

that would wrap around her heart and make her hope for something that would never happen. "Don't make promises, Matt. Just give me tonight."

TWENTY-TWO

HOT HEADQUARTERS WAS LOCATED IN a nondescript secure compound they shared with a post communications facility. An array of satellite dishes sat along one side of the hardened structure. Electromagnetic pulses couldn't get in or out, making what went on inside secure from enemy interference.

Behind several layers of security—RFID, mantraps, lasers, and fingerprint analysis—the military's most elite counterterrorist force gathered and trained for missions ranging from the standard hostage rescue to ops considerably more complex. Colonel Mendez oversaw the program, and he'd been bucking for a facility that belonged solely to HOT for the past few years.

Matt hoped the colonel got it. He'd never know, however, because he wasn't going to be here. Regardless of what happened, he'd made a decision. And he was surprisingly okay with it. He'd loved this job for so long, but it wasn't the only thing he loved. There was more to life than HOT, and he'd realized it as he'd lain in bed with Evie. His job fulfilled him, but she made him feel so much more. With her, he felt as if he belonged. There'd been no emptiness in his soul, no regret, fear, or anxiety.

She'd fallen asleep against him, her soft breath on his skin, and he'd been overwhelmed with emotion. She was safe, and that was all that mattered to him. His childhood friend, his tormenter, his Evie.

He strode through the last layer of security—as an escorted guest—and down a ramp to HOT's ops center. His escort, a private first class who'd known him for the past year, saluted him and pivoted on a booted heel. It wasn't strictly kosher to leave him unescorted when his badge had been revoked, but the PFC was gone. Matt appreciated it more than he could say. He'd stride into the ops center with a guest badge, but he wouldn't have the embarrassment of an escort into what used to be his territory.

He passed through the last door and into the hub of HOT. Communications guys sat at desks with giant screens overhead. Colored dots detailed where each of the HOT squads was located at any given moment. He couldn't help but notice that his team's dot was currently inactive. The officer of the day looked up as Matt rolled through and nodded.

Matt headed toward the set of rooms that housed his team. Kev, Billy, and Jack were at their desks. Chase, Ryan, and Nick weren't there yet. The guys snapped to attention and offered him a salute. Two desks remained empty, their occupants gone and their slots not yet re-assigned to new men.

Matt returned the salute and continued to his office, unable to talk with anyone just now. He knew their eyes followed him, knew they were concerned, but he needed these few moments alone. He'd already made his decision, but he wanted to feel what it was like to be a part of this place one last time.

He stepped inside his office and put his briefcase on his desk. He didn't sit down. His Army greens were crisp, confining. He was unaccustomed to wearing them. In the field, he wore a combat uniform that moved with him like a second skin. He placed his beret beside his keyboard and looked around one last time.

Typically, the hearing would take place at the JAG office, but HOT had a thing about associating with the regular Army—they didn't. So the hearing to determine his competency would take place here, in HOT HQ. He glanced at his watch. An Area Defense Council attorney would arrive soon to represent him. He smiled grimly to himself. No private shark lawyers like Mrs. Doucet allowed. If she had been, well, who knows?

He closed his eyes as he leaned against the desk and thought of Evie. He remembered silky smooth skin, raspy breathing, and a woman who rocked his world like no one else ever had. He'd made love to her as many times as he could that night. He'd put Misty Lee's brothel toys to good use too. Who knew hot cinnamon oil, a leash or a studded collar could be so fun?

Day-um, what a night.

And what a morning, too. He'd slipped away before first light, when the woman he'd spent the night loving lay tangled in the sheets, gently snoring. He'd left thinking that he had things to do before he could come back to her. He had to get his life in order here before he could ask her for more.

If he had to sit at that damn desk in Girard Oil headquarters, he'd do it. Provided the choice was still his, of course. The board could recommend a court-martial, and then Leavenworth was a sure thing for a while. He'd cross that bridge when he came to it.

Matt's eyes snapped open as he sensed another presence. Colonel Mendez stood inside the door, glaring at him.

"You've caused a lot of trouble, son. I hope you got a piece of ass out of it at least."

Matt tamped down on the urge to strike. Yeah, like punching a colonel would help his case any. "I did what was necessary to save lives, sir."

Mendez blew out a breath. "Horseshit. You were dazzled by a woman. And you compromised HOT assets to perform an unauthorized mission."

"I'm willing to accept the consequences, sir."

Mendez cocked an eyebrow. "Are you now?"

Matt stood at stiff military attention. "Sir, yessir."

"Goddamn it, boy, knock it off." Mendez flopped into a chair. "You make me tired, you know that? I had you pegged for this job someday. You were due to make major soon. Light colonel would come in due course, and HOT could've been yours."

"I fucked up."

"Damn right. What are you planning to do about it?"

Matt took a deep breath and closed his eyes briefly. When he opened them again, Mendez was watching. "I'm resigning my commission, sir. Effective immediately—if the board will accept it."

Mendez rocketed to his feet. "What? You can't possibly want that, Matt."

"I do, sir."

"The woman?"

Matt swallowed hard. The woman. Evie. "I'm in love, sir."

Mendez's eyes glittered. "You better be damn sure, soldier. Don't give up your career for a piece of pussy."

Matt stiffened. "Sir, I respectfully request you shut the fuck up."

Mendez let out a bark of laughter. "Okay, you got it bad. I see that. But there's still the hearing to get through."

"I'll accept whatever they decide. And I won't contest I used HOT assets to aid a civilian."

"That'd be a fucking shame then."

Matt shook his head. "I'm not following you."

"If you admit to that, then I got to admit I authorized it. And then Kev and the boys will have to admit they were involved. That cell'll get mighty crowded out there in Leavenworth. And if you think I'm sharing a shower with you, stud, you're crazy. You've been eyeing my ass since you came to work here."

Matt couldn't help laughing. "Respectfully, sir, your ass notwithstanding, I'd rather shower with a rabid monkey."

Mendez laid a hand on his shoulder. "We're getting orders, son. HOT's moving to D.C. We're going deep black, deeper than we've ever been. I need you there, leading your team. We have so much to do in this crazy world these days. The Freedom Force is still out there, still making plans to kill innocent people. We're gonna get Ibn-Rashad, and any other terrorist shitbag that gets in our way. I need your help to do all these things."

Matt let out a shaky breath. It's what he wanted, what he'd always dreamed of. But what about Evie? What about his plans for the future? How could he have everything he wanted without compromise? "I have to get through this hearing first. I'll decide what comes next when it's over."

"Fair enough," Mendez replied. "But you just remember that no relationship built on lies ever succeeds."

"Sir?"

"Assuming you get through this hearing in one piece, you better be damn sure resigning your commission is what you want. Don't lie to yourself. You'll end up blaming her for it, and that's not fair to her or you. Take time to be sure it's the right choice first."

Matt's chin dipped in a firm nod. "Hoo-ah, sir."

Mendez glanced at his watch. "They're waiting for us. You ready, kid?"

"Mm-mm, look at that boy, all grown up and better looking than a man ought to be."

Evie's gaze snapped to the front of the beauty parlor. The ladies were looking out the picture window where a dark-haired man climbed from a silver BMW. He stood there for a second, staring at the shop like he was about to enter a nest of vipers.

Her stomach dropped to her toes and her pulse kicked up.

God, he looked good. Tall and gorgeous in jeans and a white T-shirt that set off his tanned skin and clung to the ripples of hard muscle she'd personally explored with her tongue.

Her heart slammed painfully against her ribs. Her mouth dried up like baked dirt. Four weeks. He'd crept away in the early dawn hours while she'd slept and she hadn't heard from him again. She'd known that last night was all they'd had, but she'd still been stunned to wake alone.

She'd thought they would say their goodbyes face-to-face. That they'd part with a last kiss and touch. But they hadn't. After she'd realized he was gone, she'd given herself a good talking to. She'd known going over there that day what would happen if she did. She'd walked right into the lion's den. Willingly.

She couldn't blame him for doing what he'd said he was going to do. So she'd picked herself up and got on with the task of rebuilding her life.

She'd sunk so low as to call him once, but he hadn't answered his phone and she hadn't left a message. She'd worried he might have gotten tossed into prison for helping her, but she'd seen Misty Lee Girard a few times and finally broke down to ask if they'd heard from Matt. He'd called home once, she said, to tell them he was moving to Washington D.C. Since Leavenworth was in Kansas, Evie figured he'd gotten away with using his connections to help her. She'd been thankful for that.

He finally seemed to make up his mind after striding back and forth a couple of times and headed toward the door.

Butterflies swirled in her belly. But this time she wasn't hiding in the stock room. This time, she'd stand right here and wait. If he wanted a haircut, fine. If he wanted to talk to her, fine.

She could handle it. They were friends, nothing more.

No one knew how she ached inside, not even Mama, Julie, or Sarah. Evie and Matt were heroes in Rochambeau. No one stopped to think for two seconds that her heart might be broken, despite the picture the wedding photographer took that was featured on page one of the *Rochambeau Bee*. The one of her and Matt kissing before they'd taken off to the guesthouse for that night of incredible sex.

Her heart turned over just remembering what he'd done to her. What they'd done to each other. She bent over and picked up a magazine, fanning herself. It was August. Notoriously hot.

"You gonna be okay, sugar?" Mama asked softly as she sidled up. Sarah stood on the other side of her, reached out, and squeezed her hand.

"You want me to tell him to get lost?" Sarah's dark eyes flashed with anger.

Evie looked at them both in shock. Okay, so much for no one knowing. They'd never said anything, but clearly they'd known.

"I'll be fine." She put an arm around each of them and hugged them close.

"Why don't I just tell him we don't cut gentlemen's hair anymore?" Mama held her scissors in one hand. Her wrist was still encased in a splint, but it was healing well. Somehow she managed to cut hair as long as the style wasn't too complicated. She couldn't do perms, but she'd hired two new stylists who took up the slack for her. The shop was doing better than ever, in fact.

Evie smiled. "No, I'll handle it. You go back to cutting Mrs. Landry's hair."

The bell tinkled then and Matt stood on the threshold, scanning the shop. "Afternoon, ladies."

"Afternoon," they said in chorus with a lilt on the last syllable.

The instant he found her, she felt a jolt right down to her toes. The shop got oddly silent, the ladies' heads moving as their gazes ping-ponged between Matt and Evie. She wanted to disappear.

"Can I talk to you?"

Evie tossed the magazine onto a chair, forcing a smile. "Sure."

Sarah reached for her hand one more time, and Evie gave her an answering squeeze before crossing the floor. Matt held the door open and she passed outside with him. He walked over to a bench beneath a magnolia tree a few feet away. He sat. She crossed her arms and stood looking down at him. The air was hot, still, and a bead of sweat trickled between her breasts.

A car without a muffler rumbled by on the street and Matt finally looked up and met her gaze. "Will you sit with me?"

"I'll stand, thanks."

He took a deep breath, then blew it out. "You're probably pissed at me, right?"

"What makes you think that?"

"I left without saying goodbye."

"No, you said goodbye. Several times in fact."

"I had orders."

She nodded. "Yes, the hearing. You told me about it. How did it go?"

He dropped his gaze to his clasped hands. "I was cleared. They said it wasn't my fault my team members

361

died. But I still blame myself for it, Evie."

She wanted to reach for him. She didn't do it. "I think that's natural, but maybe it wasn't your fault, you know? You told me it's a dangerous job. Surely those men knew it too."

His jaw tightened. "Yeah."

Evie drew in a breath. "Well, that's good you were cleared." He loved his job. She was happy for him if he could continue doing what he wanted. And yet she was sad too. Because he couldn't see past what he wanted to do to think she could be a part of his life anyway. He'd taken the choice away from her.

And that made her angry.

"It's certainly not bad." He shoved a hand through his close-cropped hair. He'd gotten it cut since he was last here. It was super short—and yet it looked hot on him. "I'm not going about this well."

"What is it you're trying to say, Matt? Just say it and be done with it, okay? I have to get to work soon."

"Work?"

"I took a job over at Charlie's. I'm teaching him how to make some new dishes. We're adding to the menu."

His smile made her heart skip a beat. "That's awesome, Evie."

"Yes. I'm waiting tables too. For the tips," she added. "Maybe I'll save enough to someday start my own place again."

It wasn't likely, waiting tables, but she was no longer sitting and waiting for a way out of Rochambeau. Whatever the future held, she'd deal with it. If that future was here in Rochambeau—well, she could think of worse fates. She was too strong to let it worry her anymore. Something she'd realized over the last few weeks was that Rochambeau had never been the problem. She had. And she'd finally made her peace with that.

She sank beside Matt on the bench, as far away as she could get.

But he captured her hand in his, rubbing the skin of her wrist with his thumb. Her skin sizzled and she tried to pull away. He held on a moment. Then he let go, sighing.

"I'm sorry. For everything. I shouldn't have left the way I did."

Evie tucked her hands between her knees. "You had to go."

He looked up, his gaze capturing hers. She saw something in the gray depths, something that made her chest ache. "I resigned. Or I tried to. For you."

Her heart gave a little hiccup. "What?"

"They wouldn't accept it."

"Wait a minute." She shook her head in disbelief. "You can't resign from the military."

"Well, you can as an officer, but they don't have to accept it. I figured the stuff that happened here had pretty much sealed my fate so far as my job went. I thought they'd be only too happy to let me go."

"But they weren't."

He shook his head. "No."

Frustration swirled inside her. "I never wanted you to resign your job. It's clear you do something important. How could I ask you to stop when what you do saved Sarah? You help people, and you're good at it. I wouldn't ask you to stop."

"I didn't think I could ask you to live with the fear."

"That's supposed to be my choice, don't you think?"

He was looking at her steadily. "Yeah."

She processed that. "So you got to keep your job. Why didn't you call and let me know that much at least?"

He rubbed one hand across the back of his neck. "I've made a hash of this from the beginning." He spoke almost to himself. "But I was out in the field. Deep cover, Evie. I can't call when I'm out there. And I know I should have called before we went, but I wasn't sure what you would say."

"I'd have said 'thank God you're okay and not going to jail.' Or something like that."

He blew out a breath. "I've misjudged you, Evie. From the beginning. But I only wanted to protect you."

She crossed her arms and glared. "I can make up my own mind, thanks."

"I know you can."

This whole conversation was surreal. "So why are you here?"

His gaze was suddenly intense. "Because I couldn't stop thinking about you. Because I couldn't stop wondering if you'd still want me."

Her pulse hammered a wild drumbeat. "I think I've wanted you since I was six years old. But that's not something that's ever done me a lot of good."

"I know, and I'm sorry for every time I ever made you feel like your faith in me was misplaced."

She sighed. "You only disappointed me twice, Matt. Both times when you left."

"I seem to be good at that." He was staring across the street now, his hands hanging between his legs as he leaned forward on the bench.

Evie turned her head away, sucking back the tears

pressing behind her eyelids. "So Misty Lee told me you were moving. Is that true, or was it simply a story?"

He glanced at her. "No, we moved. To D.C. And then we went on an op."

"So I guess you're home for a visit then. It was nice of you to come see me."

His look turned hot, possessive. Heat flared in her belly at that look. It said *you're mine* and *I want you.*

"I'm not here for a visit. I'm here for you."

The air grew thick in her lungs. It took her a second to close her mouth. She swallowed and searched for her composure. "For me?"

He smiled, but it seemed forced, as if he was trying too hard to make it look natural. "Ever been to D.C.?"

"Once. Why?"

"Fuck." He shook his head. And then he was down on one knee in front of her, grasping her hands and forcing her to look at him. "Come to D.C. with me, Evie. Marry me or shack up with me, I don't care which right now just so long as you come with me."

She was speechless. Of all the directions she'd thought this conversation was going...

"Evie?" His expression was troubled. He looked... uncertain.

Matt Girard, uncertain? The most confident, self-assured man she'd ever known? She latched onto something he'd said, searching for a firm footing in this uncertain sea he'd let swallow her whole. "You're asking me to marry you?"

A shaky breath rattled from his chest. "Yes. When you're ready."

Her head was spinning. "Isn't it a little premature?

We haven't even lived together yet. For all I know, you hate the Food Network. For all you know, I'm a slob."

"I don't hate the Food Network, and I don't care if you're a slob."

Her throat was tight. "We're good together in bed, but…" She shook her head. "I don't even know if you love me."

"Jesus, Evie. Of course I love you. Would I be down here with my heart in my hands if I didn't love you?"

She was trembling deep inside. "You say that like I was supposed to know. You never said a word. That whole night together, and you never said a word."

He pulled in a deep breath. "I didn't think it was fair to tell you before I left. I didn't think it was fair to ask you to be a part of my life when I didn't know what was going to happen to me. But I didn't know what lonely really meant until I left that morning. I've never been lonelier than when I wasn't with you."

Evie figured she must look like a fish out of water. Gaping, gaping.

"But why didn't you call me at least? Tell me what was happening? I missed you so much. I practically begged Misty Lee for information—"

He squeezed her hands. "I couldn't. Not until I knew what the consequences were going to be."

Evie pushed her hair back over her shoulder. "I think I'm mad at you, Matt Girard. For making a decision that involved me without asking me what I thought."

"I know. I was wrong."

"And now here you are again, upending my world—" She drew in a deep breath, willed herself to be calm. "You said before that you couldn't ask a woman to share that kind of life. What's changed?"

He closed his eyes on a deep breath. When he opened them again, they were dazzlingly bright. "Me. I've changed. The job means a lot to me, but it's not everything. You're everything. Love is worth the risk."

She couldn't look at him anymore so she stared at their clasped hands. Yes, she'd been angry with him. But she'd missed him more, loved him more. Wanted him.

"I've had to help Mama get back on her feet." Her voice was hoarse with emotion. "And I've needed to be here for Sarah. She's really opened up to me. We're sisters now, not strangers. I've made my peace with Rochambeau."

"I'm glad for that. But I'm gonna be selfish and ask you to leave again. What we're doing in D.C. is pretty important. I'm not going to be in the field as much any-more—sometimes, but not often—so you don't have to be afraid for me. I'm directing operations from the new facility. I thought you'd like that."

"It's less dangerous?"

"Yes, though not always."

"I've been helping Charlie, and then there's my career…"

She was making excuses now, saying whatever came into her head because she still couldn't quite believe this was real.

"If you can't leave Rochambeau, I'm going back and offering my resignation again. And I'll keep offering until they take it."

The force of his conviction stunned her. "You'd do that for me?"

There wasn't an ounce of hesitation in his eyes. "I

would."

"But you don't want to work for Girard Oil."

"I'll dig ditches for a living if it makes you happy. I'll learn how to cook. We can open a restaurant together."

Evie laughed as an image of big, badass Matt chopping an onion appeared in her mind. She shook her head. Was that hope blossoming in her soul? Did she dare believe?

But what if this was an illusion? A mirage? Had she been breathing too many permanent solution fumes in the beauty shop?

"Evie, look at me."

She did. And what she saw made her breath catch. Love, shining through. For her.

He gave her that million-watt smile. "How about it? Think I can learn to cook?"

She regarded him seriously. "No, I don't think you'd make a good chef. Better stick to being the muscle, babe."

He squeezed her hands. "Does this mean you'll consider moving to D.C.?"

Her heart was going to burst. He was offering her something that frightened her, but after everything they'd been through together, after the way he'd risked himself for her—and the way she'd risked herself for him, don't forget—how could she say no now?

"I think I better. In order to prevent culinary atrocities, you understand."

His head dropped for a moment, his eyes closing briefly. When he looked at her again, his smile lit up her world. "I'll move heaven and earth to make you happy, Evie. I want you there when I wake up every morning and there when I go to sleep at night. I love you, even if you don't do a damn thing I tell you to do."

Happiness magnified inside her and spread outward in warm waves of sunshine. "Oh, I imagine I can do *some* things."

"Why don't we get started on that now?" He stood and pulled her up with him. "Because I can think of quite a few *things* I'd like you to do. To me. With me."

Evie caught a glimpse of a dozen faces pressed to the plate-glass window of her mother's shop as Matt wrapped her in his arms and kissed her senseless. Dimly, past the tattoo beat of her heart and the happiness swirling in her head, she heard a chorus of cheers.

Rochambeau loved its gossip, and there was nothing that lit the little town on fire quite like the news that the boy once voted most likely to succeed was going to marry the girl from the wrong side of town. The citizens were tickled pink because everyone knew that's exactly how it was supposed to be... even if it *had* taken several years for the boy and girl to figure it out.

They might not get married right away—in fact, they didn't—but one day, they'd be back to stand in the gardens at Reynier's Retreat and pledge their undying love. It had been fated since the moment two children met on the ancient steps of the old mansion.

THE END

Thank you for reading *Hot Pursuit*! I hope you enjoyed it. If so, please consider helping others to enjoy this book by:

Recommending it! Please help other readers find this book by recommending it to friends, readers' groups, and discussion boards.

Reviewing it! Please tell other readers why you liked this book by reviewing it at the retailer you purchased it from or at Goodreads.

Lending it! Where possible – please lend it to a friend!

Many thanks for all you do to help make this book a success!

The best way to keep up with the news from me, including when there will be more **Hostile Operations Team** books available, is to sign up for my spam-free newsletter here: http://eepurl.com/c5QFY

ACKNOWLEDGMENTS

A BOOK IS NEVER WRITTEN in a vacuum, and this one most certainly wasn't. This is one of the hardest books I have ever written, and it's also the one I refused to give up on. From the first glimmer of an idea way back in 2005 until now, this story has undergone many revisions and lots of hair pulling in order to reach the reader. I have so many people to thank.

My husband Mike, an Air Force veteran who was always there with military knowledge and advice, was (and is) invaluable to me. I grew up with the military, married into it, and have lived that life for a long time. Still, mistakes are inevitable, so if they're there, it's my fault. There are some things I chose to do for story reasons, and I'm sure the military spouses and vets will find them and know they aren't quite correct. I beg you to forgive me.

My Aloha Chapter peeps in Hawaii, who knew me back when I first started this book, and who encouraged me to keep going when the going got tough. My Heart of Dixie peeps in Alabama, who just simply rock in so many ways and who inspired me from the very beginning.

Kira Sinclair, Andrea Laurence, and Marilyn Puett read early drafts of this story and gave me so much encouragement. Jean Hovey, aka Alicia Hunter Pace, read the last draft and told me exactly what I needed to hear.

Then there are the Pixie Chicks, the 2008 Golden Heart finalists, who made the RWA conference in San Francisco so memorable. This was the book that finaled that year, and I am so honored to be a part of such a talented group of women. It took a few years, but this story is finally ready for the light of day!

I couldn't have done this without the advice and help of the Indie Pixies, who gave me more encouragement than they know. I adore you all, but I have to give special thanks to Courtney Milan. Courtney has always been ready to answer questions for me, and to give me recommendations when I needed them.

I also have to thank Robin Harders, editor extraordinaire, who took this project on and probably had no idea what she'd gotten herself into. I lovingly referred to this story as Frankenbook – and it was, because I'd pulled it apart and stitched it together so many times. But Robin read it anyway and told me exactly what it was missing. And Anne and Sara at Victory Editing helped with that last push toward perfection (elusive, but we tried!).

If you loved the cover, then it wouldn't exist without the major talents of Frauke Spanuth, owner and creative director of Croco Designs. I lucked into Frauke's orbit back in 2008 when I needed a professional website and I haven't looked back. She always, always comes through.

Ultimately, however, I have to thank my readers. You've given me one heck of a ride with Harlequin, and now I hope you'll love my HOT military guys as much as

I do. They aren't billionaires, but they are definitely alpha males. I've wanted to share this story for so long, and I'm thrilled I finally can.

It took an army to get it to you, and I hope you will adore it as much as I do. Thank you so much, and happy reading!

ABOUT THE AUTHOR

USA Today bestselling author Lynn Raye Harris lives in Alabama with her handsome former-military husband and two crazy cats. Lynn has written over fifteen novels for Harlequin and been nominated for several awards, including the Romance Writers of America's Golden Heart award and the National Readers Choice award. Lynn loves hearing from her readers.

For more information on all of Lynn's books,
visit her at http://www.LynnRayeHarris.com/books

Connect with Lynn online:
Facebook: https://www.facebook.com/AuthorLynnRayeHarris
Twitter: https://twitter.com/LynnRayeHarris
Website: http://www.LynnRayeHarris.com

Other Books by Lynn Raye Harris

FREE Digital Short
Maddie's Marine: A (Very) Short Story

***From* Harlequin Presents**

The Al Dhakir Brothers Series
Strangers in the Desert
Marriage Behind the Façade

A Royalty Duo
Cavelli's Lost Heir
The Prince's Royal Concubine

Stand-Alone Titles

The Girl Nobody Wanted
Captive But Forbidden
A Game With One Winner
The Man With the Money
Behind the Palace Walls
The Devil's Heart
Chosen by the Sheikh
Spanish Magnate, Red-Hot Revenge

An Exclusive Digital Short
His Royal Love-Child

***From* Mills & Boon Modern**

The D'Angeli Family Series
Unnoticed and Untouched
Revelations of the Night Before

Made in the USA
Charleston, SC
08 May 2016